Varina Palladino's Jersey Italian Love Story

Also by Terri-Lynne DeFino

The Bar Harbor Retirement Home for Famous Writers
(And Their Muses)

Varina Palladino's Jersey Italian Love Story

A Novel

Terri-Lynne DeFino

wm

WILLIAM MORROW

An Imprint of HarperCollins*Publishers*

HarperCollins books may be purchased for educational, business, or sales promotional use. For information, please email the Special Markets Department at SPsales@harpercollins.com.

FIRST EDITION

Designed by Nancy Singer

Library of Congress Cataloging-in-Publication Data

Names: DeFino, Terri-Lynne, author.
Title: Varina Palladino's Jersey Italian love story : a novel / Terri-Lynne DeFino.
Description: First Edition. | New York, NY : William Morrow, an imprint of HarperCollinsPublishers, [2023] | Series: Untitled defino : #2 |
Identifiers: LCCN 2022016109 | ISBN 9780063228436 (hardcover) | ISBN 9780063228450 (ebook)
Subjects: LCGFT: Love stories | Novels.
Classification: LCC PS3604.E33 V37 2023 | DDC 813/.6—dc23
LC record available at https://lccn.loc.gov/2022016109

ISBN 978-0-06-322843-6

23 24 25 26 27 LBC 5 4 3 2 1

For Ace and Dot, Michael, Karen, and Mark.

Mi famiglia. Mi vita.

famiglia (fa-meel-ya)

Italian: "family"

Used for loving, sometimes dramatic emphasis when English doesn't cut it

Disclaimer: The words in this book are an unofficial, completely amateur collection I grew up hearing and, sometimes, using. It includes research, family peculiarities, and gut instinct. If you read this thinking it's some scholarly thing, it's not. I love words, how they came to be, how they evolved over time. And I love my family. Many of the older uncles and aunts, the few grandparents and great-grandparents left still talk like Jersey Italians. Most of my generation doesn't, but we know the words. We know how to use them. We just don't always know why.

Note, this is *my* Jersey Italian. It's not American Italian. As with all things, Italians can't agree on much. Look at Italy and its bajillion dialects if you need proof. I started writing these words down when I was a little kid. Now that I'm older, I'm taking it a step further. I want to record what I can before that oldest generation is lost, and the distinct ways of these words go with them.

Some of what follows is going to seem stereotypical; I'm here to tell you that, yeah, it probably is, but they're stereotypes for a reason. Don't take that to mean all Jersey Italians fit into these parameters, only that my Jersey Italians did, do, and most likely forever will. I'm proudly claiming my culture. If you find it offensive, that's on you.

Varina Palladino's
Jersey Italian
Love Story

1

cornoot

Italian: *cornuto,* "horned"; also *corno, cornicello,*
or *cornetto;* "horn"

A cornoot is the horn made out of silver or gold, sometimes
red (carnelian), seen hanging from Italian necks and rearview
mirrors everywhere. A cornoot is used to ward off the evil eye
(*maloik*). Don't quote me on this, but I believe this all comes
from the "devil horns" sign (index finger and pinky raised) we use
as a warding gesture (*ma'cornoot,* or, *mana cornuto,* in Italian).
Many think that horn we wear is a bull's horn, but no. It's the
devil's horn. How that wards off evil, I'll never understand.
I imagine it came from a time more distant than the rise of
Christianity, from an earlier, pagan past. Etruscan, maybe. Or
Greek. We are a complicated people.

The Victrola was haunted.

Not a garden-variety haunting, like playing records at will, though it did do that, too; the antique was Robert the Doll–haunted, taken to moving itself from the parlor corner it did not like to the sunny, wavy-glass window it preferred. Things tended to fall off shelves or fly across the room when anyone moved it back to the corner, which Varina had just done in preparation for the penultimate holiday gathering of the year. Dishware on the waiting-to-be-set table clinked.

"Don't you dare, Vicky. I swear to Christ!"

It would have been easier and less hazardous to let the thing have its way; Varina would be damned if she'd coddle a possessed piece of furniture, on Christmas Eve, when she had sixteen people, not counting her and her mother, coming over to eat.

Condensation clouded every window in the kitchen, summer-hot even with the back door propped open. Everyone would be there in less than an hour, and Varina hadn't put the water on yet. She filled the enormous holiday-used lobster pot to boil the macaroni, gave the gravy a turn, adding the butter and basil before turning off the heat. Not even all the garlic she used penetrated the heavy scent of fried fish, salted fish, baked fish. Seven fishes in all, and her brother's grandkids wouldn't eat a bite of it. Thus, the macaroni and meatballs.

Heading into the massive pantry—the pride of her kitchen—Varina pretended she didn't see the cans of beets mixed in with the jars of tomatoes she'd put up late last summer, the baking supplies that never made it into their pest-proof containers. She'd get to it. After the holidays. *Focus. Macaroni.* She found several half bags, but not a single pound of anything the same. Would have been nice to know before she closed up her shop, Palladino's, at two o'clock.

Pulling her cell phone from her apron pocket, Varina scrolled past her three biological children, tapped the name she knew, without question, she could count on.

"Hey, Paulie!" she sang into the phone. "Can you believe I don't have macaroni in the house?"

"You've got a lot going on. I don't know how you still do these huge family things."

"Who's going to do it? My ninety-two-year-old mother?" She laughed. "I enjoy it. Honest."

"If you say so. I'll pop in at the store and get a few pounds. What kind?"

"Penne."

"You got it."

"You still have your key?"

"How else am I going to raid your cases after hours?" He laughed. "I'll be back in fifteen. Good?"

"Perfect. Thank you, sweetheart. Three pounds'll be perfect."

It would be too much, but better that than not enough. Christmas Eve was work, but worth it to have the whole family around her table. Eating her food. She wasn't sure how much longer she'd be able to pull it off, but it had been a good year. Fiscally. Health-wise. It wouldn't always be, but this year, it was. As long as that held, she'd be able to take some well-earned time off from the store, for the first time since she and Dino had rented a house down the shore, back in the early aughts.

Varina's belly rumbled. All that cooking and she hadn't eaten a bite. She took a fried smelt from the too-high-piled plate. Never her favorite, but it would do. In an hour, the house would be in merry chaos. At the moment, the only sounds were the *tick-glonk-tick* of the grandfather clock in the foyer, and the *tick-tick-tick* of her oven.

And Enrico Caruso's *"O Sole Mio."* Playing sullenly. From the corner.

Wiping her hands on her apron, Varina felt the crinkle of the handful of twenties she'd skimmed from the till—it wasn't stealing when it was your own till being skimmed from—and stuck them in her pocket. The pocket also containing—concealing—the page she had ripped from the brochure she got in the mail a few weeks ago. The one of a ship cutting a silvery ribbon of a river, somewhere in Europe.

She'd taken a few minutes to thumb through it. Tossed it in the trash. Took it out again. Looked again. Tore off the cover and shoved it into her apron pocket, then tossed the rest. The images stuck with her, came back to her when she tried to settle into sleep. The ports of call, the pictures of food and smiling faces and distant horizons. When the same brochure arrived just a few days ago, Varina hid it away in her dresser drawer.

"Varina, sweetheart, what can I do?"

"Christ, Mom." One hand to her heart, the other shoving money and page back into her pocket. "You scared me."

"Don't take the Lord's name in vain."

Varina pushed off the counter. "Sorry. Anyway, it's all done. I'm just waiting on Paulie to get here with the penne. I forgot it at the store."

Sylvia Spini patted Varina's cheek, her hand papery but soft. "You do too much."

"I wonder where I get it from?"

"I could have helped. I was only watching the news in my room."

And her stories before that. Varina hugged her mother. Gently. She'd always been small—five-feet-nothing in heels—but robust. Even leaning into plump. And energetic. Varina remembered her skating with the kids when those in-line skates were the craze, back in the eighties. Mom had been in her fifties, Dad had just died, and nothing had prepared Varina for the shift in Sylvia's personality.

"You earned the right to sit back and enjoy your family."

"Eh, maybe. Maybe." Sylvia lifted the pot lid, sniffed. She dipped in the wooden spoon, tasted the gravy. How many times had she done exactly that, in this kitchen? When it was hers? Now that it was her daughter's? Ninety-two. Her tiny-but-robust mother was ninety-two. Varina inconspicuously crossed herself, kissed the cornoot always there around her neck, along with the crucifix, and Virgin Mary medal; *please, just one more year.* One at a time. As if, somehow, it would keep her from leaving. "Everyone will be here any minute. I have to set the table."

"I'll set the table," Sylvia said. "You fix the gravy. It needs more salt. And would it kill you to use a splash more vermouth?"

"Okay, Mom. Thanks."

Sylvia tapped a little dance from kitchen to parlor, hands up and swaying like a conductor for the Caruso recording Vicky was still playing. Varina lifted the pot lid, dipped the wooden spoon. Her mother was right. A little more salt, a splash more vermouth. Not wine. That had been Sylvia's secret, passed down to Varina. No carrots, sugar, or honey for tomatoes, more acidic than sweet. No wine that changed the gravy's color from red to slightly purple. Vermouth was more expensive, but skimping was a sacrilege, whether for the family or for the store.

While in the pantry to grab the vermouth, Varina took a moment to stash the cash and the brochure page. She felt for the old Savarin coffee can, pushed to the back of the top shelf. It had to be thirty years old, this hiding place for loose change, then dollars. Five bucks. Ten. Not even Dino had known about it until she'd saved enough for the rental in Barnegat.

Varina peeled off the lid, cracked edges cracking a little more. She added the skimmed twenties. Closer. A few hundred more, and she'd have the money to pay for the cruise up front, the only way she could justify doing something so big, so expensive. "Be smart, Varina. Never pay for luxury with credit. If you can't afford to pay in cash, you can't afford it. Period." Her dad taught her that, rest his soul. The only credit card she had was for the store. Without it, Palladino's couldn't make the internet orders her business depended upon. But they were paid in full, like clockwork, every month. And that was that.

Varina grabbed the vermouth, splashed in a bit more. Stirred. Tasted. Perfect. Aside from boiling the macaroni and setting the table, everything was ready. Pandora was bringing her signature *pignoli* cookies; Dante, the wine. Her brother Thomas, his kids and grandkids were all bringing something. What? Varina wouldn't know until they showed up. Probably dessert. There was always way too much dessert. And bread, which she already had in abundance, straight from the Bronx. Hopefully, her sister-in-law wouldn't show up with the doughy stuff from the supermarket—again—and expect her to put it out. There was bread, and there was BREAD. Forty-some-odd years married to this family, and Catherine still didn't know the difference. Last time, Varina had fed it to the crows.

"VARINA?"

"Hang on, Paulie. I'm coming." Varina pulled her ponytail tighter. Not exactly Christmas Eve–stylish, but she was out of time. At least she had a festive T-shirt on. No way she was wearing the sweater Donatella had dropped off. Her daughter's taste was not only truly awful, but took no account of itchy heaviness. She'd rather lose the ugly sweater contest than sweat through the next several hours. How was it she worked like a mule, sweated like a pig, but never managed to lose those pounds she'd been trying—not all that hard—to lose since she was in her fifties? Maybe it was the abundance of Christmas cookies, the Thanksgiving pies, and the Halloween candy she always managed to buy way too much of, and how could she let it go to waste?

"Hey, Paulie." She kissed his cheek. "Thanks for this."

"No problem. Anything else I can do?"

"Not a thing. Oh! Maybe you can open those bottles of wine? Dante's bringing more, but you know he'll be late."

"He was still at the site trailer when I left." Paulie got the corkscrew from the drawer, slit the foil. "He works too hard."

"My son works too much," Varina corrected. "Hard is okay. Too much isn't. You'd think he'd have learned that lesson from his father."

Paulie crossed himself, kissed his fingers. "You'd think. He needs a partner. Someone to help carry the load. Mr. P had you, and he still keeled . . . sorry."

"It's all right. He did keel over." No one worried about her keeling over; Varina ran the store much differently from when she and Dino worked seven days a week, ten hours a day, when they were young, then when they thought they were. She sighed. "I wish Tom hadn't retired."

"Your brother and Dante had very different ideas about where the company is going. They'd have eventually murdered one another." Paulie laughed, lifting another cork free of its bottle. "He'll be okay. Dante, I mean. Try not to worry."

"Easy for you to say." Varina took the bottles, carried them into the parlor. Fourteen or forty-eight, Dante was her baby boy. He hadn't been *right* since the divorce, even if he'd been the one to ask for it. Varina still didn't get it. He and Pandora were very close. Good friends. Why divorce if they didn't hate one another?

"You need to have a talk with your son, one of these days," Pandora had said, a sad, loving smile on her lips. And no more.

"Pour us a glass," Varina said. "I have about twenty minutes off my feet before the onslaught begins."

Paulie obliged, followed her into the parlor, where Vicky no longer played Caruso. Silent, perhaps, but Varina could still feel her sulking. Patting the lid, she closed it gently and sat opposite the young man as much a son as those she'd borne.

"So, what have you been up to, sweetheart?" She sipped. "Any nice new someones in your life?"

"Subtle. Very subtle." Paulie laughed. "You really didn't like Arthur, did you."

"He's a lawyer. What's there to like? Besides, you didn't, and that was the important thing. Besides, that was last summer. What about now?"

"Now, I have no time to meet anyone new and nice."

"I thought construction slowed down in the cold months."

"It's this gentrification movement." Paulie sipped. "A lot of people with a lot of money they don't want tied up too long. Everything's being revitalized. All the beautiful, old architecture is being saved. I'm glad to be a part of it. Tom, on the other hand, is more of a 'raze it and build new' kind of guy. Trust me, it's a good thing he retired. And Dante loves it. Seriously loves it. You don't see him at the sites, how excited he gets about a corbel or a wavy-glass window like this one. It's actually kind of adorable."

"I'm sure he'd love that assessment." Varina took a long swallow. Sweet, then bitter. It could be a bit more mellow, though it probably would have been, had she allowed it to breathe. "Have you spoken to Donatella today?"

"Not today. Why?"

"I thought you two did nothing but text all day long."

"She texted." He set his wineglass down. "Nothing earth-shattering. She sent me a couple of funny memes I LOLed at. Something wrong? You worried?"

Always, when it came to Donatella. "No, no. Not worried. She dropped off my ugly sweater here at the house rather than the store.

I get the feeling she's avoiding me. I'm not even sure she'll be here tonight."

Paulie set his wineglass on a coaster. He took both Varina's kitchen-calloused hands in his construction-calloused ones. "Those terrible teens are way in the past. She's doing okay."

"But the terrible twenties weren't so long ago," Varina told him. "I never know where she is. And she's never had a job or a boyfriend that lasted more than a few months. That's not normal for a grown woman."

"It is for Donatella. And, you know, you don't have a boyfriend, either. You're a bit older than thirty-five."

"Don't be fresh."

Paulie kissed her hands and let them fall. "She's doing okay. Honest. I've been tattling on her since we were kids. Do you think I'd lie for her now?"

"Yes."

His head-back-hearty laughter made Varina's heart twitch. How could his parents not love him enough? How could they turn their backs on him, pretend he didn't even exist? Grabbing his chin, she kissed both his cheeks, slapped him, and stood up. "My time off my feet is over. I'm going to see if the water's boiling yet."

"It hasn't been twenty minutes!" Paulie called, following behind her into the kitchen. He rinsed the wineglasses in the sink, dried them with a paper towel. "Oh, before I forget." He reached into his pocket, pulled out a wad of cash. "Rent. I know it's a little early, but with the holidays and all, I figured . . ."

"Stop it." Varina pushed his hand away. "I've been giving you January's rent for Christmas since you moved in upstairs. Don't be silly."

"And I attempt to pay you anyway, every year," he said. "Seriously, I was a depressed, homeless kid back when you took me in. I'm all growed up now. It's not like the rent is even fair to be-gin with."

"I own this house, free and clear." Varina pushed his hand away again. "You living upstairs costs me almost nothing. It makes me happy to know you're there. I've always felt bad about taking any-thing at all."

"Now who's being silly." Paulie bent to kiss her cheek. "Thank you. Again. Merry Christmas."

"Merry Christmas to you, sweetheart."

"I'm going upstairs to put my ugly sweater on. Be right back."

She heard him tromp up the stairs, moving around in his apart-ment. Paul Rudolph Vittone. Her Paulie. He'd grown up just down the block. His parents had been friends of hers and Dino's, back in the day. Drinks on the patio. The occasional dinner out. They'd often joked, maybe dreamed, the best-friends status between Donatella and Paulie would turn matrimonial. Varina had known when they were teens that wasn't happening. How his parents never guessed, she, to this day, couldn't fathom. But they hadn't, and he'd told, and they'd shortly thereafter moved to Florida, telling their only child he wasn't welcome to join them. Varina and Dino had taken him in the same day.

"I don't get it," Dino had said, rubbing the top of his head, a habit Varina always suspected contributed to the bald spot there. "Do you know how many times I caught him and Dona suckin' face? How can he be fanook?"

"Young hormones are young hormones, I guess," Varina had told him. "I don't know."

And she hadn't. Not then and not now. Donatella tried to explain it to her, that he identified primarily as homosexual, though occa-sionally was attracted to a woman. It sounded confusing; she could only imagine it was to him, too. One way or another, it didn't matter. Paulie was Paulie, and she loved him. Period.

"Varina!" her mother called from down the hall. "I'm coming to the kitchen now! I don't want to scare you!"

"Wiseass," Varina mumbled, but she smiled. A car pulled into the driveway, the headlights illuminating the old garage out back.

"That's probably Tommy." Sylvia clapped the tips of her fingers together. "Always on time."

"Ten minutes early," Varina corrected. Tom would come around back. They'd both grown up here, where the front door was for guests, and the back door for family. She stood at the open door, basking in the cold air, watching her brother, Catherine, and two of their teenage grandkids get out of the car.

"Oh, look. One of the twins brought his girlfriend." Sylvia stood in the doorway beside her, barely taking up any space. "Do we have enough chairs?"

"I'll get another from the cellar."

"How will you squeeze it in? It's already too crowded."

"The more the merrier, Mom." Varina tried not to sigh.

"We should have done this at Davide's house. What does a single man need with all that space if he can't host his family for the holidays?"

Broken record. Davide and his Bergen County McMansion. No wife, no kids to populate it. Praise for the posh chain of hair salons, the success, the glamorous clientele, came only at church or bingo, repeated back to Varina by one of her mother's few remaining friends.

"Because this is where we've always had Christmas Eve," Varina said. "How come you complain about my kids all the time, but never Tommy's? You'd think they all walk on water."

"Because you're my daughter," Sylvia said, opening her arms to her son, coming up the back steps. "Tommy! Catherine! Merry Christmas!"

fanook

Italian: *finocchio*; literally, "fennel"

Fanook/finocchio is a derogatory term for "homosexual." There
doesn't seem to be any definitive reason why homosexual men
are "fennel." Italians have a lot of food words that are also insults.
The best explanation I've seen for this one goes way back to
the Middle Ages' slang use of *finocchio* to refer to a silly, mean,
treacherous, worthless, despicable man. It's not a far stretch to
figure out how that transition went.

Interestingly, fennel, as in the bulb eaten for digestive purposes
after a big meal, is pronounced in my family, *fanoik* (fan-oyk),
while the derogatory slang for homosexual is *fanook*. I never put
the two together, and I guess that explains the need for different
pronunciations. "Hey, Uncle Gaggutz! Pass the fanook!" could
totally ruin Thanksgiving.

The Palladinos were not his family. Not biologically. They were *famiglia,* because they didn't get stuck with him; they chose him. Mr. P had become a little uncomfortable around him, once he came out—Paulie hated that concept, as if declaring one's sexual preferences was anyone's damn business—but never once turned him away. That, he was certain, had more to do with Varina than any sort of enlightened tolerance. Mr. P was old-school, from a time when fanooks stayed in their closets where they belonged. Paulie suspected there were a few gay skeletons in the Palladino and Spini closets. There always were.

"Hey, Paulie," Davide called from down the long table. "Don't hog all the bread, will ya? Pass it down."

Damn, that man was beautiful. Old-time, silver screen beautiful. Rudolph Valentino, only updated into a perfectly tumbled metrosexual women loved and men were intimidated by in ways they didn't want to acknowledge. Despite his flamboyance and chain of hair salons, Davide Palladino was not one of those gay skeletons, proving stereotypes often missed key details.

He passed the basket, though he wanted to wing a chunk down the table, make them all laugh. But Varina wouldn't laugh. And neither would Mrs. Spini, that scary old bird. Paulie had never truly won her approval; then again, he didn't think anyone ever had. Only Mr. Spini. Her Tommy. Her son. He was, as far as she was concerned, as close to the second coming of Jesus Christ as the world was ever going to get.

"I guess Donatella's not going to make it." Pandora leaned closer to whisper. "Any idea why?"

"She's Donatella." At least she was in Wyldale, as far as he knew. She'd taken up residence in the old apartment over the store around Thanksgiving. Very typical. Donatella always made it home from wherever she was for the holidays, vanishing for a day or two now and then in the interim. Pushing his glasses up higher on his nose—he really needed a new pair—Paulie motioned to the beautiful young woman beside Pandora. "Who's this? I don't think we've met. Can't be Gabriella. She's only five or six."

"Funny." She nudged him. "I can't believe my baby girl is in college."

"Can't be." Paulie shook his head. "I won't listen to your lies."

"I'm nineteen, Paulie." Gabriella rolled her eyes, but she smiled, too. "And I'm only half an hour from home, so . . . yeah, not exactly flown the coop."

"Nest," Pandora corrected. "Smart mouth."

"Hey, Gabs." Paulie pointed. "Would you pass me the smelts."

She crinkled her nose, leaning away from the plate she passed him. "Oily fish, fried in oil. How do you eat these things?"

"With my mouth." Paulie tipped a couple of the small, perfectly breaded and fried fish onto his plate. "On a fork, if I'm feeling civilized."

Pandora fist-bumped him. "Kids today, huh?"

He'd always liked her best of all the in-laws. Maybe because she was Greek, not Italian, though Varina insisted they were mostly the same. "One just civilized the world earlier than the other" was her favorite joke, back in Pandora and Dante's courting days.

"Dante's looking a bit wrecked, isn't he?" she said.

Paulie chanced a glance; looking directly at the sun was never a good idea. "He's been working long hours."

"So, what else is new? He didn't even wear the ugly sweater I got for him."

"Dante? Wear an ugly Christmas sweater? Do you even know your ex-husband?"

"I did. I do. Anyway, being divorced doesn't mean I don't worry. That I don't care."

"Everyone worries about Dante. He's too much like his dad. Driven."

"And stubborn," Pandora said. "What most people don't know about Dante Palladino could fill a book, Paulie. Believe me."

He did. Paulie knew a few things, too. Like how Dante looked with only his desk lamp illuminating the contours and hollows of his face. How he pushed fingers through his hair while he worked on blueprints and left it all standing up. How he glowered at his workers instead of screaming at them, the way Tommy did. How, when Dante smiled, the whole world got a little brighter.

Gathering dishes, Paulie scraped the leavings from one into the other until he had a stack too big for anyone not construction-muscled to carry. He hefted them into the kitchen, where Catherine rinsed before Varina loaded stuff into the dishwasher. In the dining room spilling into the parlor by way of banquet tables set end to end, the men cracked nuts, crunched on fanoik, and argued. Davide and Dante, Tom and his son, Michael. Michael's twin sons, still in their teens. Paulie helped the women instead, because it was the polite thing to do. Because it was archaic for men to sit around while the women cleaned up. Because he was, after all, not a Palladino or Spini man, not by blood or marriage.

"Paulie, would you take the garbage out back?" Varina called over the din of women from teen to crone scraping, packaging, chatting, and laughing.

He set the dishes down on the counter, picked up the garbage bag.

"Thanks, sweetheart. Then go sit with the men."

"Will do."

The blast of cold air after the sweltering kitchen felt incredible. Paulie just stood on the top step, letting it hit him. Tiny ice crystals not quite snow pinged his face. Another Christmas Eve. Another New Year right around the corner. Another year.

His cell phone chirped—crickets, to remind him of summer and the shore. Pulling it from his pocket, he saw Donatella's icon flashing. He tapped it. "An actual phone call? No text?"

"Shut up, Paulie. Listen. Okay?"

Oh, shit. Not again. He pushed his glasses up onto the top of his head, rubbed his eyes. "Sure. Hey, what's wrong?"

"You got to come get me. They say I can't go, but you talk to them. Can you do that for me?"

"Who, Don? Where? Have you called your mom?"

"Vaffangul! Don't tell my mother!"

"Okay! Okay! Where are you?"

Silence. A hiccup. "I'm at the lockup."

Sweet Jesus. "What happened?"

"It's a long story. I got to go. Just come get me. And don't say anything!"

"Fine. I won't." And he wouldn't. Not this time. There was no way he was ruining Christmas Eve for Varina. "I'll be there as soon as I can."

"Now, Paulie! Shit, I can't stay here. It's disgusting. I swear, I'll get AIDS or something."

"Very PC, Dona. Cool. I'll be there soon."

Paulie tapped out of the call. Frustration coiled in his gut. He'd been rescuing her since they were five and she climbed down into the storm sewer to get a quarter she'd dropped. Paulie got a piece of rebar he found in the alley beside the liquor store and pulled her back up. It was one thing after another ever since. If her family hadn't basically adopted his sorry, discarded teen ass, he'd have stopped rescuing her long ago.

That was a lie. Paulie would never stop, because he'd always love her. She'd always love him. That's the way it was with them. With him and the Palladinos.

Heading inside, he put his glasses back on, tucked his phone back into his pocket. How to bail on the festivities without causing suspicion? He could think of only one surefire way of getting one over on Varina. He didn't like lying to her, but this was for her own good. He'd confess after Christmas. Maybe New Year's.

"Hey." He ducked to kiss her cheek. "I got to jet. Do you mind?"

"What is it?" She grabbed his arm, hauled him into the slightly quieter pantry. "What's wrong? Did Donatella call you? Where is she?"

Thank goodness it was dark in there. "It's not like that. It's . . . I have a date."

Her whole body relaxed. "Paulie!" And then she smacked his arm. "You said you haven't met anyone new."

"I didn't want to get your hopes up."

"You could have invited him."

"I only just got the call." Partial truth felt a little better. "It's probably not going to come to anything. We only just met. He said he'd call, but you know how that goes. It's just a drink."

"On Christmas Eve?" She jiggled him. "Go, sweetheart. Have your drink. No one will even notice you stepped out."

They would. Every one of them. And they'd probably figure it was Donatella he'd ducked out for, but not one of them would say so. Not even Mrs. Spini, whom Varina would have ignored, in any case.

"THEY SAID IT'S A NEW BAIL LAW, OR SOME CRAP," DONATELLA, HAND-cuffed to a waiting bench, told him. "No more bail. I have to go before a judge and, once whoever deems I'm no threat to society, I get kicked on my own recognizance until my trial."

"And if you're deemed a menace to society?"

"I said *threat.*"

"Whatever. What happens then?"

"Then I stay in county until my trial. But it's not going to come to that. Get me out of here, Paulie. Please."

He'd already talked to the arresting officer, the clerk, anyone who would listen. *It's Christmas Eve. Come on! Have a heart.* To no avail. "Don, listen." He wanted to take her hand, but the guard standing close enough to knock him off his chair didn't look like he'd allow it. "It's after ten on Christmas Eve. You're stuck here until tomorrow."

"A judge will come in on Christmas Day?"

"Apparently. Public intoxication, assault, resisting arrest, and vandalism are one thing. Violating a restraining order is another. You might not get out."

"I didn't violate it on purpose. I didn't know Fucking Chucky was even in that bar."

"Fair enough, but you did know it was his girlfriend's cell phone you threw at him, and you did follow them out to their car and smash his windshield."

"Says who?"

"Says everyone in the bar. You're screwed, Don. Time to lawyer-up. You have one?"

"Just the schmuck I used last time. Do you know anyone?"

"I might." Paulie heaved a slightly dramatic sigh. At least Arthur would be good for something, if not for him. "You know, you could have just come to your mom's feast of seven fishes with everyone else."

"I'd rather be in jail than eat with all them condescending a—"

"Hey. That's my *famiglia* you're talking about." Paulie chanced a nudge. The guard narrowed his eyes, and he backed off. "They can't tell me what time your hearing is tomorrow, but you call me as soon as it's over. I'll make some excuse and come pick you up. Okay?"

"Fine." She sniffed, wobbled a little. "Thanks."

"You'd do the same for me."

"I *have* done the same for you." She laughed, and it wobbled, too. And then Donatella's face crumbled. "Why am I such a fuckup, Paulie? I fucking ruined your Christmas. I've ruined everyone's holiday."

"No, you didn't." He glanced at the guard, eyebrows raised. The large man nodded, and Paulie took Donatella into his arms. "No one's even going to know until Christmas is over. Shh. It's okay."

"It's not. I know it's not. You shouldn't make excuses for me. You're part of the reason I'm still a mess." But she laughed, kissing his cheek, pulling away. "I'm still a little drunk, too."

"Obviously."

Donatella wiped her nose on the back of her hand. The guard handed her a box of tissues. "Thanks," she told him, smiling through her tears. The guard melted, just a little. Donatella had that effect on people, especially men of the protective persuasion. Though not as small as her grandmother, she wasn't much bigger. Huge eyes, almost like those big-eyed children on the posters she'd had in her room as a kid, would have been out of place on anyone else. Donatella's round cheeks and deep dimples pulled them off. Too well. It was hard to say she was pretty, not traditionally. *Alluring* was more like it. She attracted men like Davide attracted women. Neither of them was very adept at choosing the good ones. But while Davide navigated bad relationships with charm and finesse, Donatella typically ended up a hot mess. Case in point, Fucking Chucky.

"I don't want to go back in that cell."

"I know. But you have to."

She looked up at the guard. He frowned, but he nodded.

"I guess this is it, then." Donatella leaned forward, kissed Paulie's cheek. "Thanks for coming. For trying."

He stood up. "You call me tomorrow."

"Yeah, yeah. Go. Maybe there will be a few cannoli left."

"If there are, I'll put one aside for you."

"Make it two!" she called after him.

Paulie didn't turn and wave, but waved over his shoulder. He couldn't look at her, couldn't see her handcuffed to the waiting bench, small and slouched, half drunk and crying. There wasn't a thing he could do that he hadn't already.

For the eleventy-bajillionth time since they were five.

3

Madonn'

Italian: *Madonna mia;* literally translates as "my Madonna" (the Virgin Mary)

Typically used as an expletive of frustration, whether from anger or worry, petitioning the Madonna for relief, rather than a curse. *Madonn'* is an acceptable expression of displeasure when around older relatives who'll throw a shoe at you for other, less savory curse words. (Italian mothers and grandmothers are especially notorious for their shoe-throwing skills, much like ninjas with their *shuriken.*)

The wheels her Joseph put on the bottom of the Victrola—back when they still danced every evening after supper—made it easy to move. Sylvia pushed it from the corner to the window, chose a thick 78 from the cabinet base, and slid it from its fragile, blue-paper sleeve. *La Sonnambula:* "Come per me sereno" sung by Amelita Galli-Curci.

Bellini had always been a favorite, both his and hers. All the great Italian composers for listening—while sipping something sweet, amaretto or sambuca—after the children were in bed. Dancing always sounded of the forties, sometimes the fifties. It was a more romantic time, for Sylvia, if not the world. She was no fool, and never blind to the reality. All those people dead, only to have that damned McCarthy use their sacrifice to justify his witch hunt. Oh, how she'd wanted to protest, to speak out, but it wasn't done, and so she hadn't.

Still, they'd been the happy years, the late forties through the fifties. They'd married so young, her Joseph a skinny but dashing almost-twenty-year-old. Sylvia had only been twenty when Tommy was born nine months and three weeks after the wedding; twenty-two when she had Varina in 1950. They were the happy years, if hard. Uncomplicated and peaceful. Try as she might to pinpoint where it started veering into difficult and contentious, Sylvia never could. Rather, she didn't like where the pin pointed.

"Oh, it's you." Varina entered the room, a dishcloth in her hands. "I thought Vicky was at it again."

"It's only me." Sylvia held out her hand. "The dishes can wait. Come listen with me."

"I'm just about finished."

"Varina." She wiggled her fingers. "Come listen with me."

A long sigh, but she did as asked. "I always loved this one."

"Me too."

They stood together in the middle of the parlor lit only by the lights on the tree, swaying. All the furniture still pushed up against the far wall, the banquet tables folded along with the card chairs, left a wide space to dance, if dance they would.

"Aren't you tired, Mom? It's after midnight. Don't you want to get some sleep before it all starts again tomorrow?"

"I'll sleep when I'm dead."

Varina crossed herself. "Don't say that."

"Why not?" Sylvia shrugged. "I'm ninety-two. This might be my last Christmas."

"Mom, please."

"*Please* what? It's true. Not talking about it doesn't make me any less close to death."

"What is there to talk about? You're healthy as an ox, and you have all your marbles. Do we have to discuss your eventual demise at midnight on Christmas Eve?"

No, they did not. Varina didn't understand what it was to be so old. Sylvia hoped she would, someday, both so her daughter would have a long life, and so she could say *I told you so!* from the grave.

"It's actually Christmas now," she said. "But, okay. No death talk. What do you still have left to do?"

Varina tossed the dishcloth over one shoulder, glanced kitchen-ward. "Nothing that can't wait," she said. "I'm going to bed."

Alone.

Sylvia kept the word in her mouth—this time—letting it ratchet around inside her skull instead. It was Christmas, after all, and even she had a limit to her meddling. Varina would insist she didn't want a man, anyway; she'd had a good one and wasn't taking any chances on another. Oh, her stubborn, opinionated, delusional daughter would laugh, but Sylvia knew the truth. Stuck in her ways was what she was. And frightened. Varina had been alone too long. A dozen or so years since Dino—whom Sylvia always liked—keeled over at the store. Time enough to be alone. Time enough left to escape a cold and lonely decrepitude. Like hers.

"Mom? Earth to Mom."

Sylvia backed away from fingers snapping in her face—blinking, blinking, blinking, at the elderly woman doing the snapping—into focus, out of memory. She looked like Sylvia's sister, Rose, but no. Rose had never gotten as old as the disheveled, gray-haired woman waiting for her to speak. Oh, yes . . . "Madonn', Varina. Who taught you to be so rude? It wasn't me, that much I know."

"You spaced out."

"I was listening to the music."

"Okay. No reason to get so—"

"And when in God's name are you going to do something about that hair?"

"My hair?" Varina smoothed stray, still-curly tendrils. "I didn't have time to do anything with it, Mom. If you didn't notice, I just had a million people over for Christmas Eve dinner."

"Would it hurt you to put a little color in it? Salt-and-pepper ages you. You don't have the complexion for it. It makes you look old."

"It makes me look seventy. I have no issue looking my age, Mom."

"You could look like a slightly younger seventy."

"And I suppose you look a slightly younger ninety-two with your jet-black football helmet of hair," Varina snapped.

Now it was Sylvia smoothing her hair, which was not smooth at all. It practically crackled with hair spray. "My hair has always been this color."

"Are people supposed to believe it's still natural?" Varina sighed. Sylvia knew that sigh. She was about to be humored. "Look, Mom. It's late. I don't want to fight, especially about something as stupid as hair. I'll think about it, okay?"

"You do what you want." Sylvia sniffed. "You always have. You're still so pretty. You have a nice figure. But if you don't want to attract a man, far be it from me to offer any advice."

"And here we go again! Good night, Mom. See you in the morning."

Sylvia stood alone in the parlor, illuminated by the Christmas tree lights and serenaded by Vicky. Lifting the needle, she let the silence settle around her. Tears welled. She'd gone and upset her daughter, after she'd worked so hard to do not only the traditional feast of seven fishes, but macaroni and meatballs for the ingrates who wouldn't eat fish on Jesus' birthday. Sylvia had told herself not to, and had been so good all night, even when Paulie left to haul Donatella out of whatever mess she'd gotten herself into now. It was all that finger-snapping. It had startled her, put her off.

"Is it so terrible that I don't want her to be alone when I'm gone, Vicky? Is it?" No answer. Vicky never spoke when spoken to, only when she was moved to do so. Sylvia had been trying for years to engage the haunted old thing. A lark, at first. More earnestly, the older she got. If she could only find out who was haunting it, and how they'd gotten there, Sylvia was pretty sure she could die happy.

"Merry Christmas." She closed the lid, shuffled to her room just down the hall. It had been Tommy's, once upon a time. After Joseph died, Sylvia had moved out of the master bedroom. Not that it was any different from the other two bedrooms in the house. No master suite, like in the houses and apartments Dante built. Just a room she'd shared with her husband for forty years. Good years. Bad years. Better years. Now it was Varina's room, her tiny childhood bedroom turned into a guest room that never saw any guests.

Smearing cold cream on her face, Sylvia stared down the ancient crone in the mirror. "You behave yourself tomorrow, you hear? Be good. Leave Varina alone. I mean it this time."

She wiped away the day's makeup, revealing an even more

decrepit crone underneath it. Studying the lines and age spots in the magnifying mirror, Sylvia tried to find evidence of her younger self. The one who'd made dresses for Donatella. The one who'd Rollerbladed with the boys, after her Joseph died, because falling flat on her ass made her feel alive. The one who'd loved her husband, and hated him, then loved him again. All she could find was a sour old woman with unnaturally black hair, and more opinion than she had sense to keep in her mouth.

Wagging a finger at her reflection, she snapped off the light. Bed awaited. Empty, cold, but comfortable. Varina had bought her one of those memory foam mattresses, the kind with the downy topper. She was a good girl, her Varina. A dutiful daughter. She'd make a good wife for someone who didn't mind the gray in her hair.

4

Mannaggia dial!

Italian: *Male ne abbia il diavolo!;* literally, "Curse the devil!"

It means pretty much the same thing, used by Jersey Italians, but it seems more like "May the devil curse you!" We can be a direct people. My grandmother pronounces it *mannagia di owl.* It was confusing, as a kid, because I couldn't figure out what my bad behavior had to do with owls.

Christmas morning had become anticlimactic once the kids grew past the age of waking early to see what Santa left. Christmas Eve was the big thing. Christmas morning, just Varina and her mother barely speaking over coffee and leftover pastries, would have been pretty depressing were it not the only calm she'd have the rest of the day. Mass at ten o'clock, then home to pick up all last night's leftover desserts. From there, over to the Spini and Son warehouse, where Dante, Pan, and Gabriella would have the conference room decorated, and Davide's caterers would have tables set and food in warmers.

Thank the baby Jesus in his manger, because there was no way she could do both Christmas Eve and Christmas Day, like she used to.

Varina sipped her coffee, thumbing through the heavy-paper brochure that felt as expensive as the advertised trips themselves. She'd almost decided upon which river cruise she was going to take. It was either Lyons to Avignon, or the Castles of the Rhine. They were the shortest. A week was all she could afford, financially and mentally. Pandora would take care of the store, Paulie would take care of her mother, but there was only so much control Varina could hand over. At least, the first time.

"What is that? A cruise?"

Varina flipped the brochure closed. "I got it in the mail," she said. "Looks nice."

"You taking a trip?"

Yes. "Nah. No time. It's nice to look, though."

"Let me see."

Varina handed it over. Reluctantly. Her mother thumbed through. "This is one of them old-people cruise lines."

"I am an old people." Varina laughed.

"Don't say that."

"What? That I'm old? It's not a swear word, Mom."

"If you're old, what does that make me?"

"Ancient." Varina got up, kissed the top of her mother's head, and swiped the brochure back. "Come on. We'll be late for church if we don't get moving."

Varina took the time to fix her hair. It really was pretty, she had to admit. Thick and curly, her hair had always been her best feature. Dino said it was her eyes, big and brown and heavily lashed. Those lashes had thinned; her hair had not. So, it was salt-and-pepper. Big whoop. Varina wasn't going down her mother's path. Sylvia had always been a little vain. Then again, she'd been quite beautiful in her prime. She still was. If only she'd stop dyeing her hair and caking on the makeup as if ninety-two-year-old beauty didn't exist.

"Ready, Mom?"

Sylvia came out of her room, purse clutched in both hands, wearing the green Christmas dress she'd been wearing for as long as Varina could remember. The orthopedic hose and shoes were a recent addition, but the pearl and ruby Christmas bells were pinned to the collar, as always.

"You look pretty, Mom."

"So do you, sweetheart. Your hair is lovely."

"Thanks. Ready?"

"No lipstick?"

Don't sigh. Just smile. "I'll warm up the car."

It wasn't a long walk; Varina would have actually preferred it. The sky was the kind of crystal blue written about in happy holiday stories. No snow, though, unless she counted the now-gray stuff piled and melting around the edges of Wyldale's streets and buildings. Moot point. Mom couldn't make the four-block walk; she'd swoon at the mere suggestion. Getting the car out now and then was necessary, anyway. Varina walked pretty much everywhere. Such were the perks of living in a sort-of-urban town with its heels dug firmly into the 1960s. Local shops, for local people, thrived, especially now with all the socially conscious youngsters moving in. *Shop Local* was practically the town motto, even though The Garden State Plaza, Paramus Park, and Riverside Square—now changed to The Shops at Riverside, an appellation Varina would never succumb to—were all near enough, as well as an abundance of ShopRites, Foodtowns, and Pathmarks. Wyldale's downtown still housed the butcher, the baker, and the candlestick maker—it was a Yankee Candle, but still—alongside the boutiques and vegan bakeries and expensive coffee shops. And it housed Palladino's, her little Italian specialties grocery. A neighborhood staple. Some even called it the sun around which all of Wyldale revolved. Maybe that was her kids who called it that. Varina didn't remember.

The church was packed. Of course. Varina couldn't complain. She was an Easter/Christmas Catholic, herself. She spotted Dante first; his height made that easy. Pan and Gabriella, beside him. In the pew behind, Davide, Paulie, Tom and his extended family. Her brother waved them over, indicating he'd saved a spot for their mother on the end, just like she preferred. Varina passed her off, then wended her way to Davide and Paulie, who parted to let her sit between them. She kissed their cheeks.

"Merry Christmas, boys."

"Merry Christmas, Mom," they said in unison, smiled, and shoved one another behind her back.

"Behave." They'd always been friends, Paulie and Davide, despite the ten years between them. Paulie had even worked, in those early days—when Dino wasn't yet square with the whole idea of his youngest son being a hairdresser, not that he ever truly was—in Davide's salon. Donatella had, too, which was the reason Paulie quit, but that was water under the bridge. More water. Varina didn't even want to think about how much more Paulie would let wash before finally cutting her out of his life.

She took his hand, and Davide's. Kissed the backs of them. These boys. These beautiful, magnificent boys.

"Hey, make room." Donatella squeezed her way past her brother, kissing him quickly as she did, then her mother, settling between Varina and Paulie just as the procession music boomed. "I almost didn't make it."

"Where were you?"

"Long story." Donatella hugged Varina's arm. "Merry Christmas, Mommy."

The Donatella-shaped knot, so familiar she barely noticed it anymore, unwound. *Safe.* Probably in trouble, but right there, clinging to her arm just like she'd been doing since toddlerhood. Varina kissed her youngest child's curly head, closing her eyes and whispering, "Merry Christmas, baby."

She met Paulie's gaze over Donatella's head; his smile did not reach his eyes.

THERE WERE NO LITTLE ONES IN THE FAMILY TO RUN AROUND THE Christmas-decked conference room, causing a ruckus. Not like the old days. The great-grands were mostly teenagers and young adults too young for baby-making, although Sylvia had been younger than many of them when she had her first. These were different times. Now, young people got jobs or went to college or both, not even marrying until their thirties. If ever. They lived together, had babies out of wedlock, raised them together until they were no longer compatible, then parted ways with the help of a mediator and child support orders.

If that weren't confusing enough, there was Dante and Pandora, hosting Christmas Day dinner as they'd done for the twenty years of their happy—everyone thought—marriage. His hand on her waist, Pan smiling up at him, and laughing at the things he said when she didn't even have to, their divorce was beyond comprehension, so Sylvia had stopped trying to comprehend it. Instead, she pretended they were still married, that nothing had changed. At her age, she got a pass.

"You okay, Mom?" Thomas, her Tommy, touched her elbow. "You want some wine?"

"No thank you, sweetheart." She lifted her paper cup, trying not to grimace. Wine. In paper. *Barbarians.* "I still have—"

"Mikey!" He bolted out of his chair. "I swear to Christ if you don't get those mamalukes in line I'll crack their heads!"

"They're just having fun, Pop. Leave off."

"We don't waste food in this family, no matter how many cars you buy." Tom pushed his chair in. "Sorry, Ma."

"It's okay, Tommy." But he was already confronting his son and grandsons, the twins no longer tossing rolls at their cousins but barely containing their laughter. Her son and his son were shouting at one another, hands screaming just as loudly. Sylvia tried not to smile, hiding it in a sip of wine from the paper cup when she couldn't. She didn't like to see Tommy so red in the face. Just like his father, that one. Quick to fly off the handle over the silliest things, quick to laugh. She worried for his blood pressure that he wouldn't get checked, or if he had, it was bad enough for him not to admit it.

"Hey, Nonina." Donatella slipped into her uncle's vacated seat. "Can this family get any louder or what?"

Sylvia patted her hand. "Did you have fun last night, sweetheart?"

"Last night?"

"You didn't make it to the feast of seven fishes. I imagine you were off having one of your adventures."

Donatella pulled apart her uncle's dinner roll, ate it tiny piece by tiny piece. "Something like that," she said. "Was Mom really mad?"

"Angry, sweetheart. Dogs go mad. People get angry."

"Nonina, jeez."

They laughed together.

"She was worried, not angry," Sylvia told her. "You should call when you're not going to show up."

"I'm thirty-five. I have a life. When do I stop being the baby?"

Never. "A mother worries. You'll understand, one day."

"I doubt that." Donatella picked up her uncle's fork, twirled the spaghetti into a bite-sized ball. "If Dante didn't show up, she'd figure he was stuck on a job. If Davide doesn't show up, he's with a woman. But me? I'm in a ditch somewhere. Mom needs someone else to focus on."

"Well, sweetheart, maybe if you didn't give her plenty to worry about . . ."

"Hardy-har-har. As if Davide is any less likely to die in some horrific way. Skydiving! Or stabbed by a stingray like Steve Irwin, which I'm still not over, by the—"

Sylvia smacked the back of Donatella's head.

"Ow!"

"Mannaggia dial! Don't say things like that."

"What? Will that make it come true?" Donatella rubbed the spot, pouting. *Precious.*

Sylvia hid another smile in a sip of wine. "Who is Steve Irwin? An old boyfriend?"

"The crocodile guy? You remember."

Vaguely. She shrugged.

"That's what Mom needs, you know."

"A crocodile?"

"Very funny, Nonina. No. Not a crocodile. Mom needs a boy-friend."

As if this were news. "She was very happy with your father."

"He's been dead thirteen years."

"Fourteen."

"Exactly. I loved my dad. I know she did, too. We all loved him. But Mom needs more in her life than that store. And me."

And me. Not that she didn't enjoy her daughter's attention, only that Sylvia being one of the three things Varina's life revolved around, and ninety-two, did not bode well for Varina.

"She'd never agree," Sylvia said. "I've tried to interest her in men from the church."

"There are all kinds of dating sites for the young at heart," Donatella said. "But I guess there's no chance she'd sign up for one."

"Never in a million years. We'd have to do it for her." A finger in the air. "Now that's an idea."

"Nope," Donatella said. "Those dating sites don't allow that sort of thing, for obvious reasons."

Not to Sylvia. Sometimes people just didn't know what they wanted, or needed. There were ways, though. Old-fashioned ways. The wheels in her noggin creaked into motion. Yes, Varina would blow her stack if she ever found out, but maybe, if they played it right, she'd be happy, too. Sylvia pulled her granddaughter in closer. "We would have to be sneakier."

Donatella chuckled. "I like the way you think, Nonina."

"Because we are two of a kind, sweetheart."

"Me and you?"

"You'd be surprised." Sylvia pinched her arm. "What about a flyer? You know, like they do for guitar lessons and lost dogs."

"A flyer? How is that sneaky?"

"I don't mean put her picture up all over town with her phone number. We could put something like, 'Single, sexy, seventy-something looking for romance.' Instead of her phone number, put yours, then you could screen the men who answer. We don't want her ending up with an ax murderer."

"You know…" Donatella bit her thumbnail. "That's not a terrible idea. But not my phone number. Considering she pays for my cell, I imagine she'd recognize it. Maybe I can create an email address. But how do we get her to go out with them?"

"Oh, you'll figure it out. You're a smart girl."

"Me? This was your idea."

"You started it."

Donatella went back to savaging her thumbnail. The twins were tossing rolls again, but Tommy and Mikey were now at the far end of the long table, playing pinochle with Dante, Davide, and Gabriella.

"It's in her best interests, right?" Donatella said. "I mean, it's not just about getting her off my back. I really do want her to be happy, and I don't think she is. Mom needs a life that isn't her family or that store. She needs romance and excitement and something that's just hers."

"Absolutely. I agree." Someone to talk to, to sleep beside, to love. What woman doesn't want that? "Think about it. I will, too. Next week, after New Year's is over, we'll have coffee at that fancy-schmancy coffee shop you used to work at and see what we've come up with. What do you say? Matchmakers?"

Donatella put up her pinky. "Matchmakers."

Sylvia hooked her crooked pinky around her granddaughter's. "Don't breathe a word. If she finds out…"

"I won't. I pinky swear."

"Good girl."

"Nonina?"

"Yes?"

"Pick a different coffee place. I kind of can't step foot in The Bean's Knees. By court order." Donatella looked beyond Sylvia, to Paulie, as it turned out, motioning for her. "Looks like I got to go."

"All right, sweetheart. I'll see you soon."

And, like Tommy moments earlier, Donatella was gone. With an apology but not a backward glance. Sylvia helped herself to more wine, pouring it into the barbaric paper cup. In her day, there'd been no such thing as disposable plates and cups and utensils; not for the Spini family. There'd been no dishwasher, either. None but her. She'd cleaned for hours after everyone else had gone home to watch television or play with new games. Joseph would be snoring in his favorite chair, a hand tucked into his waistband. Varina helped, once the children were old enough to fend for themselves; and then Donatella came along ten years after Davide, and that was that, until her daughter had taken over the family gatherings, sometime after Joseph died but before Dino did. Sylvia couldn't remember anymore. The years were running together.

Sitting back in her chair—a cushioned one Dante had brought out for her, from his own office—Sylvia sipped and observed. All these people, men and women, children, all there because of her. She was their matriarch. Without her, none of them would be there. Not even in-laws like Catherine and Pandora; certainly not Paulie, who'd probably have ended up being one of those street-gays with AIDS had it not been for Varina, who would not be at all, if not for Sylvia Cioffi and Joseph Spini falling in love, getting married, having children who nearly destroyed them both.

She raised her cup. "Merry Christmas, Joe. Merry Christmas." And took a long sip. And longer. And poured another paper-cupful. What did it matter if she got drunk? She was ninety-two. They'd think she was losing her marbles. Or cute. Either way, they'd be right.

5

baciagaloop *(ba-cha-ga-loop)*

Italian: Baciagalupo; best I can find is it's an Italian surname that translates loosely as "to kiss a wolf."

In Jersey Italian, it means "dufus," or "fool." That may or may not stem from the Abbott and Costello (Jersey boys, from Asbury Park and Paterson, respectively) character, Mr. Bacciagalupe. He was a barber, a baker, a grocer, a record store owner, a peanut vendor, a chef, to name a few, depending upon the episode, played by Ignazio Curcuruto (stage name: Joe Kirk) a Sicilian-American actor. Whatever his role, he was generally slapstickish and buffoonish. As if J.I.s needed yet another way of calling someone a fool.

Y ou could ask one of your brothers. They both have the money."

Donatella heaved a long, weary sigh. The party had moved; the Spini family going their way, and the Palladinos congregating at the familial home, above which Paulie lived, and where he now sat, drawing circles in the curls at her temple.

"Couldn't we put it on your credit card?" she asked. "I'd pay it off. I swear."

No, she would not. Paulie had learned long ago to at least pretend to be as broke as she was all the time. It was the only way to keep the friendship alive, and money in his bank account. "My card limit is only something like twelve hundred bucks. Sorry."

"Oh, yeah. I forgot." Another long, heavy sigh. "I don't want to ask her."

"I don't see that you have a choice. It's your brothers or your mom."

"I can't ask my mother for money she doesn't have. Not even I'm that much of an asshole. Besides, if I don't ask Mom, she doesn't have to know about this."

"Then your brothers it is. Which one?"

She groaned, snaking her arm across his abdomen, nestling deeper into his side. If he didn't love her so much, he'd be more pissed, but he did, and he was closer to sad just then. Chaos found her, even when she wasn't the one causing it. At least half of the trouble she got into was misplaced loyalty, altruism, or empathy. The other half? All Donatella. Bad decisions compounded by the impulse control of an otter. He kissed the top of her head.

"If you're going to catch them, you'd better get downstairs before they leave."

"I don't wanna."

"Don."

"Can't you ask for me?"

"No way."

"Fine. Chicken." Donatella uncurled from his side. "Bok-bok!"

"Look who's talking."

She blew him a kiss. "Wish me luck."

Paulie stayed on the couch, feet up on the coffee table, until the sound of her footsteps on the stairs drifted away. Sitting forward, rubbing his face, he attempted to squelch the guilty conscience telling him he was the worst friend ever, sending his oldest and dearest to her scary brothers when he had the money to help her. In their thirty years of friendship, he'd only drawn two lines when it came to Donatella Palladino. He would never work with her again, and he'd never lend her money he wasn't willing to lose. That brief but disastrous stint working with her in Davide's salon drew the first line after she'd swiped expensive spa products and sold them to pay for a weekend in Atlantic City: "Don't worry so much. He'll never notice the difference. How can he know what was used in-house and what wasn't?"

But Davide wasn't just gorgeous, he was smart. He'd never accused Paulie, but he knew that *he* knew, and that made it almost as bad. Donatella was young and wild and contrite. She'd paid him back some of the money, and because she was his baby sister, Davide forgave her. He would not, however, employ her again. Ever. Paulie hadn't been fired, but he did quit. The embarrassment was too much. And then Dante came to his rescue, offering him an errand-boy job with Spini and Son Construction. The rest, as they said, was history. All in all, it turned out to be the best thing that ever happened to him, employment-wise, anyway. Personally? He wasn't so sure. Being in Dante's orbit day in and day out was as compelling as it was maddening.

The second line was one of common sense, of which he'd gained enough of to keep it firm. That amount of money would kick-start the beginning of the end of their lifelong friendship. When it all went south, he'd lose not only Donatella, but her family. His family. Because even if he was *like* family, he wasn't blood.

Watching the tree lights blinking blue and red, yellow and green, Paulie considered taking it down, right then and there. Christmas was over. The whole Little Christmas thing—religiously observed on January sixth, there in the ungentrified, still–Italian Catholic section of Wyldale, New Jersey—annoyed him. Maybe because he liked the holidays, but not the religion that deemed him an abomination. At least, that's what his parents claimed before turning their backs on him. No Christmas present sent in the mail. Not even a card. Only a phone call once in a while. Always his mother, never his dad. Paulie hadn't spoken a word to him in seventeen years.

Shaking it off, he poured himself a glass from the opened bottle of wine Mrs. Palladino had pressed on him before he went upstairs: "There's so much here. It'll go to vinegar before I can use it." For her, he'd leave the tree up until January sixth. He didn't want her worried he was depressed or something when he was actually pretty happy, all in all.

Knuckles rapped on his door, the familiar, cartoony staccato that made him smile. Paulie opened the door, whipping off his glasses. "Hey, Dante. Everything okay downstairs?"

"Huh? Oh." He shook his head. Dark eyes, dark hair, Dante had the signature and perpetual five o'clock shadow Davide did, that Tommy had. The deep cleft in his chin made all the deeper for the unshaveable black patch of it, however, was all his own. Unlike his younger brother's, Dante's tumbled look was genuine, not artfully created. Davide couldn't hold a candle to him. "Everything's fine. Dona's talking to Davide about some shit."

The wealthier brother. The wilder one. The one who'd hold it over her head, but keep his mouth shut.

"Oh, good." Silence. "Did you need something?"

"Nah. I, uh, I brought you something."

Dante stepped back on the landing, picked up a cardboard box from the top step. Something inside meowed.

"A cat?"

"A mama cat and two kittens," Dante said. "Someone left them at the site trailer. I found them this morning. Gabby wanted to keep them but she can't. School and all. She thought you might want them."

Paulie took the box from Dante's hands, brought it to the coffee table, and set it down. Lifting the flaps, he found a black and white cat and two obviously newborn kittens. One was mostly black with white patches and tufty-white ears, while the other was mostly black but for a dot of white near the nose and another on the top of its head. "Who leaves a mama and her babies at a construction site on Christmas?"

"Fucking baciagaloops, that's who." Dante scritched mama-cat's chin. She lifted her furry face, instantly purring. "Sweet." He let his hand fall. "So. You want them?"

A cat had never even been a thought on Paulie's far horizon. Three cats? He'd never had pets. Not even a caterpillar in a jar. He could count on zero fingers the times Dante had been in his apartment. And now here he was, bearing needy animals on Christmas like a handsome, kindly saint.

Paulie's heart beat a little too fast. Reaching a tentative hand into the box, he scritched mama-cat the way Dante had. She pressed herself into his touch, purring louder. "Yes."

"Yes?"

"Yes, I want them."

"Yeah?"

"One hundred percent, yeah. I'm going to have to take them to the vet tomorrow. Can I have the morning off?"

Dante laughed. "What'm I going to say? No? Sure. Take the day. Consider it your Christmas bonus."

"I already got my check. You're not getting it back."

Waving him off, Dante backed away. "There's a bag of dry and a couple cans of cat food in the box, under the blanket. Gabby took care of her this morning. You should have enough until you can get to the store."

"Great. Thanks, Dante. And thank Gabriella for thinking of me."

"Will do. Right. See you day after tomorrow, kid."

"See you."

Paulie whumped into the couch, staring at the box containing three cats he never in a million years would have guessed he'd have that morning. Two pointed ears poked out of the top, then a furry, black face with white markings around one eye and under her chin.

"I'm sorry whoever did this to you is such an asshole," he whispered. "I guess it was nice they let you keep your babies . . . and didn't drown all of you." Mama-cat hopped out of the box and onto the couch beside Paulie. "You're not going to bite me, are you?"

She rubbed up against his outstretched hand. Paulie ran his fingers over her head, along her spine. So soft. Obviously well cared for. This was no stray, but someone's no-longer-wanted pet. His nose tingled. Paulie rubbed it until the sensation ebbed. Now mama-cat was sitting in his lap, purring. Calm. Sweet. Grateful. Braving the possibility of claws and teeth, Paulie scooped her up and held her close, but lightly. She didn't seem to mind.

Another knock, this one not cartoonishly staccato. Carrying the cat to the door, he opened it with one hand. "Oh, hey, Gabs."

"Dad forgot these." She held up a bag of cat litter and a mortar pan. "I couldn't get a litter box at the grocery store this morning. Dad had a bunch of these lying around."

"I'm sure it's fine." He waved the cat's paw. "Thank you."

"You're welcome."

"You want to come in?"

She peeked around him, this perfect girl as much her mother as her father. "The kittens sleeping?"

"I think so. Here, take mama back to them while I set up the litter box."

Mama-cat shifted from his arms to hers without skipping a purr. Paulie picked up the litter box and bag, turned in circles. Where to put it? The bathroom seemed appropriate. He set the mortar pan in the corner, under the cabinet where he kept all his toiletries. It was a little overlarge, but it fit well enough to make do.

"Bring her here, will you?"

Gabriella did as asked, setting mama-cat into the litter box. She sniffed, squatted, buried, and left them both staring after her, heading back to her kittens, already at home.

"She have a name yet?" Paulie asked.

"I was calling her MaryJane, after Sister MaryJane. Because she's black and white. Get it?"

"Very witty." Sister MaryJane had been a young nun when he was a kid. Kind and devoted and surprisingly unconventional, ideologically speaking. He scooped up the cat, settled her into the box with her kittens. "Did you know she's who I came out to first?"

"I did not." Gabriella smiled. "That's awesome. She's awesome. Well, she was. I still can't believe she died. She wasn't that old."

"Cancer's a bitch."

"Yeah."

Paulie fidgeted. "She was with me when I told my parents. Her and Donatella."

Resting a hand on his shoulder, Gabriella gave it a squeeze. "I'd say I named her well, then."

"Perfectly."

"What about the babies?"

"I guess I'll let the vet tell me if they're male or female, then fig-ure it out."

"No, I meant, are you keeping them?"

"Huh?"

Gabriella sat on the couch, reaching in to pet MaryJane, now nursing her kittens. "They're too young to go now, but I'm sure you can find homes for them once they're big enough. This apartment is a little small for three cats. You'd have to make room for three lit-ter boxes. Four, if you're going by recommendations. And cat toys. Towers and scratching posts and fluffy balls with catnip in them. I researched it."

Paulie sat beside her, slipping his until-then-forgotten glasses back in place. Separate MaryJane from her babies? The babies from one another? "I don't know if I'll be able to part with them."

"It's up to you."

Voices rose angrily through the floor. Gabriella cocked her head. "Uh-oh. Looks like Christmas is over."

Maybe Davide hadn't kept his mouth shut after all. Damn.

"I'd better get downstairs and drag Dad out before his blood pressure goes up."

"I'll stay here with my cats, if it's all the same to you."

"Good call. Merry Christmas, Paulie. Happy New Year." She kissed his cheek. "I love you, you know."

His heart stitched. "I love you, too. Merry Christmas."

She rolled her eyes in the direction of the argument escalating downstairs, and left with a soft click of his door. Paulie hunkered lower in the couch, closed his eyes, and listened to the muffled shout-ing. The Palladinos labored under the belief that the louder one shouted, the righter it made them, which actually worked to some extent, as the righter each and every one of them thought they were, the louder they screamed.

He'd been planning on going back downstairs, or at least over to Donatella's apartment above the store to see how she made out. No way he was going now. Whether or not she got the money she needed, he'd find out in due time. After everything had died down. The lines he drew and held between himself and the Palladinos were precarious, but necessary.

MaryJane climbed out of her box and onto his lap; his hand automatically smoothed her soft fur. Downstairs, voices lowered, doors slammed. Cars backed out of the driveway. They were all gone, probably even Donatella. He held his breath, listening for her slow trudge up his stairs. Nothing. Paulie sighed, a strange but pleasant harmony to MaryJane's purring. He rubbed under her chin, lifting it for more. Peace was a cat, half asleep and purring on your chest. Trying to somehow magically pull some of MaryJane's contentment into himself, Paulie only managed another harmonious sigh, pulled his cell phone from his pocket, and texted Donatella.

6

goomad'

Italian: *comare;* literally, "godmother"

Mistress, paramour, a little slide on the side. It was once a given that a married man would have a goomad'.

svogliadell' *(svoo-ya-del)*

Italian: *sfogliatella;* a layered dough pastry in the shape of a shell, with a custard filling

The *f* sound often becomes a *v*, for some reason. Like fox and vixen in English.

A cell phone pinged. Varina picked her head up out of her hands. Donatella's cell phone lit up, there on the table where she'd forgotten it when she slammed out of the house, all righteous indignation and tears. Pulling it closer, she read Paulie's text: You ok?

Varina sniffed, wiped the tears from her cheeks, texted: She's not here. Forgot her cell phone. She'll be okay. Thanks. Then she switched the phone off. Not even Paulie could make her feel better just then. In truth, she didn't want to feel better. Donatella was in trouble—expensive trouble she was no way allowing either of her sons to pay for—Varina wanted just a few minutes to wallow in self-pity.

"You okay, sweetheart?"

Varina jumped in her chair, banging her knee on the underside of the dining room table and choking on her own saliva. "Why"—*cough, cough*—"are you always"—*cough*—"sneaking up on me?"

"Oh, stop." Sylvia pulled out a chair and sat beside her. "Not a great end to a nice holiday, huh?"

"Not at all." Varina ripped the paper napkin she'd balled in her hands. "What do I do with that child, Mom?"

"She's not a child."

She sniffed. "I know."

"Do you?"

"She's *my* child. She lost her father so young—"

"It's no excuse!" Sylvia took a deep breath. "Look, sweetheart, I love her. We all love our Donatella. But if she never has to pay the price for her actions she's never going to—"

"You want her in jail?" Varina burst. "Is that what you're saying? I should let them lock her up?"

"You going to shout at me, now?"

Varina clamped her mouth shut, breathed heavily through her nose.

"Maybe," Sylvia said, "thirty days in the clink will straighten her out."

"This isn't some old TV show where the wardens and the inmates are all friends. This is prison, and prison is dangerous."

Silence, but for the ticking of the grandfather clock. If it weren't for the fact that she violated an order of protection—filed and won by a man twice her size and a complete asshole, to boot—community service might have been in the offing. But Donatella had not only violated it, she violated it big. Varina pushed up and out of her chair. There was no use in rehashing it. Dante and Davide had railed against Donatella. It had been like watching a pair of pit bulls snarling at one of those fluffy white dogs that always had a bow in its hair. Varina knew they were right, that her mother was right—Donatella was never going to stop getting into these messes if someone else always cleaned up for her. But this was different. This was life-altering, and Varina couldn't let it happen.

"Go on to bed, Mom." Varina kissed one cheek, then the other. "I'm just going to put things away in the kitchen."

"Can I help you?"

"No, thanks. There isn't much. I'll see you in the morning."

Varina puttered about the kitchen, opening and closing drawers and cabinets, until she heard the door of her mother's room close. She counted to fifteen, breathed a heavy sigh, and ducked into the pantry. From the highest shelf, she pulled the slightly rusty coffee can. She peeled open the cracked lid. From the $8,800, she took the $2,500 Donatella needed to avoid thirty days locked up.

Tucking the wad into her apron pocket, Varina tried not to cry. No Europe in the spring for her. Fall, maybe. Hopefully. That would be nice. Nicer, even. It was okay. It was fine. She'd waited this long, what was another few months? But she cried anyway, cursing Dino for leaving her alone with all this. The store. Mom. Donatella. The weight of adult children she would never not worry about. The house, sturdy and standing among all the other neighborhood houses there since the turn of the prior century, was nevertheless becoming a weight on her shoulders. Always something that needed doing, repairing, replacing. Even with a contractor son, there was only so much she could ask of him. Would ask of him. It was all she could do to keep up, financially, emotionally, physically. And now a full six months of savings, savings she'd skimmed and scraped from the till, was going out the door because her daughter had gone to a bar instead of the family feast of seven fishes.

"Maybe she's right. Maybe thirty days away would straighten her out."

Even as she said it aloud, Varina knew she could never see it through. Six months from now, it would be something else. And something else. And something else skimming from her stash in the coffee can. She was never getting to Europe, never sailing down brown rivers, eating local delicacies, and dancing to local music. Not if she didn't put herself first, for once in her life.

Sliding the coffee can back onto the top shelf, Varina sniffed back her tears. No use crying over it. Dino was dead and gone, and this was hers. All of it. She wasn't letting Donatella go to prison, not even for thirty days, but she was, by hook or by crook, going to Europe in the fall. There was only one way to ensure it that she could think of, and Varina would do it. Even if it went against her every grain.

SYLVIA OPENED HER DOOR A CRACK, PEEKED OUT. QUIET. DARK. Varina had finally gone to bed. Going quietly from her room to the kitchen, she cringed when the floorboards creaked, but her daughter didn't stick her head out of her room, asking what she was doing up. In fact, Sylvia could hear her snoring all the way from the pantry.

She took out the step stool and, very carefully, stepped up one, two steps. Reaching for the coffee can, always a stretch for her, Sylvia managed to catch the edge and swooped it into her waiting arms.

"Pretty spry, if I do say so myself." She'd always been on the athletic side, even if everyone from her parents to her siblings to her own husband and kids thought she was as fragile as she was small. There were times Sylvia forgot her age and tried to hop over a puddle or climb the stairs at a trot, but she'd never broken a hip, and she'd never keeled over, so she still was not as fragile as everyone thought.

Without opening it, she could tell the load was lighter. Tears welled. Poor Varina. All her years of saving, for what, Sylvia had never known until that morning. A cruise, of all things. Varina had thought herself sly, unreadable, but Sylvia knew. She'd seen it in her daughter's eyes, in the way she tried to make light of the brochure.

Taking the folded twenty-dollar bill from the pocket of her housecoat, she crossed herself with it before tucking it into the coffee can. Varina had never noticed the odd ten or twenty Sylvia occasionally added to her stash. It wasn't much, but it was something. What did she have to spend even what little extra money she had on? Her daughter took care of her, made sure she got to the doctor and the beauty parlor and bingo once a month. She was a good girl. She deserved to be able to take her cruise. Maybe she'd meet someone, and wouldn't that be nice.

The back door creaked open. Sylvia froze. Floorboards under the ancient linoleum squeaked. Shoving the coffee can onto a shelf, she grabbed the broom and flew out of the pantry like an albatross with a busted wing.

"Stay back!" She brandished the broom handle. "I'll use it!"

"Nonina, it's me. It's Donatella."

"Madonn', child. I could have killed you." Sylvia's racing heart zinged a little more than she could ignore. Donatella might have snorted. Sylvia chose to ignore that. Hand pressed to her chest, she took her time putting the broom back. And the coffee can. She could hear her granddaughter in the dining room, quietly but still too noisily looking for something. By the time Sylvia emerged from the pantry, Donatella was already headed back out the door.

"Go to bed, Nonina." She kissed her cheek. "It's late."

"What are you doing here at this hour, anyway?"

"I left my cell phone. I was waiting for the lights to go out before sneaking back in to get it. I didn't want to face anyone."

"Not even me?"

Donatella hugged her, one-armed. "Never you. You're always on my side."

"I'm not this time. You shouldn't take money from your mother. She doesn't have it."

"I didn't hear her offer."

"She'll give it to you. You know she will."

"I thought you said she doesn't have it."

"She'll find it." It wasn't a complete lie, and she did want Donatella to at least feel some remorse. "You mark my words."

Donatella's arm fell away. She groaned softly. "What am I supposed to do?"

"Stop." Sylvia told her. "Just stop all this. Get a job. Don't drink so much. Pick better men. Think, Donatella. Think before you do these things. You can't feel your way through this world. It just doesn't work, believe you me."

The words echoed through the years. Shouted by her own mother. Her father. Well-intentioned sisters. By Joseph. They hurt, coming out of her own mouth. She'd nearly broken herself on them, and would have before succumbing, until she'd come too close to breaking her children instead.

"I try, Nonina." Donatella sniffed. "I swear I do."

"Try harder." Sylvia took her nearly-as-tiny granddaughter into her arms. Strong arms, even now. At least, that's the way she saw them. "Now go home. Get some sleep."

Donatella wiped her cheeks and nose with her fingertips. "In better news, I came up with a pitch for Mom's flyer."

"Did you?"

Like a light switch, she flipped. "We don't want to be obvious, right? Like, it's not as if I'm going to put these flyers up where Mom will see them, even if she probably won't suspect."

"Yes, that's true."

"So, I thought I'd put them up in places she'd never go. Like the VFW or the hipster eateries and bars."

"Get on with it, sweetheart. It's late."

"Right. Sorry. Okay, so considering all that, what do you think about 'Is your grandfather single and looking for love?' Catchy, right? And it'll get a wider pool, you know? Like, other people my age looking to pair their dads or grandfathers up with a nice woman."

"Well, sweetheart." *Tact, Sylvia. Tact!* "It sounds a bit . . . pornographic."

"It does not!" She laughed. Softly. "It's *love,* not lov*ing*! We don't want men looking for a goomad'. Or simply for friendship. I think it's perfect."

It did have a ring to it. And even if Varina did happen to see it, she'd never suspect.

"It'll be great," Donatella said. "You'll see. I have it all mocked up, even created an email address for it. I'll print one out and bring it when we go for coffee. Jumbaloon's? Tomorrow?"

Ah, svogliadell'. The flaky, crunchy layers. The custard center. The dusting of powdered sugar. Impossible to eat without getting half of it all over your blouse, but she'd skip breakfast to have one. Without Varina noticing, of course. "Yes, tomorrow. I'll meet you at eleven. If I drink coffee after noon, it keeps me up at night."

"There's always decaf."

"Bite your tongue."

Donatella laughed, kissed her cheek again. "I love you, Nonina."

"I love you, too, sweetheart."

"I'll do better. I swear. I'll make it up to Mom. We're going to find her a man. A good man, and then she'll be so happy, she won't even think about what a fu . . . screwup her daughter is."

Sylvia closed the door softly. Twisting the dead bolt took a little more than her wrist freely gave, but she managed. And she was tired. So tired. The day had been lovely. The evening had not been. All the shouting and stress had taken more out of her than she'd realized, because no matter how young she still felt inside her head, she was an old woman who had enjoyed and endured more life than she ever planned to.

The *scratch-scratch-scratch* started as she passed through the parlor on her way to her bedroom. Then the bells, and *It's three o'clock in the morning/We've danced the whole night through/And daylight soon will be dawning/Just one more waltz with you . . .*

Sylvia stumbled on a memory, of dancing with Tommy, his little feet on hers, but only stumbled.

"Good night, Vicky. Merry Christmas."

She closed the door and could no longer hear the music. It wasn't like Vicky to be so considerate. Maybe she'd had enough, too. Or maybe she wasn't just a haunted old Victrola, but a haunted old Victrola with a heart.

7

jumbaloon

Italian: *ciambellone;* a doughnut-shaped, frosted cake

In Jersey Italian, a jumbaloon is an obese person. The similarity to the words *jumbo* and *balloon* in English is probably just a coincidence. Here's another case of using food words to insult someone. To be fair, many of these words are also used affectionately, like this one. I don't want to give anyone the impression Italians/Jersey Italians are complete assholes all the time.

oolee

Italian: *voglia;* "wish, desire, longing"

An oolee, in my experience, specifically applies to food. One could have an oolee for cake, or spaghetti, but not for a Cadillac or a new pair of shoes.

There were only two other people in the office when Varina entered. A young travel agent, speaking with a woman around Varina's own age, unnaturally red haired—though she might have been once, given her fair complexion—and dressed to the nines in a white, tailored dress with big, black buttons. Very chic, though perhaps several decades out of date. Retro, Donatella would call it. Expensive, she thought, and that maybe she was making a big mistake.

"I'll be with you in a moment." The travel agent poked her head over the top of her cubicle.

"No rush." Varina took a seat, taking in the travel posters of palm trees and ships, mountains and beaches, cities and cities and cities all lit up or spread beneath cerulean skies. The well-dressed woman—who wore way too much makeup . . . said the woman who wore none—came out from behind the cubicle. Varina rose to her feet, as if she were a gentleman.

"Taking a trip?" The woman slid her arms into a wool coat that matched her dress.

"I am," Varina said. "One of those river cruises."

"Oh, they're lovely." Gloves now. Leather. "I've been on several. Any one in particular?"

Varina pulled the brochure from her messenger bag. "Either the one from Lyon to Avignon, or the Castles of the Rhine. Have you done either?"

"Both." She laughed, a free and merry sound that seemed out of place in this woman's throat. "You can't go wrong with either, but I love the Lyon to Avignon cruise so much, I go every other year. I just booked this year's."

"Really?"

The woman leaned in a little closer, tugging her glove into place. "Don't go in the summer," she said. "Spring or fall. Winter is less expensive, but for a reason. Me, myself? I prefer the autumn. The sun's just a different kind of warm then."

"Thanks for the tip."

"Ms. Cooperman?" The travel agent came around her cubicle. "Oh, good. You're still here. I need some information from you, if you don't mind."

"All my information is in your computer."

"Yes, yes. But I'm new, and I don't have all the access codes I need to get to it. If you don't mind waiting to book until after the New Year, I can—"

"Oh, for goodness' sake, fine."

"I'm sorry," the agent said to Varina. "It's going to be another fifteen minutes or so. Do you mind waiting?"

"Don't be silly." Ms. Cooperman yanked off her gloves. "I can do it myself. Do I look incapable to you?"

"Of course not."

"I use a travel agent because I've always done so, and I'm loyal to this particular office, not because I can't book my own travel arrangements online."

"I'm sorry, Ms. Cooperman. I didn't mean any offense."

"Well." She took off her coat. "Apology accepted. Now show me to the right computer and I'll key the information in while you help this nice lady book her cruise down the Rhône."

"If you'll have a seat in there." The younger woman pointed to her cubicle. "I'll set Ms. Cooperman up at a computer. And your name is?"

"Varina Palladino. Varina is fine."

The agent's smile was a little strained. Varina felt sorry for her. She was working the day after Christmas, in an otherwise empty office. She had to need the money, something Ms. Cooperman was probably overlooking.

"Thank you for waiting. I'm Patrice."

"That's a lovely name."

"Thanks. I've always liked it. I'll be back in a moment, and you can tell me what can I do for you."

NINE THOUSAND.

Two hundred.

Dollars.

Cruise, airfare, and three extra days in Cannes, because, after all, if she was going to spend that much on a trip to France, she was getting her money's worth. The store would be fine. Credit card in hand Varina thought she might vomit.

"Is that the card you'll be using?"

Sweat beaded her upper lip. "Does it all have to go on at once? Can I do installments?"

"I'm afraid not with this line," Patrice said. "There are other lines that do the same trip. They're older ships, but still very nice."

Tears stung. Varina dared them to fall. "No. This is the one I want." She handed over the card.

Patrice took it with a sad smile. "You sure? Once this is booked, you'd have to have a medical reason for canceling."

"I'm sure." Varina's heart thumped with every keyboard strike. Aside from the $2,500 she paid the court, she'd put every penny from her coffee can into the bank. The minute she got home, she'd make a lump payment, before the boiler could go, or the roof could leak, or Donatella could get into trouble again. The interest wouldn't be too bad. She'd pay it off in a few months. Somehow.

"You're all set!" Patrice handed back her card. "I'll get all your tickets and vouchers closer to the trip. Make sure your passport is up-to-date, and good for at least six months after the trip. Are you excited?"

Varina's heart fluttered. She laughed. "I am!"

"That's wonderful. I'm so happy for you!"

"I am, too. Thank you, Patrice."

"You're very welcome. If you have any questions, or there is any-thing I can do for you, just call." She slid a folder across her desk. "My card is in there, as well as all kinds of tips and tidbits about your trip. It's all available online, if you prefer. Many of our clients like to have the hard copy, but I do encourage you to go online and mosey around the site. You can see what the excursions are, and see which ones you're interested in. There are informational walking tours every day, as part of your package, but you will need to book the time you want. Oh! And menus! The food on this line is amazing. The closer you get to depar-ture, the more fun, interactive things you'll be able to see online."

The fluttering in Varina's chest warmed her cheeks. It was done. The worst was over! And she was more excited than she'd allowed herself to be. "Thank you again." She rose, extending her hand. "I'm sure I'll be calling you."

Ms. Cooperman was rising to her feet as Patrice and Varina came out of the cubicle.

"I'm so sorry," Patrice gushed. "I didn't realize you were waiting."

"I was, but not for you, dear." She smiled Varina's way, wagging a finger. "I remember you."

"Me?"

"You catered at least six or seven parties for me in the last decade."

Cooperman. Cooperman. Varina scrambled to place the name with the customer.

The redhead laughed. "You look like you just swallowed a bug! It would have been under my late husband's name. Visser."

"Jacob Visser!" Nice man. Flirty. She'd always dealt with him, never his wife. At least, not that she remembered.

"That's him."

"You said *late*." Varina moved closer. "I'm so sorry. I wasn't aware he'd died."

"It's been two years. I'm Ruth, by the way."

"Oh, sorry. Varina."

"Palladino." She winked. "I know. Your meatballs are to die for."

"You shop in my store?"

"My housekeeper does. I send her to get me something delicious at least once a week. You've been feeding me for years."

"That's so funny!"

"What's funnier is that you just booked the same cruise I did."

"Well, you spoke so highly—"

"No, I meant the same, exact cruise. Same week."

"For real?"

Ruth nodded. "You want to grab a cup of coffee? There's a great bakery just around the corner."

"Jumbaloon's?"

"That's the one." Ruth checked her watch. "If we get there before noon, there should be a jelly doughnut or two left."

"Not jelly doughnuts. Bom'blon'!" Varina pulled the door open, gesturing Ruth through. "Call it a jelly doughnut to Iggy's face and she'll go Soup Nazi on you."

IS YOUR GRANDFATHER SINGLE AND LOOKING FOR LOVE?

Sylvia thought the man in the dark suit was a little too old and the rose he held a little too corny for her daughter, but she didn't want to squelch Donatella's sincere attempt at creating the flyer for their secret campaign. "What is this email address?" She squinted. "I can't make it out."

"Stillgotallmymarbles-backslash-seniorbachelorette. It's a Gmail account."

Sylvia nearly choked on her coffee. "Very witty, sweetheart."

"You think?" Donatella took back the flyer. "I wanted to get across the applicant needs to have a sense of humor. Should I make the contact info a little bigger?"

"That would be good," Sylvia told her. "And, while you're at it, what about a slightly younger man in a button-down shirt instead of the suit? More casual. Like your mother."

"You have to trust me on this, Nonina. He's perfect. Nothing about him says *macho*. The suit and rose imply romance. That's what we want for Mom. A romantic gentleman with a sense of humor."

"You don't think he's too old?"

"It's just a public domain pic I got from a website, not someone for Mom to date."

"I suppose." Sylvia ate the last bite of her svogliadell'. She'd pay later for indulging, but it was absolutely worth it. "And you'll screen the men who respond?"

"Of course. I'm not going to have my mother dating losers. If they pass my inspection, I'll tell them to go to Palladino's and strike up a conversation with the lovely lady behind the counter. If there's a click, he'll ask her out and it'll be up to her to accept or refuse. What do you think?"

Sylvia swallowed the pastry with her last sip of coffee. Another no-no, but it was still before noon. It should be okay. "I think Varina will kill us both if she ever finds out."

"She won't find out. And if she does, hopefully it will be because the gentleman in question was honest enough to tell her and it'll be a funny 'how we met' story for them to tell at parties."

"Your mother doesn't go to parties."

"Well, maybe she will once she's happily in love!" Donatella threw up her hands. "Do you not want to do this anymore?"

Sylvia was indeed having second thoughts, and not entirely because she was afraid of her daughter's reaction. Her fears were selfish ones; she kept them to herself. "Of course, I do. This will be good for her."

"All right." Donatella checked the time on her cell phone. "It's almost noon. I'm going to fix the font and print out a bunch of these. I scoped out a few places where the older guys hang out, but where Mom would never in a million years step foot. I can have them up before supper."

"Are you coming over tonight?"

Donatella hung her head. "I don't want to, but yes."

"Don't be ungrateful, sweetheart."

"I'm very grateful." She picked up her head, eyes full of tears. "I can't begin to say how grateful I am. But . . ."

"But?"

"But it breaks my heart, Nonina. It breaks my heart that I broke *her* heart again, and that she found some way to scrape together the money for fines I incurred to keep me out of prison. I don't know if I can face her."

"Don't be a coward. You be there tonight, on time, and tell your mother how grateful you are. And you tell her you're going to get a job, a real job, and pay her back."

"I plan to do just that."

"Don't plan it, Donatella." Sylvia squeezed her granddaughter's hand. "Do it, even if you have to help out at the store to work it off."

"She won't let me work there. Not after I forgot to lock up that time."

And the ensuing robbery. As well as the food she gave away to friends, casual acquaintances, and nice faces. The inability to make change correctly. The coming in late and leaving early and breaks that lasted several hours. Sylvia took a deep, mental breath. "Well, the insurance company wouldn't reimburse her, sweetheart. You can hardly blame her."

"I'll be there, Nonina," she said. "Cross my heart and hope to die."

"Don't say that."

"I'm going to go. Is Uncle Tommy coming for you?"

"Any minute."

"Then if you don't mind, I'm going to jet. I have to face my mother, but I don't have to face Uncle Tommy. You know Dante told him everything."

"Of course, he did. We keep no secrets in this family." *In theory.* "Go ahead, sweetheart. I'll see you later."

Donatella kissed both her cheeks. "I love you!"

"Love you, too."

It was one of the rare times Sylvia wished she had a cell phone. She told Tommy to pick her up at 11:45 sharp. If she had a cell phone, she could call and tell him to come ten minutes earlier, thus saving her from sitting around like a chooch. A second cup of coffee would be the end of any sleep she might get that night. Another svogliadell' would lie on her stomach at least three days. But she could get her son a little treat, bring something home for Varina.

Purse in hand, she headed for the counter just as the chime rang, as the door blew open, as Varina entered the bakery with an elderly yet statuesque redhead. Sylvia turned, then turned again, like a chicken with no head and no sense of direction.

"Mom?"

Varina's hand kept her from spinning a third time. She looked up, felt her jaw go slack. Her mouth wouldn't work. Her brain spun the way her feet had. Try as she might, her bits and pieces would not align.

"It's okay, Mom. I'm here."

"We can do this another time," the redhead was saying, though her mouth seemed to move slower than the words hitting Sylvia's ears.

Deep breath. Just one, deep breath. "It's fine. I'm fine, sweetheart. You surprised me. That's all. What are you doing here?"

"The better question is, what are you doing here?"

"I had an oolee for svogliadell'. Tommy is picking me up."

"Did he bring you here?"

"Of course. You know I can't drive."

"Why didn't he stay with you?"

Sylvia bit the inside of her cheek. Just say she'd met Donatella? No, that was too suspicious. There was only one way out. She drew back her shoulders, lifted her chin. "I am not so old and senile that I can't manage a cup of coffee on my own, Varina. Now are you going to continue being rude? Or are you going to introduce me to your friend?"

Her daughter's cheeks pinked. "I'm sorry. Ruth, this is my mother, Sylvia Spini. Mom, Ruth Cooperman."

"How do you do, Mrs. Spini?" Ruth pulled off her very expensive-looking glove, held out her hand.

"I'm well, thank you, Mrs. Cooperman."

"Ms. Cooperman. But you can just call me Ruth."

"All right, Ruth." A tap on the window. Tommy waved from outside. "I'll leave you ladies to your kaffeeklatsch. Donatella will be over for supper, Varina. Bring home something nice from the store."

"I'm doing leftovers, Mom."

Sylvia sniffed. "Fine. I'll see you later, then."

Varina kissed her cheek. Sylvia darted—carefully—for the door before her daughter could walk her to it like some feeble thing incapable of making it that far. Outside, Tommy had his hands jammed into the pockets of a windbreaker suitable for spring, not

December. "You'll catch your death!" she scolded, though even she knew no one got sick that way. It was what her mother said to her, and hers before that. Tradition was tradition.

"Was that Varina in there?"

"Yes."

"Why can't she take you home?"

"She's with a friend. What? Is it too much for a mother to ask her son for a ride? It's only a few blocks. I'll walk."

"C'mon, Ma. Don't be like that. I got people back at the house. Catherine was pissed at me for leaving."

"What people?"

He squinted skyward, as if checking the rather obvious weather. "Just people, looking over some plans."

"That Catherine has something to say about? Since when?"

"Since never. That's why I got to get back."

"Well, you're already out. Now take me home like a good boy. And buy yourself a winter coat! You have the money."

Tommy held the car door open for her, like the good son he was, closing it carefully once she was settled inside. Warm. So warm. Leather seats. Electronic *blips* and *bips* she had no names for. Her boy had done well for himself. For his family. So had Varina. Sylvia Spini was proud of them both.

"Seatbelt, Ma. It's the law."

"It's only a few blocks. Cars didn't even have seatbelts in my day."

"Today is your day, too. Seatbelt."

"Fine." She tugged at the buckle. "It's stuck."

"It's not stuck. Here, I'll do it."

Tommy reached around her, pulled the belt down, and buckled her in. As if she were a child.

His cell phone *blinged* or *tinged* or whatever sound that wasn't a ring it made. Despite laws saying it was illegal to use it while driving—like it was illegal to ride without a seatbelt—Tommy didn't let it go through the car, like she knew it could. Sylvia looked out the window the whole ride home. She waited for him to come around to her side of the car and open the door, not even attempting to unclick the seatbelt on her own. Staring straight ahead, she let her son do it for her.

"You got your key?"

Sylvia fished her house keys out of her purse, handed them to him. Tommy walked her to the door, unlocked it, and handed back the keys.

"Thank you, Tommy. I'm sorry it was an imposition."

"Nah, it's okay. Anything for my best girl. I got to get back, though, before Catherine blows a gasket."

"Tell her hello for me."

"Will do!" he called, heading back down the steps, to his car, and away.

Sylvia shut the door, shut out the cold still shivering through her. Keeping her coat on, she moved through the house more slowly than she would have were she warmer. A cup of tea would hit the spot, but no. No more caffeine today. Soup. Soup would be nice. Maybe it would help with the svogliadell' lying like lead in her stomach.

8

Now this is very cool. Take these three words:

gabaruss'

Italian: *capo rosso;* "redhead"

Strangely enough, this one doesn't seem to have any insult intended. Shock me.

gabadost'

Italian: *capo tosto;* "hardhead"

This one is typically accompanied by a smack upside the head, just to make sure the point's been made.

So *gaba/capo* = head. Obviously. But there's the third word:

gabagool

Italian: *capicola*

An Italian salted pork cured with red or black peppercorns for a sweeter heat, or paprika if you like it really spicy. It can also be used to call someone an idiot. (Again, shock me, and not ironically this time. There might be a theme here.)

You might think the *gaba/capi* here doesn't go with the others, or it's just a coincidence, but no. It's not. Gabagool/*capicola* is made from the head (*capo*) and neck (*collo*) of the pig. See? Words are so cool.

You sure you don't want a glass of wine, instead?" Paulie dunked the tea bag in hot water. Six o'clock was cocktail time, in his book. Usually, in Donatella's, too.

"Just tea, thanks. I've sworn off drinking."

"Again?"

"Shut up, Paulie."

He handed her the cup, sitting beside her on the couch, glass of wine in his hand. "So, what do you think of my babies?"

She glanced into the box where MaryJane and her kittens—both boys, according to the vet—slept. "Very . . . fuzzy."

"You don't like cats?"

"No, I do." Donatella sipped her tea. "I'm just in a pissy mood. Sorry."

"What do you have to be pissy about?"

"I got arrested. Duh."

Paulie did his best not to roll his eyes. "You also got out of it with a little embarrassment and familial angst."

"You don't think that's enough to put someone in a bad mood?"

"I'd think you'd be more grateful that your mother found the money to keep you out of the lockup."

Donatella sank lower in the couch. "I am grateful. And that's part of it." Big sigh. "I hate being a constant disappointment. I don't want to be this way, you know."

"Then why are you?"

She slumped lower, and sideways, onto his shoulder. Paulie took the cup from her and set it onto the coffee table, alongside his wine, and resettled her against him. Snuggling into him, Donatella pressed her nose into his neck. "I wish I knew," she said. "I just don't. I try so hard, Paulie. No one believes it, but I do."

She was right. No one, including him, believed it. He didn't understand how someone could make the same mistakes over and over, and somehow expect a different result. "You'll have to make it up to her."

"I'm in the process of doing that."

"Oh?" He picked up his head, tried to look her in the eye, but Donatella only nestled in deeper.

"Don't ask questions. Just trust me."

"You going to pay her back?"

She snorted. "I put in an application at Jumbaloon's today. They're looking for a counter girl who can also help out in back when necessary, and I have bakery experience."

Bakery experience that ended with her being banned from The Bean's Knees for life. Still, it was a start. "When will you hear something?"

"Probably before New Year's. They're really shorthanded, and

I've known Iggy forever. That could be good for me, or bad. But I think good. She'll hire me."

"Well, good. Glad to hear that. That mean you're sticking around for a while?"

"Yeah, I guess."

Paulie twirled a curl around his finger. "Don't sound so enthusiastic or anything."

"No, I am. It's just . . ."

"Just?"

"It's a counter *girl* job. You know?"

"It wasn't that long ago I took an errand *boy* job with your brother."

"That's because you have a crush on Dante. And, shut up. You've already earned your way to . . . what is your job title, anyway?"

"Nothing official. I'm still a jack-of-all-trades. And I don't have a crush on your brother."

"Oh, please." Donatella tickled his ribs.

"Stop!"

"Paulie and Dante sitting in a tree!"

"Donatella, stop!"

And she did, settling into his side again and snuggling in close.

It wasn't a tree. It was in a coat closet, one drunk New Year's Eve. Paulie kissed the top of her head, lingered there in the soft sweetness of her. The truth, the lie, the fantasy. He held her closer. "You know I am enamored of anything Palladino."

"Ew, my mom?"

"Don't be disgusting, Don. She's like my mother."

"What about me?"

"You know I adore you."

Her hand on his abdomen caressed the muscle there. "A girl still likes to hear it every now and then."

Paulie's body responded as it did with few women, but always with Donatella. Ever since their teens. Ever since they were each other's first. He leaned in, nipped her lip. "I thought you weren't a *girl*."

Donatella pulled his glasses from his face, pushed him backward into the couch, her hand breaching the waistband of his jeans. He'd thought, once upon a time, he could renounce his sexuality and make a life with her, somehow fixing both of them in the process. But he couldn't. It wouldn't have been fair to her, or to him, because being gay wasn't just about sex.

"This is a bad idea," he murmured against her kisses. "Don, seriously."

"Why?"

Let me count the ways . . . "It's an unhealthy fallback we both decided was—"

"It's just sex." She unzipped his pants. "What's the point of this relationship if there are no perks involved?"

"Love? Devotion? Friendship?"

"I could get a dog for all that. This?" She squeezed him. Paulie groaned. "Yeah, this is a perk. Sex without strings attached for us both. Come on. It's Christmas."

"Christmas was—" Yesterday. Paulie knew better. Donatella never took no for an answer. He didn't really mean it anyway. He pulled her shirt over her head. His own. Their bodies fit against one another. Inside. This was how it was with them. How it had always been. Not, he hoped, how it always would be. He loved her. He adored her. He would forever. But Paulie wanted happily ever after. Husband, house, kids, and—apparently—cats. Someday. Not today. Today, it was Donatella. Sex without strings attached. A little time outside of her latest mess, and the lies he told himself.

"MOM?" VARINA KNOCKED ON HER MOTHER'S BEDROOM DOOR. SHE could hear the news playing softly, and her mother's even softer snore. "Mom? Dinner."

"I wasn't sleeping!"

Rolling her eyes—since Sylvia couldn't see her—Varina went back to the kitchen. Heaven forfend Sylvia Spini admitted to sleeping at any hour not between 9:00 P.M. and 6:00 A.M. She had always been that way, for as far back as Varina could remember. Sleep equaled lazy, and lazy equaled unworthy of the home she made, the children she cared for, the husband who worked hard all day. Varina had realized her own descent into that madness too late to save herself those groggy days when the boys were little. By the time Donatella came along, she napped when the baby napped and made no excuses for it.

Seven o'clock. Varina did her best not to sigh in that disappointed way her mother sighed. She put away Donatella's plate and silverware. Her daughter kept as many dinner dates as she broke. This was nothing new. Everything just *felt* different, like the swell before the surge. Something big was coming, Varina felt it from the tips of her toes to the ends of her salt-and-pepper hair.

France.

Not Italy. Italy would have been too cliché. A bubble of excitement rose up from her belly. She smiled, the sort that lifted the shoulders an inch or two higher.

"What are you so chipper about?"

Varina nearly dropped the glass she'd been returning to the cabinet. "For the love of Christ, Mom!"

"You're jumpy lately."

"You're extra skulky lately."

Sylvia sat down at the table. "Where's Donatella?"

"Your guess is as good as mine. Eat. If I reheat this stuff again, it'll be like cardboard."

Sylvia grimaced, but she dug in like a college student into a home-cooked meal. Varina ate more slowly, trying not to be overly concerned about her mother choking. She poured her water without being asked, just to be safe.

Leftover turkey and all the fixings was one of Varina's favorite meals, even when it was catered, not homemade. It was good, she had to admit, though the gravy wasn't as thick and oniony as the one she made at Thanksgiving. Light. *Elevated,* as the TV chefs said. Varina preferred rich, hearty, peasant food; she'd make an exception when she was in France.

"What are you up to?"

Varina nearly dropped her fork. "Me? Nothing. Why?"

"You're sighing like a leaky radiator."

She was not sharing her secret. Truth be told, she feared sharing it. To spend that amount of money on herself was bad enough, but traveling alone? Heresy! Sylvia Spini would blow hotter than Vesuvius. Women did not travel alone. Ever. That's just the way it was, even when one was a seventy-year-old widow who'd been running her own business and seeing to the needs of an entire family for more years than she cared to count. Her trip was the one thing Varina was keeping for herself, to herself, until it was time to leave for the airport.

"Too much holiday, I guess."

"Liar."

"Mom, really. Can we just eat in peace?"

"Can't a mother be concerned about her daughter?"

"There's nothing you need be concerned—"

"Who was that gabaruss' in Jumbaloon's today? You going funny on me now?"

"Funny?"

Sylvia rocked her hand, nearly transparent eyebrows raised.

"Ferchrissake, Mom."

"She's not your type."

"I have no interest in women. Not romantically. What is with you tonight?"

"Nothing."

"Now who's the liar?" Varina took a deep, deep breath. *Be as patient with her as you want your kids to be with you one day.* "Are you upset Donatella didn't show?"

"Afanabola with that girl."

"You don't mean that."

Sylvia set her fork down, pushed her—empty—plate away. "It doesn't matter. I'm going to watch *Murder, She Wrote,* and go to bed."

She had every episode. Home-recorded on VHS. There was no telling her about streaming, or DVDs, which took up much less space. Videotape was enough of a leap into the future for Sylvia Spini.

"Leave that," Varina told her when her mother picked up her plate. "I'll clean up when I'm done."

"Oh, sweetheart. I'm sorry. I don't want to leave you eating alone."

"Honestly, Mom, it's fine. The shop opens bright and early tomorrow. I'm going to finish up, clean up, and hit the hay myself."

Sylvia didn't argue, only nodded sadly and left Varina alone. She supposed she might have pressed a little harder, tried to find out why her mother was so upset about a fairly common occurrence. What did it matter, though? Her mother had been looking forward to seeing her favorite grandchild, and that grandchild hadn't come.

It didn't bother Varina that her mother had a favorite; she was only smugly satisfied it was one of her offspring to get the designation. She'd always found Tommy's kids—like Tommy—a bit obnoxious. It would have pissed her off to have her good boys passed over for one of them.

Sylvia's bedroom door closed; Varina grabbed her purse from the hook on the wall and took from it the paperwork from the travel agency. Setting aside the frightening tally for trip and airfare, taxes and fees and transfers, she pulled out the daily destination sheets full of menus and excursion options.

Embarking in Lyon, France, September twenty-ninth. After six full days sailing through Provence, via the Rhône river, she would disembark in Avignon on October sixth. From there, three days in a hotel overlooking the Mediterranean in Cannes, France. Home again on October tenth, a new woman. A woman who used a credit card, one who'd traveled, one who would continue to travel. Italy. Spain. Croatia. Japan. Anywhere her hard-earned money could get her. No more banking for the next catastrophe; Varina Palladino would be a woman freed late, but better than never.

9

pastafazool

Italian: *pasta e fagioli;* literally, "pasta and beans"

Pastafazool is comfort food at its best, often made of leftovers, back in the day, beans added for protein. Basically: small macaroni (*pasta,* to the infidels), tomato sauce, onions, garlic (goes without saying, but I'll say it for the infidels that call macaroni pasta), olive oil, beans. My cousin says you have to go to the deli counter and ask for the end of a proscuit' to use, but pretty much any salted pork will work. (I hope she never reads this.)

chooch

Italian: *ciuccio;* "pacifier"

In Jersey Italian, a chooch is a big baby. Typically affectionate, as in, "Get over here and give me a hug, ya big chooch." It can also be a Jersey Italian version of the southern phrase "Bless your heart, but . . ." as in, "Hey, chooch! Never use canola oil instead of olive for making cutlets."

It seemed like everyone had a secret these days. Varina with her wistful sighs and her gabaruss' girlfriend. Donatella going AWOL for two days, only to show up with a kiss and a promise to get the flyers distributed. (She'd only laughed when Sylvia suggested they switch *grandfather* for *grandmother,* because Varina had turned into one of them lesbians.) And now Tommy, calling out of the blue to take her to lunch in the middle of the week. Something was up, and Sylvia didn't like it one bit.

She stood at the window, watching for Tommy's Cadillac to pull up the driveway. He'd be up the steps and opening the door before she could even reach it, like the good son he was. No honking horns for his mother. She'd raised a gentleman.

Tires crunched in the gray, exhausted snow. Sylvia made her way to the door. Christmas was truly over. Even Little Christmas. The tree and its ornaments, packed into the boxes they came in fifty years ago, were in the cellar. So was the wooden manger, along with the requisite, tissue-wrapped figures. The Magi and their camels. The Angel Gabriel. The Holy Family. Sheep and goats, though the donkey that carried the laboring Mary was long since lost to time.

How many Christmases had those figurines seen? More than she had, certainly; her mother had given the Nativity set to her just before she died at the daring age of ninety-seven. She'd carted the manger and figurines across the ocean, wrapped in newspaper and straw, because they'd belonged to her own ancient and stubborn grandmother, left behind.

The figures were chipped, mostly the camels, goats, and sheep, because the children had always played with them even though Sylvia scolded. The Angel Gabriel's wings and trumpet had broken off numerous times and been glued back in place. Melchior's nose was missing, a chunk of Balthasar's robe. Gaspar's hands, once clasped together in adoration, had broken off, never to be found.

The Holy Family, though, were faded but intact. Sylvia had always seen that as a sign, though what it said, she would never say out loud and tempt the fates.

Her son was loudly scraping his shoes clean on the stoop. Dabbing the corners of her eyes, she couldn't let Tommy see her cry. He'd think there was something wrong, and there certainly was not, even if, in all probability, her last Christmas was already behind her.

"Hey, Ma. You ready?"

"Do I look ready, sweetheart?"

"Where's your coat?"

Sylvia lifted her chin. "What do I need a coat for? I'm only going to the car."

"You still need a coat." He lifted one off its hook. "This one yours?"

As if she would ever wear a purple coat, even at Christmas. What did her son think she was? A kook? "That's Varina's. The black one is mine."

Tommy held it up for her. Sylvia slipped her arms into the lined sleeves. Such a nice coat. Old, but they didn't make things like it anymore. Joseph had bought it for her such a long time ago, though she couldn't remember if it had been a Christmas gift, or for her birthday, or an out of the blue gift because she'd admired it. He did that, in those first years, and in the last. Not so much so in those between.

Tommy helped her down the steps, opened the passenger side door. "Where's Catherine?"

"Catherine?"

"Your wife, sweetheart. Isn't she coming?"

"Nah, Ma. It's just me and you. Me and my best girl. I thought I told you."

"No, you did not. Is Catherine upset with me? Is it because she didn't like the salt-and-pepper shakers I got her for Christmas?"

Tommy closed the door, came around to the driver's seat. "I just wanted some time alone with my mama. Something wrong with that?"

"I notice you didn't say anything about the salt-and-pepper shakers."

"She loved them! You know she has a thing for ducks."

The very reason she'd bought the hideous little things. Sylvia wagged a finger. "Are you two fighting?"

He groaned. "No, we're not fighting. Look, can't we just have a nice lunch together? I used to take you out all the time, just me and you. Remember? I thought it would make you happy."

Those lunches Sylvia had cherished, once upon a time. "Of course, it does." She reached up to put a hand to his always-stubbled cheek. "You're a good son."

She remembered the lunches slightly less clearly than when those lunches stopped for no other reason than her son's success, which made her very happy, indeed. Wasn't that what a mother wanted for her son? Busy, busy, busy. With the construction company he'd inherited from his father. With his kids. His wife. His life. Though what his excuse was now that he wasn't quite so busy eluded her.

"You just passed it, sweetheart."

"What did I pass?"

"Portofino's."

"We're not going there, Ma. I'm taking you to Scordato's."

Scordato's? Her face warmed. She pressed a palm to her cheek. "But it's so expensive."

He squeezed her hand, grinning like a chooch.

What a generous man. Such a good son she'd raised. Sylvia's cheeks were still pride-warm when he pulled into the lot, and handed the keys to the valet.

"No joyriding, got me?"

"Yes, sir."

"Good." Tommy slipped him a few bills. "Park it close."

"Yes, sir."

Tommy ordered steak Scordato. Sylvia opted for a bowl of pastafazool, and a side salad that took her longer to eat than her son his steak. They talked mostly about his grandchildren, her great-grandchildren. Who was doing well in school and who was not; who'd gotten a job, in trouble, a new boyfriend. It wasn't that Sylvia couldn't keep track of them, just that she barely knew most of the great-grandchildren. Tommy's Angelina and her family lived in Tennessee, where Catherine's people were from. Mark was in Florida with his wife and kids. Only Michael had stayed close, with his wife and their twin sons. But Michael was now divorced, like Dante, poor boys. She'd always loved Pandora, but Mikey's Vanessa—Sylvia didn't use the word often, and only when she really meant it—was a bitch. Wherever they were, the grands and great-grands were in stages of their lives that made their ninety-two-year-old nonina out of sight, out of mind. She understood. She really did. That didn't mean she had to be happy about it.

"What do you think? You have room for dessert?"

Sylvia had barely finished her pastafazool. "I could go for a scoop of raspberry sherbert."

"Sherbert?"

"Just a little something sweet."

Tommy waved the waiter over. "My mother will have a scoop of raspberry sherbert. I'll take a couple gannol. They fresh?"

"The cannoli are always made to order, sir. But I'm afraid we only have sorbet, not sherbet."

"You got raspberry?"

"We do."

"Ma?"

"That'll be fine, sweetheart."

"And a double espresso," Tommy called after him. "With a twist a' lemon."

Sylvia folded over her soiled napkin and replaced it on her lap. The waiter should have taken it with their lunch dishes and left her with a fresh one. The service in Scordato's was starting to slip.

"This was very nice, son," she said. "Thank you. The perfect pick-me-up."

"What? You depressed?"

She tried to make light. "No, no. Just the after-holiday blues. You know."

"The holidays are fun and all, but it's good to get back to regular." Tommy picked at something dried on the tablecloth, focused in that obvious, avoidant way he had.

"Okay, Thomas. Out with it."

"Out with what?"

"Whatever it is you buttered me up to tell me."

"It's nothing."

"Thomas Alfred Spini, now!" She didn't have to slam her hand on the table. It was implied.

He stopped picking. The waiter appeared just then, setting down their desserts and her son's espresso. Tommy made a show of giving the lemon rind an extra squeeze. He took a bite of his cannoli.

Sylvia put her hand—did that gnarled thing used to diaper him? Comfort him? Feed him farina?—atop his. "Tell me what it is, son."

Tommy turned his hand around, brought hers to his lips and kissed it. "Catherine and me, we're . . ."

"You're getting divorced! I knew it. That's why she's not here. I thought she was acting funny over the holidays."

"No, we're fine. We're good. In fact . . ." He took a sip of his espresso. "We're buying . . . we *bought* a place in Florida."

Had he taken the glass of water in front of him and thrown it in her face, Sylvia could not have gasped louder, or with more horror.

"Don't look at me like that, Ma."

"Why would you do such a thing?" If she could fly out of the restaurant like a jilted lover in one of her television stories, she'd have flown like the wind.

"Our son is there, and our grandkids. I'm tired of the cold, and as long as I'm around, Dante's going to keep pulling me back into the business. But listen, Ma. Ma!"

She tried. Oh, how she tried! But her head buzzed and buzzed with everything she never wanted to consider.

"We want you to come with us."

The buzzing silenced, instantly and without echo.

"What?"

"We want you to come to Florida with us." He smiled, big and hopeful. "The place we bought? It has a whole suite that would be just for you. Brand-new construction in one of them neighborhood things. A . . . a . . . community."

"For seniors?"

"Kind of. Fifty-five and over. But that's what makes it great!"

"Florida is where people go to die, Thomas."

He laughed. "It's where people go to retire. Snowbirds. Ever hear that expression?"

"No."

"Well, that's what we'd be." He kissed both her hands, again and again. "The business is going to kill me. And I'm retired! Catherine, she . . ." He looked away. "She made me promise to make changes before it was too late. This is a big change, but a good one. And our place is near all them amusement parks. Angelina and the kids are already planning a big trip to stay with us."

"What about Mikey?"

Tommy sat back in his chair. "I asked him to come, too. He says no. Custody stuff. He's got to stay close. But he'll bring the boys down lots. You'll see him more there than you do here."

She might not see Michael outside of the holidays, but she *could*. There was a difference between seeing someone, and being able to see someone.

"Is Varina in on this?"

"Varina?" He blew through his lips. "No way. I didn't want to open that can a' worms unless you for sure wanted to come with us. No sense having that fight unless I have to."

He was right, of course. Varina would fight this tooth and nail. Her daughter was nothing if not devoted.

"I'm too old for such a change, Tommy."

"Who says?"

Who, indeed? Her parents. Joseph. The children. All gone. All grown. Now? "My time for such adventures has passed, sweetheart. My home is here. I can't die in a strange place after living my whole life here."

"Don't say that. You're not going to die."

"I will someday."

"Come on, Ma."

Sylvia reached across, patted her son's hand. "I do appreciate you asking, though."

"We mean it. For real."

"I know you do, sweetheart." She patted his hand again. The cup of raspberry sorbet was mostly melted. Sylvia dug out a fairly solid bit and ate it. Tommy devoured his cannoli in four bites, swallowing them down with the dregs of his espresso. He looked so like his father, though he got his stature from her father-in-law. Tall, tall man. Five-eight or -nine. And solid. *Svelte* would never be a word used to describe anyone in their family, apart from Davide, who worked out with a trainer six days a week.

Her son, her little boy, with steely hair like Varina's, deep lines in his face, and age-spotted hands, was an old man, by her family's standards. Men who got to be sixty were rare enough; few reached seventy. Tommy was seventy-two, and his health was not good. Florida would probably be wonderful for him, though she was close to certain it would kill her to lose her son at this stage in her life. Then again, how much life did she even have left anyway?

"You mad?"

"Angry, sweetheart. And no. Of course not. I want only your happiness."

Falling back in his chair, Tommy dramatically clutched his chest. "For real? Catch me, I might pass out."

"Oh, stop." She smacked his beefy shoulder. "You're terrible."

He straightened. "Am I?"

Sylvia opened her mouth, the sarcasm that passed for affection dying before it could escape. "Never once in your entire life, Thomas Alfred Spini. You're a good boy. A good son." It wasn't his fault she lived longer than anyone expected, stalling everything until they could do and be what they wanted without inconveniencing her. "I will come visit, and I'll stay a long time. Maybe the whole winter. I promise."

"Yeah?"

"Yes, son. I promise." But she'd never travel alone, and Varina wouldn't leave the store long enough to fly down to the inferno that was Florida. Donatella would go. Tommy could afford to spring for the airline tickets. There was all manner of trouble that granddaughter of hers could get into down there. She'd seen news footage of half-naked people doing God-knows-what in Miami. That would absolutely appeal to her wild Donatella. It certainly might have appealed to Sylvia, once upon a time.

Tommy paid the check, assisted her from her seat. He kept hold of her elbow through the restaurant, held her coat up for her to slip into. It was cold outside, but Tommy must have had the valet start the car when the waiter brought their check, because it was toasty inside.

Back home, her son walked her to the door. She tapped him to her level so she could kiss both his cheeks. "Thank you, sweetheart."

"Any time." He opened the door.

"Tommy?"

"Yeah?"

"When?"

He took her elbow and propelled her into the house. "February or March," he said. "Whenever the place is done."

Sylvia nodded, smiled a smile that had to look as strained as it was, and stepped inside. "Say hello to Catherine for me."

"Will do. Love you, Ma." He closed the door. From the window, Sylvia watched him hurry to his car, get in, and drive off. It had to be a relief, to have that over and done with. She could be glad, at least, for that stress to be off his heart.

"I love you, too, Tommy."

Hanging up her coat, Sylvia let the tears fall. Varina wasn't there to see, to worry, to ask what was wrong. By the time she got home from the store, Sylvia would have built up enough ire over the situation to hide in. Now, alone in this house steeped in her family, she'd weep without shame.

The scratching, then the skip. Sylvia closed her eyes, waiting.

Sul mare luccica l'astro d'argento/Placida è l'onda/Prospero il vento . . .

Enrico Caruso's voice filled her stuttering—just a little—heart.

Venite all'argine/Barchetta mia/Santa Lucia/Santa Lucia...

The possessed Victrola sat in the front window, playing its demon heart out. Vicky loved the Caruso records best. In truth, so did Sylvia. Songs in a language she'd heard all her life, but never spoken. The voices of long ago. The sounds of her people from a tiny town outside of Naples no one could ever agree upon the name of. Piccola. Piccino. It was a family argument for years; now the only one left to argue it was Sylvia.

O dolce Napoli/O suol beato/Ove sorridere volle il creato...

Sylvia swayed, one hand in the air, like a dancer. She sang along with Vicky and Enrico.

"Tu sei l'impero dell'armonia/Santa Lucia/Santaaaaaaa Luciaaaaa!"

10

Fanabola!/Afanabola!

Italian: *Vai fa Napoli!;* literally, "Go to Naples!"

In Jersey Italian, it can mean "Go to hell!" Considering my people are Nap'letan', I should find this more insulting than I do. Apparently, it's not Naples itself considered hell enough to make into a curse, but the extreme poverty in Naples at the turn of the twentieth century that had many southern Italians and Sigilian' (sij-lee-an, aka: Sicilians) seeking better horizons in the United States. Many, if not most, Italian Americans have roots in southern Italy and Sicily.

W e l ... n ... d our fir ... ish!"

Cell phones. Sylvia had no use for them.

"Donatella? Is that you? I didn't understand a thing you just said."

"S'me. Ha ... on." More crackling, then, "Can you hear me now?"

"Yes, sweetheart. I can hear you."

"Is Mom there?"

"It's two in the afternoon. Why would she be here?"

"Just checking, because we landed our first fish! I'm sending him over to Palladino's to woo Mom right now."

Sylvia's heart stuttered. It did that more and more often lately. "You've met him? Is he nice?"

"Of course, and of *course!*" Donatella laughed. "I wouldn't have approved him otherwise. He's very handsome in the way Mom likes men, which is to say, very Italian looking in a—" her voice lowered and thickened "—'I used to be a beefcake' way."

"Your father was not a beefcake."

"If you ever noticed he was, I'd be worried." Her voice muffled again. "He's going to ask her for cipollini, which I brilliantly confiscated from the shelves and storeroom. It'll make her interact with him longer. I also swore him to secrecy about our little matchmaking scheme."

"On a stack of Bibles? Because if he blabs, we're finished."

"He won't, because then he will be, too. Besides, I had him sign a nondisclosure agreement. I thought of everything."

No. She had not. Neither had Sylvia. It had all seemed like such a nice, simple idea. "And if he blabs anyway, you suing him?"

"Like I have money for a lawyer. But he doesn't know that. Relax! This is going to be great. You'll see."

Classic Donatella. "Sweetheart, I—"

"Listen, Nonina, I got to go. I'm at work."

"All right. Come by later. We'll talk more. And I'd love to hear how the job is going."

"If I can. Love you!"

"Who was that?"

"Oh!" Sylvia clutched the phone to her chest. "Varina! You could have killed me!"

"You're so dramatic." Varina took the phone from her mother, put it on its cradle. "Who was it?"

"Donatella. What are you doing here? Why are you not at the store?"

"What did my daughter want?"

"She was just . . . just . . . apologizing for not coming to dinner again."

"That does sound like Donatella."

"So why are you home?"

Varina unwound her scarf. "I left Gabriella in charge for a little while. It's good practice for her."

"Practice?"

"For . . ." Varina tossed her scarf over the back of a chair. "For next summer. I'm hoping she'll be able to work in the store, give me a bit of a break so I can do something other than work."

"Like go out for coffee with your gabaruss' girlfriend?"

"Stop calling her that."

"It's not an insult. She does have red hair." *From a bottle.*

"Her name is Ruth, and she's my friend."

"Fine. Ruth. You've been spending an awful lot of time with this Ruth person."

"I like her. We have a lot in common."

"Isn't she a Jew?"

Varina laughed. "Why does that sound like a racial slur when you say it?"

"Don't be fresh."

"Yes, Mom, she's Jewish. So?"

"You're a Catholic."

"And?"

Sylvia threw up her hands. It didn't matter; what did matter was that a suitor was on his way to Palladino's to woo her maybe-lesbian daughter, and here she was at home. She had to call Donatella. But how to do that without blowing everything?

"I need a sweater." She rubbed briskly at her arms. "I think I feel a chill."

"I'll get it for you. How about a cup of tea?"

"I'll put the kettle on while you get the sweater."

Varina kissed her cheek. The moment she was out of the kitchen, Sylvia picked up the phone, dialed Donatella's number.

"Mom?"

"It's Nonina. Listen, your mother is here. Call Gabriella and tell her to call Varina and say she has to go."

"But—"

"Just do it!" Sylvia set the headset in its cradle just as Varina returned with her sweater.

"You didn't hang it up right. It was doing that *boop-boop-boop* busy signal."

"O . . . kay." Strangely cheerful Varina went into the pantry, came back with tea bags. "Didn't you put the kettle on?"

"Oh. I forgot." She really had. "I'm sorry. I guess I'm slipping a little."

"Don't be ridiculous. You're sharp as a tack." Varina took the kettle from the stovetop, filled it at the tap. Before she could get it onto the burner, the phone rang. "Sit, I'll get it."

Sylvia refrained from crossing herself, though she did so mentally.

"Oh, hey, Gabby. How are . . . oh. No, no, it's okay. I was just going to have tea with Nonina. No, I'll head over right now. Your paper is more important."

Varina hung up the phone. Her sigh, on this occasion, was not wistfully happy, but wistful nonetheless. "I'm sorry, Mom. I have to go back to the store. Gabby forgot she has a paper due tomorrow."

"That's so unlike her," Sylvia said. "Maybe I'm not the only one slipping."

"Funny." Varina fixed her mother's tea, put the other cup back into the cupboard. "I'll be home around six. I'll bring manigott' from the store. Sound good?"

"Yes, very." So heavy, all that cheese. Couldn't they ever just have baked chicken? She'd have to go easy. "We'll have tea another time. Or maybe, you'll take me with you when you go for coffee with the gabba . . . with Ruth."

"I'd like that, Mom." She kissed Sylvia's cheek, grabbing her scarf from the back of the chair. "Love you. See you later."

"Love you, too, sweetheart."

Wrapping both hands around the hot mug of tea felt good on her fingers. She blew across the top, took a tentative sip. Sweet, just the way she liked it. Varina was so good to her. Better than she deserved, considering what she'd done all those years ago. Sylvia closed her eyes against the thought, the memories always fresh no matter how many years passed. The station wagon that still smelled like the fruit punch Tommy spilled in the back seat, her overnight bag on the passenger seat, and a road so open it had made her weep.

Sylvia got up, careful not to spill her tea. It was long ago, and everything turned right in the end. She'd been a good mother, a good wife, and she'd been happy, for the most part. She wanted happiness for her son, and for her daughter. Before she breathed her last, Sylvia would make sure they were.

Heading for her room to watch her stories, Sylvia Spini patted Vicky—again in the front window, but silent—on her way past. Her world was a bed, a chair, and a dresser. A television and a VCR that played recorded episodes of *Murder, She Wrote,* complete with commercials. It wasn't a suite in a fifty-five-and-over community in Florida, but it was home.

IT NEVER FAILED. HEAVEN FORBID SHE TAKE *ONE* AFTERNOON OFF. Just one. How was she going to manage a whole week and a half away from the store? She'd have to close it, and that couldn't happen. Varina couldn't afford the lost revenue. Could she? Too bad none of her kids had gone into accounting.

Tapping Ruth's number on her Recents list, Varina picked up her pace. Gabriella had sounded close to frantic about a paper she should have had done long before tomorrow's due date. Her mother was right. That was very unlike her conscientious granddaughter.

"Hello?"

"You'll never guess what happened when I tried to take an afternoon off work."

Ruth gasped dramatically. "Catastrophe?"

"Close."

"Want me to come over? I'll sit in a quiet corner and drink coffee, there for you to vent to in quiet moments."

"You're lovely. But no. The shop's only open another few hours. I'll manage."

"You sure?"

"Positive. We still on for this weekend?"

"I already got the tickets," Ruth said. "I adore *Into the Woods,* even if it's just a local performance."

"You're such a snob."

"When you've seen everything there is to see on Broadway, *dahling,* there's nothing that will ever compare." Ruth chuckled. "I'll pick you up at five thirty. We'll have an early dinner."

"What did I ever do without you?"

"That's the question for the ages. Toodle-pip!"

"Toodle-what?" But Ruth had already hung up, and Varina was out of breath from half running the blocks between home and store. Tucking the phone into her pants pocket, she pushed open the door. The bell—the same one she and Dino put up before opening the doors of the shop—chimed.

"Nonnie! I'm so sorry." Gabriella already had her coat half on. "I'm such a ditz. I can't believe I forgot all about my paper. This very nice man is looking for cipollini, and I think you're out." She kissed Varina on her way out the door. "Love you!"

"I'll be with you in a sec." Varina nodded to the man waiting at the counter. "Sorry about that. Grandkids, right?"

He laughed softly. "I have a few myself."

Tossing her coat over the chair in the back-room office, Varina grabbed an apron from the hook. She was still tying it on as she came out. "Now, what were you looking for? Cipollini?"

"Yes, the ones in olive oil."

"I just got some in." She came around the counter, went to the shelf where they should be. "That's strange. I couldn't have sold a whole case already. Let me check in back." She did, unsuccessfully. "I'm sorry. Not a single jar in the store. I'll have to order more. If you give me your name and number, I'll call when they come in."

He gave his name. "Louis Barbizzi," she said. "I know that name. Is your wife Anntonette?"

Louis looked away. "Was. She died a couple years back. The big C."

"Oh, I'm so sorry." She remembered clearly now. Anntonette and Louis Barbizzi. She'd been a loudmouth but pleasant enough. He'd been the strong, silent type. "We used to sit at baseball games together, when our boys were on the same team. Your son is . . . Larry, right?"

"Right, right." He smiled. "Yours is Dante."

"That's one of them. The other is Davide."

"I think I remember. Yeah."

"I have a daughter, too, though she came along way after our baseball days."

"Ah." He grinned. "An oops baby."

"That'd be Donatella." In every sense of the word.

Silence fell, suddenly and uncomfortably. "Well," Varina said, just as Louis told her, "I only just moved back here, from south Jersey."

"Oh?"

"Yeah." He shrugged. "Toni and I, we got a place down the shore when I retired. But she got sick and . . . well, I just wanted to come home, you know?"

"I understand."

More sudden and uncomfortable silence. Then, "You look almost the same," Louis said. "Older, of course, but just as pretty."

"I . . . uh . . . thanks?"

"Sorry, sorry." He actually blushed. "It's been a long time since I asked a woman to go out with me."

Varina's heart sank to her belly before jumping up into her throat. *Holy Mary, Mother of God.* "Is that . . . are you asking me out?"

"I . . . am? I mean, yes. I am. Is that too forward of me?"

It absolutely was, but Varina found herself warming in that pleasant way of a surprise gone right. She knew him, after all. It wasn't as if they were strangers. Was she as uninterested in men as she claimed? Or was it all about spiting her mother's constant harping? Worse, was it because she feared they were uninterested in her? Only one way to find out. "I guess it's not if I say yes."

"Really?"

She laughed. "Sure, why not. What do you have in mind?"

"Dinner, Saturday night? Is that too boring?"

"I can't Saturday night," she said. "Previous engagement. But I can do tomorrow."

"I can't do Friday," Louis told her. "Taking my grandson and grand-nephew to a basketball game."

"Oh, that's sweet." Varina bit her lip. Did she actually want to go out with this man enough to be bold about it? It would make her mother's day, that was certain. It would at least get her off her back a little. And, maybe, actually be fun. "Well, how about tonight?"

"Tonight? I . . . uh . . ." Louis straightened, and he smiled in a gentle way that set Varina's pounding pulse at ease. "That'd be great. Is it too old-fashioned to say I'll pick you up at seven? Or do you want to meet someplace?"

"It's not old-fashioned, but I'll meet you." Just in case. "Have you been to Frankie's lately?"

"Not since coming back north."

"There's a new owner, but the food is still great. I'll meet you there at seven fifteen."

"Seven fifteen. You got it." He headed for the door, paused with his hand on the knob. "I'm looking forward to it."

"I am, too," Varina said, and found she actually meant it.

The bell over the door jingled. Varina let go a long, deep breath. Louis Barbizzi, of all people. Countless evenings, swatting away gnats and mosquitoes while their boys played ball, she'd thought him nice but a bit henpecked. Kind of beefcake, blunt about the features, he'd never in a million years have been her type. But here they were, decades later, going out on a date.

A date. Varina leaned heavily against the counter, pulling her cell phone from her pocket.

"You again? What do I have to do to get rid of you?"

"Ruth, I . . ." Varina gulped.

"What is it? Varina, what's wrong?"

Another gulp. "Nothing's wrong. I . . . I have a date."

11

buttann'

Italian: *puttana;* "whore" or "prostitute"

Fun fact: Puttanesca, the popular pasta sauce, literally translates to "of, relating to, or characteristic of a prostitute."

A food of, relating to, or characteristic of . . . yeah. Cool (←sarcasm).

Puttanesca itself is fairly new, having made its way into Italian cuisine in or around World War II. One story is, it got its name from the rather pungent scent of anchovies, olives, and capers being reminiscent of the particular scent of a mid-century Italian prostitute. There are some who prefer the story about a famous restaurateur throwing the first puttanesca together for a late-night group of hungry customers who asked him to make *una puttanata qualsiasi,* or, to throw together whatever ingredients he had on hand. That story seems to go with the linguistic evidence that says the name derives from the way Italians use the word *puttana* as an all-purpose profanity, sort of like Americans use the word *shit.* Thus, puttanesca might have originated with someone saying, "I just threw whatever shit I had into a pan."

S o, you got this?" Dante leaned over Paulie's shoulder, his finger on the plans for the kitchen renovation. "You sure? I wouldn't ask, but Georgianna left me hanging."

Paulie breathed deeply through his nose, as much for courage as to smell Dante's scent. Tom Ford's Neroli Portofino. Unisex. Expensive. Too expensive for Paulie to buy for himself, but not too expensive to buy his boss for Christmas, because a Dante who smelled of bergamot, mandarin orange, lemon, rosemary, neroli, and amber was even sexier than one who smelled of sawdust and the outdoors, but only marginally.

"She had a baby, Dante," he said. "It's not her fault the little guy came a month early."

"Yeah, well, she was behind. She's always behind. I been looking to replace her anyway. She always relied on you for a reason. You got a good eye."

"Thanks." Paulie's heartbeat thumped like a dog wagging its tail. "I'll do my best."

"I know you will." Dante straightened, smiling crookedly. *Adorable.* "I have faith in you, kid."

"When are you going to stop calling me kid?"

"When you're not one." He laughed, ruffling Paulie's hair. "I'm sending the inspector in a week from Thursday, so . . ."

"Yeah, yeah. I got it. I'll get this started first thing in the morning. Are the appliances ordered?"

"In the warehouse. Let Birdie know when you need them, he'll bring them over."

Dante headed for the door of the site trailer. They'd been months working on this building, a new warehouse for a stone and block company, and the last contract from Tommy's reign. Dante had no interest in the schools, supermarkets, and apartment buildings his grandfather, and then his uncle, had been locally famous for; he'd already started moving Spini and Son Construction into home and downtown renovations before his uncle retired—their biggest bone of contention. This last job was a bitch-and-a-half, mostly because it was a favor called in, and Tom was bowing out before it was finished.

"What are you doing here?"

"Huh?" Paulie turned. Donatella and Dante hugged in the doorway.

"Can't I come visit my favorite brother?"

"Davide is your favorite."

"He is not. I love you assholes both the same. Paulie's my actual favorite. He here?" She stepped into the office. "Oh, there you are!" She kissed Dante's cheek. "I won't keep him. Promise."

"He's all yours." Dante bowed out, saluting Paulie.

Donatella bounced into the office, sat on the edge of his desk. "Where are your glasses?"

"I'm wearing contacts."

"Since when?"

"Since recently," he said. "Glasses are annoying when you're sweaty all the time." And when you were constantly taking them off the moment certain people entered the room. "You're wrinkling the schematics."

She pulled the papers out from under her, smoothed them on her thigh. "Sorry. You done for the day?"

"Just about. I need to look over these and make sure I have what I need to get started on this kitchen tomorrow."

"For the condemned Victorian Dante bought over on Greensway?"

"That's the one. And it's no longer condemned. Well, it won't be after we pass all inspections."

Donatella groaned. "I love that house. It's so . . . vintage."

"Built in 1902," he said. "The plan is to keep that vintage feel but modernize it. Want to help me pick a color scheme?"

"Really?" She hopped down. "Yeah, sure!"

Paulie showed her the sample charts for tile, flooring, and cabinets, and how to mix and match the contemporary with the vintage to make it new and fresh rather than a strict interpretation of the past. Donatella had a good eye, which he'd always known. Yet another thing she could be good at if she would only focus.

Settling on white marble counters, a green milk-glass tile for the backsplash, navy blue lower cabinets, and white uppers, they stood back to admire their artistic vision.

"You really love this shit, don't you," Donatella said.

"Not the construction part as much as the design part. I'm good at it, if I do say so myself. Dante has a vision for restoring all the old buildings and homes in Wyldale. He's good at tearing things down and putting them back together again, but if the interiors were up to him, it would be all-white everything, all the time."

"Davide is the creative one."

"Definitely. Dante has vision, though. He amazes me."

Donatella purred, "He does, does he?"

"Stop." Paulie shuffled his schematics into a pile. "Seriously."

"Come on! When are you going to admit it?"

"When there's something to admit."

"Fine, fine. Don't get your panties in a twist."

"I wear boxer briefs."

"I know." She waggled her eyebrows, fingers digging into the hollow of her hip. "Damn."

"What's wrong?"

"I have this stitch in my side. Right here." She pressed a little lower in her groin. "It's been bugging the crap out of me for days. Damn, I'm getting old. Maybe I need a new hip."

"Probably, O ancient one." He rolled up his papers, slipped them into a cardboard sleeve. "Want to grab some dinner?"

"I just ate about a million doughnuts at work. And a cupcake."

"Sounds healthy. Want to keep me company while I eat? I'll buy you a soda."

"Make it a glass of wine and you have a deal."

"I thought you swore off drinking."

"It's one glass!"

"Fine. Done. I'm thinking tacos."

Paulie locked up the trailer and together, they headed for the parking lot. Donatella didn't have a car—probably no license, either, though she'd been cagey about whether it was revoked or simply suspended—but the construction site was only a few blocks from downtown. Wyldale wasn't a bad area; he still didn't like knowing she'd walked by herself through the least savory parts of it. This, Paulie kept to himself to avoid the verbal castration she'd otherwise unleash.

"Ah, the old Pinto." She tapped the electric-blue hood. "I can't believe you still have it."

"It's a beast." He shrugged. "It gets me where I need to go."

"We got into some trouble with this thing, once upon a time, huh?"

With it. In it. Her dad caught them making out in it more than once. Paulie and Donatella both lost their virginity in it, when they were fifteen. He thought, back then, she was his forever, which turned out to be true; just not in the way either of them suspected.

"After you, my lady." He opened the door for her, just as another car pulled into the lot.

Gabriella slammed to a halt next to his car. "What the hell, Don?"

"What's the matter?" Paulie asked.

"Donatella knows." Gabriella got out of her car, arms crossed over her chest. "I don't like disappointing Nonnie. She was looking forward to an afternoon off. What was so important you had me lie to her?"

"It's a secret." Donatella hunched deeper into the white bench seat of the Pinto. "Don't make me tell. You'll find out soon. I promise."

"Nothing doing. No way! Spill it, or I'm going back there to tell her you made me lie to her."

"Oh, this is juicy, whatever it is," Paulie said. "Gabby, get in the back. Donatella's going to tell us all about it."

"THE PUTTANESCA WAS BEAUTIFUL. THE COMPANY?" VARINA TOOK A sip of her coffee. Decaf, of course; it was after nine. The hour and a half spent being reminded of why she and Dino hadn't socialized with the Barbizzis outside of baseball games had been enough to call it an early night. With Louis, at least. Ruth was another story. "Let's just say he's not ready to be dating and leave it at that."

"He talked about his late wife, huh?"

"From the moment we ordered." Varina sighed. She did that a lot lately. "It's not that I had high hopes, only that it would have been nice to have a positive first stab at dating."

"Maybe you shouldn't be stabbing it, then."

"Oh, hush."

"It really is too bad." Ruth dunked her cookie. "At least you were brave enough to try. I don't know if I'd have been."

"Get out of here! You'd have done it, and without all the jitters I had."

"You have a much different vision of me than I have of myself."

"Then let me keep my delusions." Varina swiped a cookie from the plate between them. "I need a brave friend to keep me sane. These are excellent, by the way. I wonder if this place would be interested in providing them for the store."

"Stick to the story, woman."

Varina wagged her half-eaten cookie. "Well, it was a first. Maybe I'll try it again sometime."

"You going to tell your mother?"

"She knows I went out on a date." She shrugged. "She had such high hopes. She's been after me to find a man for years."

"Why do mothers always want to marry off their daughters?" Ruth asked. "Mine did the same to me, rest her soul. Jacob wasn't a year in the grave before she started trying to fix me up."

"They just want us to be happy, I suppose."

"I was never happy married. The last two years have been wonderful."

"Should you be saying that?"

"Why not?" Ruth took another cookie. "It was my business that made us wealthy, we had no children, and he was unfaithful from day one. I stayed married because that is what one did. I sure as hell am not going to play the grieving widow. What about you and your husband?"

Varina pressed her fingertip into the crumbs on the table, wiggled them onto the plate. "His name was Anthony," she said, "but everyone called him Dino. We were happy. We made a great team."

"How romantic."

"It was, in its own way." Varina brought her cup to her lips, rested them against it. Memories stung, tickled her nose. "We were high school sweethearts, with all the drama and mush that goes along with that. Don't get me wrong, it was sweet, but what came after we were married and started having kids? It was a real partnership. We made a family and a business all at the same time. There was no 'man is the head of the household' bullshit, like my parents. It wasn't me that was the 'heart of the home.' It was us, together. We might not have been like turtledoves, but what me and Dino had? It was much better."

"I'm sorry you lost him so young."

Varina sipped. "I am, too."

"You could have been taking this trip with him instead of me."

"Nah, probably not." Travel. She'd thought about it, in quiet moments, but there had been precious few of those. First the blur of babies, then boys with baseball practice and soccer games; and just when they were getting self-sufficient, Donatella had come along and the process started all over again. With her, it had been softball and soccer, dance class and play rehearsals and never enough money, because all that stuff cost a fortune.

Varina had been happy. Dino, too. Their kids were everything. The store. One another. They had so much more than most. Still, the truest fact remained—she and Dino weren't turtledoves, and they weren't adventurous romantics who'd have traveled through Europe, let alone taken a cruise through France. A week down the shore had always been their speed. Now she was on her own, and her speed had changed. Apparently. She checked her watch.

"I should probably go. If I get home too late, my mother will call me a buttann' and not speak to me for a week." She grinned. "Then again . . ."

Ruth laughed, but it faded. She put a hand on Varina's. "I didn't upset you, did I?"

"No. You didn't." She closed her hand around her friend's. "I miss Dino. Every day. But he's gone, and you and I are going to France. I can't wait."

"Me either. I didn't think these cruises could actually excite me anymore. It's different, when you have someone to show the things you love."

Funny, how that happened. Varina let go of Ruth's hand. "I'll see you Saturday. Five thirty."

"Five thirty."

Ruth offered to drive her home, but Varina walked, like she walked just about everywhere. Louis had offered her a ride, too. Prolonging their date, or, worse, having that awkward good-night in the car was the last thing she wanted to endure. She'd shaken his hand outside the restaurant, told him she'd had a lovely evening and to take care of himself, and that would absolutely be that.

Steeling her resolve on the back stoop, Varina shoved the key in the lock and opened the door.

"How did it go? Did you have a nice time? Did he try anything fresh?"

"I'm not even in the door, Mom."

"Then come, come." Sylvia hauled Varina in by the arm. "Tell me all about it."

"There's nothing to tell." She took off her coat, unwound her scarf, and hung them on the hook. "He's a nice man, but he's not ready to date. Even if he were, he's not my type."

"What type is that, sweetheart?"

"The type that can have a conversation that doesn't revolve around his deceased wife."

"Oh." Her mother slumped. "That's too bad. But maybe next time will be better."

Varina laughed. "There won't be a next time."

"I meant with a different man."

"This was the first guy to have any interest in me in years, Mom. I doubt there will be another one anytime soon."

"You never know." Sylvia wagged a finger. "These things tend to snowball. Once the eligible gentlemen out there know you're on the market—"

"Sweet Jesus, Mom. I'm not a fresh ham. I'm done with this conversation."

"Fine."

"Don't be like that."

"I'm not being anything but tired. It's bedtime."

Varina looked at the clock; she'd been longer with Ruth than she meant to be. "It was sweet of you to wait up."

"It's what mothers do."

Indeed. "Night, Mom."

"Good night, sweetheart." Sylvia offered her a cheek. Varina kissed it dutifully, lingering in the powdery scent of her mother longer than she probably should have. Sylvia tended to see such gestures as something more morbid than intended, though she wasn't wrong about the motive. Did her kids love her as much as she loved her mother? Silly question. Of course they did. Of course.

Shutting lights as she went from kitchen to parlor to hallway, Varina halted in her tracks. The Victrola hunkered like a guilty child in the front window. She was close to certain it was her mother who moved it from place to place, though Sylvia swore she never did.

"Fine, stay there," Varina told it. "I'm too tired to argue."

Scratch-scratch-scratch.

"Don't you do it."

The almost-strain of music skidded to a halt.

"Thank you. Now go to sleep."

While she changed into her nightgown, Varina could have sworn she heard a softer-than-soft waltz playing, but when she stepped out into the hallway to go brush her teeth, there wasn't a sound to be heard but the floorboards creaking underfoot.

12

benedeeg'

Italian: *bene dire;* "to bless"

I always thought *benedeeg'* meant "Thank God!" I suppose it sort of does, because that's the way it's used.

The *r* in *dire* drops off and, in this case, becomes a *g* in Jersey Italian. It's kind of magical, really.

goombah

Italian: *compare;* "comrade"

Synonymous with the more recognizable *paesan'* (*paesano*), and not to be mistaken for the Super Mario Bros.' Goombas, though the reference cannot be accidental.

Nordic of them worked out. Four men sent to Palladino's to woo and win Varina, and not one of them had lived up to her daughter's lofty expectations.

"I have no idea why the store is suddenly pickup central, but it has to stop." Varina put a piece of baked chicken—chicken! benedeeg'!—onto Sylvia's plate, followed it with potatoes and carrots, nice and soft. "I tried it. I did! But I absolutely, positively know now, I don't want to date. Ever."

"You're just not trying hard enough."

"Mom, don't."

"But, sweetheart, if you would just—"

"Color my hair? Lose a few pounds? Wear some makeup? You want me to change who I am to please a man I don't even want?"

"Of course not."

"Good. That was the right answer, even though you don't mean it. I know you have something to do with this, so don't sit there looking all innocent."

"Me?" Hand to her chest, Sylvia did a pretty good job of feigning innocence, if she did say so herself. "You think I'm out there soliciting dates for you like a primp?"

Varina's brow furrowed, then she groaned. "It's *pimp*, Mom. And yes, I suspect you're doing just that. Somehow. All these men aren't showing up out of the blue."

"Four, Varina. Four men. I'd hardly call that a lot."

Another groan, this one more wistful. "Please, let's just eat and forget about yet another horrific date in the annuls of my recent, and now finished, dating experience."

Sylvia ate her chicken, trying to loosen up her jaw. Donatella wasn't adequately screening these men. All of them goombahs, but not the right kind. Varina needed someone like Dino: an Italian man who wasn't that traditional kind who had patriarchal notions about the roles men and women played in a relationship. She'd gotten lucky with Dino; how to tell her picky daughter that kind of lightning didn't strike twice?

"I'm sorry, sweetheart. I didn't mean to be harsh or critical."

"You never do."

"That's not fair."

"Isn't it?" Varina put her fork down. "I've gone out on more dates in the last month and a half than in all the years since Dino died. Do you think I did it for me?"

"Are you saying you're doing it for me?"

"That's what I'm saying."

"And are you telling me you didn't get just a little excited every time? A little hopeful? I see more than you give me credit for."

Varina pouted, and in her face Sylvia saw the child she had been, the one who felt so much more than she let on. Reaching across the table, she took her daughter's hand. "Are you okay, sweetheart?"

Varina squeezed, and let go. "I'm fine. Burned out. Bummed out. I just don't want to talk about it."

They finished eating in silence. Varina cleaned up, as always, leaving Sylvia to go watch an episode of *Murder, She Wrote*. Instead, she put on a record, turned it up just enough, and called Donatella from the phone in the parlor.

"Mom?"

"No. Nonina. Listen, sweetheart. I only have a minute."

"Okay. Shoot."

"Hold off for a few days. Your mother is burned out on bad dates."

"Um . . ."

"What?"

"I already told one of them to go to the shop tomorrow."

"Well, that's good. Tomorrow is Monday."

Silence, then, "I don't get it."

"The shop is closed Monday."

"Oh, right."

"Get in touch with whoever it is and tell him to hold off a week. And anyone else who calls."

"Will do."

"Will you really?"

"I said I would."

"Mom?" Varina called from the kitchen. "You want tea?"

"No, thank you, sweetheart!" She lowered her voice. "I have to go. Your mother already suspects I have something to do with the men coming to the shop."

"Bye, Non—"

Sylvia put the phone into the cradle none too gently just as Varina came into the room. She pretended to dust the table.

"What are you up to?"

She looked up, innocent as pie. How many times would Varina buy it? "Me? Nothing. I'll dust tomorrow while you're at the shop."

"Tomorrow is Monday."

"Oh, yes. Yes, it is. Well, then you dust."

"I won't be here either, though."

"Where will you be?"

"Ruth and I are going into the city." Varina tossed the dish towel over her shoulder. "Lunch, MoMA, maybe dinner, too."

"Ms. Moneybags is going to send you to the poorhouse with all this fancy-schmancy stuff."

"Mom."

"Sorry, sorry. You go, sweetheart. Have fun. I'll stay home by myself and dust."

"You're impossible. You do know that, right?" Varina came

closer, put her arms around Sylvia and hugged her gently. *Fanabola.*
Another my-mother-will-be-dead-soon hug. But she leaned into it
anyway, because Varina was probably right.

"You could come with us," she said. "Ruth is dying to meet you.
She says you can't possibly be as hilarious as I make you out to be."

"Me? Hilarious?"

"That's Ruth being kind." Varina laughed. "Really, Mom. Come."

"That's too much adventure for me, sweetheart. But thank you.
Another time."

"I'll hold you to that."

She would. Eventually, Sylvia was going to have to have coffee or
lunch with the gabaruss' Jewess who had enamored her daughter.
There was more going on there than Varina was saying. Were it not
for the fact her daughter had been going out with men lately, she'd
truly wonder about that whole lesbian thing. Or maybe her guilty but
well-intentioned conscience was making her suspicious.

Heading to her room, Sylvia ignored the pops and creaks in her
knees, her ankles, as best she could. The day was done. Supper was
over. Another night of Angela Lansbury solving crimes in small
towns that could never possibly see so many murders, and bed. She
sighed. What else could one expect at ninety-two?

"—NINA." DONATELLA WHUMPED BACK INTO THE COUCH, PUT HER FEET
in Paulie's lap. He massaged them. As of today, she had officially
lasted longer at Jumbaloon's than she had at any job over the last few
years. Not that he was counting. Paulie was starting to see the signs,
though; it wouldn't be much longer before her feet got itchy. She'd
be gone a month, two, six. Just when everyone thought she'd never
come back, she would. Though used to her disappearing for months
at a time, Paulie always missed her, if not her chaos.

He asked, "Something wrong?"

"I have to call Mr. Yu off for tomorrow." Donatella wiggled her toes. "I forgot the store is closed on Mondays."

"How could you forget that?" He laughed. "Palladino's is older than you are. And you worked there!"

"Until I left the place unlocked and we got robbed and the insurance wouldn't pay because I'm a negligent fuckup."

"Yeah. I remember."

"So does my mother."

"Shouldn't she?"

Donatella groaned. "What am I going to tell Mr. Yu?"

"Just put him off until Tuesday."

"I can't. Nonina says Mom is burned out on bad dates. Mr. Yu is so nice! Remember him, from back in high school? Jenny Yu's grandfather who practically raised her."

"Oh, right. He came to all the plays. I remember him smiling a lot."

"I think he has a hearing problem. Anyway, he's not a goombah. I was thinking maybe that's what's wrong with all the men I sent over to the store, you know?"

"Or maybe it's just too many, too fast." Paulie really dug into her arches. If he could get her through another day at the bakery, and then another, maybe she'd get used to being on her feet for long stretches, and not quit. Maybe she'd stay. "He'll understand."

"But I have *such* a good feeling about him, Paulie. Jenny does, too."

"You told Jenny Yu, who you haven't seen in a decade, about your matchmaking scheme?"

Donatella dug her heels into his thigh.

"Ow!"

"It's not a scheme. I met her in a club the other night, and this led to that. I showed her the flyer and she thought it was a great idea. Then she offered up her grandpa, who's been alone longer than Mom. They like the same things and did I mention he's not a goombah?"

"You did. But I think the last name would have tipped me—"

Donatella bolted upright, her heels now—accidentally, probably—jamming him in the balls. "Sorry, sorry! Oh, Paulie, I'm so sorry. I just had the best idea ever."

Paulie only groaned, flopped sideways on the couch.

"I'll be right back."

Donatella scrambled for her laptop. By the time Paulie could breathe again, she was back, grinning maniacally.

"What did you do?" he managed to croak.

"I told him not to go to the store."

"That's your best idea ever?"

"No." She chuckled. "I told him to go to the house!"

"Are you insane? How's he going to explain that?"

"We've tried sly—"

"What's this *we* stuff?"

"It's time for the direct approach. He's going to tell her the truth. His granddaughter and her daughter thought they would hit it off."

"And showing up at the house is better than a phone call how?"

"They're old! Fashioned. Old-fashioned! This is the way they did things back in their day. Besides, Mom would never be rude. She'd at least talk to him. I'm one hundred percent positive they'll hit it off. Or she can tell him good day. But I don't think she will."

"You're kind of an idiot," Paulie told her. "At least your heart is in the right place. You know the jig's up after this, right?"

"Just for a little while. If it doesn't work out with Mr. Yu, I'll give it a rest for a week or two. I'm kind of floored by the amount of activity I've gotten. Who knew there were so many single grandfathers looking for love in the area?"

"That many, huh?"

"More than there are eligible grandsons, I'll tell you that. I don't send them all to the store, you know. I screen very carefully. There are some real kooks out there. One guy asked if she was a good house-keeper. Can you imagine?"

"Men are pigs."

"Ha, ha. Speaking of men . . ." She slid up to his side, resting her elbow on his shoulder. "How'd your boyfriend like the kitchen we designed?"

Paulie chose to let her innuendo slide. "Dante loved it. Then again, he'd have probably said that no matter what I did. As discussed, he's not the creative type."

"Did you take pics for me?"

"I forgot."

She smacked his arm.

"Kidding." He pulled out his phone.

Donatella scrolled through them. "Damn, Paulie. This is beyond gorgeous. I never would have imagined all this from the tiles and shit we picked out."

"You should come see it in person, before it sells."

"It'll go that fast?"

"We've already had a few interested parties, and the house isn't even finished yet."

"The gentrification of Wyldale, by Spini and Son, featuring kitch-ens designed by the soon-to-be-famous-on-HGTV Paul Rudolph Vittone." She poked him. "Sounds a bit bougie, doesn't it?"

Paulie took back his phone. "Yes and no. Dante is doing some up-scale work, but he's keeping the integrity of the town intact. Lower-income neighborhoods will stay lower-income neighborhoods, just renovated at a price people can afford."

"Doesn't seem like he's going to make a lot of money on those."

"He'll make enough on the higher-end neighborhoods. I told you. He has a vision."

Donatella curled into him, whispering in his ear, "And he's shared this vision with you? How special."

"Jeez, will you stop?"

"Is it so wrong to want to see my brother and my best friend live happily ever after?"

"He's not gay, Don."

"What about that kiss?"

"We were very, very drunk. He and Pan were newly married. And besides, he doesn't even remember." Or he pretended not to, so Paulie pretended, too.

"Bi, then," Donatella persisted.

"Dante's an all-or-nothing sort of man."

"Jeez! Can't a girl get one gay brother?"

"You have me."

Donatella knelt on the couch beside him. "I have you. Always."

"Always and forever." He kissed her cheek. Then the other. Then Paulie kissed her mouth. Talking about Dante did things to him he'd rather not have done to him. She kissed him back, but not with the depravity he'd been hoping for.

"Sorry, pal." She put a hand on his chest. "Not tonight. I'm getting my period and I feel like someone shoved a cheese grater in there."

"Wow." He leaned back. "That's . . . some visual. Good mood killer."

"You love me."

"I do." Paulie kissed her nose, pushed out of the couch. "I'd better get going. You have work early, and I have to tuck in my cats."

"Ugh. Don't remind me. About work, I mean. How are the little furballs doing, anyway?"

"MaryJane is awesome. Like she's been with me forever. Chooch and Pastafazool are getting big. They'll be ready to leave Mama soon."

"And will you be able to do it?"

He put his coat on. "I don't know. I have time yet."

"If you keep them, you have to get those boys fixed. And Mary-Jane. You don't want more kittens in the house."

"Gross, Don."

"It happens!"

"G'night!"

"Good—"

Paulie closed the door on her *night*. Hands jammed in his pockets, he walked the blocks between Donatella's apartment over the store, and home. It was cold, and there was no one out at that hour. A car passed. No more. No one. Paulie didn't like being alone, even on these streets he knew so well, where everyone knew him and had most of his life. That was part of the problem. They *knew* him, and not all of them liked him. *Fanook* had never died out; he'd heard it muttered. Shouted. He didn't think anyone would hurt him physically, but he didn't know for sure. It made dating in general problematic. Arthur had been the one longish relationship in all the years since Paulie's outing. They'd met down in Cape May, both in their twenties, then. Neither had felt the need to move for the other. The occasional visit lasting a few hours or a few days—Arthur called them fuckfests—had been enough for both of them, until it just wasn't. Paulie really did want happily ever after, and Arthur definitely wasn't it. The only one who could be wasn't even—

His cell phone chirped as he entered his apartment. He tossed his keys into the little dish on the front table. "Hello?"

"Hey, kid." Dante's voice jolted his heart and warmed his ear. "Sorry to call so late."

"No problem, boss. What's up?" Paulie put him on speaker. The number on his screen was not Dante's. Peggy Fauci? Who the hell was that?

"I just wanted to tell you how great that kitchen turned out. I'm really proud of you."

MaryJane wound about his legs. "Thanks."

"I mean it." He sounded half asleep. "Really gorgeous."

A woman's muffled voice. Music that sounded a lot like that adult contemporary jazz stuff Dante claimed to hate. "Boss? You okay? Where are you?"

"Fine, kid. I'm fine. With a friend. I was just thinking of you. I mean, about the kitchen, and how great it turned out."

The woman's voice rose enough for Paulie to think he heard, "That's what you were thinking about while we were—?"

"I was thinking you might want to expand to bathroom design," Dante said, louder now. "The Jack and Jill and the powder room are already done"—white and black, yes, Paulie had seen—"But the master en suite still needs doing."

"Yeah?" Paulie's insides quivered. He pushed his glasses up higher on his nose. "Sure, I'd love to take a crack at it."

"Good. It's yours. I'll meet you there first thing tomorrow. I'll show you what's what."

"Great. Thanks, boss."

Silence lingered slightly longer than comfortable. No woman's voice on the other end, even if Dante still used her phone. Paulie's imagination ran away with him, and he thought he might be sick. He took a breath to speak, but Dante beat him to it. "Could you call me Dante, kid? *Boss* makes me feel . . . old."

The roiling in his gut eased. A little. "I'll call you Dante if you stop calling me kid. It makes me feel . . . infantile."

Dante laughed softly. Wearily. "You got it. Paulie."

"Paul would be even better."

"Let's not get crazy, now."

And Paulie laughed softly, too. "Okay, Dante. I'll see you in the morning."

"Ciao, bello."

Tapping out of the call, Paulie stared at it long after the screen faded to black. "Did we just have a moment?" he asked his cat. She only blinked up at him. "You're right. I'm an idiot. Come on, my love. Time for bed."

Paulie checked on the kittens. He'd gotten them a used playpen from Ditto, the secondhand shop on Walnut. They got into everything if he let them run loose. So far, they hadn't climbed out, but it wouldn't be long. He hoped, with MaryJane accessible, food and toys and a litter box, they'd be happy enough for another week or so. Then, he'd have to make a decision.

Burying his face in MaryJane's fur, Paulie closed his eyes. He wouldn't read anything foolish into Dante being with this Peggy Fauci person. It was work Dante thought about. Constantly. That Paulie was involved had been coincidence. He'd been especially distracted, lately. Not himself. Almost . . . sad. Then again, he'd always been the tall—for a Palladino—dark, and brooding sort. He'd seemed happy with Pandora. Happy enough. Settled. They were good together. Good parents to Gabriella. The divorce came as a shock to everyone who knew them, even, Paulie believed, Dante himself.

He put MaryJane into the playpen with Chooch and Pastafazool, who immediately snuggled in to nurse. She purred, glancing up at him with come-hither eyes. Paulie scritched under her chin. "Night, girl."

Purr-purr-purr.

His head barely touched the pillow before he was asleep, and dreaming of tile and grout, fixtures and claw-foot tubs. And a sad smile on lips that, one drunken night, had kissed him so tenderly in a coat closet on New Year's Eve.

13

mi scuzat'

Italian: *scusatemi;* "excuse me," "apologies"

Sometimes whittled down to a simple *m'scooz* or even *'scooz*.

agida/agita *(ah-jih-da)*

Italian: *aciditá/agitare;* literally, "acidity/agitate"

Indigestion, or mental upset. *Agida* is typically used to express displeasure with a situation or person, e.g.: "Stop drumming your fingers! You're giving me agida!"

I always wondered if Italians in Italy use any versions of these words. Interestingly, they kind of do. Neapolitan Italians reduce (I learned that term from a linguistics video) words from Standard Italian, dropping many of those beginning or ending vowels. Jersey Italians, who are mostly from the Naples region, just took it to a whole new level.

Sylvia wasn't dusting, even though she'd told Varina she would. Her dusting days were over, as were her vacuuming days, her dishwashing days, "pretty much anything that had to do with housework" days were over. She made her bed. She kept her room tidy. She did her own laundry. That was enough.

Her daughter left earlier that morning, for her fancy-schmancy day in the city with Mrs.—*mi scuzat'*—*Ms.* Moneybags. Tommy was busy, as was Pandora, and Gabriella was back at school. Donatella was—gasp!—working. Sylvia thought about calling Davide to come get her, but she didn't need her hair done, and besides, he drove too damn fast in that car of his. A Vespa. No, a Viper. That was it. Sylvia had no desire to ride in something that dangerous sounding.

Staring out the window like a child on a rainy day, Sylvia thought, maybe, she'd just watch her stories. She hated watching them with commercials—no one had yet caught on that she actually did know how to work the DVR—but she had nothing else to do. Passing through the parlor on her way from kitchen to bedroom, she almost caught Vicky in the act.

"I see you!" She wagged a finger at the Victrola, caught halfway from corner to window. "You know my daughter accuses me of your antics, don't you? Fine. If I'm going to be blamed . . ." Sylvia moved the Victrola into the window. "There you go, you haunted old thing."

Longing welled. Hers? Or Vicky's? Was there a difference? They were both still functioning long after their useful days had ended, trapped in bygone days and memories, of dancing and parties, broken hearts and new love.

Sylvia took a record from the cabinet. "The Blue Danube" waltz, by the Philadelphia Symphony Orchestra, conducted by the great Leopold Stokowski himself. She and Joseph used to dance with the children to this one. They'd never been interested until they heard it play on a carousel down the shore. After that, it was an after-Sunday-dinner dance together that continued many years.

She blew imagined dust from the record. This was music, from a time when conductors were celebrities in and of themselves. Leonard Bernstein, Cab Calloway, Mitch Miller. Or maybe, it could be, they were simply caught in the same past she was. There were probably even famous female conductors now. There were famous female everythings.

But the music. The music! The sound quality was poor, and sometimes it skipped, or wound down and garbled before the end of the record. Yet the ever-present scratch of the needle on vinyl evoked her youth. Picnics accompanied by a portable and newer version of Vicky. Parlor parties in the houses of friends long dead. Sylvia was the last of them still breathing, remembering, keeping their ghosts from withering, forgotten. Lifting her arms, she floated and spun. Carefully.

Ding-dong.

The front door. Another sound out of the past. A package? Maybe a Christmas gift from a not-errant-after-all grandchild—Angelina sent a card, but not even a fruitcake to go with it!—lost in the mail. Leaving the record playing, she looked out the sidelight window.

And elderly Oriental man stood on the stoop, straight and composed, holding a bouquet of daffodils. He had to be at least as old as Sylvia herself. Maybe older. Delivering flowers? On a winter day as cold as this? Probably for one of Varina's rejected suitors, vying for a second date. Sylvia opened the door. "Aren't you a little old for a delivery boy?"

"Excuse me?"

Sylvia pointed to the flowers. "Are those for Varina?"

He smiled, the channels of his wrinkled face becoming chasms. "They are. Are you Varina?"

"Me?" She laughed. "I'm her mother."

"Pleased to meet you, Mrs. . . . ?"

"Spini."

"I'm John. John Yu. May I come in? It's rather cold out here."

"Oh. Yes, yes. Come in." She pointed to the doormat. "Wait here, please."

Sylvia took the flowers from the man, took them to the kitchen, and put them hastily into a vase. Taking two dollars from the spare change jar, she crossed herself, praying whatever single grandfather looking for love sent the flowers would be given a second chance.

"Here you go." She held the tip out to John Yu. "Thank you."

He smiled, his expression puzzled. "What is this?"

"Your tip."

"My . . . oh!" John laughed, the sound something between a baritone and a tenor, just like his voice. "I'm not a delivery person. I'm John Yu. My granddaughter and yours thought Varina and I would be a good match. They sent me here to meet her."

Her belly quivered. "You're a single grandfather looking for love?"

"Well, that sounds a bit untoward, but I suppose—"

And now it simmered. "Donatella sent you?"

"Yes, that's her name."

"Is she insane?" Sylvia threw up her hands. John Yu took a step back. "Silly question. Of course she is. Mannaggia dial! That child's going to give me agida until the day I die!"

"I'm sorry. Have I done something wrong?"

Sylvia put both hands on top of her head, as if that might keep her stack from blowing any higher. Taking deep breaths, she did her best to compose herself. "No, Mr. Yu. You have not. My granddaughter did. She should never have sent you here."

"I was originally supposed to go to the store. Palladino's? Just a few blocks from here. But my granddaughter, her name is Jenny, told me to come here instead. The flowers, I'm afraid, were my idea."

"It's a nice touch. Nice touch." She let her arms fall to her sides. "I'm sorry, Mr. Yu. My granddaughter should never have given out our address to a stranger. And, besides, pardon my bluntness, but you are far too old for my daughter."

"I am eighty-nine years young."

"Don't give me that old line." She laughed. "Neither of us are anything that even remembers young."

He chuckled, too. "How old is your Varina?"

"Seventy. Not young either, but too young for you."

"You may be right about that." He put his hands in his pockets, cocked his head. "'The Blue Danube' waltz. Philadelphia Symphony Orchestra?"

"It is."

"I have the same recording."

The record ran down. Sylvia waited, but it didn't start up again. Very unlike Vicky to behave. "Do you have a possessed old Victrola, too?"

He laughed. "No, I'm afraid not. My grandchildren have digitalized all my music and put it on my phone." He pulled it from his pocket. *Tap-tap-tap.* "See? My music list."

Wonder of wonders. "But it can't sound the same."

Scrolling the list, he stopped it with a finger. Tapped. The scratchy "Blue Danube" waltz began all over again, from his phone, not Vicky.

"Close." Sylvia raised a crooked finger. "But there's nothing like the real thing. Come."

John Yu followed Sylvia into the parlor. She cranked Vicky up, set the needle carefully down, and waited. *Scratch-scratch-scratch,* and . . . She smiled. He smiled.

"See?"

"You are right, Mrs. Spini. There is nothing quite like that old sound." He held out his hand. "Shall we? Unless, of course, there is a Mr. Spini who will object?"

Was she still able to blush? That was what the heat in her cheeks was, wasn't it? She did not press her hand to the sensation; maybe he wouldn't notice. "My Joseph is long in the grave, God rest him." She placed her hand onto his. He gave a little bow, and led her into a waltz she'd not danced in more years than she cared to remember.

"You're a very good dancer," he told her.

"Yes, I know. Thank you. You are, too."

"We come from a time when such things were expected."

"That's true. Were you born in this country, Mr. Yu?"

"I was," he answered. "My family has been in the United States since the early railroad days. You?"

"I'm first-generation American," she told him. "And only barely. I was born three months after my mother came over on the boat."

"Just your mother?"

"And me." Sylvia shrugged. "Papa was already here, along with the older children. That's how it went, back in those days. He was here over a dozen years before my mother and I arrived. He took my oldest sister after his first trip home, left my mother pregnant with my second sister, came back for her when she was seven, left Mama pregnant with me. By then she'd had enough being separated. She made the crossing when she did so I would be an American."

"That must have been a difficult crossing for her."

"She used to tell me it was, when I was little and naughty, thinking it would make me behave to know how she suffered for me. I found out, years after she died, that my father insisted she cross in style. She had her own cabin, and daily meals served on white linen."

John Yu chuckled softly. "Were you a brat?"

"Oh, I was." She chuckled, too. "Wild, is what I was. At heart, anyway. I think my father knew that, and he felt sorry for me, having to fit into a mold I wasn't meant for. It wasn't easy being a girl like me, in the time I was raised. It's still not, I don't think."

"I could say the same, but about being Chinese. It was especially hard, during the war. It didn't matter I was Chinese, not Japanese. All of us were lumped together, considered enemies. It's better now, though."

She sighed. "My papa spoiled me so. By the time I was born, there was more money, less stress. My two sisters, rest their souls, worked from the time they were seven. I went to school, even got my high school diploma. I had dresses and sweets and dolls. It was no wonder I was such a brat."

The record played, and on they danced and talked. Vicky kept the turntable turning even after it should have run down. It was good, having someone to talk to about a time she remembered more clearly than she did last week, someone who knew what she knew, about things familiar and beloved, even if, at the time, they hadn't been. That's what reminiscing was, as far as she was concerned, a thing one did with a smile and fondness.

Eventually, the recording played out, the *hiss-hiss-hiss* at the end echoing the *scratch-scratch-scratch* of the beginning. John Yu stepped back, bowed slightly at the waist. Sylvia managed a halfway decent curtsy. Crossing to the Victrola, she lifted the needle.

"Thank you for the dance," Mr. Yu said.

"You're welcome. Thank you for the conversation."

"My pleasure."

The grandfather clock ticked too loudly. Sylvia patted her hair, as if it had somehow mussed in all the excitement.

"I suppose I should be going." He started for the door.

Sylvia intercepted him. "What shall I tell Varina about the flowers?"

John Yu smiled, those channels becoming chasms in that most pleasant way. "Tell her they were given to you by a new admirer."

"Me?" Her hand moved to pat her hair again; Sylvia curled her fingers into her palm instead.

"If it's not rude. Or too forward."

"Oh, not at all. I . . . thank you, Mr. Yu."

"You are very welcome, Mrs. Spini."

Sylvia opened the door for him, standing on the mat where he'd stood, holding that lovely bouquet, watching him go carefully down the steps. "My knees." He tapped his leg. "They're not as young as they used to be."

"You just be careful."

He reached the bottom without incident. "Good day, Mrs. Spini."

"Good day, Mr. Yu."

But he did not go. Sylvia waited, already feeling the chill creeping up her arms.

"If it's not too bold, may I call on you again?"

Oh my. Oh my! "That would be lovely. We can dance again. I will make you tea. Or coffee, if that's your preference."

"Coffee, but decaf, if you please."

"I understand, believe me."

"I will bring something sweet to go with it."

"That would be nice."

"Shall we say . . . Wednesday?"

Wednesday, as in the day after tomorrow? Sylvia rubbed the chill from her arms. "Wednesday," she said. "Two o'clock?"

"Two o'clock."

The chasms of his smile ate up his entire face. "I will see you then, Mrs. Spini."

"You may call me Sylvia," she told him.

"Then you must call me John."

"Good day, John."

"Good day."

And off he walked. Slowly. His posture excellent. Sylvia stepped back inside, closed the door behind her, enjoying the fluttering that chased the chill from her ancient bones.

Putting the kettle on for tea, she spotted the hastily put together vase of flowers. While the water heated, she arranged them nicely, tied the bow from the bouquet around the vase itself.

Tell her they were given to you by a new admirer.

Sylvia hugged herself to keep from trembling. An admirer. So strange and lovely and, she felt, sincere. The vivid yellow and orange, green and white, against the bright blue of the bow reminded her that spring was near. Spring in a vase, brought to her—well, Varina, but things changed—by a lovely Oriental man who waltzed divinely. Not the way she'd seen her day going. Not the way she'd anticipated their encounter ending up, considering how it began.

14

Ashbett'!

Italian: *Aspetta!;* "Wait!"

Also used as a way of affectionately telling someone to be quiet. Or passive-aggressively telling them to shut up.

Maloik!

Italian: *Malocchio!;* the evil eye

It's a stare practiced and perfected by Italians of all kinds. And Greeks. They've mastered it, too. If it has ever been leveled upon you, you know it. To counter the maloik, make the ma'cornoot (*mana cornuto,* in Italian) or, the "devil" sign, by making a fist and leaving up index finger and pinky. Combine it with a very specific spit, that being no actual saliva flying from your mouth, but a very pronounced "too-too!" and you'll be safe.

She'd pretend it was on purpose, that's what she'd do. Varina lifted the mirror so she could see the back of her hair that was just as purple as the front. Something resembling a laugh but feeling more like a sob welled up from her heart and out her mouth. This is what came of letting her mother's constant nagging get to her.

"Don't blame your mother," she said to the purple-haired woman in the mirror. "It's your own fault for choosing red. And for being too chicken to go to your son's salon. Your fault."

Setting the mirror down, Varina wiped the tears from her cheeks. There was nothing to do about it now; she had to get to the store, purple or no purple. She tied a kerchief at the nape of her neck. It didn't hide her hair, but it made it less noticeable. Maybe she could get an appointment with Davide later in the day. Pandora might cover for her at the store. Varina didn't relish hearing her son's lecture about the damage box dyes do, but he was a good boy. One withering look would probably be enough to shut him up.

On her way out the door, she called Ruth. "I did something really stupid."

"You went on another date?"

"Ha, ha. No. As a matter of fact, the sudden abundance of eligible bachelors wandering into Palladino's asking for products I don't carry or are out of stock has dried up completely."

"That sounds kind of fishy to me."

"The only thing fishier is where they all came from to begin with, which, by the way, my mother definitely has something to do with. I just don't know how yet. But that's not it." Varina took a deep breath. "I dyed my hair."

"Your mother got to you, huh?"

"Ashbett', ah?" She laughed. "Maybe a little. But I'd been thinking about it, to be honest, and not hating the idea, but . . ."

"Oh, no. You did it yourself."

Silence.

"Varina! Your son owns the most successful hair studios in three counties!"

"I know!" She groaned. "And that's not the worst of it."

"I'm listening."

Varina huffed and puffed, only then realizing she was walking so fast she was nearly jogging. Slowing down, she took a deep breath. "It's a little embarrassing, and I don't want you to think less of me."

"I couldn't possibly think less of you. And I mean that sincerely, not sarcastically."

Another deep breath. "I went for red." And then in a rush, "You have the most beautiful red hair and I thought, if I'm going to do it, I'm going to really do it, but it's not red like yours, it's more like mahogany if mahogany were purple. Actually, violet, and I tried washing it out because it's one of those temporary dyes, but it's not washing out at all, only getting more pink, and now I have to go to work and I'm so embarrassed I just want to cry!"

And then she was crying. Half jogging down the street, on the phone, crying like a little girl who dropped her ice cream cone.

"Varina, stop walking."

She stopped.

"Take a breath."

She took one.

"Now another."

And she did.

"First of all, my red comes from years and years of salons attempting to replicate my natural color, and it's close but not exact. It was your son's salon, as a matter of fact, that got this close. Second, it costs me a small fortune every three weeks to be maintained. I've often considered letting it go white, more often since meeting you. Your hair is lovely, Varina, those curls I'd happily pay a fortune for if my hair were thick enough, and that perfect mix of black and white. So, don't be embarrassed about wanting what I have, because I want what you have. Third, your grandkids are going to think you're the hippest thing ever. And your daughter is going to go bananas. Live with it today, and see how you feel. Tomorrow, if you still hate it, make an appointment with your son and he'll put it to rights."

She was right. Of course, Ruth was right. Varina started walking again, more slowly, less frantic, even if her heart was still beating a little too fast.

"Want to have dinner tonight?" Varina asked. "My house?"

"You cooking?"

"Of course." Varina laughed. "I know you've had my cooking from the store, but I'll make something I don't carry there. Believe it or not, I make an amazing turkey meat loaf. Soy and ginger and garlic. It's delicious."

"Your mother eats turkey meat loaf?"

"Absolutely not, that's why I suggested it. She's going out for dinner. Again. My brother always did his dutiful-son thing once a week. Now that he's moving to Florida, he's packing them in. She's been out twice already this week."

"Wow. Maybe she has a boyfriend."

"Let's not get crazy, now."

The women laughed together as Varina slipped into the alley leading to the back of the shop. Putting the key in the lock, she couldn't believe how much better she felt. "Thanks for talking me off the ledge, Ruth."

"That's what friends are for."

"I'll see you tonight. Come over around six. Mom will be back by seven thirty, the latest. You'll finally get to meet her."

"I'll bring wine, then," Ruth said. "Lots of wine."

VARINA GOT A FEW LOOKS, BUT NO ONE ASKED ABOUT HER HAIR. NO one made faces, or remarks under their breath. Now and again catching a glimpse of herself in the chrome counter, she had to admit she kind of liked it. Where her hair had been pepper was still pepper, but where it had been salt, it was now a pale violet. She took off the kerchief before noon.

Lunch hours were always the busiest, but in the winter months, usually slower. In warmer weather, Varina needed extra hands for the lunch rush that extended into the dinner hours. Why cook when you could pick up a meal prepared by Palladino's, complete with fresh bread from the Bronx? Going away in October was going to be a little harrowing, considering it was one of her busier times of year, but Varina would manage, by hook or by crook.

Today, however, for whatever reason, it was order after order. In person. On the phone. Thank goodness she hadn't opened herself up to online business. Yet. Gabriella was on her to move into the computer age, but Varina could barely keep up as it was. The profit margins weren't big enough to warrant extra employees, and she couldn't bring herself to raise her prices high enough to hire them. Who would buy that meal prepared by Palladino's if they could go out for dinner for just a little more? No, her prices had to stay relatively the same, or she'd lose those regulars who kept her in business. She'd seen far too many downtown businesses fade away over the years to fool herself—loyalty was loyalty, until the purse was hit too hard and the customers took their business elsewhere.

The bell over the door jingled again, and she was behind three orders.

"Be right with you!"

"What did you do to your hair? I love it!" Donatella came around the counter, an apron already in hand. "What's next?"

"Ronnie. Chicken cutlet hero."

"Got it." She kissed Varina's cheek, then, "Hey, Ronnie! Long time no see. You want that hero hot or cold?"

Mother and daughter handled customers side by side for the next hour. Varina had forgotten just how nice it was to work with Donatella. It wasn't that she was inept, just irresponsible. Her presence lit up the whole place, as well as the customers who hadn't seen her in a while. Some recognized her from Jumbaloon's, where she served doughnuts and coffee with the same infectious smile. Rather than being exhausted when the bell stopped jingling, Varina felt energized.

"So?" Donatella untied her apron. "The hair?"

Varina ran fingers through it. "Would you believe me if I told you I did it on purpose?"

"Not in a million years."

They laughed together. All Donatella's chaos made it easy to forget the good stuff.

"Let me guess, you decided to go red and instead of asking Davide, you tried doing it yourself."

Varina grimaced.

"Oh, Mom!" Diving at her, Donatella hugged her around the waist. "You're nuts. Have you called him?"

"No," she answered. "I haven't decided if I hate it yet."

"Really?"

"Is it that bad?"

"No! It's amazing! I think you should keep it. You look awesome."

"Ruth said you'd go bananas."

"How would she know?" Donatella feigned a pout. "I've never met Ruth. Do you complain about me all the time?"

"Why would you say that?"

"Because you have a lot to complain about?"

"Sweetheart, no."

Reaching into her pocket, Donatella was trying not to smile; Varina could tell by the way she pressed her lips together, just like she did when she was a child in church, trying not to giggle. She slapped her hand onto the counter, leaving behind crumpled bills. "Bada-bing! There you go."

"What's this?"

"One hundred bucks. I'm paying you back, like I promised."

Varina pulled her hand back. "You don't have to—"

"Mom, stop." Donatella picked up the bills and put them into the cash register. "Seriously. I know you don't like taking money from me, from any of us, even though the boys have more money than the Catholic Church, but I want to do the right thing. I want to pay for my own dumb mistake."

Tears stung. Varina held them in check. She touched her daughter's cheek. Pulling her errant child, her misbehaving, old-enough-to-know-better daughter into her arms. "I know you worked hard for that money."

"No harder than you did." Donatella kissed her cheek. She doubled over slightly, fingers pressed to her groin. "Damn."

"What's wrong?"

"That stitch in my side. I swear, if it were any higher, I'd think it was my appendix."

"You probably pulled something," Varina told her. "I bet you lifted something heavy at work."

"That mixer can be a real bitch. Have you ever seen the size of that thing?"

"I'll take your word for it. Why don't you go lie down?"

"Yeah, I will. I told Paulie I'd stop in and check on his cats. He's stuck at the job site until all hours, finishing up a bathroom."

"Hey, why don't you go check on the cats, and rest at Paulie's awhile, then come down and have dinner with me and Ruth. I'd love for you to meet her. I'm making that soy-ginger turkey meat loaf you love."

"Oooo, yes. Thanks, Mom."

"Six o'clock."

"If I don't show up, bang on the ceiling. I might be asleep."

"I'm not banging on any ceiling." Varina tsked. "Set the alarm on your phone."

"Fine, fine." Donatella kissed her cheek. "Love you."

"Love you, too, sweetheart."

And she was gone.

A whirlwind that left a hole in the air, and everyone breathless in her wake.

Varina opened the cash register, took from it the hundred dollars in crumpled bills Donatella had shoved in there. Money her daughter had earned. Money her daughter needed to live on. Money Varina didn't really need, not even to take her trip of a lifetime. One way or another, she'd sock away the necessary money. What would Donatella go without because of this hundred dollars?

Crumpling the money into her fist, Varina refused to cry. As her own father used to say, her daughter would never have coffee without any cake. This payback was a good thing, a step in the right direction. Maybe, after more than half a lifetime of perpetual adolescence, Donatella was, at long last, growing up.

PAULIE CHECKED FOR A TEXT FROM DONATELLA. FIVE TWENTY-FIVE, and nothing. Damn. She wasn't answering. He should have known better than to trust her to do as she promised. The cats were probably fine, but Chooch and Pastafazool had gotten out of their playpen last night. They still seemed too little to be out and about; there was nothing kitten-proof about his home. MaryJane would see they stayed out of trouble, right?

Sigh.

The bathroom was nearly finished, and only just in time. Prospective buyers would be there in the morning, and he'd promised Dante upside down and inside out that it would not only be done, but staged. It wouldn't take long to accomplish. The fixtures would be quick, and then all the knicks and knacks that would make it pop. He could go home, check on the cats, have something to eat, and be back before eight, finished by ten. Maybe eleven. Or he could call Varina and ask her to check. Or he could trust MaryJane to take care of her babies.

Hurrying to his car, he rang Donatella instead of texting her. It went straight to voicemail, which meant her phone was turned off. Fantastic. Paulie hung up without leaving a message he'd regret, then have to leave a second message apologizing for. How it happened that she let him down and he ended up apologizing, he still didn't quite get. It happened, though. Often.

It only took ten minutes to drive across town. Paulie thought about ducking into Palladino's to pick up something for his supper, but the shop would already be closed, and he didn't have the key on him. Too bad. He could have gone for Varina's chicken piccata and broccoli rabe sangweech on a wedge of that bread from the Bronx. Tomorrow. He'd order it in the morning and ask her to bring it home for him if he didn't get back before closing.

Pushing his key into the lock, Paulie found it already open. The kittens were sleeping. With Donatella. On the couch, curled into a sweet ball of fluff and curls, watched over by MaryJane, perched on the back.

Paulie closed the door as quietly as he'd opened it. Kneeling on the floor in front of the couch, he pushed the curls from Donatella's face. The kittens didn't stir.

"Hey," he whispered.

She grunted. "What are you doing here?"

"I . . . uh . . . just came home to grab some dinner."

Donatella yawned, scooping the kittens into a safer position before sitting up. "You thought I didn't keep my promise."

Why lie? "You didn't answer any of my texts."

"Because I turned my phone off to catch a few winks. I feel like shit, and I'm exhausted. I worked at Jumabloon's from five thirty this morning until noon, then helped Mom out at the store until four." She checked her clock. "I'm supposed to be having dinner with her and her new girlfriend in about fifteen minutes. That's why I'm still here."

"Oh."

"Oh? Is that all you have to say?"

"I'm sorry?" Paulie said. "I'm sorry you've let me down so many times in the past that I thought this was just another time."

"Wow, thanks."

He laughed. "Come on. Seriously. I'm sorry. And thanks for checking on them."

Donatella scooped a still-groggy Pastafazool into her hand, nuzzled his tiny head. "They're so cute."

"Too cute."

"You thinking of keeping them?"

Paulie sat beside her, picking up Chooch. "I just don't think I can. It's not fair to them. I can't let them out, and this place is just too small."

"But you're keeping MaryJane."

"Of course."

She kissed Pastafazool's nose. "I can help you find homes for them."

"Thanks."

"Sure. Hey, why don't you come downstairs with me and have dinner with my mother."

"I really don't have time. I have that bathroom to finish for Dante before—"

"Come on. You have to eat. And you know there will be plenty. We can take these little guys down, give their mama a break, and then we have an excuse to hit the high road after getting some food."

"You're a piece of work, you know that?"

"A work of art is what you mean." Getting up, kitten in hand, Donatella doubled over. "Dammit. Take him." She handed Pasta-fazool to Paulie, clutching at her groin. "I feel like serious shit. If I don't get my period soon, I'm going to explode."

"You still haven't gotten it?"

"Huh? Why?"

"Didn't you say something about that a couple weeks ago?"

"I don't remember. It hasn't been that long. Shit, Paulie. I know how to use birth control. Don't scare me."

He laughed. "I'm just saying! Sometimes these things—"

"Don't! I'll maloik you and your whole family if you say it out loud!"

"I'm sure it's nothing." Paulie handed her back the kitten. "Remember when you forgot to take your tampon out and—"

"Gross. I remember. Ugh, I'm not going to the gyno for that again. You can do it for me."

"No way. I love you, woman, but no friggin' way."

"We'll see." She headed for the door. Picking up a tiny paw, she waved it in MaryJane's direction. "See you later, mama-cat. Rest while you have the chance."

Paulie followed after her, closing the door on MaryJane, who followed meowing after her kittens. His heart pittered a little, already somewhat breaking over the prospect of taking them away from her. But isn't that what cats did? If Dante hadn't brought them to him, the boys would be weaned and then go off on their own, never to see their mother or each other again. MaryJane must have litters that had already done just that. Which reminded him, he had to have her spayed. Paulie made a mental note to call the vet in the morning.

Donatella paused at the door leading to her mother's part of the house. "Just so you're aware, Mom's hair is purple. Don't act shocked." And she opened the door. "Mom! Paulie's eating, too. I hope you have enough!"

15

stunad' *(stoo-NAHD)*

Italian: *stonato;* literally, "out of tune"

In Jersey Italian, *stunad'* is more along the lines of "confused," like: "I just bumped my head and I'm all stunad'." Or, when you've tripped over the cat and fallen down the front steps: "What are you, stunad'? Didn't you see that cat on the stoop?"

How one word became the other is obvious, and kind of cool. Very cool.

Capeesh?

Italian: *Capisci?;* "(Do you) understand?"

So common in American English vernacular, *Capeesh?* is universally understood to mean exactly what it means. Answering, "Yeah, I got it," is very *Medigan* (American). If you want to be classier about it, answer with the Italian *Capisco* ("I understand"). That'll really throw them. It might also get you punched in the mouth for being a smart-ass. As I might have mentioned—we are a complicated people.

S o . . ." Ruth sipped her wine. "That was interesting."

They'd gone through two bottles over supper with Paulie and Donatella, opened another when Sylvia got home and briefly joined them before retiring to her room.

Varina lifted her glass. "You see why I need a vacation?"

"I never doubted that you needed a vacation, but . . ." Ruth lifted her glass, too. "Here's to Provence in the fall."

"Donatella's not always that hyper."

"Yes, she is. I don't even know her and I know that's true. She has a nervous energy, like she's not settled inside her own skin. Your mom does, too."

"My mother?" Varina shook her head. "I don't think that's true."

"You're too close to both of them. She took your purple hair well, though."

"Surprisingly. I think she was just tired. And she was being polite because of you. She calls you Ms. Moneybags, you know."

Ruth tilted her head back, laughing. "Oh, that's wonderful. And she remembers *Ms.,* does she?"

"She remembers to correct herself." Varina laughed with her. "I think she likes you, though."

"I think *like* might be too strong a word. Anyway . . ." She tapped Varina's hand. "Have you decided what you're going to do about your hair yet?"

Varina touched her curls. "I think I'll give it another day."

"If you still have purple hair when we go to France, I'm getting a tattoo, just so you're not hipper than me."

"You could go purple, too," Varina teased. "Or blue."

"It took too long to get this color right to screw with it."

"Tattoo it is, then."

Silence settled over them, the comfortable, comforting kind of being with new friends who felt more like old and dear ones. Ruth played with the stem of her wineglass. "Paulie seems like a real sweetheart."

"He is."

"But he's . . ." She waggled her hand back and forth.

"Yes, he's gay. Is that a problem?"

"Only for Donatella."

"Not really." Varina sighed, sipped her wine. "I don't understand it completely, their relationship. It seems complicated, and yet, it's apparently simple to them. They love one another deeply, they're just not *in* love, and never will be. You know?"

Ruth shook her head. "Kids today, huh?"

"I think they're very brave. It's not like this sort of thing didn't exist when we were their age, it just existed where no one could see it. No one wanted to see it. Paulie being Paulie taught me many things I never considered before."

"That's always a good thing," Ruth said. "Minds opened in that direction are kind of rare for our generation. What did your husband think of Paulie? Did he know him?"

"Paulie and Donatella have been friends since kindergarten. Dino, he . . ." Varina's nose tingled. "He did his best. He was always kind to Paulie, and I think he genuinely loved him. But the whole gay thing was so foreign to him, so taboo. You should have seen the gasket he blew when Davide said he wanted to go to beauty school."

"Because he thought that meant his son was gay?"

"I think it was more that Davide wanted to do a woman's job, to be honest. We've never been in doubt about Davide's sexuality. Believe me. But it's kind of the same macho thing. And it's really funny, hearing myself say that, because Dino was never the kind of man who believed my place was in the home and girls couldn't play soccer."

"Sounds like he was a conflicted soul."

"I suppose he was."

"Let me ask you." Ruth fiddled with the stem of her wineglass. "What if Davide had been gay? Or Dante? Would he have disowned them, like Paulie's parents did?"

A question Varina had asked herself a dozen or two thousand times in the intervening years. "No. He loved his sons. He'd have come around."

"But you paused."

"Did I?" Varina finished the wine in her glass. "Neither of my boys is gay, anyway, so it's a moot point."

"I suppose it is." Ruth checked her watch. "Yikes. It's later than I thought. Let me help you with these dishes, then I should run."

Varina followed her into the kitchen, a stack of dishes in hand. "Just leave those there on the counter. I can get them all in the dishwasher if I do it just right."

"I haven't washed a dish since . . . probably college," Ruth said, "so I'm not fighting you on that count. Not even for graciousness' sake."

"You're exaggerating."

Ruth crinkled her nose. "Maybe a little, but not by much. Honestly, Varina, I have no idea how you do it now, let alone did it with three children. A business, a home and family. Extended family. I'm exhausted just thinking about it."

"Simple. I never thought about it." She turned on the faucet, let it run to get hot. "I'm sure your life was busy in a different way."

"Busy, yes. And sometimes mind-numbingly aggravating. There is no way I could have run my modeling agency without staff taking care of the rest of my life. The heights of the fashion world are unkind, at best, but exciting. And exhausting."

The hair, the nails, the perfect put-togetherness that was Ruth Cooperman. Of course.

"Close your mouth, you'll swallow a fly."

"Huh?"

Ruth chuckled. "Just something my grandmother used to say. Your mouth is hanging open."

"Oh, sorry." Varina turned off the water. "I didn't realize . . . we never really talked about your business. What you did before you retired."

"I'm not retired."

"But . . . all the traveling. And you're always free when I call."

"Because I make myself free," Ruth told her. "Oh, I don't go into the offices in the city much these days, but they're still my offices. My staff. My models. I have a reputation as somewhat of a dragon, but I'm respected in the field. At least, feared."

"You? A dragon?"

"You've only known me a few weeks, my dear," Ruth said. "And in a social context. I don't think you'd like Businesswoman Ruth Cooperman. I've glued things to models in places that should never be glued. Trust me."

She couldn't help it; Varina was agog. She'd known her new friend had money, and was somewhat . . . forceful, but a dragon in the fashion world with offices—plural—in New York?

"I just thought you should know about my alter ego."

"I'm Italian. You think your dragon heritage scares me?" Varina laughed. "As long as you don't try gluing anything to me, we're fine."

"Those days are over!" Ruth threw her hands dramatically into the air. "I'm my name now, my reputation, and little more than a figurehead signing all the paychecks." She checked her watch again. "I really do need to get going. Dinner was delicious. I know it's not an Italian specialty, but you really should consider selling that meat loaf in the store. Okay. Dashing. Toodle-pip!"

"Text me when you get home!" Varina called after her. Watching

Ruth through the kitchen window, she saw her pinch the bridge of her nose, stumbling slightly to a halt. In the cracked and heaving driveway, Ruth Cooperman stood perfectly still for a moment. Two. Then back went her shoulders and up went her chin. She yanked open her car door—a Lincoln, a bit of luxury that made more sense to Varina now—and got in. A rev, lights flicking on, and she was gone.

THE BATHROOM WAS DONE, COMPLETELY STAGED, AND READY FOR viewing. Paulie had taken pictures with his cell phone to show Donatella. It had turned out even better than he imagined. Texting the photos to Dante, he trudged up the stairs leading to his apartment.

Crickets immediately chirped. Paulie answered his phone. "Hey, Dante."

"Those pics are really great. Really great job. I mean, really great."

"But is it great?"

Dante laughed softly, the sound purring from Paulie's ear to his groin. "I can't believe I had this talent right under my nose all these years and never took advantage of it."

"I'm not sure how to take that."

"Shit, Paulie. You know what I meant."

"I'm teasing." He leaned against the railing, listening to the silence.

"We should get together," Dante said.

"We should?" *Stop it heart. Please.*

"To talk about your place in Spini and Son."

"Oh."

"It's not that I don't appreciate all you've done the last few years, but I'm not wasting your design skills nailing up studs and Sheetrock."

"Yeah?"

"Yeah, Paulie. What're you, stunad'?"

"Tired. I'm only just getting home."

"Dedication. That's what I like in a man. In my men. My workers," Dante fumbled. "Once people see what you did in this house, everyone's going to want a piece of you. I'm telling you, Paulie, you're going places. I just want to make sure you're going there with me. With, uh, Spini and Son."

"Where else would I go? You know I'm like a barnacle where your family is concerned."

Dante grunted something like laughter. "I'd like to make that official, contract and all. We'll go to Scordato's. We'll talk over steaks and Manhattans. My treat."

Paulie rarely ate beef, and despised bourbon. "Sounds great. When?"

"What's today?"

"Thursday, for another hour and a half."

"Tomorrow work?"

"I'm free and clear, unless my asshole boss has me working until ten thirty again."

"Another crack like that and you get no overtime, capeesh?" But he laughed again, a sound Paulie couldn't imagine getting tired of. "Above and beyond, kid. Thanks."

"So now I'm *kid* again?"

"Sorry. Paulie."

"Can't get you to go for Paul, huh?"

"You've always been Paulie. You'll always be Paulie. Even when you're an old fucker with five hairs on your head and four teeth in your mouth."

"Sounds like I'll age well."

Was this another moment? Paulie tried not to be ridiculous, and failed miserably. "See you at the house tomorrow," he managed to say. "Ten, right?"

"Ten, yeah. Take the morning off until then. Get some sleep. Night, Paulie."

"Night, Da—" The call booped out. "—ante."

Slipping his phone into his pocket, Paulie made it the rest of the way up the stairs without hitting his floaty head on the ceiling, or tripping over his own winged feet. Maybe it was just that Palladino spell life had put on him, when he was a kid with no one in the world who loved him. Who cared. Maybe because neither Dante or Davide had ever called him fanook, and had purportedly beaten the living snot out of those who had. As much as Paulie loved Davide, not to the extent, but in the same way he loved Donatella, it had always been Dante who—

The door to his apartment whipped open. "Where the fuck have you been?"

Kittens tumbled onto the landing. "Don't let them out, Don." He scooped both kittens into his arms. "Close the door." And she did. Depositing the kittens into the playpen—that they immediately climbed out of—Paulie turned his attention back to the quivering form of his best friend. "What's wrong?"

Donatella thrust something small, like a pen, a pink pen, into his hand.

"What's this?"

"Read it."

Not a pen; a pregnancy test. *Pregnant.* Clear as day. Paulie held it out to her with two fingers. "Did you pee on this?"

"Don't joke. Look what it says, Paulie! Look!"

"I see."

"And?"

His shoulders slumped. "And what, Don? It was bound to happen eventually. You're not exactly a nun, or careful. I'm here for you, whatever you decide. If you need to—"

She grasped his shoulders, her fingers digging into muscles so tired they instantly cramped. "I haven't been with anyone since Christmas."

"Good, that narrows it down."

"It narrows it down to you, Paulie."

His stomach heaved and his face got hot and something like hope and joy and fear and despair pricked him from the inside. "Me?"

"That night after Christmas, remember? Right there on your couch? Ringing any bells?"

Bells rang. They gonged and gonged inside his head. Paulie's knees gave out. He dropped onto his couch, narrowly missing Mary-Jane. Donatella sat beside him.

"Aren't you on some kind of birth control? I know I've picked up your prescription for you. Many times."

"I ran out around Thanksgiving, and forgot to refill it," she said. "But there wasn't anyone after Fucking Chucky, and then that night I got arrested, I swore off men for good."

"But we . . . it was the next day!"

"I said *men,* Paulie. Not you. But I guess that's pretty dumb, huh. Being gay doesn't make you sterile or anything. Not that I thought that. I guess I just wasn't thinking at all." She groaned onto his shoulder. "Just when I was getting my life together! I even paid my mom back some of the money she put out for me."

Paulie slid an arm around her shoulders. He kissed her curls and there lingered, eyes closed and heart beating like rain on a roof. His conversation with Dante felt like years in the past, a moment lost. A chance not taken.

"We'll handle this," he told her. "We will."

"We don't have much choice."

"First, we go to the doctor."

"Clinic. I have no money. I just gave all my spare cash to my mother."

"Don't worry about that. I'm going to be making more money, now that Dante wants me to be his designer."

"Yeah?" She sat forward to face him. "Oh, Paulie. That's great."

"Thanks. He's taking me out for steaks and booze tomorrow night to talk details."

"A date?" She waggled her eyebrows.

"Stop." He nestled her back into his shoulder. Her breath tickled his neck. His heart *boom-boom-boomed* in his ears. *Baby. Baby. Baby.* His. And Donatella's. His brain pushed through the booming, wrapped around this concept, this child of his blood and bones that he'd never imagined because he hadn't imagined he could. Pulling her closer, Paulie held her tighter. The hopes and plans he'd had on the other side of the door, before Donatella opened it and thrust the future into his face, crumbled, making way for this most unexpected and impossible thing. "I'm . . . wow, Don. I'm going to be a daddy."

"Not if I decide I don't want to be a mommy."

Everything inside him froze. Every muscle clenched. He was a modern man. He believed in a woman's right to choose, even now when it would shatter his heart to pieces.

Donatella went limp against him. "Don't be upset, Paulie. I'd only mess this up like I mess everything up, and then a poor little baby would be messed up, too."

A deep breath through his nose, pushed out softly through his lips. "Is that what you want?" he asked. "Are you sure?"

Her body trembled. A sob burst from her lips. Donatella clung to him, words mixing with her tears so he understood not a one.

"Shh, it's okay. I'll be okay." He pulled her into his lap, this tiny woman he loved more than anything. "It'll be okay."

It wouldn't be. Paulie could find no way for it to be okay unless Donatella stopped being Donatella, not for now but forever. He didn't see it happening. But this baby was. Unless she decided it wasn't. And that was, for Paulie, the worst possible scenario.

16

schiatanumgorp
(ski-yat-an-oom-gorp)

Italian: *schicciarmi lo stomaco;* "crush my stomach"

A bit dramatic, as usual. Jersey Italians use it for an extreme form of agida, typically caused by a loved one's bad behavior, for which even a thrown shoe is no remedy.

This one might be specific to certain neighborhoods in New Jersey, as I've only heard it among family and friends. How *stomaco* became *gorp* is a mystery, though I suspect it's related to *gut*.

Related Jersey Italian words are *schiat'* (ski-yaht) and *schiatuz'* (ski-yah-tooz), both best understood when used in a sentence:

"You're making me schiat'!" translates to, "You're turning my stomach!"

Whereas, "I'm all schiatuz'," translates to, "I'm tied up in knots."

Again, this might be specific to certain (very dramatic) neighborhoods in New Jersey.

W e need to renew our campaign to find your mother a man."
Sylvia set a cup of ginger tea on the table beside Donatella's
resting, groaning head. "Are you listening?"

"Yes, Nonina."

"Pick up your head and act like a human."

"I told you, I don't feel well."

"That's what happens when you stay out all night drinking."

Donatella picked up her head at that. "I wasn't. I didn't."

Sylvia felt her granddaughter's forehead, then gave it a little
smack. "Gabadost'!"

"Ow! What?"

"You have no fever. Don't lie to your grandmother. Now drink
your tea."

Donatella slurped from the teacup, barely lifting her head enough
to do so. Sylvia suppressed the urge to smack her hard head again.
Maybe she really hadn't been out all night drinking; and maybe the
pasta water would salt itself on Sunday. Sighing, she sat down.

"Have you gotten any more calls?"

"Messages, Non," Donatella said. "I didn't give out my number."

"Oh, yes. I forgot. Any more messages?"

"Lots. Well, four."

"Good, good! And?"

Another slurp. "I haven't screened them yet. You told me to
hold off."

"You haven't even contacted the gentlemen in question?"

"No."

"Mannaggia dial!" Sylvia would have bolted up from the table,
had her muscles and bones cooperated. As it happened, she only
managed to thump her chair a little. "I counted on you to stay on
top of this."

"But you told me to hold off!"

"A week or two! It's been . . . forever!"

Donatella cocked her head. "No, it hasn't. A week and a half, at most."

Sylvia held her indignant pose as well as she was able, counting the days in her head since John Yu appeared on her doorstep with a bouquet of daffodils meant for Varina. The days went so fast when he visited, and yet slowly in between. Their first dinner date together had been every romantic notion she'd ever had, complete with the single rose he'd brought her, just like the grandfather looking for love in Donatella's flyer. She'd put it with the daffodils, still in their vase with the bow. Pressing a hand to her fluttery heart, the silly thing, Sylvia would have smiled had she not still been holding that indignant pose. Her own current happiness proved she'd been right all along: Varina needed a man.

"Nevertheless," she said, "we need to get back on this. Your mother hasn't been out since those first four. Time to get her back up on that horse."

"Five."

"What do you mean?"

Donatella slurped. "Five. Unless . . . didn't she go out with Mr. Yu?"

Sylvia froze, mid-sip of her own tea. She set the mug down slowly. "I don't think so."

"That's weird. I sent him here to the house. My friend Jenny, that's his granddaughter, said it went really well. Her grandfather is suddenly super-chipper, anyway."

"Oh . . . uh . . . there was an Oriental man who stopped by with flowers. Your mother wasn't home."

"Nonina." Donatella groaned. "Food and rugs are Oriental. Mr. Yu is Chinese."

"We always called them Orientals." Sylvia picked up her tea again, blew across the top. "Or Chinamen."

"Sweet Jesus Christ."

"What? What did I say?"

Donatella groaned her head onto the table again. "You can't use those words, Nonina."

"Who says?"

"The twenty-first century says. It's insulting."

"Don't be silly. I would never insult Joh . . . an Oriental person."

"Chinese."

"It's the same thing."

"No. It's not. And that's why it's an insult."

Sylvia set down her mug, wrapped her fingers around it so they wouldn't shake. "But I don't *mean* for it to be." And she didn't. Oh, she didn't! How many times had she used the word in John's presence? Several times, she was sure. "Doesn't that count?"

Her granddaughter pulled herself up on her elbows. She really did look tragically unwell. "In some ways, it's even worse," she said. "Because it was so ingrained in everyone's heads, it didn't even register to those not of East Asian descent. During World War Two, the Japanese were sometimes referred to as Chinamen, even though we were fighting to help liberate the Chinese from Japanese atrocities. Words matter, Nonina. Do you understand?"

"I'm not sure."

"Okay." She tucked her hair behind her ears. "Think of it this way. How did you feel about Italians being referred to as dagos?"

Sylvia gasped. "It's not at all the same!"

"It's exactly the same, because Italians coming into the country were lumped together with Spaniards, who were called Diegos. *Dago.* Get it? It's marginalizing. Whether you refer to all East Asians as Orientals or Italians as dagos, it's taking away identity and replacing it with something generic, lesser, mocking. It lets people treat others like they don't matter."

Silly heart; now her stomach was joining in. "But I didn't mean any of that, sweetheart. I never did."

"Of course, you didn't." Donatella gripped her hand across the table. "We're all accidentally racist without even knowing it. But once you know, you have to change or instead of being an accidental racist, you're one on purpose. Like insisting on using an inappropriate term just because you always have. See?"

"I think so." How could she apologize? What could she say that wouldn't make it worse? Tears stung. Her lip trembled. Sylvia sipped her tea in an effort to hide it, but Donatella caught her anyway.

"Oh, Nonina!" She came to stand behind her, wrapping her up in a gentle embrace. "It's okay. This is just between you and me. I won't tell anyone you're a racist. I promise."

It was too late now; Sylvia Spini was crying. A rare event, but once it happened, there was no stopping it. "You don't understand. I'm sure I used the word *Oriental* in his company, on more than one occasion. I'm sure of it. Oh! I'm sure!"

Donatella squatted down beside her chair. "Who?"

"John!" She wailed. "He's so kind and so good, and such a lovely dancer, and I insulted him without meaning to, and he never once said anything. He didn't even wince!"

"John. John Yu?" She glanced in the direction of the daffodils. "You dirty little buttann'! That's why you're so interested in renewing the grandfather scheme. You stole my mother's man!"

"Stop." Sylvia batted her, laughing through her tears. "He's too old for your mother. He's practically my age."

"Really?" Donatella groaned to her feet, pressing at her side. "I didn't think about that. I guess he would be more your age, considering Mom was ancient when she had m . . . oh."

"Moe? Who's Moe?"

Her granddaughter shuffled across the kitchen. She fingered the daffodils, her shoulders hunched. So young. Everyone was, to Sylvia, but Donatella? She'd always been the baby, coddled and summarily dismissed. This, Sylvia Spini knew, because Sylvia Cioffi had been the same. And that's why she'd always—secretly—loved her, not most, but best.

"Donatella?"

She turned with a smile and a watery laugh, high-pitched and trying entirely too hard. Changeable as the wind. "I'm glad you've found a nice man to spend time with, Nonina. And I'm even more glad I had something to do with it."

"Just don't tell your mother."

"Why not?"

Sylvia didn't quite know. "I will. Soon. It's nice, for now. Having this secret romance."

"Have you kissed him?"

"Ashbett'!" She had not, but Sylvia wanted to. Very much. "Just promise me."

"I promise. As long as you promise not to use the word *Oriental* ever again."

"Unless I'm talking about food or carpets."

Donatella took her teacup to the sink, rinsed it. "It's really fascinating, you know? How even the most innocent words become insults. Like *fat*, or *retarded*, or *old*. Words aren't bad, in and of themselves. They become insults because of the way people use them. The intention."

Whatever melancholy had captured Donatella, let her go. Sylvia remembered such mood swings. Remembered when she forgot everything else. She said, "I never thought about it."

"Most people don't. I do. I think about a lot of things no one else does." Donatella sighed. "Usually in the middle of the night."

Sylvia remembered that, too.

Silence but for the *tick-glonking* of the grandfather clock. Sylvia half expected Vicky to start up some kind of dirge, but she kept silent. For once. Donatella leaned in to kiss her cheek. "I'll get back on the grandfather thing."

"Good girl."

"I'll come by on Monday. We can go over the new recruits before I send any to Mom."

Monday, she was seeing John. It would take all day to prepare, visit, and then recover.

"Not Monday," she said. "The store is closed, though your mother rarely graces me with her presence on her day off anymore. How about Tuesday?"

"Right. I keep forgetting. I'll come over after my shift. Around two thirty?"

"That would be fine, sweetheart."

Sylvia waved her granddaughter out the kitchen door with another kiss blown and a shouted "I love you!" She felt breathless and light-headed with this secret shared. This lesson learned.

"Oh, John." She rubbed her soft belly. "What have I done?" And she wasn't seeing him until Monday. Several days of schiatanumgorp to contend with, because this she would not forget like she forgot her grandchildren's names, what day it was, and if she left the light on in her bedroom.

Rinsing her teacup and putting it in the sink, Sylvia felt that flutter in her chest again. She paused, hand pressed to her heart. No pain, just the flutter, and not entirely uncomfortable. She waited. And waited. No more flutter, not even when she thought about how she would have to apologize for using a racial slur because she'd been accidentally racist. Because even at the supposedly wise age of ninety-two, a woman could learn.

17

ginzo *(hard g)*

Shortened form of *Guinea*, a derogatory term for a person of Italian descent, referring to the Guinea Coast of Africa, and implying Italians are not "white." (That comes with a whole lot of baggage to unpack, and is totally not cool, but if I started in on that, this entry would be more like a dissertation covering the many forms racism takes.)

This is a tricky one, because it varies from community to community. Call an Italian a guinea or ginzo or ginz, and you'll get punched. But food? We're proud of our ginzo food. Ginzo Christmas. Ginzo Thanksgiving. There are ginzo movies, ginzo cars, ginzo fashions. Just note, *we* can use ginzo. You non-Italians cannot. Unless you want to be punched.

setedi *(SEHT-duh-dee)*
Italian: *sedeteti;* "sit down"

Same. No connotations. Just garbled together in Jersey-speak.

R ay? Ray Pimintiero?" Varina tapped the man on the shoulder.
He turned. "It is you. Remember me? Varina Palladino. Well,
I was a Spini when we knew one another in school."

Furrowed brow became a smile. "Varina!" He laughed. "I knew
the name sounded familiar."

"What?"

Ray laughed rather stuntedly, pointing to the lettering on the
door. "I meant Palladino. So, you and Dino got married, huh?"

"A couple years after graduation."

Raymond Pimintiero, one of those alpha boys all the others
looked up to, good at sports, popular with the girls, wealthy family,
actually remembered her. And Dino. And that they'd been sweethearts. Shocking, actually. Aside from St. Francis's Summer Camp
for Catholic Youth, they'd definitely not been part of the same social
circles.

"You here for something specific?" she asked. "Or just browsing."

"I, uh . . . cipollini?"

Again, with the cipollini. What was it with the cipollini lately?
"I'm afraid I'm out. But I'll be getting some in this week. Are you
local? Last I remember, you were down in Tennessee or something."

Ray nodded. "I moved down there after the divorce. I'm back
home about a month, I guess. Just bought a place in one of those fifty-
five-and-over communities. We all come back home in the end, eh?"

"Some of us never leave."

"You been here all this time?"

"All this time," she said.

Silence fell, along with a pair of slightly awkward smiles.

"Anyway," he said. "Got any fresh mutz?"

"You're in luck. Just pulled it a little while ago."

He followed her to the counter. The balls of mozzarella were still
warm in their containers.

"That's one thing you just don't get in Tennessee," he said. "All this ginzo food. I've missed it. I'll take two."

"Wet or dry?"

"Wet. And a loaf of that semolina." He leaned elbows on the counter, his lopsided smile evoking chalkboards, the ketchup scent of a cafeteria, and sunshine on tall grass. "You know what? You got a little basket or something? I need to stock up."

VARINA BRUSHED A TINY BIT OF MASCARA ONTO HER EYELASHES. THE tube had to be two years old. If her eyelashes were just a little thicker—like they'd been in younger days—she wouldn't have caved to makeup at all. As it turned out, she was just a little vain. Scrunching and floofing her curls was as far as she'd go, coiffure-wise. She still wasn't sure about the color. It wasn't quite purple anymore, but it wasn't redhead red. Either Ray hadn't noticed or he didn't care, because he hadn't looked askance even once during the half hour he spent in the store stocking up on old Italian favorites.

Putting on her coat, she shouted to her mother watching television in the parlor, "I'm going to the movies with Ruth!"

"You have a good time, sweetheart."

Varina called Ruth the moment she hit the sidewalk. "This is all your fault."

"Why, hello to you, too, my dear. What's all my fault?"

"I'm going on another date."

"I thought you swore that off."

"It's been a few weeks. Besides, I had a little crush on this guy, way back when we were kids. I figured, why the hell not. And that's what's your fault. Ever since I met you, I've been doing things I never would have before. You're a bad influence on me."

"Is your hair still purple?"

"A little."

"Need I remind you, you met me at a travel agent, booking a cruise through Provence? I'm a result of your bad behavior, not the cause."

"That's not what my mother says."

Ruth laughed. "I'm sure. Why are you out of breath? You haven't even met up with him yet?"

Varina slowed her pace. "You're very wicked."

"I do try."

"I walk too fast when I'm nervous. At this rate, I'll be schvitzing when I get to the restaurant. Did I use that right?"

"Perfectly."

"Remind me why am I doing this before I chicken out."

"Because you had a crush on this guy when you were a kid. And your mother thinks you're a lesbian."

"That prospect is looking better every day."

"Don't be silly. Lesbians get all gussied up and worry about schvitzing and stress over dates, too."

"I imagine so." Varina blew out a long breath. "Thanks, Ruth."

Slowing her pace again, because she was once again nearly jogging, Varina considered making some excuse and going home. Better yet, actually go to the movies with Ruth instead of lying to her mother. It had been nice talking to Ray, reminiscing about camp—which he remembered her being part of only after her prodding—and the good old days when they had absolutely nothing in common. Then he'd asked her out to dinner. Casually. As a way to continue their conversation without customers interrupting it. At least, that's how it had felt.

"You know what was the weirdest thing?" she asked.

"Tell me."

"He remembered Dino and I were sweethearts, but never asked about him. Why did he assume I was single?"

"Maybe because you don't wear a ring?"

"I never did."

"I don't think he'd be aware of that."

"True." Varina stopped walking, moved to the edge of the sidewalk so the kids blasting music through their earbuds could pass.

"Darling, you're being a goon. Just go out on your date and have fun. You're not obligating yourself to marriage, or even sex. Unless you want it, that is. Sex."

"Don't start that again."

"If only I could. Unlike you, I don't have men coming out of the woodwork begging me to go out with them."

"It must be that dragon-lady reputation."

"Very possible."

"Isn't that what's weird, though?" Varina asked. "All of a sudden, at my age? All these dates? It's weird, right?"

"It does seem a little strange," Ruth answered. "But you know what they say about strength in numbers."

"I'm pretty sure that's not what the expression is referring to."

"But you know what I meant. Don't be difficult. You'll never catch a man if you're difficult."

Ruth laughed, and Varina laughed with her, dispelling the agida building since she said yes. "You're the best."

"I know."

"Should I ask him outright if my mother set us up?"

"Only if you really want the answer," Ruth said. "Just have fun. And call me later. I want to know how it goes. Toodle-pip!"

Slipping her phone into her bag, Varina spotted Ray outside The Blue Pig. Its neon sign colored him an electric shade of blue. Hands deep in his pockets, head bowed and lost in thought, he didn't see her until she was nearly on top of him. He smiled that chalkboard, tall-grass smile.

"For a second there, I was back in high school," he said. "You look the same."

"Liar." She laughed. "But thank you."

"I mean it. Not that you still look sixteen or nothing, just that I can still see her. You. Anyway…" He opened the door, standing aside to let her in first. "I hope you like barbecue."

"COME IN, COME IN."

Sylvia hustled John Yu into the house for the first time since the day they waltzed, right there in the parlor. He still drove, thank goodness—they'd been out, several times—and had been able to come over the moment Varina left for her "movie with Ruth" that was actually a date with Raymond Pimintiero, that nice boy Sylvia remembered from Varina's high school days. Funny, how clearly she remembered him the moment Donatella mentioned his name, standing at the podium on graduation day, delivering the valedictorian speech. Things happened that way, more and more often. A name. A smell. A commercial jingle on one of her VHS tapes. And there it would be, a memory clear as day when she could barely remember what she'd watched on the news the evening before.

"I don't know how long Varina will be out, but we'll have a couple of hours, I think."

John shucked off his coat, hung it on a hook. "We could go back to my house, if you'd prefer."

"I couldn't!" Sylvia pressed a hand to her chest. "I'm a lady. Besides, I want to waltz with you again. I have a record on the turntable, all ready to go."

"Of course, of course." John kissed her cheek. Sylvia closed her eyes, imagined turning her face at just the right moment to feel his lips on hers, rather than her cheek. Soon. Soon. It had to be just right, this time, surely to be the last time for a first kiss.

"Can I get you anything?"

"Not a thing, thank you." He gestured to the Victrola. "Shall we?"

The turntable was already spinning when Sylvia went to turn it on. She winked at the old demon, set the needle onto the grooves. "Vienna Waltz." Johann Strauss. Sweeping. Lovely. A little too fast. She'd only considered how much she loved the recording, not how quickly her feet—and his—would have to move. John Yu bowed. She did her best curtsy. And he took her into his arms.

Did Vicky slow the tempo? Or was it something even more magical? A deceleration of time. A dip out of sync. Whatever it was, Sylvia floated on it. Floated back and back, to when she was Sylvia Cioffi first learning how to waltz. To fox-trot. Even to rumba, cha-cha, and tango, without her father's knowledge. He'd never have allowed such dancing. Never have paid for those lessons. But Sylvia had learned.

She was leading, and fully aware. Instinct honed at the age of fourteen, when there were only two boys in the class, and the girls often had to dance with one another. John picked up her cues as if they'd been dancing together for years. And maybe it was true, in some version of life she'd yet to live. Sylvia Cioffi and John Yu, who might have lived in the very same town but never met, because he was Chinese and she was Italian.

The record wound down and—thank God, or Vicky—did not start back up again. They were both a bit winded, slow to speech. John still had her in his arms, looking at her with a strange but dear expression.

"You would be the belle of the ball at Sunset Downs. We have dinner and dancing every Wednesday evening. No one dances like you."

Sylvia patted her hair. "I'm sure that's not true." But of course it was, after all those lessons.

"Join me next week. Let me prove you wrong."

Dinner and dancing? "That would be lovely. Except . . ."

"Except?"

"What will I tell Varina?"

John slumped a little, though his arms still held her near. "Would she mind, so much, to know we see one another?"

"Oh, dear, no. I never meant to imply that."

"Then why am I a secret?"

"Because . . . because . . ."

"Is it because I'm not Italian?"

Sylvia opened her mouth to deny his words, to assure him. This was it. Her moment of confession . . . Why, oh, why couldn't her memory have failed her now?

"Setedi." She gestured him to the couch. "Sit, sit."

He did as she asked, rising again when she sat beside him. Like the gentleman he was.

"I will admit," she said, the agida already souring her stomach, "that had my children brought home anyone not Italian when they were kids, I'd have been upset. I was furious with my grandson when he married a Greek."

"Oh."

"Please, listen."

He nodded.

"Believe me when I say, it has never once, from the moment we met, been a thought in my head. It truly hasn't. I've been much too smitten."

He smiled at that, the wrinkles of his face becoming chasms her fingers wished to trace.

"Although," she said, trying not to squirm like a schoolgirl caught misbehaving, "I've recently learned that I'm an accidental racist."

"An accidental racist? I don't think I've ever heard that term before."

"I hadn't either. My granddaughter told it to me when I referred to you as . . ." She winced. ". . . Oriental."

"Ah, I see." Still smiling. He leaned a little closer. "I still think the word *colored* in my head. I know it is not the proper word today, but it was the one used when I was young. We are both accidental racists."

"But you keep it in your head. I'm afraid I didn't. I'm sorry if I offended you."

"Apology accepted."

"Then I did?" Tears stung. Sylvia bit her lip to keep it from trembling.

Chasms. "I honestly don't recall." John took her hand, kissed it. "I have also been too smitten to notice."

"Oh, John." Sylvia gripped both his hands, their fingers intertwining, the boles of old trees grown together. "I do care for you very much."

"Then why am I a secret?" he asked again.

Because it was so magical this way. To feel young and rebellious, not because he was Chinese but because they were ancient and falling in love. Something no one even considered possible. She said, and it was conveniently true, "Because Varina doesn't know about the campaign to find her a man. How will I explain you without spilling the beans?"

John's eyes fell to their clasped hands. His thumb caressed her knuckles as if they were the fine bones under smooth skin before housework and child-rearing and age gnarled them. "I see your point," he said. "It would mean too much storytelling to keep up with."

"And I can barely keep up as it is."

She laughed; he laughed, too, their heads coming together. *Do dootz!* She used to play with her children. Her grandchildren. The

great-grandchildren. *Do dootz*. Forehead touching forehead, until
the hard knocks of toddler enthusiasm made her see stars.

"How about this?" John kissed her fingers. "Let's start again."

"Start again?" What had they been talking about? Sifting
through spilled memory, she scrambled for a thread to follow back.

"Yes. Let's meet for the first time, all over again. Under different
circumstances."

Oh, yes. Yes. Varina. The single grandfathers—without whom
Sylvia would never have met this beautiful, wonderful man holding
her hands so tenderly—and keeping them secret. Sylvia's whimsical
heart flittered. "That does sound romantic. How do we do that?"

"Well . . ." He cocked his head. "It would have to seem accidental.
Is there anywhere you go frequently? Someplace I can accidentally-
on-purpose be?"

Bingo? Too public. And she did not put it past Jeannie Rosato
to swoop in and attempt to steal him away. She'd always been the
man-hungry sort. Church? Still too public. Someplace smaller. More
intimate. Less likely to be populated by too many people she knew.
Who knew her.

"What about the bakery where my granddaughter works?" she
asked. "I'd need a ride, anyway. And she already knows about you, so
bringing her into it isn't a stretch."

"Perfect! What do you say? Tomorrow?"

"Hold that thought." Sylvia picked up the handset from the tele-
phone table beside the couch, where a phone had been in residence
since this house first had such a thing.

"Donatella?"

"Hey, Nonina. What's up?"

"Are you working tomorrow?"

"Afternoon shift, why?"

"I need you to take me to the bakery with you."

"Why?"

"Ashbett', I'll explain tomorrow. What time?"

"I go in at one."

Too late for coffee, but if she went light on lunch, she could get something sweet. "Perfect. Don't forget me."

"I won't. What are you up to?"

"I love you, sweetheart. Bye!" She hung up the phone. Her face ached. Sylvia hadn't smiled so much in years. "All set. Meet me at Jumbaloon's at one o'clock."

Chasms and chasms and chasms. Sylvia could fall happily into each one. It took every ounce of ingrained decorum to keep her fingers from trailing their paths from brow to eyes, eyes to cheeks. Her heart pittered, and it pattered. Breath came in short just-remembered bursts. His eyes, brown and yellowed around the edges, never blinked. Only looked into hers just as yellowed about the edges. Lashes thinned to nothing. Lids spotted by age. He was so beautiful. The way he held her gaze said he found her beautiful, too.

Those eyes, those chasms, blurred and then vanished as he leaned nearer, as Sylvia's eyes closed. Their lips met. Not lush as teenagers first exploring. Not plush as adults navigating old, arousing ground. Thin lips, creased by years of smiles and frowns and fretting and fury, met in a kiss of longing without weight, of passion without the scorching heat, of memories doing for them what their bodies could only remember.

Sylvia's flittering heart thumped, more of a squish into an over-stuffed chair than palpitations battering her ribs. John's lips held hers and held hers, moving in ways that made hers move in kind. Perfect. At last, perfect. She'd waited all her life for such a kiss. And then he was pulling away, his eyes still closed while hers opened wide.

Scratch-scratch-scratch . . .

The waltz from *Faust*. Sylvia could have laughed aloud, were he not rising, his hand outstretched.

"May I have this dance?"

Sylvia put her hand in John's. The music, lively, sweeping, and again too quick for their old legs to keep up. *Vicky, you wicked thing.* But John led her this time, their bodies out of tempo but their hearts keeping time.

Sylvia Spini danced with her eyes closed, unwilling to see herself in the mirror over the sideboard. To see was to know, and she didn't want to. Not right this moment. Just for this dance, in the arms of this man she already loved, she wanted only to pretend they were young and in step and had a whole lifetime ahead of them.

18

Ffangul/Vaffangul/Baffangul

From the Italian, *vai fare en culo;* literally:
"go do it in the ass"

"Fuck! / Fuck you! / Go fuck yourself!"

These go by degrees, the first a strong but comparatively mild expletive, the second being more heated, while the third is when there is usually a shoe flying at you as well.

Che fa ghist'? *(kay-fah-GHEEST)*

Italian: *Che fa questa?;* "What are you up to?"

I've been asked this question way too many times in my life.

Dinner was delicious, and Ray was nice company. Varina ate too much—the portions were enormous—savoring every mouthful. She'd never been one of those women who pretended to be full after a few mouthfuls in some strange show of feminine decorum; she certainly wasn't starting now. Ray shared bits of everything on his plate and wasn't shy about picking from hers. A bit too familiar, intimate, but he didn't seem to be anything other than enthusiastic.

Varina insisted on going dutch when the bill came. To his credit, after an uncomfortable moment in which, she imagined, he had to tamp down his more traditional impulses, Ray agreed.

"Mind if I walk you home?" he asked. "My stomach's asking, not my chivalrous nature."

"I don't mind at all." Although she had planned on calling Ruth for the walk home. "It's only a few blocks."

"Do you always walk?"

"As much as I can," she answered. "It used to be the only time I had to myself. Now?" She shrugged. "It's habit. And I like it."

He didn't offer his arm, for which Varina was grateful. She liked him okay, but whatever crush she might have had on him as a teen stayed back in the 1960s; there was nothing even resembling romantic happening for her. Ray simply walked beside her, hands deep in his coat pockets and head down, just like she'd seen him outside the restaurant a couple of hours ago. She'd never have pegged him the contemplative type, although she'd never really known him as a kid, in hindsight, as tentatively feeling out the world as she had been. She'd pegged him as just like all the other boys who flocked around him. Maybe he had been. Or maybe he'd just pretended to be.

"So," she said, "I'm curious."

"About?"

"You haven't said anything about my hair."

He looked up. "What about it?"

"It's purple?"

Ray shrugged. "It's your hair."

Not a compliment, false or otherwise. Honesty. "I get a few odd looks, but mostly, no one seems to even notice."

"Times have changed. People are . . . freer."

"And we were children of the sixties."

"Italian children of the sixties." He chuckled. "Which means we were kind of stuck in the forties, right?"

"True."

But she hadn't been. Not with Dino. Even if they mostly kept it to themselves. It was easier not to rock the boat, and live life their way in private. "I like the changes. The progress. It's a different world."

"Not really different," Raymond said. "Everything's just more visible. You know?"

Varina thought of Paulie. "I do."

They'd chatted over dinner. Face-to-face, skimming over the shallow surface of family, St. Francis's Summer Camp for Catholic Youth, and old high school friends neither of them had thought of in years. Varina now knew he'd been married and divorced twice. First time, for twenty-seven years, and the second, seven. He had three grown children, a few grandkids, and, before returning to New Jersey to be closer to them, after forty-six years in advertising, had spent the first years of his retirement in Nashville.

"I played piano on open-mike nights, and painted local wildlife stuff. Nothing great, or anything, but I liked it."

And there she'd seen it, even as he skimmed that shallow surface, the reaching for something while other things pulled. In a thousand years of guessing, not only would Varina never have guessed valedictorian, golden boy Raymond Pimintiero was the contemplative type, neither would she have imagined him playing piano in Nashville, or painting ducks on a pond.

"Do you still paint?" she asked him.

"I wasn't sure you heard that part." He grinned. "I do. Not as much. I've been pretty busy since coming home."

"Funny, isn't it? That this is still home? You haven't lived here since you were in college, right?"

"Since I got married." He put up a finger. "The first time. Which was right after college. Yeah, it is funny. I didn't even mean to say it. Just . . . did."

"It's a good town."

"I don't live here in Wyldale, though," Ray said. "I live in Fort Lee. Sunset Downs. It's one of those fifty-five-and-older communities. The kids thought I'd like it."

"And you don't?"

"It's all right. For now. It's kind of nice being one of the young guys on the block."

"My brother's moving into one of those communities in Florida."

"Tommy?"

"You remember him?"

Ray shrugged. "Who doesn't? He was kind of a big deal football guy when we were kids."

Varina remembered Tommy playing football, not him being any sort of superstar. Another dream bypassed? "So, what were you doing in town today if you live in Fort Lee? Slumming?"

"Reminiscing, I guess." He laughed. "It's . . . I sort of . . . I didn't have any intention of . . ." And then he let go a long breath. "It's kind of a weird story. I'll tell you about it sometime."

If she ever went out with him again. Varina only smiled and nodded. "This is me." She pointed to the house—home sweet home—across the street.

"This where you grew up?"

"Mostly. I bought the place from my mother after my dad died."

A figure in the window, noted in her periphery, ducked out of sight when she turned to look. "That was probably her in the window. I guess I'm caught."

"Caught?"

"I told her I was going to the movies with a friend."

"You're such a rebel."

Varina laughed. "Just smart. She can be pretty insufferable."

"It's nice, though, you still have your mom."

"I'm lucky, I know." *Though sometimes . . .* "Well, night, Ray. It was good seeing you."

"It was good seeing you, too, Varina."

No attempted kiss. No hedge for a second date. Varina couldn't decide if she was relieved or insulted, before a car rolled down her driveway, the lights not going on until it was in the street and blinding them.

"Who the heck could that have been?" She squinted at the license plate. As if her night vision were good enough to see it. "At this hour?"

"It's only nine," Ray said. "You didn't recognize the car?"

"I don't think so. Maybe I better get inside and see what's going on."

"Right. Good night again."

"Night."

Varina went around back. The door was unlocked. Going inside, hanging her coat on a hook, she called, "Mom?"

No answer. She sighed, shook her head. "Mom?" She called again from the parlor, where the Victrola skipped at the finished end of a record. Varina turned it off. "What have you two been up to?" She closed the lid, knocked on her mother's bedroom door.

"I can't hear you, sweetheart! I'm . . . watching the news."

"Can you come out a sec?"

"What? Sorry! Can't hear you!"

"Mom. Are you all right? I saw a car leaving our driveway?"

"What? I'm fine. Just in here watching my shows. I'm not dressed. We'll talk tomorrow."

The volume went up. "Ffangul," Varina muttered under her breath, then, "I'm knocking until I see your face. Open the door, Mom."

The volume went down. Some creaking ensued. The door opened a crack. "There? Satisfied?"

"Che fa ghist'?"

"Nothing. You're making me miss my show. Good night, sweetheart." She closed the door. "I love you!"

"You're up to something. I know you are."

"Nighty-night!"

Varina crossed herself before thinking the thoughts attempting to form. No ax murderer had done away with her annoying mother then made his escape in a darkened car. For the moment, it was enough. Going back to the kitchen to put the kettle on for some tea, she tapped on Ruth's number.

"How'd it go?"

"Fine, fine. Listen. Remember what we were talking about? That there's something funny going on around here?"

"Yes. Why?"

"It's more than my mom potentially fixing me up with men. I just saw a car roll down my driveway and take off. And she won't come out of her room."

"Sounds like she might be a drug dealer. Could she have turned your place into a crack house without you knowing?"

"Very funny. That was just so strange."

"I'll give that to you. It's very strange. Could it be someone was casing the place?"

"My place?" Varina laughed. "Doubtful. But maybe I should call the . . . oh, no."

"What? What's wrong? Is someone in the house?"

"No, no." Her belly sank. "It was probably Donatella, or something to do with her. My mother's always covering up for her. I know it's to spare me, but . . ." She sighed, fingers rubbing sparkles behind her eyes. "She is always upstairs with Paulie. What could she have gotten into now that my mother is covering up?"

Silence, then, "Or maybe it's just that your mother has become a drug dealer."

Varina laughed, in spite of herself. "I guess you don't want to hear about my date then, since I'm apparently a drug dealer's daughter."

"I never judge. My mother was a jewel thief. Spill it!"

Varina told Ruth about about Ray, their memories, the perfectly lovely date. Her friend listened, as always, without interrupting. What had she done all these years without her?

"Any sparks?" Ruth asked.

"Nope. But he's a nice man. I think we could be friends."

"You trying to replace me?"

"Who could replace you?" Varina crooned.

"Good. Just remember that."

They laughed, but Varina wasn't feeling it. Not entirely. "My tea is cold, and I'm beat. I'm going to watch the boob tube a little while."

"Boob tube." Ruth chuckled. "Only you would call it that."

"I still call aluminum foil tin foil, too."

"Isn't it?"

"Not since the twenties, or something. Some things just . . . endure." She poured her tea down the drain. "Thanks for listening."

"I rarely have anything better to do. And I meant that sincerely, not sarcastically."

"It's funny, how often you need to add that." Laughter, now, that she felt. "Night, Ruth."

"Toodle-pip, Varina."

Heading into the parlor, Varina yawned and stretched her arms over her head. Long day. Good day. Weird night, but only after a nice dinner with an old sort-of-friend. She resisted the need to listen outside her mother's bedroom door, making sure all was well. It was. She knew it was. Instead, she curled up in her chair, her father's chair, she scrolled through the channels, settling on an old episode of *Northern Exposure,* ten minutes in.

Maggie and Joel. Chris and Ed. Shelly, Maurice, and Holling. It had been her favorite show, hers and Dino's. They'd been roughly the same ages as the stars, back then. They'd snuggle in the television's blue and flickering glow, captivated by this quirky show about people so unlike them, in a place they couldn't imagine. The world had been theirs. Young, but not too young. In their prime, with a little girl barely school age, and two boys more in their teens. A good business, a nice home owned outright. The nineties had been magical years Varina often counted as her best.

On the screen—flat, not like the box her mother insisted was fine, just fine—Joel and Maggie sparred. It never got old. Swallowing the thickness from her throat, Varina turned the volume up just a little. Her mother was hard of hearing; it wouldn't bother her at all.

"MY GRANDMOTHER'S UP TO SOMETHING."

Paulie lifted out of his doze. "Huh?"

"She's being really cagey. I'm supposed to take her to the bakery with me tomorrow."

"Why is that cagey?"

"How is it not?" Donatella sagged back into the couch. "She says we'll talk tomorrow."

"Then you just have to make it through tonight," he teased. "Seriously, how wicked could it be?"

Donatella waggled her eyebrows. "She has a boyfriend, you know."

"No way."

"Yup. She stole one of the grandfathers looking for love. I bet it has something to do with that. What else could it possibly be?"

"Drugs?"

"Yeah. Must be drugs." Donatella shoved him. "You want to go out or something? I'm bored."

"There's nothing to do. Let's just watch a movie."

"You're already asleep. I don't feel like sitting here watching you sleep."

"You don't have to. You can watch the movie."

"Ugh, Paulie!"

"I'm tired," he said. "It's cold outside. Let's snuggle."

Paulie wriggled his arms around her, put his head on her shoulder. Held her. Held her back. They hadn't talked about it. At all. He was trying to give her time. Space. Headspace. Whatever it was she needed. And maybe, just maybe, if he avoided the subject, so would she.

"I know what you're doing."

Dammit. Paulie snuggled in deeper. "I don't know what you're talking about."

"I'm not stupid."

"Of course, you're not. You're one of the smartest people I know."

She didn't get up or push him off, but every muscle bunched, ready. Paulie knew this Donatella best of all. He'd fed off her frenzy, once upon a time. Both of them young and stupid and wild and hurting in some way. Allies against a world they didn't fit in. Somehow, abandoned and unloved Paulie Vittone had found his niche; adored and coddled Donatella Palladino never had.

"I have an appointment at the clinic tomorrow morning. Before work."

Paulie closed his eyes. *Oh, please. Please, no.* "Do you want me to come with you?"

"No," she said. "I need to do this alone."

"How are you getting there?"

"Don't worry about it."

"Don, I can drive—"

"You have to work. I got it covered, okay? It's not going to take long. I have to be at work at one, anyway." She relaxed a little, picked up the remote. "Want to watch an episode of *Game of Thrones*?"

"Sure."

He wouldn't open his eyes. Wouldn't look at her. He'd bawl. He'd beg. He'd be everything he didn't want to be. In truth, Paulie didn't know what was right. All he knew is that he wanted the baby she carried more than anything he'd ever wanted in his life. And it wasn't his decision to make.

19

braggiol' *(bra-jole)*

Italian: *braciola* (*braciole,* plural)

While braggiol' is a flat piece of meat, seasoned, rolled up and tied, then cooked in the Sunday gravy, it, along with sausiche (Italian: *salsiccia;* "sausage"), is a euphemism for the adult male phallus, for reasons I'm sure are clear.

While we're on that subject . . .

pishadeel/pishee *(pee-sha-deel/ pee-shee)*

Italian: *pesciaolino;* "small fish"

Or "penis"; most specifically, one belonging to a little boy. The *deel/ee* makes it diminutive. I always thought it was a familial thing, until I finally watched *The Sopranos* and heard Tony use it the same way my *famiglia* does. Validation was mine.

facciabrutt' *(fa-cha-brute)*

Italian: *facia brutta;* "ugly face"

While it can be used as an insult, it's also used affectionately
when the face in question is undeniably beautiful. Italians are
nothing if not passive-aggressive, even in their love. It could also
be a "don't tempt the fates" sort of ward, like knocking wood.

Varina inspected herself in the mirror, satisfied. She—
eventually—enjoyed the happy accident she'd had with her
hair, but she really liked her salt-and-pepper better. Maybe she was
getting too old and set in her ways, but the pinky purple felt like
she was trying to be someone she wasn't, like the attempt at being
a redhead.

"Be careful. The gavadeel' is hotter than the braggiol'." Davide
set her plate onto the workstation top, handed her a fork and napkin.
She'd brought his favorites—homemade cavatelli and hand-rolled
pork braciola—even if his trainer forbid the carbs. He wouldn't take
a dime for doing her hair; the least she could do was feed him. And it
was as good an excuse as any for a one-on-one dinner with her son.

"So, why red?" he asked with a mouthful of too-hot meat.

"I thought I told you not to ask."

He grinned.

Varina pushed food around on her plate. "A whim," she said. "A
friend of mine has the prettiest red hair, and Nonina put it in my
head that I look old the way I am, as if old is a bad thing to be. It's
a privilege many don't get. Anyway, I knew if I asked you, I'd hurt

your feelings if I didn't like it, then be stuck with it the rest of my life, so . . ." She shrugged.

"I could have given you a red no one would ever know wasn't yours," he said, "but I would have advised against it. Your coloring is all wrong. And you're absolutely beautiful as you are."

"That's my good boy." She patted his cheek, perfectly balanced with scruff and perpetual—though never overdone—tan. Her Adonis of a son. He'd be insufferable if he didn't have the charm to match.

"I'm glad I could fix it for you," he said. "It's not always successful."

"I had no doubt." She ate a little. "The friend I said has the prettiest red hair owes it to you, you know. She said it took ages to get a match to her natural hair, but you did it."

"Me, personally?"

Varina laughed. "No. I think she goes to your salon in Guttenberg. I don't know the name of her stylist."

"I work out of there a lot. What's her name?"

"Ruth Cooperman."

Davide choked, coughing. Varina leapt off her chair, pounded his back. "Honey? Sweetheart? Can you breathe?"

He held up his hand. It took a few tries, but he cleared his throat. "Ruth Cooperman. That's your friend?"

We're going to France together. "Yes."

"Since when?"

"Around Christmas. Why? Do you know her?"

"I can't believe you do." He coughed through a laugh. "I've seen her, of course, but I only know *of* her. And that she's my most glam client."

"What do you know about her?"

His eyebrows raised. "I'm sure she's very nice."

"That bad, huh?"

"She can make or break salons like mine by either using them or making sure no one does. I'd better give Jeanette a raise for getting her hair color right. If I had the goolies to muscle Jeanette out, I'd have taken her myself long ago."

"You're such a liar." Varina swatted him. "You could charm the scales off a snake."

"Not before that one had me skinned and made into shoes."

"Stop."

"I can't believe my little mama is friends with the Dragon of Fifth Avenue. Don't tell her I called her that."

"I'd never. That's mean."

"Don't fool yourself. A woman like her enjoys a title like that."

"You don't know Ruth the way I do."

"And you don't know her reputation the way I do."

"She's not her reputation."

"That's not what you always taught us." Davide picked at his food. "Remember when I said I wanted to go to beauty school? I thought Dad would have a stroke, right there in the kitchen."

She tried to smile. "Your father got over it."

"Only after I told him it was a great way to meet girls."

Not even then, but Dino tried. Because of Paulie, he tried harder than he otherwise might have. Men didn't have to be construction workers. They could be hairstylists, too. The concept was just too alien, no matter how otherwise evolved he tried so hard to be.

"He was very proud of you. Of your success."

"I know. Even if he never came to one of my places for a haircut. Anyway, this braggiol' is spectacular, but there's no way I can eat it all. Who do you think I am? Uncle Tommy?"

And, like that, the uncomfortable subject changed. Typical Palladino. Spini, too, if Varina were being honest, because she let it go. "Give it to me. I'll put these together and you can have it another night. Or for lunch."

"Bring it home to Donatella. She'd probably appreciate a free meal."

"Be nice."

"What?" Davide dodged Varina's swat.

"Your sister is trying. She paid me back a hundred dollars already."

"Ooo." He twiddled his fingers like a villain. "A whole hundred. Better open an account in the Caymans."

Varina grabbed his face between forefinger and thumb, a lightning strike perfected over many years with four, counting Paulie, children. "I mean it. Be nice. Your sister is trying." And then she kissed him. "Facciabrutt'! I'm going home. I'll see you for Sunday dinner."

"This Sunday?" Davide rubbed his cheeks. "I can't."

"It's the second Sunday of the month. *Famiglia* Sunday dinner. No exceptions." She scraped what was left of her dinner into her son's, snapped the container closed, and handed it to him. "If you're a good boy, I'll invite the Dragon of Fifth Avenue."

Eyes wide, chin low, hands in prayer, Davide batted his eyes like a lovesick cow in the cartoon shows of her youth. "Yes, Mommy."

Kissing him again—one dimple, then the other—Varina savored the swell of love. He'd always been a naughty thing, but a good son. A good man. Too bad he'd be a terrible husband, and a worse father. Not everyone was cut out for it. Two of her three children hadn't been, apparently.

"Sunday! Two o'clock!" she called over her shoulder. Zipping her coat up over her chin, Varina stepped out into the cold for the two-block walk home. The temp was bracing, but not painfully cold. How long before it became too much for her? The ancient Buick in her garage barely moved from its spot. It probably needed a tuning, at the very least. Or maybe she'd trade it in for one of those tiny smart cars that ran on electricity instead of gas.

Ludicrous. As if she would buy a new car when she already had one, besides being perfectly capable of walking most places she needed to go. She wasn't destitute, by any means, but neither was she the Dragon of Fifth Avenue.

Pulling the phone from her pocket, she tapped on Ruth's icon.

"I told you never to call this number," Ruth joked. It was always a joke. Never a hello.

"Do I have the pleasure of speaking with the Dragon of Fifth Avenue?"

Ruth snorted. "I'd have thought your son would have shared that information with you long before now."

"He didn't know we're friends until five minutes ago. Should I be scared?"

"Maybe."

"I'm not."

"Well, good. You shouldn't be. Why didn't he know we're friends?"

"I haven't shared you with my kids yet. Well, Donatella, obviously, but she and Davide don't talk much. Even if they did, it wouldn't have come up. My son tells me you probably like the title."

"I do. It's kind of fun to watch people wither when I enter a room."

"I'd love to see that one day."

"I'll invite you to Fashion Week. It'll be illuminating, I assure you."

"When's Fashion Week?"

"Oh, Varina. Really?"

She laughed. "How would I know? As you might have noticed, I'm not exactly a fashionista."

"How nineties of you." Ruth tsked. "I'll be honest, though, it's one of the reasons I love you the way I do. You have even less interest in my world than I do, and that's saying something."

Varina stepped off the curb, looked both ways. "If you're no longer interested, why do you do it?"

"What else am I going to do?"

No family. As far as Varina could tell, no friends but her. Ruth had a point. "Come for our family Sunday dinner," she said. "I want to see my son wither in your presence."

"Hilarious."

"Seriously," Varina said. "It's nothing formal. Just me forcing my kids to see me and one another once a month. Oh, and my mother will be there, too. And probably Paulie . . . and Pan. Probably not Gabby, but maybe."

Silence. Varina's pace slowed. "It was just a thought. No pressure." Then stopped when the silence lingered. "I've overstepped."

"No, no. Not at all." Ruth sniffed.

"Are you crying?"

"Don't be silly. I'd love to come for Sunday dinner. What can I bring?"

"Wine, unless you like the stuff that comes by the gallon."

"I'll bring several bottles."

She laughed, and so did Ruth. Relief warmed Varina's face. "I'm home. I'll see you Sunday. Two o'clock. Oh, and my hair is no longer purple, so you're off the hook about that tattoo."

"Thank heavens." Ruth laughed. "I would have gone through with it, you know."

"I have no doubt, O dragon. See you Sunday."

"Toodle-pip!"

"Bye—"

But Ruth had already hung up.

Phone in pocket, hand rifling around in there for her house keys, Varina hopped from foot to foot to keep warm. The door flew open.

"You could have knocked. I was afraid you were a burglar trying to . . . oh! Your hair is back to normal. Thank goodness!"

"I knew you were lying when you said you liked it." Varina kissed her mother's cheek on the way through the door. She closed it behind her, locking all the locks. "No cracks about the salt-and-pepper?"

"Why would I say anything bad about your beautiful hair?"

Varina shouldered out of her coat, hung it on the hook. It wasn't worth the words to remind her. "Did you eat something?"

"I made a can of soup."

"Mom."

"Ashbett'! I couldn't even finish the whole thing. There were crackers, too."

"You don't eat right unless I make it for you."

"Then we're even for all the suppers you didn't eat because you'd already snuck Burger King and McDonald's."

"It was White Castle, and I was a teenager. You, Mother, are ninety-two."

Sylvia mumbled something Varina didn't catch, but caught the drift of, as well as the telltale hiss of a record winding down on the Victrola's turntable.

"Is that you? Or is our demon at it again?"

Her mother's hand fluttered to her hair, then her cheek before falling to her chest. "I was listening to music. I got scared when I heard you at the back door."

"Why would you be scared?"

"Maybe because I'm ninety-two."

The eye roll just happened, even though Varina had sworn, having been the recipient of many an offspring eye roll, that she wouldn't do that to her mother. "Well, go listen. I'll clean up in here and—"

"I can clean up. You go get changed."

"It'll only take . . ." Varina halted mid-grab for the faucet. Bowls.

Salad plates. Glasses. Forks and spoons and butter knives. Two of everything. "What's with all the dishes?"

"I…" *Hair, cheek, chest.* Sylvia insinuated herself between Varina and the sink, turned on the faucet. "I can't hear you with the water running. Go get changed."

The lunches and dinners Tommy said never happened. The car rolling down the driveway. Now this bit of insanity. Enough was enough. Reaching around her mother, Varina turned off the water.

"What's going on, Mom?"

Sylvia didn't look at her. "Why do you have to be so nosy?"

"I learned from the best."

"Don't be fresh."

"Mom."

"Mannaggia dial!" She threw up her hands. "You've gotten so bossy."

Varina followed her mother out of the kitchen, through the parlor, and down the bedroom hallway. Sylvia opened the door to hers, poked her head inside. "You can come out now."

From the mauve interior of her mother's room, an elderly man emerged. Sheepish and smiling, he bowed his head, fingers to brow, as if tipping his hat. "Hello."

"Hi?" Varina stepped back so he could come into the hall.

"Varina, this is John Yu. John, my daughter, Varina, who has gone and spoiled everything."

"Don't be harsh, my love."

My love? "Hello, John. Pleased to meet you."

"The pleasure is mine." Gentle, not soft, his voice sounded like his smile looked. "I've been anxious to meet you."

"Which you would have done on Sunday, if my daughter weren't so nosy."

"Sylvia."

"Mom."

Unison. Varina liked him already.

"Perhaps we should take this to the parlor," he suggested, "where we can make proper introductions?"

"Good idea." Varina gestured them ahead of her. John's hand rested on the small of Sylvia's back. Guiding. Protective.

Scratch-scratch-scratch.

"Not now, Vicky."

Again, unison. This time, mother and daughter. Varina took her mother's hand.

"Did you think I'd be disapproving or something?"

"No," Sylvia answered. "I was enjoying my secret romance, is all."

"And I spoiled it." Now she felt bad. "I was worried, Mom."

"About what?"

"You've been acting strange. And the car rolling out of our driveway last week scared me." She turned to John. "I imagine that was you?"

"It was." His smile widened. Deepened. "I must admit, I felt like a teenager being caught in his sweetheart's bedroom."

"Why didn't you just tell me?" Varina asked her mother.

"I told you. I was going to introduce John to the family on Sunday."

Sylvia Spini's need for drama rarely fell short of spectacular. At least, that's what Varina remembered. It had been so long, with only hints and peeks of it the last decade or three. Pulling her mother into her arms, she kissed the top of her head, pulled back and kissed both cheeks.

"You're a piece of work, you know that?"

"Takes one to know one."

Varina laughed. John laughed, too. And then Sylvia joined them, trying like hell not to.

"It's early yet," she said. "How about I open a bottle of wine and you two tell me how you met?"

"Just a small one," John said. "I'm driving."

"Fair enough." Varina started for the kitchen, hiding a smile as best as she could. For all her talk of Varina finding a man, Sylvia had gone and done it for herself. She couldn't wait to tell Ruth.

"I told you she was nosy."

"She loves you," John whispered back. Though neither one of them was actually whispering, even if they thought they were. Varina pretended not to hear them, instead went into the pantry and took a bottle of wine from the shelf.

scumbari *(shkoom-BA-ri or skoom-BA-ri)*

Italian: *scumbari*, as far as I can find, is Calabrese for "disheveled," or "out of place" (either literally or figuratively). This word sometimes comes with waggling eyebrows and a "too hot to handle" wave, implying promiscuity.

Finoot'!

Italian: *finito!*; "finished!"

While this can also be used in a triumphant way, as in you finally finished all the laundry, it's more typically said angrily, accompanied by a brushing off of the hands—twice, no more or less—and walking away. No shoe will be thrown, in which case, you're in real trouble.

The 1902 Victorian on Greensway got two offers on the first day: one at the asking price, one slightly lower. Dante accepted the lower, made by a couple with two little kids, rather than the higher, made by an older couple who wanted it as a rental property. Paulie might have warned it was a slippery slope, a sort of profiling that might be viewed as unethical, but he didn't. Dante envisioned not just re-vitalizing Wyldale's architecture, but the city itself. The last thing he wanted was the sort of gentrification that was—as far as he was concerned—ruining Brooklyn. Wyldale had always been a working-class, family place. If Dante Palladino had anything to do with it, it would stay that way. And for that alone, Paulie couldn't love him more.

"You almost ready?" he called to Donatella, in the bathroom the last half hour. "You can't keep the door closed that long. The cats are going to poop on the floor."

She came out of the bathroom dressed with more care than he'd seen in a while. Her hair was half up in a messy bun, but neater. The curls slightly tamed.

"You look nice."

She touched her hair. "Not scumbari, is it? Nonina hates my hair this way."

"Nonina will always find something to criticize. You know that."

"True." Donatella looked away. "By the way, and speaking of cat poop, the obstetrician said I can't go near the litter box. Toxoplasmology . . . or something. Maybe you should find a place other than the bathroom for it."

Obstetrician? Paulie's breath caught in his throat. Couldn't budge. Couldn't move. He managed a small sip of air and "You didn't do it."

Donatella pushed past him. "Didn't do what?"

"You had an appointment. With the clinic."

"I think that's what I was just talking about. Duh."

"I thought you . . . I was afraid you were going to . . ."

She turned on him, tears glistening but not falling. "I did. I was. But I couldn't do it. So, like it or not, Mr. Vittone, you and I are having this baby."

Again, his breath caught. He let it stay inside him, let it build and build until his lips tingled. Pulling Donatella into his arms, he did his best not to cry and failed miserably.

"I'm not getting married or anything." Her voice muffled into his shoulder. "I can't do it to you, and I won't do it to me. We'll do this our way, Paulie, just like always."

Just like always scared the piss out of him, but Paulie was used to scared. He'd spent most of his life afraid of something.

"You want to move your stuff in here?" he asked, letting go.

"What stuff? All I own is in a box under my bed."

"Fine, bring your box and put it under my bed. You're here all the time anyway."

"Won't that cramp your style?"

He laughed, slightly maniacally. "What style? I have no love life. You know that."

"And now for sure you won't." Donatella averted her eyes. "I don't want to fuck up your life, Paulie."

"Oh, honey, you did that when we were five and I was pulling you out of that sewer."

"Storm drain."

"Same difference." Paulie took her shoulders in his hands, gave her a little shake. "I'm really happy about this, Don. You have no idea."

"I think I have some." She smirked up at him.

"Was I that obvious?"

"A little. Okay, a lot. But that's not why I'm going through with this. Not entirely, anyway. Just partly. And I don't want to tell anyone yet. It's too soon."

"Okay." Paulie had no idea what they were going to tell everyone anyway. *Hi, remember me? Your sister's gay best friend? Well, I knocked her up and we're having the baby together but not getting married just in case I find a boyfriend or she ... she ...*

She takes off? Falls for another Fucking Chucky? Decides she wants to be an archaeologist? Out of the frying pan, into the fire.

The breathless sensation expanded rather than contracted, like he was breathing in and in and in and in and couldn't exhale to save his life. It wouldn't happen. It couldn't. She'd never. The baby would ... it would ... it had to somehow ...

Paulie's cell phone chirped, setting loose all that air, his thoughts a balloon let go to career haphazardly.

"It's Dante." Donatella, oblivious, handed him his phone. "Better take it."

Paulie tapped into the call. "Hey."

"I wanted to go over a few things without all the chaos. Can I come up now for a few? Or maybe after dinner?"

Paulie closed his eyes, checked his breathing. Donatella had scooped Chooch into her arms. She was sniffing his tufty head, scritching under his chin. It would be all right. She would be. They would be.

"Yo, Paulie. You still there?"

"Yeah. Sure. Sorry. We have fifteen minutes now. That enough?"

"Plenty. I'll be up in a sec."

"I guess I'm going down ahead of you." She set Chooch on the couch. "My brother's corrupting you."

"It's just a few minutes."

"Today. He'll drag you into his 24/7/365-except-Christmas life. Just you wait and see."

"I won't let him." He steered her to the door. "Tell your mom we'll be down at two on the dot."

Paulie opened the door just as Dante was about to knock. "Hey, Dante."

"Quesadich, Paulie?" He stepped aside for his sister to pass, stooped to kiss her as she did.

Pressing a hand to his cheek, she breathed in deep. "Mmmmm! You smell like Mom's chicken piccata. Yes! Don't be too long. You know how she gets."

Paulie waved Dante into his apartment, shooing the kittens out of the way. They never missed a chance to dart into the hallway, where all sorts of wonders were apparently just out of reach.

"You still got them, huh?"

"I keep telling myself I need to find them homes. I just feel so bad, splitting them up."

"They're cats."

"They're brothers."

Dante chuckled. "I don't think they know that."

Paulie shrugged. They did, just like MaryJane knew they were her offspring. "So, what did you want to talk about?"

"This." Dante pulled a roll of papers from his back pocket. "We said we're making it official. Legal."

"Oh, right." He took the contract, discussed and ironed out over steaks—which were actually quite good—and Manhattans—which he'd had to choke down—and got a pen from the drawer in his kitchen. A contract binding him even further to the Palladino family. To Dante.

"You sign, then I will. We need a—" He smacked the paper. "Fanabola! I should have had Donatella stay and witness."

Paulie signed anyway. So did Dante. It was official, but unofficially so. Paulie wasn't really sure why Dante insisted on a contract that stated they both had the option of a thirty-day release. What was the point of a contract if, in the language of the thing itself, it could be broken? Which he'd never do. He'd get to design home interiors for good money, plus benefits, for a man he . . . respected, whose vision he shared. They'd have to pry his stiff, dead body off this job.

"I guess that's done, then." Dante rolled up the papers. "I'll have Mom witness."

Silence expanded in the little apartment, making it feel claustrophobic. For Paulie, at least. Dante was texting with someone, probably Pandora, because he was smiling. He looked up, sliding his phone into his pocket. "We're going to do great things for this town, you and me."

"I . . . yes. We are."

"I've been thinking," he said, moving further into the apartment rather than toward the door. "Maybe it's time to retire Spini and Son. With Uncle Tommy down in Florida, we're not doing those big projects anymore, the ones that rely on the reputation he and Poppy built, you know? I'll keep the corporation and shit, but was thinking of doing renovation business under a new name."

"What name?"

Dante shrugged, but he took a card from his cell phone case, two-fingered it to Paulie.

Timeless Renovation and Construction
Authentic and environmentally conscious
restorations, one home at a time.
Dante Palladino: Proprietor

Paulie looked from the card to Dante. He looked . . . worried? No, Dante never worried. Expectant. "This is . . . it's amazing."

"Yeah? You think? Not too fancy-woo-hoo?"

"Not at all." Paulie laughed, clapping Dante's shoulder. "It's perfect, man. It's beautiful. It says it all, in very few words."

Like Dante himself.

"It's about time I crawled out from under all that other shit. All them ugly-ass block warehouses and strip malls?" Dante brushed his hands together. "Finoot'! I can't do it anymore. The thought of it makes me schiat'."

"I never knew you were that unhappy."

"Yeah, no one did." Dante looked him square in the eye. "There's a lot no one knows."

Paulie's gut twisted. "I'm, uh, glad you're happy, Dante. Really glad."

"I'm getting there." He smiled, a little sadly, Paulie thought. "Let's get downstairs, eh? If we're late, Mom'll have a conniption."

Paulie gestured Dante through the door first, blocking Chooch and Pastafazool from scampering out. Dante, the job; Donatella, the baby. The whole Palladino family itself. He had everything he wanted, everything he needed, but only sort of. Only halfway. Like always. Paulie was dizzy with it all. With the happiness and the fear and the futility of love that went every which way but how he wished.

21

Statazeet! (sometimes, Statajeet!)

Italian: *Stai zitto!;* "Be quiet! Shut up!"

bas'nigol' *(bas-NEE-gol)*

Italian: *basilico:* "basil," the herb

I have no quippy comment about this, so instead I'll record the old family story about my great-something uncle Basil and aunt Mary. He was five-feet flat and ninety pounds, dripping wet. She was close to six feet tall and never under two hundred pounds. She was, by all accounts, the sweetest woman who ever lived, and the undisputed queen of crude. She loved nothing more than shocking people by wondering aloud about the state of her pussy, and how often men handled their own pricks (two of her favorite words). She delivered these inappropriate bombs so innocently, it was hard to tell if she actually meant what she was saying (she 100 percent did). Aunt Mary lived to 105. Her last words were "My asshole hurts."

J ohn, you sit right there, next to Mom." Varina held out the chair
for him. "Comfortable?"

"Very, thank you."

"Don't fuss, Varina," Sylvia grumbled. "Where's Dante?"

"He's up with Paulie. They'll be down in a minute." Donatella
breezed in, kissed her grandmother's cheek, then John's. "I didn't
know you were coming."

Varina narrowed a look that Donatella did not see—because
Sylvia was trying to fix her hair—but would have told her she had
some explaining to do. Her daughter had apparently known about
her mother's secret romance from day one, their meeting having
happened right there in Jumbaloon's. That her grandmother swore
her to secrecy was a given, and that's what stung most; their bond
had always been stronger than Varina's with either one of them.

The front doorbell rang.

"Got it!" Davide practically dove for the door. He opened it, standing aside and sweeping the bottle of wine and cake box from Ruth's
hands in the same, graceful motion. "You must be Ms. Cooperman."

"And you must be Davide." Ruth winked at Varina. "You weren't
exaggerating. He's gorgeous."

Her son—charming, suave, confident Davide—actually blushed.
"Let me take your coat."

"Thank you."

Varina took the wine and cake. "You didn't have to do this."

"A lady never attends a dinner party without bringing something." Another wink, and a whisper, "Especially if she doesn't care
for wine by the gallon."

"Everyone, this is my friend, Ruth."

"We've met," Sylvia said. "But Ruth hasn't met my John."

And, like that, Ruth was sucked into the family, same as John had
been. Varina took the wine and cake into the kitchen, peeked in the

box. Chocolate cake, big enough for a small army. She was already salivating.

"Hey, hey!" Davide called out. "Look what the cat dragged in. If it isn't the family workhorse, blessing us with his presence. I think I see a little sawdust in your hair."

"Better than the goop you got in yours," Dante returned. "Aren't you worried about the extra pounds when you weigh in at Weight Watchers?"

"Basta." Varina stepped between her squabbling sons. "I mean it." Then to everyone: "Setedi! Setedi! Food's getting cold."

She set down a platter of piccata. Pandora and Paulie both helped with the green beans and roasted potatoes.

"That smells as amazing as it looks." Ruth rubbed her hands together. "I don't think I've ever seen chicken pounded so thin."

"My mom makes the best piccata you'll ever eat," Davide told her. "Chicken is chicken. It's all about the sauce."

"It's just butter and lemon." Varina passed the platter around. "Nothing special."

"Yeah, right." Pandora laughed. "There's a metric ton of garlic. And capers."

"Shallots," Donatella chimed in. "I know she uses shallots. And Italian parsley, not that crappy kind that tastes like grass."

Sylvia took a bite, smacking her lips. "I taste wine. Maybe vermouth. There's no wine in true chicken piccata."

"Try all you want," Varina told them. "You'll never guess my secrets. I'll take them to the grave."

"You have to tell us one day," Pandora said. "How else are we going to keep it in rotation at the store?"

"You mean after I die."

"Ashbett'!" Sylvia crossed herself. "Don't say such a thing. Especially on a Sunday."

"Pan has a point," Paulie said. "You need to teach someone all your recipes."

Varina didn't dare tell them there were no recipes to pass on. Some of this. A little of that. Ingredients varied by the quality of them. Old garlic tasted different than new garlic. As Donatella said, Italian parsley was different from curly. She never knew how much of anything to add until she smelled it, the scent somehow telling her how it tasted, how all the aromas mingled to inform her palate how everything would combine. She could make anything work, but it had nothing to do with recipes, and thus couldn't be taught. One had to simply *know,* and there was only one person in the family who did; unfortunately, she was currently in college studying English. Varina knew, though. She knew beyond all doubt Gabriella's future was in food. Maybe it wouldn't be the store, but it was in her blood, same as it was in Varina's.

As they did most second Sundays, her culinary skills worked their magic. The boys behaved. Mom was her chatty, overly-critical-but-in-a-funny-sort-of-way self. Everyone did their best to include John in the conversation, and Ruth was the woman she'd met at the travel agent, not her Dragon of Fifth Avenue reputation. Davide was completely enthralled by her. Donatella seemed strangely serene, and Paulie, distracted, but in a stunned way, not a bored one. Chatter. Laughter. A Sunday dinner to beat all Sunday dinners. Varina even toyed with the idea of telling her family about her trip—how natural would it be, considering Ruth's presence—but didn't. Not now. Not yet. Maybe in September.

"That was amazing, as always." Davide patted his stomach. "I'm going to have to do an extra hour at the gym tomorrow."

"So, four hours instead of three?" Dante asked.

"Statazeet, chubs. It wouldn't hurt you to do some cardio."

Varina rose to collect plates, her *basta* glare leveled.

"Sit, Mom," Pan told her. "You've done enough. Come on, you jamokes. It isn't Christmas. You're helping."

Paulie was first on his feet. "We'll stack them in the sink. We know you're particular about how they go into the dishwasher."

"It's only because—"

"—you know how to get it all in!" everyone but Ruth and John chorused, laughing. Varina couldn't love them more. Not a single one of them.

Davide, Donatella, and Dante got up as well, gathered dishes and glasses, forks and knives and dirty napkins. Ruth sat back in her chair, patting her flat stomach with a perfectly manicured hand. "That was, by far, the best meal I've ever eaten."

"You're exaggerating." Varina waved her off. "But thank you."

"She's not exaggerating, sweetheart," Sylvia said. "It's bas'nigol', isn't it."

"It's . . . what? Oh! No, there's no"—she turned to Ruth—"basil"—and back to her mother—"in it. You'd see it."

"Not if you put it in cheesecloth."

"Bouquet garni," Varina supplied. "True, but no. If I put herbs in, I put them in. You'll see—"

A crash of dishes and cutlery falling cut her off. Varina was half-way to the kitchen before she finished saying, "I'll be right back." Voices were lifting. Davide. Dante. Donatella. Of course. Pandora and Paulie separated them, already looking defeated. On the floor, a pile of her now-broken dishes, and what food had been left on them. "What's going on in here?"

"I didn't pawn Daddy's crucifix!" Donatella faced her brothers, fists clenched. "I'm tired of them insinuating I did."

Not this again. Varina pressed fingers to her eyes. "You three need to stop right now."

Davide put up his hands, backing toward the dining room. He

and Dante exchanged a glance. The needling that started soon after Dino's death still had more than enough life in it all these years later.

"I've told you both a thousand times," Varina claimed for that thousandth time, "Daddy lost that crucifix a couple of years before he died."

"I'm sure, he did." Dante now exchanged a glance with Pandora, and he, too, headed for the dining room.

Donatella glared after her brothers, fingers sweeping under her chin. "Baffangul! Come on, Paulie."

"Wait! We didn't even have dessert yet."

"I'm not going in there with those two."

"Donatella." Varina cautiously dared touch her tightly wound daughter, grasping both her shoulders when she didn't pull away. "Ignore them. You let it bother you, and that's why they keep doing it."

"They're infantile."

"Stop reacting, and they'll stop goading you."

"Why is this on me?" Donatella pulled out of her grasp. "They're assholes to me, and I'm the one who has to diffuse it?"

She had a point. Varina slumped. "How did this even come up again?"

"Davide started it." Pandora sighed. "Dante picked it up. They're both shooting for bear today."

"Loaded for bear," Varina corrected her.

"It's a horrible expression either way," Donatella snapped. "There's no reason to hunt bear anymore. It's barbaric!"

"What does that have to do with anything?" Varina asked.

"It's just an expression," Pandora murmured. "Jeez, Don, what flew up your butt."

"Don't you start on me, too."

"What did I say?"

"Girls," Varina said. "Please. What are Ruth and John going to think of us if we can't—"

Pandora ducked as Donatella blew. "What the hell do I care what anyone thinks? That's it! Baby or no baby, I'm done with this family!"

Baby? Varina stepped into her path. "What did you just say?"

Donatella tried to get around her. "Get out of my way, Mother."

"What's gotten into you?"

When she was small and easily contained, Donatella would violently shake. With fury. With terror. Sometimes, joy. Unable to contain her emotions, unable to control the result. Varina hadn't seen it so intense in a long time, not since those raving, rampaging teen years. Donatella shook now, still small but no longer containable.

"Sweetheart," she soothed as she'd never had the patience for back then. "Hey, come on. Take a deep breath."

She should have known better.

Donatella was small and not necessarily strong, but the shove took Varina by such surprise that she stumbled backward, landing hip-first, wrist-second on the linoleum floor. Her daughter stepped over her and out the door, slamming it behind her.

"Go after her," Pandora told Paulie. "I'll take care of Mom."

"I'm fine." But she wasn't. Her hip hurt, probably just bruised. The wrist, however, throbbed. Pandora helped her to her feet just as Dante blew back into the kitchen.

"What happened?"

And then there was Davide, lifting Varina from the other side. Pandora told the boys what happened; she heard with only half an ear. Broken heart. Probably broken wrist. *A baby. A baby, a baby, a baby.* Was it true? Varina had to hope it wasn't.

"You shouldn't keep bringing that up," Pandora was scolding.

"Even if she did, who cares? It was almost twenty years ago. No one can ever make a mistake with you two. As if you're so damn perfect."

"That's no excuse for what just happened," Dante said. "And I wasn't the one who started it."

"You finished it, though. You always have to have the last word."

"This isn't the time or place for this, Pan."

"It never is. It never was." She settled Varina into a chair, kissed her cheek. "You okay, Mom?"

"Fine," she lied. "Please, sweetheart, would you check on Ruth for me. What a nightmare this is."

"I'm sure her family is just as nuts."

"I don't think she has one."

"Good for her!" Pandora laughed, but it was high and wobbly.

"You two." She pointed to her sons, then the kitchen chairs on either side of her.

Obedient, if unhappy about it; these were men, not boys. Men she'd raised. Men she was proud of, most of the time. Propping her throbbing, probably-not-broken-after-all wrist on the table, she let go a deep sigh.

"I'm not going to defend her," she said. "Donatella is who she is, just like you two are who you are. You're adults, and I'm tired of mothering you. All of you." Another deep breath. "If we can't get through a Sunday dinner or a holiday without this kind of thing happening, I'm not doing them anymore."

"Are you kidding me?" Davide shook his head. "That little brat shoves you to the ground and Dante and I are—"

"She didn't shove me down," Varina snapped. "She shoved past me and I fell. The two of you, going at one another, starting in on Donatella, and in front of guests! When are you going to grow up?"

"Mom," Dante said, "we were just kidding around. It's what we do. We always have."

"And you're the only ones who find it funny. Don't include Donatella."

"She's not a baby anymore, Mom," said Dante, and then Davide, "I can't believe we're the monsters here when—" but Varina cut them both off.

"She's never been able to just brush it off like you two do, and you know it." Varina rested her chin on the heel of her uninjured hand. Were her wrist not throbbing, she might have covered her ears instead. "Maybe you boys should head out."

Dante and Davide pushed away from the kitchen table. They kissed their mother, murmured apologies and I love you's. In the dining room, they did the same for their Nonina, before bidding a polite good-bye to John, to Ruth. And then they were gone. Pandora, too. The house was silent. Not even Vicky dared utter a single sound.

Varina rested her head on her arms, folded on the table. Thoughts wouldn't behave. She let them have their way with her. Tears welled; one or two might have fallen before her mother and Ruth joined her in the kitchen, pretending they couldn't tell, and she picked up her head.

"I'm sorry, Mom. This . . . I don't know what happened. Is John okay?"

"He went home." Sylvia brought her a dish towel packed with ice and placed it on her still-throbbing, though not as much anymore, wrist. "He has a big family, too," she said. "He understands. At least we got that over with."

"What?"

"The inevitable."

Ruth brought over the cake box and three forks, handed them

each a utensil, and untied the string. They wordlessly dug into the massive, decadently chocolate cake. It was exactly what Varina wanted in that moment. Exactly what she needed. Her mother. Her best friend. And chocolate cake.

"I'm really sorry, Ruth."

"Don't be." Ruth waved her chocolate-slathered fork in the air. "If my family were this sort of loony, I might still be on speaking terms with them."

"What do you mean?"

Ruth ate her bite of cake, rolled it around in her mouth before swallowing. "This is love," she said. "This is hot and messy and seemingly out of control, but it all comes from a place of love. My family is cold. I go years without speaking to my sisters, for no particular reason other than I have no interest in them, and they have no interest in me. There's the occasional phone call, a congratulations for a grandchild born or something. I honestly couldn't say when I saw any of my family last."

"Weren't you ever close?"

Another bite of cake. "If we were, I don't remember. Maybe when we were little?"

"Was there a fight? Should I not ask?"

"It's fine," Ruth said. "Not that I recall. Just a drifting no one cared to alter."

"But what about your mother? Your father?"

"Mother was the same. Daddy?" And now Ruth smiled. "What I remember is lovely, but he died when I was just a little girl. My mother remarried soon after, to a man who had no patience for little girls missing their daddy. Anyway, don't apologize for your messy family. Between my cold, distant relations and the absolute malevolence of Jacob's family, yours is a day at the beach."

An electronic *bing* turned them both to Sylvia. She held up a cell phone. "It's John," she said, "making sure I'm all right. Isn't that sweet?"

"Very," Varina answered. "When did you get that?"

"This?" She waved the phone like a flag. "I asked Tommy to get me one. It lets me talk to John whenever I want."

Sylvia pecked out her response with one crooked finger, shoulders hunched, smile twitching her lips, then spreading to crinkle the corners of her eyes. Varina wanted to hug her, to tell her how truly happy she was that she'd found someone to love again. Just then, her heart was too heavy, her head too full. *A baby.* She had to have heard that wrong. Had to.

"How can I help?" Ruth glanced about the kitchen. "It looks like your daughter-in-law did most of it already."

Pandora. How she loved that girl. "I can manage what little is left." She sighed. "I guess I'm in the market for new dishware. I loved those dishes. They were made in Italy."

"I'm sure you'll find new ones you like." Ruth got up, gathered the forks. She closed the box and set the cake in the fridge. "I bet you can even find the same ones online."

"Yeah, probably."

Ruth put a hand on her shoulder, leaned down and pressed a cheek to hers. "Tomorrow is Monday. Want to have lunch?"

"Sure. Sounds good."

"It'll all be okay." She whispered in Varina's ear, "Only seven months to go."

Her mother was slightly hard of hearing, but Varina shushed Ruth, smiling and nodding anyway. *Provence. Seven months. Why couldn't it be tomorrow?*

"I should get going. You stay put," Ruth said as Varina started to rise. Oh, her hip ached! "I can see myself out." She leaned closer to Sylvia. "It was good to see you."

"Fanabola! No need to shout in my ear."

She and Varina exchanged an eye roll over her head. Ruth twiddled her fingers. Varina twiddled back.

"Toodle-pip!" And, as always, Ruth was gone in a rush of air and a waft of perfume.

Varina suppressed the urge to put her head back on the table, in the comfort and solitude of her crossed arms. Instead, she rearranged the now-soggy dish towel, melting ice still wrapped inside. Her wrist only hurt a little. Her hip would hurt longer, she was certain. Cutting off those thoughts before they could go any further, she pushed away from the table.

"A very British way of saying good-bye," Sylvia said, "probably deriving from an English dialect word meaning 'to wander off,' such as 'I'll be toodling along now.'"

Varina sat back down. "What are you talking about?"

Her mother held up her cell phone. "*Toodle-pip.* I looked it up. See?"

Taking the phone, Varina noted the entry, though she'd inherited her father's eyesight, not her mother's, and couldn't read it without her glasses. She handed back the phone. "You're something else, Mom."

"Of course, I am, sweetheart." Sylvia took back the phone, tucked it into her dress pocket. "I'll clear away the crumbs here. You go relax a bit. You know Donatella will be back to apologize any time now."

And she would be. Irrational, impulsive, brutally shortsighted, Donatella had, as her generation coined, big feels. She'd not just feel bad for pushing her mother, she'd be desolate, contrite, and self-loathing. It was all part of the deal, the pattern, since earliest childhood. Varina was tired of mothering that, too. She didn't want to care about the consequences of cutting her children all off, of throwing up her hands and saying she was done. But she did. It was partially her fault for letting them all get away with it their whole lives.

Varina limped to her room. It was early, but she was ready for the day to be over. Nightgown, slippers, fluffy robe. Maybe she'd make a cup of tea and watch something old on television. Something that lied about what being part of a big, loving *famiglia* truly entailed. Or maybe one like Ruth's, that might be cold and distant, but was sure as hell a lot simpler.

scarol' *(SHKA-role)*

Italian: *scarola;* "escarole"

The green, leafy vegetable (delicious with garlic and white beans, sautéed in olive oil) is also slang for "money," like *dough* in American English.

oobatz'

Italian: *pazzo;* "crazy"

Coincidentally, there's a word that differs only in one letter— *oogatz'* (*cazzo*, in Italian), which literally means "dick/cock." What it means in Neapolitan slang, as well as Jersey Italian slang, is "nothing." For example:

"Hey, Angelo, what did you get for Christmas?"

"Ma caught me in the boiler room with Tina. I got oogatz.'"

I'm going tomorrow. I'm making an appointment right now."

Donatella was already on her phone, thumbing her way to an abortion she'd only hours before told him she couldn't go through with. Paulie snatched the device from her. "This isn't a decision you can make to spite your family."

"What happened to supporting me in any decision I make?" She tried to grab the phone back.

Paulie held it behind his back. "This isn't a decision. This is anger. Don't do this in anger. You'll regret it the rest of your life. Please, Donatella. Try to be rational."

"How can I be rational with those two for brothers?" she said, having no real idea just how irrational a statement that was. "They won't let me forget a single, stupid mistake I made. Not one. Not even ones I didn't do, but they think I did, but I didn't! Don't they know I live with every mistake I've ever made pummeling my brain, day after day? Night after night? Like I need them to remind me. Did anyone have to tell three-hundred-pound Uncle Vito he was fat? Well, I don't need anyone to tell me I'm a royal fuckup. That's why I can't have this baby, Paulie, not spite."

He took several deep breaths. Behind his back, he turned off her phone and slipped it into his pocket. Taking her into his arms, he held her close.

"You're ferocious, you know that?"

She laughed despite herself, burrowing more deeply into him.

"You don't think you'd be as ferocious a mother?" he asked. "You don't think you'd fight for your child with the same ferocity you show the world?" He put her from him. "You've made mistakes, Don, maybe more than others. You have a bad temper, but you also have the biggest heart of anyone I've ever known."

"You have to say that."

"No, I don't." He sat her down, then took the cushion beside her.

"Listen," he said, "I want this baby. I won't lie and tell you it doesn't matter to me. It does. More than I ever realized, to be honest. But that doesn't change the fact that if I didn't think you were capable, I wouldn't ask it of you. Ever. I'm asking, Donatella. If you decide, in calmer moments, you just can't, I'll respect that. But please don't take something from me just to spite people you actually love very much, but are momentarily angry with."

She sniffed. "Stop making sense."

"One of us has to." He jiggled her shoulders. "You get to be the fun one. I'll be the responsible one. It'll be a good dynamic."

"I . . ." Tears spilled. Donatella trembled, not the scary way she had downstairs, but the kind he knew better. "I want this baby, Paulie. Since going to the doctor, I've actually been excited. Like, everything is better. I feel better. I already love her so much."

"Her?"

"It's a girl. I know it."

"Okay. And?"

"And then shit like what happened downstairs happens, and I get so scared. What kind of person pushes her seventy-year-old mother down?"

"It was an accident."

"It was not. I mean, I didn't actually mean to push her down, but I didn't not mean it either. I wanted her out of my way. Who does that, Paulie?"

She was calm now, moving into the self-deprecation he could have predicted like garlic did bad breath. Paulie took heart in Donatella's confession—the first—that she actually wanted the baby. Loved it. *Her.* He breathed easier, easing some of the guilt from his own shoulders.

"Want some tea?" he asked.

"Herbal," she answered, and then she smiled, and relief settled more comfortably in. "I'm sorry, Paulie."

"I know."

"You shouldn't have to talk me down off a ledge every damn day."

"Hormones," he told her, though that only accounted for the last couple of months. Handing her the blanket from the back of the couch hid the trembling of his own hands. The joint in his sock drawer beckoned. He rarely did it now, though he'd done it often when he was a kid always on the same edge Donatella remained on. Paulie only kept an emergency stash for those overwhelming days when the churning wouldn't stop.

He made her tea. He tucked the blanket around her. He sat by her side. They watched an episode of *Game of Thrones*—which she'd watched in its entirety and was making him watch now that it was over, even though he had no desire to—and then another because Donatella had fallen asleep on his shoulder, and he couldn't reach the remote.

After eleven, she still hadn't stirred; Paulie eased out from under her, his arm asleep and aching.

"I was dreaming," she murmured.

He waited. Curled into a ball of wild hair and blanket, Donatella said no more. Paulie went quietly into the bathroom to brush his teeth. Chooch and Pastafazool followed him, batting at his toes and tumbling over one another while he bent over the sink. Brush, rinse, spit. Paulie plonked the toothbrush into its holder, there beside the one Donatella kept at his place. His heart stitched. He rubbed the spot, but it was no use.

It was going to be a long seven months.

Picking up the kittens, one in each hand, he nuzzled their little heads. They smelled of kitten, a sweet, slightly dusty scent. No longer milky. MaryJane had weaned them, and Paulie'd had her neutered along with her little sons. No more kittens. Not for any of them.

Pastafazool wriggled, trying to break free. Paulie set them both down, knowing now what he'd known all along—he wasn't giving up any of the cats. Somehow, he'd manage in his little apartment. Or maybe, if things worked out in some way not a disaster, he'd buy one of the blue-collar, working-class homes he was helping to renovate, and give them more room to roam.

Donatella wasn't on the couch when he came back through the living room. The blanket was still warm, but she was gone and the door was slightly ajar. Paulie closed it, leaving the chain undone. He hoped she'd be back. He hoped . . .

A long, *long* seven months.

In his bedroom, he paused at the dresser. Instead of taking out his pajamas, he opened his sock drawer that reeked of the single joint within. Taking it out to the fire escape, he lit it before he was all the way out the window. Soothing, like an oversized sweatshirt or the sound of crickets or the wind or the ocean. The joint was so old, Paulie didn't even know its effectiveness; he didn't care either.

Below, across the street and three houses down, he spotted Dante's truck—no one else Paulie knew drove a red 1987 Dodge pickup, a rust bucket he kept running because it had been his grandfather's—parked under a streetlight. Dante sat behind the wheel. Paulie's stupid, stitching heart pinged. Buzzed just enough, he climbed down the fire escape, crossed the street, knocked on the window. The doors unlocked. Paulie went to the passenger side and got in, joint still in hand.

Dante didn't say a word, so Paulie didn't either. He just smoked his joint, wondering when he'd be scolded or teased or told to get out of the car. Then Dante reached across and took it from his fingers, taking a deep drag and holding it in. And another before handing it back.

Paulie put up his hand. "I'm good."

"You sure?"

"Yeah, finish it."

Dante did, as silently as he'd told Paulie to get into the car, to share his joint. That's how it was with him. The necessity for words fell short of the capacity of Dante's intent. It used to drive Pandora nuts. Paulie kind of liked it. It made a comforting contrast to Donatella's frenzy.

Blowing out the last drag, he tossed the roach out the window. "I want to show you something."

"Okay."

He pulled the glistening, golden something from the ashtray, handed it to Paulie.

Holding it up to the streetlamp light coming through fogged windows, Paulie watched the crucifix sway on its chain. Mesmerizing, and momentarily beautiful. The epiphany worked its way through the marijuana haze. "Your dad's."

"Yup."

"You've had it all along?"

"In a manner of speaking." Dante took the chain from him. "I found it in a pawnshop in Jersey City, a year or so before he died."

Paulie's heart sank into his stomach.

"I never told him. I never told Mom. It seemed better to let them think Dad lost it, though I'm pretty sure they had their suspicions."

"And you're sure it was—"

"Her name was on the pawn slip."

Ffangul. "You've kept it hidden, all this time?"

"What else am I going to do with it?" Dante put the crucifix and chain back into the ashtray.

"Why are you telling me this?"

"I don't know what trouble she was in at the time, but she never had the scarol' to get it back. I only knew to go looking because one of my crew said he saw a cross like my dad used to wear in a pawn-shop near his place. He thought maybe I'd want to buy it for him, to replace the one he lost and never stopped talking about." Dante shook his head. "She never copped to it, Paulie. Not even to you, apparently, because you're a terrible liar and you really didn't know."

"That's why you showed me? To see if I knew?"

"Kind of. But more because..." Dante let go a deep breath through his lips. "I never told anyone. Not even Pan. I guess, with what happened tonight, I needed someone else to know. Someone else I trusted not to tell my mother. It'd break her heart, Paulie."

"I know."

"Maybe one day, I'll be able to give it to a grandkid or something, but if something happens to me before I can do that, you know what it is. Where it is. I realize it's a selfish impulse, but, you're . . . you know. You're *Paulie*."

No. He didn't know. Not where Dante was concerned. They'd never even been friends, even if they were sort of like brothers.

Dante's hand rested on the armrest, so near to Paulie's it would only take a pinky's twitch to touch him. Instead of taking that hand and holding it tenderly, Paulie smacked it twice, harder than necessary. "It's okay. I get it."

"Yeah? Good. Okay."

Paulie felt the dismissal coming. "What are you doing here, Dante?" he asked before it could. "Were you planning on coming up, or hoping I'd see you out here?"

"Both." He grunted. "Neither. I didn't think it through. What the fuck do I know, eh? My sister makes me oobatz'."

"Yeah, me too."

"But we love her."

"We do. Very much."

"Could you tell me why?" Dante laughed. So did Paulie. And for a moment, inside the marijuana-fogged Dodge pickup almost as old as Paulie himself, all was right in the world. Right enough for him to look at Dante, not the usual sideways sort of averted glance, but full-on. Right into the eyes looking back at him, punching Paulie in the face with a truth he'd only half believed. Until now. It wasn't a crush. It had never been a crush. Paulie loved him. Loved Dante. And always had, from the time he was the kid caught furiously making out with Donatella.

Dante's smile faded to a ghost. Confession burned Paulie's tongue. *Tell him, you big chicken.* He bit it back. It would make everything awkward for no reason, because if wishing didn't unmake someone gay, it sure as hell didn't gayify them either. Contract or no contract, he'd be out of a job. The job of dreams he'd never known he had. His means to providing for a child he never knew he wanted.

"Donatella's pregnant."

The words fell out of his mouth. Unintentional. Unplanned. Dante's ghost smile vanished. He closed his eyes, lowered his chin to his chest. He said nothing. Paulie wasn't even sure he was breathing, though of course he was. It was Paulie who held his breath.

"How far?"

"A couple of months."

"What's she going to do?"

"Have it. At least, that's what she says today."

"Fuckin'-A." Dante pushed a breath through his lips. "Fuckin'-A."

"Dante?"

It took a moment, but he looked up.

"There's something else you should know. Something I want you to know before . . . I want to . . . shit. It's mine. The baby's mine."

Another moment. "You're shitting me."

"Nope."

"You? And Dona? But you're—"

"Yeah."

"And you still—"

"Apparently."

Dante tugged his lower lip, eyes on the dashboard. "Fuckin'-A," he said again. "I guess it's better than any of the guys she's dated. You're going to do right by her."

"I'm trying to."

Dante fell silent, but his gaze never faltered. Dazed, and maybe a little relieved. Leaning across the car—Paulie held his breath—Dante opened the door on the passenger side. Finally, dismissed.

"I'm looking at houses all this week," he said. "I won't be around. I like your plans for the McBride Ave house. Framing's all done, so get started working your magic, kid. I'm counting on it being even better than the Greensway house."

The cold air coming in shivered through Paulie, cleared the condensation inside the cab. He got out of the truck, held open the door. "Okay, boss."

Kid. Boss. Paulie could almost cry. Dante pulled from the curb before he could close the door all the way.

SHE'D ALWAYS BEEN A SIDE-SLEEPER, BUT HER HIP HURT NO MATTER which side she tried to get comfortable on. Varina stared at the ceiling, her thoughts going back and again to Donatella shoving her aside, then stepping over her to get free. It hurt worse than she'd ever let her boys know. They already had too much fuel to hurl into Donatella's fire. They loved one another; they didn't necessarily like one another much. A shared past of memories, the solidarity of *famiglia,* kept them glued but they were often at odds. More so, the older they got. Her oldest closing in on fifty and her youngest thirty-five, they were only going to get older, less harmonious. All she had to do was look at herself and her own brother to understand that point of fact.

Varina took a deep breath, blew it out slowly. Maybe Ruth's family wasn't so different from the Spini-Palladinos after all. At least they were honest in their apathy toward one another. Varina fell just short of envious, staring up at her ceiling, trying to ignore the dull throbs in her body. Just short. She wanted to be anywhere but in her own bed, in her own house, in her own life. She wanted to be in Provence, sailing down the Rhône with Ruth. Now, not in October.

A creak of the floorboards in the hall tossed her from thinking. "Mom? That you?"

The door to Varina's room opened and quickly closed. Donatella slipped into bed beside her, curling into her mother just as she had when she was a little girl afraid of the dark.

"I'm sorry, Mommy. I'm so sorry."

"I know, sweetheart."

"I didn't mean to shove you. I should have helped you up. I was just so angry! I wasn't even thinking."

I.

Donatella used the word an awful lot. Her perspective always from within, pushing out; never outside of herself looking in. Varina stopped short of taking her into her arms; the wrist forbade it, and she was privately glad.

"I think," Donatella whispered, "I might need medication."

This was new. "What kind of medication?"

"The kind that stops me from being this way. Less impulsive. I need at least a few breaths between thought and action, you know?"

"There's medication for that?"

"All kinds."

Donatella snuggled closer in, still that tiny thing, afraid of the dark. Huge eyes. Pale cheeks. Vibrating without moving a muscle. Her little girl. Her Donatella. Her beloved *oops* a decade after she thought her family complete.

"When is the baby due?" she asked at last.

A soft sigh. "End of September, beginning of October."

Of course. Varina's stomach tightened. "Who? Please not Charles."

"Fucking Chucky." Donatella snorted. "No, not him. It's Paulie, Mom. The baby's daddy is Paulie."

Paulie? Relief overwhelmed. Hip. Wrist. Didn't matter. Varina pulled Donatella close and rocked her back and forth. She laughed and she cried and she kissed her daughter's face, those chicken pecks that used to make her children laugh. Paulie. Thank Jesus, Mary, and all the Saints! Paulie! Maybe this would be it, the life-changing event Donatella needed to snap her out of childhood. Into being a responsible adult. And it happening with Paulie was—strange, but who was she to say—fitting. They'd done everything together since the age of five; why not this?

"Should I take this as a sign you're not pissed and disappointed?"

"Why would I be? I'm not that old-fashioned. I know you don't have to be married to have a baby these days."

"What if I said I don't want to keep it?"

Varina's heart popped. She took a very slow, hopefully unnoticed breath. "You wouldn't have told me if you were planning on having an abortion, or giving it up for adoption."

"True."

That breath wanted to rush out of her, but Varina kept her cool. "What are you and Paulie planning to do?"

"The only thing I'm sure about is we're *not* getting married. We'll just do the Donatella and Paulie thing as best we can. Don't tell anyone yet, okay? We will, when we're ready."

"Of course not."

"Thanks." Donatella wriggled closer. "Paulie is so excited."

"He's going to be a great daddy."

"It's number one on the list of pros for having this baby. I know, beyond all doubt, she'll have at least one good parent."

"She?"

"Yup."

"How do you know?"

"I just do."

She had a fifty-fifty chance of being correct. No, that wasn't right, even if it used to be. Two genders was an antiquated notion. Dino would have scoffed, dismissed it as stuff young people came up with to give their parents agida. Tommy? Fugettaboudit. Varina found it fascinating at first, then so logical and natural she couldn't believe she'd ever thought in binary. How much richer was the world free of those constraints. Woman and man were just the opposite ends along a spectrum so varied and beautiful, Varina got teary thinking about it.

Something else to thank Paulie for, because she didn't know if she'd have ever thought such thoughts were it not that her love for him forced her mind to open. Embarrassing as it was to admit to her own ignorance, she let go of the shame of it long ago. Varina's mindsets hadn't exactly been her choice; remaining locked in them would have been. For the fact she'd shaken them off, she was rather proud.

Donatella breathed softly into Varina's neck, asleep. Her baby. Dear God, her baby. Closing her eyes and holding her closer, despite the pain making itself known, she was momentarily in the past. Dino was still alive. The boys, teens. Donatella barely in kindergarten, unhappy with her classmates and her teacher, who punished her for every little noise she made. She'd slept with her parents almost nightly, racked with trembling that wouldn't quit. Varina and Dino tag-teamed in the patience department; Donatella never knew. And then came the incident with the storm sewer drain that brought

Paulie into her life. Into all their lives. And like that, the night tremors went away. At least for a little while.

Kissing her daughter's curls, Varina winced. The hip was definitely going to cause issues for the next few days. She needed a few ibuprofen if she was going to get any sleep whatsoever. She managed to extricate herself from Donatella, who did not wake but rolled over, taking most of the covers with her.

In the bathroom, she took the pills, and texted Paulie that Donatella was with her, and would likely be all night. He texted back immediately, just a relieved emoji. Varina weighed the pros and cons, then:

Congratulations daddy
. . .
. . .
. . .

My lips are sealed, she tapped in, before his pulsating dots could become anything more.

☺
I'm here, whatever you need
I know. Love you
Love you back
. . .
. . .
. . .

Varina waited.

Dante knows. Don't tell Dona

Ok, she tapped back, though it left her feeling cold. So many secrets, some better kept. Like her trip to France that she was still taking, by hook or by crook.

Some were just more comfortable to keep.

Or seemed to be.

Until they blew up in everyone's faces.

23

a'mappin' *(ah-mapeen)*

Italian: *mappina;* "dish towel" or "rag"

A'mappin' is kind of like *ragamuffin* in American English, but leaning less toward "cute and adorable but very dirty," and more toward someone who is more than scumbari-disheveled, and closer to the point of being downright disreputable, e.g.: "Go change those ripped jeans. You look a'mappin.'"

bishgott'

Italian: *biscotto/biscotti* (singular/plural)

You might think of biscotti as those oblong, almond things sold in coffee shops from the artisanal locals to Starbucks, but in my world, bishgott' is specifically the Stella D'oro anisette toast you get in the grocery store.

Vicky was not herself.

In the weeks since first playing for Sylvia and John, the Victrola had curbed her spontaneous bursts of song, and hadn't once moved herself when no one was looking. Maybe it was because she spent more time in her sunny window, and, now that John was a frequent visitor, got played more often. Sylvia wanted to believe that, but didn't quite. There was something morose about the old demon, as if she might be miffed, or even jealous. She'd get over it. She had before, and would now, because Sylvia had no intention of indulging her.

Aside from that, Sylvia was happy. Not just happy; blissfully so. Cliché as it was, there were no other words to describe the heady feeling of being loved, of belonging. She enjoyed her Wednesdays, dinner and dancing over at Sunset Downs—a bit precious, name-wise—with a complex full of people her own age, with the same kinds of aches and complaints, joys and blessings. Being among her own assuaged the loneliness Sylvia never recognized for what it was. The need for like minds. Like bodies. Like pasts, no matter the ethnic background. It didn't hurt that being John's sweetheart—and *that* had come with many a scornful glance and whispering—among so many widowed made her somewhat of a celebrity.

Sylvia didn't even feel the need to sling guilt at her family like mashed potatoes at a diner anymore. Not at Tommy for moving to Florida, or her grandchildren for not visiting enough. She had John, her love, to talk to and have meals with, to look forward to seeing when they were apart. Sylvia Spini was never lonely. Not anymore.

Lifting the Victrola lid, Sylvia caressed the wood. Varina had recently buffed it with beeswax and lemon oil; not only did it feel like velvet, it smelled divine. She propped the lid, gave the crank a few turns, and lowered the needle onto the record already on the turntable.

Caruso, of course, singing Verdi's *Rigoletto*. "Bella figlia dell'amore." "Fairest daughter of the Graces." Sylvia could never remember the names of the other singers in the quartet. John had. He always seemed to know who sang what songs, when, and with who. Maybe because it was right there in his phone, complete with links to the things he wanted to learn about. Sylvia meant no disrespect, but who were the others when Enrico Caruso stole every stage he'd ever stepped foot upon?

Sitting in the wingback nearest the Victrola, Sylvia closed her eyes and listened. So beautiful. Sun streaming through the wavy glass. She was like a cat, warming herself in the melodic sunshine; if she could, Sylvia would have purred.

Whump! Whump! Whump!

"Nonina! It's me. Let me in. It's freezing out here!"

Another moment, hand to heart, waiting for it to cease pounding, and Sylvia pushed to her feet. She didn't need to spy Donatella through the window to know who waited upon her doorstep. Sylvia yanked open the door. "What the devil has gotten into you?"

"What?" Donatella stepped inside, kissing her grandmother's cheek as she passed. "I couldn't find my key."

"Madonn'! You could have texted me." Sylvia closed the door, then gave it an extra shove so she could twist the dead bolt. "I'd have unlocked the door before you came down."

"I forgot you have a phone."

"Where is your coat?"

"I only came down the stairs." Donatella rubbed her arms. Her hair stood on staticky end. She wore sweatpants and a sweatshirt Sylvia was certain her granddaughter had owned since high school. There was even a softball logo on the hip. And though her cheeks were rosy from the cold, she had rings under her eyes.

Sylvia put a hand to Donatella's forehead. "What's the matter with you?"

"Quit it, Non." Donatella swatted her hand away. "I'm fine. Can't a loving granddaughter come visit her grandmother on her day off?"

"You look a'mappin'."

"Gee, thanks. Listen, Nonina." Donatella lifted the needle from the record, and closed Vicky's lid. "We have a problem."

"We do?"

"Can I get a cup of tea first?"

"Of course, sweetheart. Of course." Sylvia led her to the kitchen, put the kettle on. Donatella's leg jiggled in that nervous way she had.

The kettle whistled. Sylvia put tea bags into mugs and poured the hot water. Donatella dunked her tea bag over and over, as if that somehow helped it to steep faster. Lifted it out with a spoon, wound the string around, pulled it tight no matter how many times Sylvia scolded that doing so only made the tea bitter. Donatella scooped in the sugar, splashed in the milk. Her own tea ceremony since childhood.

"So, what are you here to talk about?"

"Huh? Oh, yeah." She placed her phone on the table between them. "Take a look."

"Oh! This is our flyer." Sylvia picked it up. "I don't understand."

"It's been made into a meme on Facebook and Twitter."

"A what?"

"A me—it's a thing, Nonina. It's gone viral."

"Viral?"

Donatella groaned. "Someone took a picture of it, and put it on the internet. Others thought it was funny or whatever and shared it. Now it's been shared thousands of times, and I can't keep up with the email flooding into that email address."

"Oh. That doesn't sound good."

"Some are from men, or their representatives, as far away as California. Most are from people who have no interest in dating Mom. A lot of kooks out there, I'll tell you. However . . ."

"However?"

"If it's viral on social media, it's going to be viral locally among those who've seen the flyer for themselves, you know? It won't take long before they start putting two and two together."

"How would anyone know it's Varina?"

"She's been on a few dates." Donatella sighed. "And old men gossip, too."

"What about your nonexposure agreement?"

"First, ew. Second, it's a non*disclosure* agreement that we both knew was flimsy at best."

Sylvia had, at any rate. "Maybe she won't put two and two together."

"And maybe I'll chop off all my hair and start wearing camo."

"You're really not making a good case for—"

"She's going to be so mad!" Donatella whumped her head to the table. "We're dead."

"Angry, sweetheart. And no one's dying over this."

"Mad, angry, whatever. How can you be so cool about it?"

Because I'm too happy to be otherwise. "It's just a few men wanting to date her."

"We have to shut it down," Donatella went on. "But we can't, really, because it's out there. What do we do?"

Tea properly steeped—five minutes, according to the Galloping Gourmet—Sylvia removed the bag. Sugar. Milk. Not a ceremony but a preference. Blowing over the top, she tried to find advice or thoughts to help the situation she'd gotten her daughter into. She still wished Varina would connect with one of those grandfathers looking for love, as she had connected with John. Sylvia understood loneliness a little better, but she'd also discovered just how revitalizing love could be.

"You want bishgott'?"

Donatella sighed, slumped a little. "Sure."

Sylvia got the tin—same one she'd had since Christmas 1944, when Stella D'oro was still family-owned and in the Bronx—from the pantry. Donatella pried off the lid. She dunked until the bishgott' was mush, barely getting it into her mouth before it flopped onto the table.

"Should we just tell her?"

Tea went down the wrong pipe. Tell Varina? Not only would she be angry, she'd completely stop going out with the men who wandered into the shop, out of principle if nothing else.

"It'll die down"—*cough, cough*—"don't you think?"

"You don't know the internet, Nonina. Once it's out there, it never dies. Ever."

"Maybe delete the email address, take down the flyers, and give it a wait-and-see. A week or so."

"You think?"

It would buy a little time, at least. "It's worth a try, no? Maybe it's not as bad as you think."

"Maybe. But what if someone outs us?"

"Outs?"

"Tattles, Nonina. Forget about the flimsy nondisclosure thing. Now there'll be grandfathers going in unrehearsed."

"It sounds so tawdry when you say it out loud."

Donatella laughed. "It is, when you think about it. What were we thinking?"

What, indeed? Only, Sylvia was still thinking it. That maybe, just maybe, one of the grandfathers would turn out to be her daughter's John. "There's still a chance we'll get out of this without her ever finding out." Sylvia handed her another bishgott'. "Besides, once you clear the evidence, it'll be our word against a bunch of old men. Who's your mother going to believe?"

"The old men." Donatella laughed, a squeaky, hopeless sound. "I meant well."

"We both did. If she ever finds out, Varina will know that."

"Why does everything I do blow up in my face?" Donatella took another bishgott' from the tin, slid it closer to Sylvia. "Put these away before I eat them all."

"I have more."

"Wrong response." Dunk, dunk, mush. "Thanks, Non. You always make me feel better."

"It's the primary job of any grandmother." She took the tin back to the pantry. "Want to watch an episode of *Murder, She Wrote* with me?"

"Like we used to." Donatella's face lit up, almost banishing the dark circles under her eyes. At least, her cheeks pinked again. "Can we stream it on the big TV? Then we can snuggle on the couch."

Breaking with tradition, Sylvia acquiesced. She'd streamed a few episodes herself, sharing her love of the program with John; she still liked the grainy VHS recordings better, when she was alone and feeling nostalgic. She had to admit, that happened less and less, lately.

Donatella wrapped herself in the throw blanket on the back of the couch, tucked her legs underneath her. She'd already queued up an episode. Sitting beside her granddaughter, Sylvia put her arm around her tiny shoulders. Donatella leaned closer, closer, until her head was on her grandmother's shoulder, then her lap.

"Nonina?"

"Hmm?"

"Can I tell you something?"

"You can tell me anything, sweetheart."

Pause, then, "I'm pregnant."

Sylvia's heart zinged like it hadn't in weeks. Thoughts raced. Words wouldn't come out of her mouth, not to congratulate or scold or ask who the father could possibly be; there were certain to be several candidates. No wonder Donatella looked a'mappin'. Cioffi women didn't do pregnancy well, except for Varina and her three, uneventful confinements. But she was more Spini than Cioffi, Sylvia had always thought. A natural mother from day one. But Donatella was a Cioffi, fawn-brown curls to size five shoes to the kind of flighty that bordered on hazardous.

"Are you mad at me?"

"Angry. And no." Her mouth worked, and wasn't that strange.

"Okay, good. Mom knows, but don't tell anyone else."

"All right, sweetheart."

Donatella aimed, pressing the Play button on the remote, and there was Jessica Fletcher on the television screen, perfectly dressed and coiffed, as always. Such cheerful music for a show dedicated to murder and intrigue.

"I love you, Nonina."

The zing of Sylvia's heart soothed. "I love you, too, sweetheart."

She petted her youngest grandchild like she'd always done, when she was little and looking for comfort. Older and looking for comfort. When Sylvia was young and less inclined to calm, she panicked first, thought second. Like Donatella. She raged and she wanted and she reacted. Like Donatella. This woman, her blood, so like her in all the best ways. And all the worst. She knew better than to pepper her with questions, demand answers. So, she didn't.

shkeeve

Italian: *schifo;* "disgust"

Pronounced *skeeve* in common American English vernacular, it was an Italian word first. *Shkeeve,* often used as a verb, must be accompanied by the proper expression of dramatic disgust to get the full effect: "I shkeeve the sheets in this hotel!"

We are also an expressive people.

Related: schifozz' (shkuh-VOATZ)
Italian: *schifosa;* "disgusting," "lousy," "gross"
In case you were interested.

So how many dates this week?" Ruth, perched on a stool behind the counter, ate olives out of the little plastic container Varina had handed her to keep her fingers out of the bowl in the refrigerator case. "Four? Five?"

"Three." Varina shrugged. She had to admit, all the attention was flattering. But . . . "It's not only bizarre, it's getting irritating."

"Then why are you saying yes?"

"I don't know." Another shrug. "Dinners I don't have to cook?"

"Very funny." Ruth closed the container. "If I eat any more of these, I'll be drinking water for days, which means I'll be up all night peeing. Seriously, Varina. Why go out with all these men if you don't enjoy it?"

"I didn't say I don't enjoy *any* of them." Certainly not Harry Spaneda, Guy Santori, and Ralph Quinero, a string of men more interested in her business, her cooking, and what kind of housekeeper she was, respectively. "The worst was Mitch Valentino. Did I tell you about him?"

"The obviously new convert and acolyte to Viagra?"

"That's him. He lives in the same fifty-five-and-older community John Yu lives in. As does Ray."

"The high school jock."

"Yes."

"Hmmm . . . are you thinking what I'm thinking?"

"That my mother might have started it but these men are now passing my name around like sticks of gum?"

"Old men don't chew gum," Ruth told her. "Sticks to their dental work."

"Stop." But she laughed. "I mean it. The men coming to my store looking for items I'm mysteriously out of had to be my mother, but this? There's obviously more to it."

"Are you putting out?"

"Ruth!"

"What? I would have, at least once or twice. If it's not that, what would the men have to gossip about?"

"Well, I'm not, so there goes your theory."

"You didn't answer my question. Why go out with them at all?"

"Curiosity?"

"Do I look gullible to you?"

Varina let go a long exhale, pretending to think about it. "I did have fun with Ray."

"Ah, the one you said could replace me."

"I never said that."

"How long ago was it?"

"Three weeks, maybe?"

"Has he called again?"

"No. And that's strange, because I really thought I'd have to let him down easy. Turns out, he has even less interest in me than I have in him."

"Have you called him?"

"Why would I?"

"Knock, knock!" Ruth tapped gently on her noggin. "Because you had fun."

"I don't want to lead him on."

"Making a friend isn't promising to love, honor, and cherish," Ruth told her. "I love you, darling, but you need more friends than just me."

"Who says I don't have other friends?"

Ruth leveled that cool, blue stare.

"Fine. You're my only friend. I don't have time for a social life."

"That's because you're constantly working."

"This store won't run itself. The catering won't get done."

"Then hire help."

"No offense, Ruth, but I'm not exactly in your tax bracket. I have a house always in need of repair, my mom to take care of, the refrigerator cases need replacing, and I have to finish paying for the cruise. Not to mention coming up with the property taxes on both the store and the house every year nearly bankrupts me. There's not a spare dime in my coffers."

"Coffers?" Ruth half snorted, half laughed. "Are we in a Dickens novel now?"

"No. Just reality. This is my reality."

"It doesn't have to be."

Varina's shoulders sagged. "What does that mean?"

"It means you're in a rut, despite the cruise that's still way too far in the future to count. If you ask me, which you will if given time, so we'll just skip ahead, that's why you keep going out with men you have no interest in. You don't want a man. You want out of your rut of work, eat, sleep, work, and an occasional afternoon with a brilliant, amazing friend. You want freedom."

Varina felt the pout scrunching her lips, quelling it before it could fully form. "When did you find time to get your psychology degree?"

"Joke all you want. It's true, and you know it. They're a convenient distraction, though, if you ask me, you could be better distracted between the sheets than in restaurants whose chefs don't begin to compare to you."

She had a point. Several, in fact. "What am I supposed to do, then?"

"Oh, Varina. Isn't it obvious?"

"No, so can you just spell it all out for me? I'm too tired for thinking."

Ruth got down off her stool. She took Varina by the shoulders. "Sell. Your. House."

Water in her face. Ice down her spine. "My house?"

"Yes, your house." Ruth gave her a little shake, and let go. "What do you need a house for? Especially one that's probably worth a small fortune but in need of more updating than you can currently afford to give it."

"Where would I live?"

Ruth pointed to the ceiling.

"The apartment? It's Donatella's."

"She doesn't live there," Ruth said. "She keeps stuff there. You've said it yourself. And with the baby coming—"

"Statazeet!" Varina waved both hands at her, as if she could waft the words back into her friend's mouth. "She'll kill me if she knows I told you."

"Oh, pish." Ruth waved back. "It's not like she's going to be able to keep her secret much longer. Anyway, she's living with Paulie, and I don't think that's going to change."

"Another reason I can't sell. Where do they all go? Paulie and Donatella? My mother?"

"Paulie and Donatella are adults," Ruth told her. "Remember your vow to stop mothering them? It's not up to you to provide housing. Besides, Paulie's making good money now. I doubt they want to live upstairs from you forever."

"And my mother?"

Ruth waggled her eyebrows. "How soon before she shacks up with John?"

"Oh, stop! She'd never."

"And why the hell not? I would, if I were her."

A blooming heat cracked the ice in her spine, in her veins. Sell her house. Sell her home. Sell the place that housed most of the family memories she had.

"I can't."

"Why not?"

"It's too much."

"Too much what? Conflict? Thinking? Relief?"

"All of the above." Varina blew out a deep breath. Selling her house would solve just about everything that needed solving in her life. Financial security. Independence. That step out of mothering and into the Varinahood she'd never actually gotten to claim.

"I planted the seed," Ruth said. "Let's see what sprouts." She checked her watch. "It's five. Let's close up and go upstairs, just to get a look at the old apartment."

"Well . . ." Varina untied her apron. "I probably should make sure Donatella didn't leave any food in the fridge."

"That's the spirit."

Ruth locked the front door, turned the sign, and switched off the neon OPEN. Varina hung her apron on its hook. They left Palladino's via the back entrance, heading up the—now that she was noticing, very rickety—steps to the apartment she and Dino had lived in, where they brought Dante and Davide home. She'd loved it there, once. She'd been so happy. Buying her mother's home had been more necessity than desire, even if she'd come to love the place as her own. But, maybe . . .

She put the key in the lock. "I'm just checking for old food," she warned Ruth, "so don't get your hopes up."

VARINA TIED UP THE TRASH BAG, TOSSED IT ONTO THE LANDING WITH the others. She'd gotten the rotting food out of the fridge the week prior—poor Ruth, she'd nearly vomited when Varina opened the refrigerator door—after she let herself into the apartment without an acknowledged hope in her heart. The rest had waited until her day off. Everything was clean, if, admittedly, a bit shabby, and she no longer shkeeved opening a cabinet or drawer. It had been so long since she'd been in the apartment; age and neglect had taken its toll in her absence. She couldn't blame Donatella entirely. For the filth, yes, not the dated fixtures and appliances, cabinets and flooring. It hadn't been new when Varina lived there, way back when, and nothing much had really changed since.

"Mom?"

She stuck her head out the door. "Up here, Dante."

He came up the steps, head bent and shoulders slightly stooped. Straightening before reaching the top, Dante shoved back whatever worries troubled him. At least, he bore them better. Her son. Her Dante. He always had carried too much of the world on his back. He bounced on the top step. "These stairs need replacing."

"Among other things."

He kissed her cheek. "What're you even doing up here?"

"Cleaning."

"Why are you cleaning Donatella's apartment?"

Because she's pregnant. Because she's working her part-time job. Because it's just easier to do it myself. "Because it's mine," she said. "That is, I . . ." Saying it out loud was a lot harder than saying it in her head. She hadn't even told Ruth. "I called you over to ask you a question, not to be questioned."

"Sorry. Ask away."

Deep, deep breath. Out, out slow. "What do you think it would cost to renovate this place? Not just a face-lift, but a whole renovation, like you do on the houses you buy."

Dante's thick eyebrows arched in that way he had when he wanted to make a smart-mouth comment but thought better of the idea. "I don't know. We talking the store, too? Or just up here? Because if you're going to reno, I'd say reno it right. Plumbing and electrical."

"Didn't we do the plumbing and electrical when we fixed up the store back in the nineties?"

"That was twenty-something years ago, Mom. It should still be good, but there might be newer codes we'd have to adjust for."

"Oh. Right. Okay, worst-case scenario. What would it cost? Just ballpark it."

Dante took in the scope of the place. Varina could see the wheels turning in his head, could almost smell the churning of his thoughts. "With me and my crew doing the work? It all depends on what you want, but you're looking at anywhere from a hundred to a hundred fifty thou."

Varina paled on the inside. "And how much . . ." *Say it out loud. Say it!* "How much do you think my house is worth?"

Dante's brow furrowed. "A mortgage? At this point in your life?"

"No, not a second mortgage. I'm thinking about selling."

"For real?"

"I'm thinking," she said. "Not necessarily doing. I have a lot to consider, but what do you think the house is worth?"

"Four hundred fifty K, easy," he said. "It's what houses in your neighborhood are going for."

"Even though it needs work?"

"After the work, it'll be worth closer to seven hundred. It's not the house people are paying for. It's the location. You're in one of the most sought-after areas in Wyldale. In a few years, who knows what it'll be worth? This close to Manhattan? Whoever buys it won't just get a home, but a friggin' great investment."

"Potentially buys it. I'm not there yet, son. I don't know if I can do it."

"Yeah, I know. Lots of memories."

"It's . . ." *The truth shall set you free!* "It's not that, really. It's your sister and Paulie. And Nonina."

"Mom, come on." He put a hand on her shoulder. "I get Nonina, but Donatella is a grown woman. And she's got Paulie to take care of her."

"I know." She hung her head. "I'm trying to be more heartless."

"It's not heartless."

"Tell me you wouldn't do the same for Gabriella."

"That's different."

"It's not," Varina told him. "Your kids are your kids, no matter how old they are. Anyway. You've given me something to think about. Thanks, sweetheart. Don't tell anyone."

"You got it."

Hands in pockets, Dante moved to the front windows overlooking the street. "I always liked living here. I liked being smack in the middle of town, where all the action is."

"I did, too."

He knuckle-tapped the wall between the windows, squatted on his haunches to do the same to the floor. "It's got good bones," he said. "I think it was built in the twenties. Construction was different, back then. More craftsman than 'slap it up and hope it stands.' I bet, we start taking walls down, there's a whole lot of treasure behind them."

"Do you really think so?"

"You'd be amazed by the things we find during a renovation."

Varina bit the inside of her lip so hard her eyes teared. "I think I could get excited by this, son."

"Yeah?"

"Yes. Very. But . . . what about Nonina?"

He rubbed the back of his neck. "That's a tough one. But we could figure it out. I could put in one of those chairlift things so she didn't have to worry about the stairs."

"Ruth says she'll probably just shack up with John."

Dante laughed. He had such a deep and beautiful laugh when caught off guard. "Ruth might be right."

"Would you . . . do you think you could work up better than a ballpark for me?" she asked. "What it would actually cost to renovate up here, update what needs updating downstairs?"

"Sure, Mom." He grinned. "I thought you weren't ready? That you wanted more time to think."

"I'm not. I do. Just let me know. Okay?"

"Okay."

"What do you say we go downstairs and grab something for supper? Nonina would be so happy to see you."

"I still got stuff to do," he said. "Paulie's meeting me over at the Dunn Street house to go over some plans."

"It's already five."

Dante laughed, this time not deep or beautiful. "My days don't end at five, Mom. Can I get a rain check?"

"Sure, son."

"I mean it," he said. "How about Wednesday night? I should have some numbers for you by then."

"Really?"

"Promise."

"Nonina will be over at Sunset Downs on Wednesday," she said. "It's their dinner and dancing evening. I'll have you all to myself."

"Sounds great."

"What do you want me to make you?"

"Surprise me."

"You got it." Varina grabbed him by his scruffy cheeks, kissed one, then the other. "You're a good boy."

Dante only nodded, eyes downcast. Varina wanted to pull him

into her arms and hold him until whatever troubled him passed. She'd never been able to hold him long enough for that. Her troubled son. His stormy mind, always kept to himself.

Varina walked with him to the door, glancing over her shoulder before closing it, and locking it up tight. The little thrill chasing itself over the surface of her skin was just enough to make her smile. To hope. To want. Even if she felt a little guilty about it.

25

Achendan!

Italian: *Cento anni!;* "One hundred years!"

A Jersey-fied Italian toast for a hundred years of health, happiness, and prosperity. Often shortened to *chin-chin*.

Paulie went with her to the obstetrician, who referred them to a psychiatrist working pro bono with the clinic. Though his insurance would cover much of her maternity care, she didn't want her brother knowing anything until she was ready for him to know, which really sucked because he actually did know, but Paulie couldn't tell her that without sending her through the roof.

The docs at the clinic were overworked, but kind. Exhausted, but competent. It took three weeks to get an appointment with the psychiatrist, and they only got that because Donatella was able to take an appointment canceled by another patient.

"Go," Dante said, when Paulie told him he had to leave. "Take care of my sister."

As always. And so, he had.

The overwhelming relief of this found appointment almost overrode the anxiety of their second, hard-won ultrasound appointment Donatella had yesterday canceled. It manifested in vision-obscuring sobs tangling his stomach the whole way home to pick her up. Waiting for *it* to happen—whatever *it* happened to be—was almost worse than the actual, inevitable event. In all the years of their friendship, he'd never worried much about *it*. Donatella was Donatella. She got into trouble he usually got her out of, or she vanished for days/weeks on end only to show up on his doorstep a little worse for wear but with a story to tell. They'd laugh and he'd admonish, but she was always fine. There'd even been long stretches wherein she got a job, held it, and he could forget about the chaos long enough for it to take him by surprise when it fell.

Everything was different now. Since the incident with her mother, she'd been on her best behavior. She not only agreed to medication, should the doctor prescribe it, it was her idea to begin with. But Paulie could sense *it* coming. Donatella did, too. He could see it in the drumming of her fingers, in the constant motion of her legs.

This time, it wasn't just she who'd get into trouble or disappear, it was the baby she carried. The appointment freeing up was nothing short of miraculous, and not a moment too soon.

She was waiting outside when he pulled up to the house to get her, a huge smile on her dimpled face, and an enormous crocheted shawl wrapped around her shoulders.

"Where'd you get that?"

"Thrift store." She slid into the car, closed the door. Opened it to free up the shawl, and closed it again.

"When?"

"I don't know. Yesterday? Day before? Why?"

Paulie pulled away from the curb. He'd never seen it before. "It's pretty."

"It hides a lot." She grinned, pulling her shirt taut across her abdomen. "See? Bump!"

He did not see. Donatella was only four months along, but if she said there was a bump, there was. Paulie rubbed her belly as if she were one of his kittens. She shrieked and wriggled and punched him in the arm.

"Seatbelt," he told her, and Donatella complied.

"LITHIUM?" DONATELLA SHOOK THE AMBER CONTAINER OF PILLS. "Isn't that what they make batteries out of?"

"I'm sure it's not the same thing." Paulie checked the rearview. She'd let him sit in on all but fifteen minutes of the two-hour appointment with Dr. Beedle, the very nice psychiatrist who asked many questions, consulted the bloodwork, and assured them she'd helped many women navigate their pregnancies without incident.

"Bipolar is a scary diagnosis to hear," she'd said, "but very treatable with medication and diligence. The medication I'd like to prescribe is safe and effective while you're pregnant, though it might make you feel a little muffled, at first. Give your body time to acclimate to it. After you've given birth, we can try newer medications that you won't even notice you're taking."

Paulie'd heard the things Dr. Beedle wasn't saying within what she did. He'd also done a lot of googling in the fifteen minutes Donatella shooed him out of the room. *Scary* wasn't even close to accurate. Nothing in the happy little pamphlet in the waiting room mentioned the horrors he found. He told himself, over and over and over again, that having a word for it didn't change anything. As always, Donatella was Donatella. He was, however, gaining respect for the old adage about ignorance being bliss.

"Paulie. Yo, Paulie." Donatella shook her pills. "Have you heard a word I said?"

Stopped at a light two blocks from home, Paulie didn't even remember pulling out of the clinic parking lot. "Sorry," he said. "I was thinking about . . . about work."

Another punch in the arm. "Always work with you. When did you get so adult?"

"Not sure." *Around Christmas of this past year.* "It was a slow process."

"Well, you're getting boring, just so you know." She pointed to the ancient, red thermos tucked between his seat and the door. "You got any water in that thing?"

"Yeah, sure." He handed it over.

Donatella tipped one of her pills onto her hand. Small. Pink. Innocuous. If it worked, it would change her. It would change them. Paulie's heart crackled, tiny fissures that would heal without any scarring. If it worked, their baby would be safe.

She raised the thermos, those dimples deepening, those enormous eyes just short of teary. "Chin-chin." And swallowed the pink pill down.

mommo

Italian: *mommo;* "dumbass"

I always thought *mommo* was a shortened form of *mammone*. In my Jersey Italian world, both meant "dumbass." Apparently, *mammone* means "mama's boy." I could see where *mommo* could be connected to *mammone*, insinuating "mama's boy" is synonymous with "dumbass" (kind of like "pussy," "sissy," or the older term, "milquetoast").

stracciad' *(stra-chahd)*

Italian: *stracciare;* "to tear up; rip"

Stracciad' is different from agida and schiatanumgorp in emotion; while the latter two are in the gut, stracciad' is in the heart, and in the head. We Jersey Italians are complex creatures of deep emotions, as well as linguistically creative. And dramatic. Did I mention that already?

I always like doing the first walking tour of the day." Ruth leaned toward Varina, pointing to the place on the computer screen. "That way, you get a good idea of what there is to do, and still have time to do it."

"I'll trust you on that." Varina clicked her way to booking morning walking tours for the entirety of their trip. Ruth did the same on her laptop.

"Should we do one of the other excursions?"

"I've done them all, and I can tell you with certainty—the first time? Stick with the walking tours. If you try to squeeze too much in you don't get to actually see anything. There's something to be said for just *being* somewhere, you know? Having a cup of coffee in a street-side café in Lyon is far different from a cup and a doughnu . . . bomb'lon at Jumbaloon's."

"I imagine so." Varina's entire body fizzed like just-popped champagne. It was getting closer. Every month, there were new preparations to be made. The marketing department had it all timed perfectly, ramping up the anticipation in regular, ever more enticing intervals. Before she knew it, she'd be on a plane, flying over the ocean. If she was this excited just booking tours, she could almost fear her head exploding when she was actually boarding the ship. If she were not practical. Which she was. But maybe not as practical as she used to be, because she was going, after all, even if her daughter was to give birth at the same time. Maybe the baby would come early. Varina could only hope. There was no rescheduling the trip. And, she reminded herself—sternly—she wouldn't even if she could.

"Arles is my favorite stop along this route," Ruth was saying. "Walking around there, taking in the town where Van Gogh painted many of his masterpieces, absorbing the antiquity. It's . . . there's nothing like it. And I can't believe I'm so excited about this. I've done this trip at least a half dozen times."

Varina closed out of her computer, the thrill still wiggling through her. Knocking wood, just to be safe.

"That's a job well done." Ruth closed her own laptop, got to her feet. "I say it's time for a glass of wine. Or do you have another date you have to get ready for?"

"I told you, no more dates. I'm done. Finoot'!" She brushed her hands, one rasping off the other. "I didn't even tell you about the man who came to the shop today."

Ruth sat again. "Oh, tell, tell."

"He didn't even go through the whole farce of asking me for something I'm out of," Varina said. "He just marched up to the counter and asked me out."

"How bold. Apparently, you said no."

"I did, and you know what he said to me?"

"I can't even imagine."

"He asked me why I advertised if I wasn't interested in giving it a shot. Then he grumbled something about me thinking I was too good for him and left."

"That doesn't sound like someone your mother would send to woo you."

"Maybe I was wrong?"

"Or maybe you were right about the old geezers around here gossiping."

"I think it's time to confront her about it," Varina said. "I should have done it long ago, but then she met John and she's been so happy. I don't want to spoil anything for her."

"But this last man . . ." Ruth shook her head. "I don't know. Sounds pretty creepy to me. Maybe closing up the store to renovate will be a blessing in disguise."

"I haven't made up my mind yet."

"Oh, Varina. You know it's—"

"Dante hasn't gotten me the numbers."

Ruth's brow furrowed. "But he was supposed to do that two weeks ago."

"He was, but he hasn't been able to. It's not his fault. He's spread too thin."

"Well, that *is* his fault. He's going to make himself sick."

Varina sighed, chin propped on the heel of her palm. "I know. It worries me. His father was the same, but he had me. Dante has no one but Dante. I know he seems like the strong, silent type, but there's so much going on in that head of his all the time. I think working himself to exhaustion is the only way he sleeps at night."

"Well, that's not good."

"No, it's not. But, anyway." She straightened. "He promised me this week, without fail."

Ruth checked her watch. "It's early, but do you want to grab dinner with me?"

"I wish. Mom finally roped me into dinner and dancing over at Sunset Downs."

"Maybe you should have taken the Neanderthal up on his offer, then."

"I'd rather dine and dance over at Sunset Downs." Varina perked up. "Hey, you want to come?"

"Oh, darling, I might love you irrationally but I'm not irrational. I'll pass."

"You're a spoilsport."

"Maybe, but my inner dragon knows the limits of her tolerance." Ruth cocked her head, eyes narrowing. "Doesn't that Ray person live in Sunset Downs?"

Varina smacked herself in the head. "How could I be such a mommo? My mother? Trying to get me to see Ray again? However shall I live with my own stupidity?"

"Sarcasm is very unbecoming, dear."

"You're the most sarcastic person I know."

"On you. On me, it's ravishing. Maybe I do want to go with you now. This is getting juicy."

"I take back my invitation."

"You're a pill, you know that? Is this the way you're going to be on the cruise?"

Varina made a face at her.

Ruth grabbed her arm, hauled her from her chair. "Come on, at least let me gussy you up, if only to taunt Ray with what he can't have."

Against her better judgment, Varina let Ruth do her thing. She had to admit, she was pleased with the results. Looking at herself in the mirror, she couldn't say exactly how she looked "gussied up," only that she didn't look the way she did when she went to work, to the grocer, to visit her kids. Maybe her outfit was slightly more put together than a blouse and jeans, even if she was indeed wearing a blouse and jeans. Ruth elevated it—pearls, earrings, a belt, ballet flats—the way Varina did the simplest peasant food.

"You're amazing." She'd given her curls an extra pat.

"And I didn't even have to glue anything onto you."

Varina never remembered she didn't much like driving until she did. At least it was still light. She parked in the visitor's lot. John had been one of the first inhabitants of Sunset Downs; his townhouse was close to the dining room, pool, and clubhouse. Varina had to admit, the place had its perks. Like a perpetual cruise, though nothing she'd ever want for herself. She enjoyed Ruth, her kids, as well as her solitude. This was right up Mom's social-butterfly alley.

"Sweetheart!" Sylvia came at her, hands raised to cup her daughter's cheeks. John hung back just long enough to give her space for those chicken-kisses.

"You look beautiful, Mom." And she did, in the floral-print dress. Sylvia Spini. In floral print. No more black or navy blue except for holidays.

"Thank you, sweetheart." Sylvia stepped back. "You look *très chic*. Are you wearing makeup?"

"No. A little mascara."

"Well, you look as lovely as always, doesn't she, John?"

"Quite." John took Varina's hand. "Like her mother."

"She looks more like her father," Sylvia said. "All Spini, that one."

Varina and John exchanged an amused glance.

"Shall we, ladies?" John crooked both arms. Sylvia took one, Varina the other.

He escorted them to the table where the lovebirds held court. There were already several others seated there. The men rose as they'd been taught in their youths, bowing slightly to the ladies not yet seated. Varina smiled, meeting each pair of eyes as she was introduced. She'd never remember all their names, but they probably wouldn't remember hers either, so it was okay. Until her mother introduced, "And this is Ray, sweetheart. Ray, my daughter, Varina."

"Hello, Varina." His grin and raised eyebrows said he was no more fooled than she.

"Fancy meeting you here. Was she as subtle with you as she was with me?"

"What did she say?" her mother asked John, nudging him in the side.

The smile Varina bestowed upon her mother almost hurt to hold. "Ray and I went to school together, Mom. We had dinner a few weeks ago. Remember?"

"Oh." Sylvia's cheeks pinked. "Did I know that, sweetheart?"

Varina knew better than to believe Sylvia Spini innocent, but it was altogether possible her mother, in that moment, was guilty only of setting her up with a man her age, not with Ray in particular.

"Maybe not," she said. "I've been out an awful lot lately."

Her mother blushed a deeper shade of pink, tipping whatever genuine innocence there was off its perch. But now was not the time to ask, to accuse. Maybe when they got home.

Dinner was served family style; it wasn't terrible, if lacking in seasoning. Once Varina got over the discomfort of the situation, she decided to get over herself and enjoy the evening. Ray was a nice man, if a little old-school in the chivalric ways Varina found irritating, which was completely illogical considering she found John's like gestures with her mother absolutely adorable.

The residents were, for the most part, sweet, interested in anything and everything she said. They poured her wine they could not drink; after a few glasses, it didn't taste too bad. By six o'clock, dinner was over and Varina was tipsy. A quarter after, and the music piped in, at first slow and barely there, then louder and more dance-worthy.

"It's not Vicky," Sylvia said, "but it'll do. Shall we, sweetheart?"

John set his napkin on the table, rose without a word, and offered his hand. A few of the others joined the dancing couples, many of whom were women dancing with other women. Men were a slightly rare commodity, it seemed, though Varina would never have believed it by the number of them soliciting dates in her store. She tried to inconspicuously spot the latest one who accused her of advertising.

"So, who's Vicky?"

Ray, having taken the seat of one of the dancers, leaned in a little too close. Varina took a sip of the not-so-bad wine. "My mother's Victrola. It's haunted. Plays when it wants to. I try to keep her in the corner of the parlor, but she likes the front window. I can't tell you how many times I've caught her there. I probably should just let her stay, but it's a thing between us now. A game." She chuckled into her wineglass. "Is that an amused expression, or a horrified one?"

"A little of both." Ray slid his arm along the back of Varina's chair. She sat forward like an awkward teenager. In her periphery, her mother waved her onto the dance floor. Subtle as a monkey on stilts. Varina ignored her.

"Varina! Ray! Come dance."

"I'm sorry." She groaned. "I suppose she means well."

"Sorry for . . . ?"

"Her matchmaking. She just doesn't give up."

"No, she doesn't." His gaze averted, he had more to say that Varina was pretty certain she did not want to hear. At least, not now. But maybe he'd be better to ask than her mother, after all.

"Would you like to dance, Varina?"

Not really. But maybe she did. Just a little. Finishing the last sip in her glass, Varina took his offered hand.

OUTSIDE IN THE SPRING NIGHT, AFTER THE DANCING WAS DONE, JOHN placed a sweater over Sylvia's shoulders. He was always doing little things like that. Opening doors, pulling out chairs, taking her hand when she had to step up onto a curb, or down stairs even though he was the one with bad knees, not her. It made him happy to take care of her. It made her happy, too. Happier than she'd ever been, heaven help her. She wished she had some wood to knock.

"I had fun tonight, Mom." Varina kissed both her cheeks. "Thanks for inviting me."

"Ray is a nice man, isn't he?"

"Mom. Don't start."

"I'm just saying."

"Well, don't. I don't want to start where this will lead, here and now."

Sylvia bit back the gentle coaxing she knew wouldn't come out as gentle coaxing. Instead, she took her daughter's hand in both of hers. Chicken-kisses worked there, too. "I like to see you happy, sweetheart. I want to know you're as happy as I am."

"My happy doesn't necessarily involve finding a man. No offense, John."

"None taken, my dear."

"Ruth and I have fun all the time."

"That's wonderful, but—"

"No but's." Varina pulled her car keys from the tiny handbag Sylvia had never seen before. "We should head home."

"All right, sweetheart." Sylvia stepped away from John, closer to her daughter. Cold seeped through the sweater he'd placed across her shoulders.

"Text me when you get home. I want to know you're safe."

"I will."

"Good night, Varina." John gave a little half bow. He leaned in and kissed Sylvia's cheek, and then the other before brushing his lips to hers.

"Good night, John."

And she was walking with her daughter to the old Buick she still remembered new, when Dino brought it home, so proud. She, herself, bought the cornoot still hanging in the rearview, to keep them safe on the roads.

Varina was talking; Sylvia didn't take in a single word. She looked over her shoulder. John waved, still watching. Waiting for them to get into the car. Another Wednesday in their past. Another day ended.

Varina opened the door for her, helped her inside. Her eyesight was usually good, but not at night; she thought she saw John turn to his townhouse. Yes, there he was. A shadow moving along the walk.

"Mom? You okay?"

"I'm fine, sweetheart. A little stracciad'."

The rectangle of light that was John's front door opening appeared, and vanished, leaving only the softer glow of his fake gas lantern.

"Didn't you have fun?"

"I did, yes."

Sylvia's nose tingled and her eyes stung; her heart flipped and fluttered.

She didn't want to go.

Wednesdays were lovely, as were the lunches they shared and the dinners and the episodes of *Murder, She Wrote* that were no longer enough. Sylvia wanted breakfasts and cold feet under the covers. She wanted a closet too small for both their clothes. She wanted to share a bathroom and a bed, passing gas, and a laundry hamper. Next month, in May, she would be ninety-three; how much longer could she possibly have to waste?

"Turn around, sweetheart."

"Did you forget something?"

"There." She pointed to a driveway. "Turn around there."

"Okay, okay."

Varina navigated the turn, pulled back up to John's townhouse. The fake gas lantern still glowed. Sylvia opened the car door.

"I can get whatever it is for you, Mom," Varina said. "You wait here."

"No, sweetheart. You can't." Sylvia stepped out; how nice it would have been to have John's assisting hand. She didn't need it, but she did like it an awful lot. Leaning back into the car, she told her daughter, "It turns out, I'm not too old for adventure after all."

"Huh?"

"Go home, Varina." She closed the door. It didn't close all the way, but Sylvia didn't think she had the courage to open it up again and not get back in. Sweater drawn closer, she walked the walk, she climbed the steps, she knocked on the door. She did not, would not, look back.

John opened it, his smile creating those chasms she loved more than she feared whatever gossip might come tomorrow.

She asked, "Do you have a spare toothbrush?"

He answered, "A whole drawer full of them."

"And pajamas?"

"I'm sure we can find something."

"Okay. John?"

"Yes?"

"Just so you know, this isn't just tonight. This is always."

Chasms and chasms she could fall into forever. Sylvia slipped her hand into his. John stepped aside, and closed the door behind her.

If Varina lingered, Sylvia didn't know it, and neither did she care.

IN AN AGING HOUSE IN WYLDALE, A DAUGHTER SAT ALONE AT HER kitchen table, the same kitchen table where she'd fed her husband and children breakfasts. Formica. Vinyl chairs. The yellow walls dulled by years and years of olive oil and oven spills. She smiled a private smile, wondering what a ninety-something first night together looked like, and immediately banished it from her brain. But not the smile. Not the smile.

And in a little brick townhouse, in the Sunset Downs complex of Fort Lee, New Jersey, an old man and an old woman slept. Her hand on his chest. His chin resting on the top of her head. They fit together like worn puzzle pieces, frayed smooth about the edges. A first night. A forever night. For however long forever lasted.

minga *(ming-ya)*

Italian: *mingere;* "to urinate"

This one can mean so many things, but it all comes down to an impolite way to denote frustration, or yet another derogatory way to show your disdain for a person. So, it can mean "Balls! Damn! Shit! Slut! Asshole!" or it can just mean you're really pissed off. Or it can be more casual, like, "Minga! You should have told me you didn't like lasagna!" It's all in the intent . . . and hand gestures. Hand gestures can change everything.

Stugots!

Italian: *Questo cazzo!;* literally, "This cock/dick/ putz!"

Another imaginative way to say, "Fuck it!" For some reason, *ffangul* will get you smacked, or your mouth washed out with soap, but *stugots* doesn't. Necessarily.

M inga! Be careful with that thing! It's older than your grandmother!"

Varina stood, hands on hips, watching the old demon being loaded into the bed of Dante's truck with a heavier heart than she ever imagined she'd have. Vicky's place in the window wasn't just empty, there seemed to be a hole in the air all around it. Varina would not cry, even if tears were trying desperately to escape her stubborn ducts.

Once she was secured in the truck, Dante handed the two young men each a twenty for their efforts. "You got the address. Deliver it inside, you got me?"

"Got you, boss."

"And I hear you took a tip from my nonina, I'll dock it from your pay."

"Got you, boss."

So young, these boys working for her son. Gruff as he was with them, he trusted them enough to do the job, in his beloved truck, no less. Reaching into the cab, Dante took something from the center console, slipped it into his pocket. He handed one of the boys his keys. "No joyriding."

"In this thing?" the kid scoffed.

"Stugots." Dante smacked him upside the head, but he was smiling. "See you back at the warehouse. One hour."

The boys got into the truck, turned it over, and backed out of the driveway. Varina kept her arms crossed so she wouldn't wave Vicky good-bye.

"I guess this takes care of your Nonina issue."

She blinked away the emotion, brought her son into focus. "Huh?"

"Nonina, going to live with John. You don't have to worry about that, if you still want to sell the house."

"Oh, right. Yes." She uncrossed her arms. "Sorry, son. I'm distracted. This happened so fast. I haven't had time to process."

Dante fidgeted from foot to foot. "Can we go inside a minute?"

Varina checked her watch. She'd closed the store for an hour after the lunch crowd to see the Victrola off; she needed to get back before the dinner rush.

"It'll only take a minute."

"Of course, sweetheart. Come on in."

Up the back steps, into the kitchen that still smelled of last night's supper—Mom's last as a resident of the house—Varina's feet felt heavy. Mired. She was happy for her mother, and slightly angry with her. One minute there—an always, a constant—and now over in Fort Lee, living with a man she'd met only a few months ago. Change was good, but hard when everything had been the same for so long.

"You know this place was built in the twenties?" Dante's hand slid up the kitchen wall. "A lot of this is all lath and plaster. And the wavy-glass window? It was probably part of another house. I bet the builders salvaged it from some demo they did, from a place built before the turn of the last century, before they could do big sheets of glass in a factory. That's why it has all the panes the upstairs windows don't. It's worth a small fortune."

"Maybe that's why Vicky loved it so much." Varina smiled back the stinging in her nose, her eyes. "She is a bit of a snob."

Dante chuckled, more of a grunt lost in thought. "I know you're pissed at me for putting you off," he said, "but there's a reason for it."

"I'm not upset with you, son."

"I want to buy the house."

Varina staggered, just a little. She pulled out a kitchen chair and sat down. "You? Want to buy this house."

Dante sat opposite her. "I'm buying houses all over Wyldale and renovating them," he said. "Granted, nothing this expensive. I don't have the capital for that yet, but this won't be to resell. I want it for me."

"For you."

"Are you just going to keep repeating what I say?" He laughed. "Yeah, for me. I didn't want my house when Pan moved out, but neither did she, and I wanted Gabriella to have her same home to come to, whenever I got her. Now she's in college and . . ." He pushed fingers through his hair. "Look, Mom, it's all kind of falling into place, don't you think? Nonina meeting John, Donatella moving in with Paulie and . . . all that, you thinking about selling the house and renovating the apartment. And me, doing houses now instead of commercial shit. I want to buy this house, make it mine."

"Do you . . ." She reached across the table for his hand. "Son, do you have this kind of money?"

"No." He laughed. "But I got a plan, and that's why I've been putting you off. I had to work all the numbers, figure it all out." Dante took both her hands. "So, here's the deal. Being that it's between you and me, you can give me a better deal on the house because there's no Realtor involved, see? That saves around twenty K right there. Then, I do the work on the apartment and store, and we deduct the cost of that from the sale of the house. I get a mortgage I can manage outside of the business, you get a newly renovated apartment and store, plus a nice bit of cash to retire on. We all win."

"We all?"

"Yeah, you, me, Paulie and Donatella."

"How do they fit in?"

Dante leaned back in his chair, his smile genuinely happy rather than sarcastic or weary. "I know you'd never just boot them out," he said, "so I found an option. I got this duplex on the other side of town, closer to the warehouse. I bought it a long time ago, before Uncle Tommy even decided to skip it down to Florida. It's outdated, but in good shape. I just never got around to it. Not much history to it, you know? I figured they can live in it while I reno the house. Then if they want the place, I'll let Paulie buy it off me. Hold the mortgage."

All falling into place, indeed, with a lot of manipulating on her son's part. "And what would you have done with Nonina, had she not moved in with John?"

"Simple." Dante shrugged. "She'd have lived with me. It's about time you got to take care of just you, you know?"

Oh, yes. She did know. And now Dante would become the Varina of the family, just like Sylvia had taken the role, way back when. Only his Nonina had met a man and fallen in love. She would likely spend the rest of her life in Fort Lee, in a fifty-five-and-over community seemingly invented for her. Paulie had always looked out for Donatella; he always would. And Varina was free to do whatever she liked, for the first time in her almost-seventy-one years.

"Numbers," she said. "I want actual numbers."

"I'd never cheat you, Mom."

She smacked him from across the table. "Mammone! Of course you wouldn't. But you'd cheat yourself. Now I need numbers and a time frame. It needs to be done before the end of summer."

"You going somewhere?"

She'd almost blown it. Accidentally on purpose? In either case, Varina chickened out. "Where would I go, eh? With the baby coming . . . don't look at me like that. I know you know. Paulie told me. But your sister doesn't know you know so keep it zipped. Anyway, I don't want to be in chaos when the time comes. Now about that time frame . . ."

"You're up to something."

"Don't be fresh. I'll give you such a paliad'."

"I'm shaking." Dante laughed. "You going to break another wooden spoon on the counter?"

She smacked him. Dante barely dodged. All those broken spoons slammed on the counter rather than their little butts. Only the worst kind of person hit their kids, as far as she and Dino were concerned, even if both her parents had done so.

The grandfather clock gonged the third quarter. Varina instinctively checked her watch. "I have to get back to the store," she said. "Get me all those numbers. If it's all good, I want to start yesterday. Are you sure you want to do this? Definitely sure? Positively?"

Dante grinned like his father used to, when amused but too tired or kind to point out what amused him. "I'm sure."

Were she the squiggling kind, Varina would have squiggled in her chair, maybe let out a happy little giggle. But she wasn't. Instead, she got up from her chair and hugged her son. "You're a good b . . . man, Dante."

He melted into her, just for a moment. Like he had when he was a boy too cool or too proud for his mother's embrace, but still needed it like air. "I'll get the ball rolling." He rose from his chair, out of her embrace. "I have to rearrange my schedule a little, but my crew can handle it."

"And the finances?"

"Don't worry about the finances. I got a good accountant who'll figure it all out."

Following her son to the door, Varina managed not to skip or twirl. She waved; Dante didn't see her, backing out as he was, arm along the back of the seat, even though he had one of those rearview cameras. And he was gone, the driveway empty, spring puddles darkening the pavement.

"What just happened?"

Dante was buying the house. She was moving back into the apartment, fully renovated and built to suit. And there would be money in the bank, plenty of it, for the first time in her entire life. Varina could hire help. Travel. Maybe not as extravagantly as this cruise in the fall. But travel. And she had Ruth to do it with, a woman she hadn't even known the same time last year, but who had become the best friend she'd ever had, aside from Dino. In fact, the only actual friend she'd had since . . . could it be? Frannie Giordano, way back in high school?

She pulled the door closed behind her. Trotting down the steps she'd been successfully trotting down most of her life, she tapped Ruth's icon on her cell phone. It rang only twice.

"Hey stra—"

"I just sold my house . . ."

scootch/scorchamend

Italian: *scocciatore/scocciamento;* "pest/brat"

While a scootch is a pest, a scorchamend is the next level of
annoying, the kind that could earn the shoe, or the smack upside
the head. The English word *scorch* seems to be involved as a
"sounds similar and can lend to the same meaning" coincidence.
Scooch (without the *t*) means to move over a little. There is a
difference, though how that came to be, I have no idea.

mooshad'

Italian: *ammosciato;* "limp," "droopy," "wilted"

Used to describe overcooked pasta, the general feeling of being
under the weather, as well as a rumpled appearance. It's a
versatile word.

T ake these back up to Joey." Paulie handed the ring of stain
     samples to the runner. "Tell him we're doing the clear coat. If
I see even a whisper of color added to those floors, I'll hand him his
goolies on a platter."

"Got it, Paulie."

It was good to be the king. At least, the crown prince.

The renovation of Palladino's had begun before April became
May. The whole building had good bones, built in an era of quality
over expediency. Of course, the plumbing and electrical needed updating, but aside from water damage caused by ancient refrigerator
units, and asbestos tile under the linoleum necessitating professional eradication, the place only needed spiffing up. The refriger-
ated cases were, at this point, vintage and way too cool to toss, thus
they were refurbished at a slightly greater but totally-worth-it cost
than buying new. They went aesthetically well with the granite
counters, the period-appropriate tile along the back wall, and the
wire racks replacing the old, less sanitary wooden ones Varina and
Dino had gotten for free from the Wyldale library, renovated back in
the late eighties. Easy stuff.

Lifting the linoleum had revealed old, chestnut wide boards, often used back in the day because of the abundance of chestnut trees
in the area, making it even cheaper than pine. Now nearly extinct,
chestnut was worth a small fortune. It also cleaned up beautifully,
giving Palladino's the sort of old-world charm that appealed to both
those who remembered the days of small, neighborhood grocers, as
well as the kitschy, younger crowd campaigning to buy local, buy
small. They were all buying, or would be when Palladino's reopened,
and that was the important part.

While renovation continued in the store, demolition happened
in the apartment. The chestnut floors downstairs were present under the layers and layers of flooring upstairs. The crew discovered

many other treasures during demolition, like the huge, plate glass window still mostly proclaiming—

Bertie's Radio and Television Repair
You break it? We'll fix it!
Est. 1941

—that had been covered up. Paulie loved it even more than the chestnut floors. He hoped Dante and Varina let him restore it rather than have it scraped off.

The crew had also found a snug but sturdy cage elevator—probably installed to more easily haul those massive radios and television sets to the second floor—behind a wall, giving access to the shop below. Because it was already part of the structure, it was grandfathered in, with provisions Dante understood but Paulie didn't bother about. The thing was fantastic, and it—as well as the plate glass window—inspired Paulie's entire design. They'd still redo the stairs, to code, on the outside of the building, but it was good to know Varina would have the elevator. For groceries, not because she would eventually age out of all those steps. Of course not.

Working daily with Dante, learning the ins and outs of construction from a higher level, calluses and blisters, sawdust and Sheetrock dust in every crack and crevice of his body, made Paulie happier than he'd ever been in his life.

At least, professionally.

"Yo, Paulie," Dante called from the "backyard." It wasn't a yard yet, only broken up pavement and cement, but it would be. Small, but green. *Ish.* If there was money left, Paulie had plans. A week, tops, and they'd be able to call the store finished. Varina could reopen, and work on the apartment could go full steam ahead. Brushing Sheetrock dust from his hair, he met Dante outside.

"What's up?"

"Is this the right tile for the back wall?" Dante held out the Pepto Bismol–pink subway tile.

"That's disgusting."

"I thought so. Well, they just delivered a whole pallet of this shit."

"Obviously a mistake. I ordered red, white, and green."

Dante leveled a glance, eyebrows furrowed.

"I'm kidding."

"Scorchamend!" He smacked the back of Paulie's head. Gently. "You want to deal with this?"

Paulie rubbed the spot, checking the invoice, just to be sure. Yes, there was his order—six-by-twelve. White and navy. Forty-eight square feet. And the name of the person who packed the order.

Pat McGinty.

Paulie went cold. Head to toe. Blood to bones. He handed the invoice back to Dante. "The pink tile wasn't a mistake."

"But you just said—"

Tapping the invoice, he waited for Dante's squint to make out the name.

"You gotta be fucking kidding me."

"Nope."

Dante crushed the invoice in his hand. "I got this." And blew out of the yard like an avenging angel.

Putting the tile back on the pallet, Paulie wouldn't give in to the lump rising in his throat, and the ire in his gut. No matter how much the Palladinos loved him, respected him, accepted him, he was still the fanook. Outsider. Other. He was certain his old pal Pat thought his joke funny. Innocent. He had to know Dante wouldn't. He and Davide had beaten the snot out of him, back in the day, for the "joke" gone too far that left thirteen-year-old Paulie with his pants down and his ass smacked raw by the varsity basketball team. McGinty, in his second attempt during senior year, after two attempts during junior, had been the captain. The Palladino boys made an example of him. What Dante probably didn't know was Pat McGinty never forgave Paulie for that, and likely never would.

"Guess you guys can knock off early," he told the tilers waiting for the verdict.

"How'd that happen?" Stan-the-tile-guy stretched, hands pressed to the small of his back. He'd been with Spini and Son since the elder Mr. Spini's days of old-school Italians, Poles, Irish, who the ever-changing working class of Wyldale couldn't shake off.

"Somebody made a mistake," Paulie said. "Dante's getting it sorted out."

"Okay. Guess that's a day, then. See you tomorrow, Paulie."

"See you tomorrow."

Stan's grandsons—both slightly older than Paulie—followed him out of the yard. They'd both been on that varsity basketball team that smacked him raw. Now he got to tell them what to do, when. Paulie was pretty sure they both knew the pink tile had been no mistake, but they hadn't laughed. Old dogs could learn new tricks, he supposed. Or they'd learned their lesson well enough, way back then. Either way, Paulie couldn't help wondering if they laughed, even under their breaths, over the pink tile.

What did he care about Pat McGinty, anyway? Mammone. Always had been, always would be. Varina taught him, "They can only upset you if you allow it," and though it seemed a bit simplistic, he believed her. Because she loved him. They all loved him. And he loved them back, even old Stan and his asshole grandsons who may or may not have chuckled under their breaths. It was kind of funny. Funnier was imagining McGinty cowering before Dante's fury. Dante, who'd hopefully outgrown the Neanderthal impulses that resulted in bloody knuckles and noses, financially thrashing

him into a sloppy ball of simpering goop. He'd take his business to
Home Depot or Lowe's before giving Pat another dime. Pat, who
had to have known there would be consequences. Grown-up consequences way worse than getting the snot beaten out of him.

Whistling rather happily, Paulie Vittone headed home. Dante
would get it all taken care of, including a contrite-if-not-sincere apology. It really was good to be someone in authority, untouchable in his
own right and not because everyone was afraid of the Palladino brothers. He had to give Dante credit for the whole avenging angel thing,
for seeing his talents, for putting them to good use, but without those
talents, he'd still be sweeping sawdust and nailing up studs, teased
when no one was looking, when he took it rather than tattled.

"You here?" Paulie chucked his keys onto the sideboard. "Donatella?"

Something grunted, and he was pretty sure it wasn't one of the
cats. He followed the sound and found her on the couch, a blanket
over her head.

"Hey." He lifted the blanket. "It's five in the afternoon. Have you
been up yet today?"

"Vaffangul."

"Nice."

"You know I worked this morning."

Oh, right. She had. Paulie sat at her feet. "You hungry?"

"Starving. I'm always starving."

He patted her butt. "Come on. I'll make us eggs or something."

"I want pizza."

"Pizza gives you heartburn."

"I don't care. I want it." Donatella pulled the blanket from her
head. "Please?"

Rings under her eyes, pale complexion, hair like a bird's nest.

Adorable and fragile and pathetic in ways only Donatella Palladino could be. Paulie sighed. "You're going to curse me later." But he pulled out his cell and ordered her favorite pizza—kalamata olives and onions, slightly overcooked—from Mommo's. "It'll be here in twenty minutes."

"Fabulous." She sat up, tried smoothing down her hair. "Everything okay? You look mooshad'."

"I look mooshad'?" He laughed. "Have you looked in a mirror lately?"

"You suck. I feel like shit."

Paulie put her feet in his lap. "Maybe it's time for you to stop working."

"No way. I've saved up a lot of the money I owe my mom. I want to pay her back before I drop this kid."

He couldn't fault her. "Just be careful, okay?"

"I'm fine."

He took a mental breath, weighed the risk. "Did you reschedule the ultrasound?"

"I will."

And he let that mental breath go, pulling off one of her socks so he could knead the ball of her foot.

"Oh, that's so good." She moaned. "You should have been a massage therapist. Or a pedicurist."

"Not a podiatrist?"

"You'd make a terrible doctor." She wiggled her toes. "No patients. Get it?"

"Oh, very funny. Remind me later to laugh." He took off the other sock. "Dante mentioned that duplex again today. We really have to start thinking about moving. Demo on this place'll be starting in a few weeks."

"We have time."

"We don't." He held on to her foot when she'd have bolted off the couch. "We have to make a decision."

"You make it." She yanked her foot away. "Like always."

No sense asking what she meant. Today was apparently a *you made me do this* day. He hated those, but he was used to them. Resting his hand, palm up, on the back of the couch, he waited. And waited. She would take it. She always did. And she claimed he had no patience.

"Sorry."

"Maybe next time, don't say the first thing that pops into your head and avoid the apology."

"The stupid medication was supposed to keep that from happening." She rubbed her face with both hands. "It just makes me feel like I'm underwater. My whole face itches all the time. I hate it."

"It's too soon for you to have acclimated to it." Though he'd seen the difference already. Donatella was calmer; also perpetually sleepy. But she didn't vibrate with all that pent-up motion anymore. She didn't twitch in her sleep. "You're doing great."

"I'm trying, Paulie. I really am."

Same song, different day. But she meant it. She always did. Paulie slumped lower into the couch, rested his head back. Eyes closed, he caressed the back of her hand with his thumb. In all their years of friendship, they'd never spent as much time together, never actually lived together for more than a couple of weeks here, a month there. The breaks from her had been, he realized, part of their success. They hadn't really been apart since Christmas. Grateful as he was for that fact, Paulie was mentally exhausted. He could only imagine what it was like for her. His caged, pregnant Donatella.

"What if I fuck up our kid? Turn her into a psycho or something."

Paulie lifted his head, doze falling away. "You won't."

"What if she turns out to be hell on wheels, like me?"

"You're not hell on wheels."

Donatella snorted. "What happens if you fall in love and want to move away from here?"

I'm already in love. "Never happen."

"What if I do?"

"We can't plan for all the what-ifs, Don. How about we deal with them if they ever happen?"

"It doesn't help for you to make sense. You know that, right?" Donatella shrugged deeper into the couch, pulled the blanket around her shoulders. "Don't pay attention to me. I'm being a bitch."

Paulie kissed her hand. "You're growing a human," he told her. "Kind of a big deal. You get a pass."

"And what about the rest of the time?" She didn't pull away, only stared until the sorrow in her eyes got too heavy to hold up. "Sorry. Sorry. Just—"

The doorbell rang. Neither of them moved. Paulie's heart broke for her. And it ached for himself. Everything was changing, and it wasn't only about the baby she carried, even if his whole world hinged upon that reality. Finally, she pulled her hand gently from his. "Pizza's here."

Paulie answered the door, paid for the pizza. How was it possible to love someone who hurt you, who frightened you, who was almost as big a danger to your happiness as she *was* your happiness? He had no answer, and likely never would. There was only now, the two of them in the apartment with his cats, about to eat pizza she would curse him for later.

29

Bondanza!

Italian: *abbondanza;* abundance

See that exclamation point? When speaking aloud this word in Jersey Italian, it's always said with that emphasis of triumph and joy.

Basta!

Italian: *Abbastanza!;* "enough"

It means exactly the same in the formal, and the pidgin. Jersey Italian chops off the first two letters, and the last three, because that's what J.I.s do.

Ninety-three.

In eight hours and a few minutes, Sylvia Spini-née-Cioffi-kind-of-Yu would be ninety-three years old. They'd celebrated, she and John, with all their friends in the dining room. As fortune had it, Wednesday dinner and dancing coincided nicely. John asked the kitchen staff if they would see to a cake, and they'd obliged. It was a party of parties, even without her children, grandchildren, and great-grandchildren. She hadn't even invited Varina. Her daughter was always so suspicious of her intentions, and she still didn't even know about the grandfathers-looking-for-love scheme. Benedeeg', the store being closed for two weeks seemed to have put an end to it. She and Donatella were off the hook.

There'd be a family party come the weekend, when everyone would be able to attend, even Gabriella, coming home especially for the occasion. Tommy wouldn't be there, and that broke Sylvia's heart just a little. How many birthdays did she have left, after all? But it was hard to be too heartbroken when she was so happy, and it was so much easier to understand her son's desire to live his own life, his way, even if it was a simple plane ride to make his mother happy on her ninety-third birthday.

It was nearly nine, but she was exhausted. Dancing always did her in. Happiness could be exhausting, too, like sorrow could be. And loneliness. Comfortable in her favorite chair, feet up on the hassock, Sylvia basked in the bondanza that was her life with John.

She'd enjoyed every decadent moment of the scandal moving in had caused. The whispers and the shushed gossip. The disgruntled widows who'd had their sights set on John Yu. No wedding, no rings, no ceremony at all. Living in sin made Sylvia feel bold and adventurous but not in the least sinful. The younger generations were right: true love was never sinful. Besides, the only monetary contribution she could make to the household came from Joseph's social security benefits; at her age, giving them up for propriety's sake was foolish. As far as she and John were concerned, they were husband and wife, and would be until the end of their days. That was enough. It was more than enough. It was everything.

"My love?" John came toward her, cell phone in hand. "I believe you got some texts while we were out."

"Oh, thank you. I didn't realize I'd left it at home."

"Are you coming to bed?"

"In a minute," she said. He nodded, that always-smile on his lips, and ambled off to their bedroom to turn down the covers and fill a glass of water he'd leave on her side table. Sylvia scrolled through the texts, all from Donatella.

7:46 Hey, Nonina!

8:02 You must have forgotten your phone when you went to the dining room.

8:13 Back yet?

8:34 You're out late, aren't you? LOL

8:37 Should I be worried?

8:41 I just called Mom. She's not answering either. Are you okay?

8:50 Hellooooo! Earth to Nonina!

Sylvia checked the time. Eight fifty-eight. She responded:

I'm fine. You still awake?

The little dots she'd come to understand meant someone was typing a response appeared immediately. Then they stopped, and Sylvia's cell phone chimed—wind chimes she'd chosen for the coming summer.

"Nonina?"

"Hello, sweetheart. Sorry I worried you. It's Wednesday. Dinner and dancing."

"Was Mom there, too?"

"Not this time. She must be out with Ruth."

"Oh, whew. It's okay. I was just watching a movie and thought it was funny. You'd like it."

"Would I?" She wouldn't. Sylvia never liked the movies Donatella suggested. Dark, gritty humor was not her thing. Always too much supposedly funny violence. "Text me the title. I'll look into it."

"Okay." Pause, then, "Did you ever feel like there were bees buzzing under your skin? When you were pregnant, I mean."

"Not when I was pregnant, no."

"But otherwise?"

Otherwise? Sylvia remembered. "Why do you ask, sweetheart?"

Silence.

"Donatella?"

The voice that answered back was small, trembling. "I think there's something wrong with me."

"There's nothing wrong with you."

"No, there is. I know there is. I've been *diagnosed*. But I think it's staying in one place too long, you know? I haven't since I was a kid. You remember what I was like back then."

Always raging, crying, rebelling. "You're all grown-up now," Sylvia told her. "You're going to have a baby in a few months. Give it time."

"What if it doesn't help?"

"It will."

"How do you *know*, Nonina?" Louder now. Wobbling. "How?"

She took a deep breath, and from the exhale tumbled, "I was a lot like you, sweetheart."

"You were oobatz'?"

"Basta, eh? You're not crazy. You're a wild soul. That's all."

"You were? A wild soul?"

"Is that so hard to believe?"

Donatella laughed, still wobbly. "No offense, Nonina, but yes."

"Well, I was. I wanted to be a dancer. I wanted to travel the world. But I got married and had my children and that need to fly died away."

"That sounds awful."

"Do you think I had an awful life?"

"Well . . . no."

"We make sacrifices for those we love, just like you will for that little one you've got in your belly. You'll see."

"I hope you're right. I don't want to be this way."

It broke Sylvia's heart to hear her say so, but John was in bed, waiting; heartbreak was indeed hard to come by. And, besides, she didn't want to think the thoughts crowding now inside her almost-ninety-three-year-old brain. Old days. Long-ago days. Heartbroken days of bees under her skin, a suitcase on the seat beside her, and the way ahead that went backward instead.

"Nonina?"

"Huh? What? I wasn't sleeping."

"You were snoring."

"I was not."

Donatella laughed softly. "You go to bed. I was just bored. You're always my go-to."

That made Sylvia smile. Her Donatella. "Where's Paulie?"

"Working late. As always." She groaned. "It's so annoying. It's always one last thing he has to finish so the next day isn't as crazy-busy, but the next day always is, in a different way, in a different house, because no one disappoints the great and powerful Dante

Palladino, especially Paulie, who has a huge crush on him. But don't tell him I said that. He gets pissy."

Sylvia didn't like the word *pissy*. It sounded disgusting, and she was never quite sure what it actually meant. "Are you still working at the bakery?"

"Barely. I'm supposed to stay off my feet as much as possible. Swollen ankles."

"Oh, that's too bad. Keep those feet elevated."

"I'm trying. It's just so boring, being cooped up here all the time. The stupid meds I'm taking make me too lazy to do anything productive."

"Medication?"

"Just something to keep me from going completely nuts. It's not the best option for me, but it is the best option for the baby. Safe, you know. But it makes me so . . . blah. I should just stop taking them. I don't think they're helping. I still have bees under my skin, but I'm too lazy to do anything about it."

"Maybe that's the point of them, sweetheart."

Donatella snorted. "Yeah, maybe." And a long sigh. "Welp, I guess I'll get back to my movie."

"Don't forget to text me the title," Sylvia told her. "Maybe John and I will give it a try."

"Will do. Night, Nonina."

"Good night, sweetheart."

Sylvia tapped out of the call, her crooked fingers shaking just a little, the way they did when she was tired after a long and happy day. All her days were happy now. Few of them were as long as Wednesdays. She pushed to her feet, switching off lights as she passed through the house and to her bedroom, where John was already in bed, asleep. He'd left the bathroom light on, so she'd be able to see. On her bedside table, that glass of water on the thick-paper coaster, a free gift from a charity he gave to. John gave ten dollars to any charity that asked for a donation. He was so good. So good.

Sylvia changed into her pajamas, washed her face, brushed her teeth, and got carefully into the turned-down bed. Lying on her side, hands folded under her cheek, she watched the adorable acrobatics of John's sleeping face. His mouth moved as if he were speaking. His cheek twitched. Under the covers, so did his legs. For a man as peaceable as he was during waking hours, his body was ever in chaotic motion while he slept. It had taken a little getting used to, but Sylvia had, and now she was grateful for it. At their ages, easy proof that the person lying next to you was still breathing was a good thing.

Placing her hand on his abdomen pulled a soft and silent sigh from her core. Sylvia touched him because he was hers, because she could, because she wanted, more than anything, to memorize the sensation she'd never taken the time to memorize when it was Joseph who was hers. She'd forgotten, within weeks of his death, what the stubble of his chin felt like. The heft of his hand. The softness of his belly.

Sylvia Cioffi-Spini-kind-of-Yu had made mistakes in her life. In her marriage to Joseph. With her children. But she'd made amends, and none of them but Joseph had been any the wiser, because they'd cooked up a story, she and he, about a surprise spa week won in a silent auction at a Saint Joseph's table the Easter prior. Everyone gossiped behind their backs; there'd been no spa, only a sanitorium for women suffering hysteria. Everyone knew how prone to drama Sylvia had always been. They let that misconception ride. It was better than the truth. That Sylvia Spini had run away from home, abandoned her children, her husband. She'd come home, where she belonged, despite the bees under her skin and her feet longing to fly. They'd made a pact to never tell. He wouldn't squelch the wild ways he fell in love with, she would behave enough to let him save face, and they would dance every night, after dinner was done, the children sleeping, just like they used to.

Past mistakes were just that—past. Sylvia would not make them again. And so she lay beside John, watching him, her own eyes fluttering, her own breath slowing, feeling for the next twitch.

sculamacaroon' *(shkoo-la-ma-ca-roon)*

Italian: *scolare la maccheroni;* "drain the macaroni"

In Jersey Italian, sculamacaroon' is an item, not an action: specifically, a colander. I thought my dad made this word up, along with many other words I came to realize were part of the pidgin. *Sculabast'* (*scolare la pasta,* or *scolapasta*) is probably more familiar to most, but I never heard of it until researching this.

e'stupeed

Italian: *essere stupido;* "to be stupid"

By now, you get the drill on the hows and whys of pronunciation, unless you're e'stupeed.

S croll down to the little longship icon and click on it."

Varina squinted. "There are at least six longship icons. Which one?"

"The one at the bottom of the video we were just watching, choochie."

"It's *chooch*."

"Oh. I thought it was choochie."

"It's not. And don't call me chooch. It's not nice."

"You call people chooch all the time."

"It's different when I do it. Oh, I got it." Clicking on the appropriate icon, the recipe for the coq au vin featured in the video appeared. "I'm making this. Want to come over for dinner on Sunday?"

"Isn't it *famililia* dinner Sunday?"

"*Famiglia,*" Varina corrected, clicking her way to printing the recipe. "Nope. Those are over. I can't have them all in the apartment. It's just too small. And Dante's already started demo on the house."

"Well, it is his now. Lock, stock, and barrel."

"It is, indeed." Waiting at the printer as if it would print faster if she did, Varina willed her heart to beat as practically as her brain. "It's time, anyway. I'm tired of pulling teeth to get them all to come. If my kids don't care enough to see one another outside of holidays, they don't."

"Is this part of the vow to stop mothering everyone?" Ruth asked.

"I suppose."

"Kudos, darling. I'd love to come on Sunday. What time?"

The door chime jingled.

"Do I hear another geezer coming to woo you?"

"Funny. No, it's been blessedly quiet. Maybe I don't have to confront my mother after all. Oh, crap."

"What?"

"It's Ray. Gotta go. One o'clock on Sunday." Varina tapped out, slipped the phone into her apron pocket. "Hey, Ray. How've you been?"

"Hello, yourself, Varina." He turned a slow circle. "The place looks great."

"I'm really happy with it. I haven't seen you here in a while." In fact, she hadn't seen him since the Wednesday dinner and dancing. "What brings you in?"

He patted his belly. "I had an oolee for ravioli. And your sauce."

"Oh, Ray." Varina tsked. "You were down south too long."

"Huh?"

"*Gravy,* not *sauce.*"

"Right, yeah."

"What kind of ravs? I have meat, cheese, or Florentine."

"Just cheese."

Varina grabbed a box of homemade—by a local supplier; there was only so much time in a day—cheese ravioli. "Unfortunately, I sold out of my gravy earlier, but there are several very good jarred varieties on the shelf. I'll show you."

Ray ended up buying a lot more than the ravioli, even if he groaned about his doctor's warning to cut down on the fat and sodium intake. Good Italian groceries tended to have a lot of both, especially the $27-a-pound prosciutto that Varina tried to steer him away from.

"Just a quarter pound of the prosciut'," he said. "That can't hurt, right?"

"I suppose not."

She sliced a quarter pound, added a few extra slices, and wrapped it up in paper. "I don't do bags," she said. "Bad for the environment. But I have some boxes in back if you need one."

"I got it covered." Ray reached into his pocket, pulled out what looked like a small, black ball. Flip, unfold, flap, and it was a grocery bag.

"How ecologically conscientious of you." She packed his groceries.

"I try." Ray paid for his things, hefted the bag from the counter. "It really does looks amazing in here. I honestly couldn't say how it's different. It just is."

"That's Paulie's genius. Paulie works for Dante. He's like my own son."

"I know who Paulie is." Ray grinned. "I live in the same complex as your mother, remember?"

Varina laughed. "Right, yes. He did my apartment, too."

"Your mother talked about that. Here in town?"

She pointed. "Right up there."

"Really? She didn't mention that part. Or maybe she did. My memory isn't what it used to be."

"Mine either."

"You have pictures?"

She did. On her phone. Varina had daily documented the magic she still couldn't believe resulted in her own apartment, built just for her. "It's closing time," she told him. "Why don't I lock up and you can see it in person."

"Yeah? You sure? I don't mean to put you out."

"Not at all. I love showing it off. Wait here." Varina locked the front door, lowered the electronic grates Dante had insisted be installed after several of his job sites had been robbed. "Give me your bag. I'll put it in the refrigerator case so your food doesn't get mooshad'."

Bringing Ray into the back room, Varina tried not to be too smug about the cage elevator she led him to.

"Now that's something," he said. "It looks really old."

"It is. Dante's crew found it buried behind a bumped-out wall I always thought was part of the heating ductwork. He says it probably got put in when the radio repair shop opened up, and was cobbled together from bits and pieces of other old elevators from the turn of the twentieth century. You know how they were back then. Nothing got thrown away. It got repurposed."

"Is it safe?"

"It passed inspection. My son wouldn't have left it here otherwise."

"I guess not." He still looked skeptical. "Kind of small, isn't it?"

"If you're uncomfortable, we can go up the back steps."

"No, no. I got it." Ray stepped into the elevator.

Varina pulled the lever to close the grate, then the other lever to send it up *clink-clank-rattling* as she suspected it had done when it was brand-new.

The elevator stopped. Varina pulled the lever to lock it in place, to open the grate.

"Wow." Ray once again turned that slow circle. "This is . . . wow."

"Pretty snazzy, huh?"

What had once been a cramped little place sectioned off into too many very small rooms was now open and spacious. An eat-in kitchen, complete with floor-to-ceiling cabinetry, and a sitting room showcasing the plate glass window—*Bertie's Radio and Television Repair*—overlooked the street. Everything done in shades of navy— "Jazzy Age," Paulie said—and white—"Lady's Glove"—with splashes of yellow and red, lent to the 1940s retro he had been going for. Even her appliances, though state-of-the-art, looked like they'd been pulled forward in time.

"This window is something else." Ray ran fingers along the newly restored lettering. "1941, huh?"

"I can't imagine why anyone covered over it."

"Probably to get more bedrooms in or something."

"There were two tiny bedrooms here," she said. "Now there's just one in the back of the apartment."

Varina led Ray to the pocket door, slid it open. Powder-blue walls. White trim. White ceiling fan. Sheer, yellow curtains on the floor-to-ceiling windows—uncovered treasures, like the elevator and the chestnut floors—open to the late-spring breeze.

"Beautiful. Really nice."

"Look in there." Varina pointed to another pocket door.

Ray opened it to a bathroom tiled entirely in white and black. "It looks like a tiny spa. This is really great, Varina. Congratulations."

"I can hardly believe it's all real," she said. "Then again, even though I've only lived here a few weeks, it feels like home. Like it's always been."

"I don't know if I ever felt at home anywhere," Ray told her. "Wyldale is home. Franklin Lakes was home. Nashville was home. None of it ever felt . . . permanent."

"I imagine Sunset Downs doesn't either."

He shrugged. "It's fine, but nah."

Silence fluttered in between them, not quite uncomfortable and only just shy of companionable. Varina hadn't had a female friend since high school until Ruth came along; she'd never had a male one aside from Dino. There had been acquaintances who came as couples somehow attached to the kids, neighbors, or church, acquaintances who fell away as kids grew up, as neighbors moved, as church became something attended only on holidays. It was true, she felt nothing like romantic where Ray was concerned, but she did like him, and maybe having a male friend was an adventure to add to her list.

"You want to stay for supper?" she asked. "I have a container of sauce in the freezer. We can have ravioli, if you want."

Ray picked up his head, pulled his hands from his pockets. "I'd love to. Thanks."

"Fill the pot and grab the sculamacaroon' from the rack. I'll go back down and get the ravs."

RUTH HAD BEEN RIGHT; VARINA NEEDED MORE FRIENDS THAN JUST HER. She and Ray spent a couple of hours eating in her new kitchen and reminiscing about the old days. It was nice. Ruth would like him. This was all so new, this having-friends thing. This having-a-social-life thing. One day soon, she'd have them both over for dinner, or they'd all go out. It would be nice to be a group, having fun and creating memories, kind of like her mother was doing, but on a smaller scale.

"I'll walk you down," she told him when he said he needed to go. The dishes in the dishwasher, pots washed—Ray dried—and leftovers packed away for him, all that remained to do was clean out the espresso pot.

"Can we use the stairs?" he asked, half joking but really not.

Varina grabbed her key ring holding keys to the store, the apartment, her car, and all her kids' houses.

Not a rickety step in the whole staircase. It still smelled of new lumber. Her whole building did. It wouldn't take long for olive oil and garlic to permeate everything, of course; the outside stairs would become weathered, but Dante had built everything to last, like the old-world craftsman who'd built the place back in the twenties. Long after she was a memory, the store, apartment, elevator, and staircase would live on.

At the bottom of the stairs, behind Palladino's, lived a patch of green. Tomato pots, a patio table, a little flower bed. Like the apartment, it was just right. Just big enough. Just hers. Dante had even replaced the back entrance door with one a bit more attractive than the old, metal service door. Come summer, she planned on spending a lot of time in her little oasis.

"Let me grab your stuff from inside," she said. When she returned, Ray had his hands in his pockets again, contemplative again. He had a way of falling into that silence, seemingly able to cut himself off from the world. "Something wrong?"

"Oh? Sorry. I was just thinking."

"I noticed."

He smiled. "Can I be honest with you?"

"Uh-oh."

And then he laughed. "Nothing sordid, I swear."

It had been such a nice evening; Varina really didn't want his honesty just then. "All right. Shoot."

Ray fidgeted like a schoolboy, foot to foot, hands still in his pockets. "This is awkward."

"You don't have to—"

"No, I do. It's . . . you're great, Varina. Really great. I know you're not interested in romance. Your mother keeps forgetting she told me that and repeats it every time I see her."

"Oh, Lord in heaven. Ray, seriously, you don't need to—"

"Just listen, okay?"

She nodded.

"I like you. I think you like me. But after two failed marriages and a few girlfriends, I've come to the conclusion that, at this point in my life, I have no interest in romance either. Honestly, I started coming to that conclusion after our dinner at The Blue Pig."

"Should I take that as a compliment?"

His brow furrowed. "What I meant is, I had fun that night. I had fun tonight. Having a nice time with a woman doesn't have to mean more than that."

"Whew!" Varina exaggerated wiping her brow. "I had fun, too. Both times."

"Maybe you haven't wondered why I hadn't called after The Blue Pig, but, I guess, I just wanted you to know there's a reason for that. One that's made me pretty uncomfortable since finding out you were . . . you are . . ." He pulled one hand from his pocket, rubbed his face. "Look, I'm not being noble or playing the long game, I swear to Christ. I'm just . . . it's just . . . you're a good woman." Ray pulled his other hand free of his pocket. In it, a folded square of white. He slipped it into hers. "You deserve better than this. I just thought you should know. Good night, Varina. If you never speak to me again, I'll understand. But I hope you do. I really hope you do."

She could only watch him half walk, half trot from the yard and vanish down the narrow driveway, mouth agape. A car engine turned over. Headlights illuminated the night. One moment. And gone. Varina stood in the dim of moonlight and the twinkle lights of her garden. She unfolded the paper Ray had placed in her hand.

Is Your Grandfather Single and Looking for Love?

Crumpled soft and frayed about the corners, the elderly gentleman in the dark suit, holding a rose, was still clear. And an email address.

"'Stillgotallmymarbles'? Are you kidding me?"

Varina's face burned hot. Her skin skittered cold.

Who had . . . ? Why would . . . ?

Why advertise if you're not going to give it a shot?

Flyers. Someone had made these flyers. Ray had seen it, answered it, and someone had sent him to Palladino's to strike up a conversation, to survey the goods before committing to a date. Just like the others had been.

Crumpling the flyer in her hand, she jammed it into her pocket. Mortification and fury chased one another through her head, over her skin, alternately sweating and goose-bumping. Varina didn't know if she should scream or weep. She did neither. She pulled her phone from her pocket.

"Mom?"

"Varina, sweetheart! You just caught me getting ready for bed."

"Good. I'm coming over. I'll be there in ten."

She didn't give her mother the opportunity to respond, just tapped out of the phone call and slipped it back into her pocket. So much for letting the whole matter die; this was just too humiliating. A flyer. A flyer! Advertised! Of course, it had been her mother setting her up; the flyer was even her speed. But she wouldn't have known how to do it on her own. There was only one person with the skills to do it, while lacking the common sense not to. She stayed up later; she'd be next.

SYLVIA CHECKED THE TIME ON HER PHONE; IT WAS GETTING CLOSE TO nine. What could be so important that her daughter had to visit now? It couldn't be good. The baby? The store? Gabriella? Maybe it was Gabriella. She'd been kicked out of school. But no, her great-granddaughter wasn't that sort.

Varina hadn't sounded hysterical, though the girl'd never had a moment of hysteria in her life. She could always be counted on to keep her head in an emergency. Like when her father dropped dead on the job, and then her husband had done the same. Varina had seen to ambulances, arrangements, even burial plots and flowers. There'd been a tone, though, one Sylvia hadn't heard before, and one she didn't like one bit.

"Are you coming to bed, my love?"

He stood in the bedroom doorway. Her John. Her mostly husband. The love of her life. He stood in his pajamas, glass of water in hand.

"Not quite yet," she told him. "Varina just called. She's coming over."

"Now?"

"Apparently, yes."

"Is everything okay?"

"I imagine it's nothing serious."

But could it be? Tommy. Oh, God in heaven! Tommy was dead. Of course she'd never say so over the phone. Sylvia's heart fluttered and flipped. She gripped the doorframe.

"Darling? What's wrong?"

"I don't know. I wish she'd just said whatever it was."

"I'll put the kettle on."

"Thank you, John. Thank you."

The doorbell rang before the kettle boiled. Sylvia stood on her side of the door, willing her heart to stop fluttering. Once she opened it, her whole life could go right down the toilet. Still, she opened it to Varina, standing upon her doorstep, holding out a flyer. Sylvia took it, brought it closer to her face.

"Oh, thank God." She hit her daughter with the piece of paper. "Don't ever do that to me again!"

"Me? Do that to you? Mom!"

"Mannaggia dial! I thought Tommy was dead!" She grabbed Varina's sleeve. "Get in here."

Varina stumbled into the house. The ramifications of the flyer in her hand trickled through Sylvia's relief. The jig was up. She was in trouble, but at least her Tommy wasn't dead.

"Tea's ready." John stood in the kitchen doorway, ancient Brown Betty teapot in hand. "Kitchen or dining room?"

"Kitchen." Sylvia waved for Varina to follow. She pointed to a chair. "Setedi."

Varina sat, the expression on her face a cross between anger and betrayal. Oh, she could give looks like no one's business, that daughter of hers. No wonder she'd never had to rely on hysterics.

"I'll leave you ladies to it, then." John set the teapot on the table with the mugs, spoons, sugar, and milk already there, though Sylvia smelled the chamomile she'd never put milk in, and neither would

Varina. All those years living together, she knew her daughter well enough to know that.

Varina said nothing, even after the door to the bedroom quietly closed. She waited. Sylvia poured them both tea. And waited. She stirred in a teaspoon of sugar. Varina curled her hands around the mug, and waited.

"I swear on all that's holy," Sylvia said, at last, "it seemed like a good idea at the time."

"YOU'VE GOT TO BE KIDDING ME." RUTH'S LONG EXHALE SOUNDED LIKE bubbles. "What could they have been thinking?"

"Neither one of them is very good at thinking things through to a conclusion." Varina navigated the streets of Fort Lee, heading home. "I suppose they meant well."

"Don't excuse either one of them."

"I'm not."

"I have to be honest," Ruth told her, "if this happened to one of my sisters, I'd be howling with laughter."

"You're terrible."

"I deny nothing. It was decent of Ray to clue you in. Are you upset with him?"

"No, of course not. I imagine he's been mortified for me, and for himself, this whole time. Here I was, thinking I was suddenly so desirable that men were coming out of the woodwork, when all along I was being advertised like the weekly chuck special at ShopRite."

"Filet mignon, at the very least. Besides, you knew there was something fishy going on and you went out with them anyway. We talked about your need for distraction from your humdrum life, except for me, remember? Don't be so down on yourself."

"I guess. Mom swears Donatella took all the flyers down weeks ago, after it went viral online. Thankfully, the renovation on the

store made the whole thing fizzle." She sighed. "I'm just so embarrassed. All those men thinking . . . whatever they were thinking."

"Who gives a flying ffangul? Did I get that right?"

"Ruth!"

"Oh, come now. If there's reason to use that word, this is it. What
are you going to say to Donatella?"

Varina tried not to sigh. Donatella had never been so fragile, so
on the edge of completely crumbling, not in all her life. The medication Paulie confided she was taking didn't seem to be doing anything
good. "I'll be getting a text or phone call any minute. I'm sure my
mother's already called her."

"And if she doesn't contact you?"

Varina's text chime tinged. She glanced at the phone in the cup
holder. "That's her now. I'm just pulling into the driveway. We'll talk
tomorrow."

"Okay. You're a stalwart lass, Varina Palladino!"

"I'm something, all right. Night."

Switching off the engine, Varina picked up her phone.

I'm so sorry, Mommy.

Same words, different disaster.

I know, sweetheart.

. . .

. . .

. . .

Nonina and I meant well.

I know that, too.

☺ I'm glad that's all over and done with.

Varina squeezed her eyes closed. Alone in her car. No one to see her tears. All over and done with? The humiliation? The flyer still out there in cyberworld, making her look like a desperate old lady unable to catch a man?

She texted back . . .

Me too.

. . . and turned off her phone.

She got out of the car, headed home via the back service entrance for Palladino's. The thought of climbing all those steps made her brain hurt only slightly more than the clanking elevator. Tossing the stupid flyer into her patio chiminea as she passed helped, but only a little.

Relief sighed from her mouth, from her body, when she stepped into her own apartment still scented by fresh wood, that would soon smell only of garlic. It wasn't even ten, but Varina was exhausted. She washed up, changed, flicked out all the lights, and climbed into bed. Her eyes would not stay closed unless she pressed fingers to their corners. Behind reluctant lids, that e'stupeed old man with his rose and shy smile leered. It didn't matter that her mother and daughter meant well; the truth proven by the end result cut deep. No one had been interested in her, they'd been looking for an easy path to a relationship that—aside from Ray—had been more about finding someone to take care of them than it had been about finding someone to love.

Burying her face in her pillow, Varina cried. Really cried. How long would it have gone on, were it not for Ray? Thank Jesus, Mary, and all the saints for his courage. She'd thank him personally, but it was just too humiliating. In time, maybe. If she ever dared to show her face outside the store again.

MORNING SOMEHOW MANAGED TO WORK ITS WAY OUT OF NIGHT; Varina's gritty eyes betrayed what little sleep she'd gotten. Schiatanumgorp sent her to the store without breakfast, would probably deny her lunch as well. Turning the sign to open, Varina wanted to call Ruth. Ruth would make her laugh about it. Varina wanted to laugh about it. Desperately. Like whistling past the graveyard.

Acid pooled in her belly, rose up to her throat. No. Not like whistling past the graveyard. That was hollow; Varina didn't do hollow. She'd never been good at pretending, even when she was little, playing with her toys. She was a grocer or a teacher, never a princess. She'd lined up books in her library—the coffee table in the parlor—not ridden unicorns through enchanted forests. Varina had always done what needed to be done. End of story. Now would be no different.

She went out back to the chiminea, fished the crumpled flyer from inside. Uncrumpled it. The old man looked back at her, holding that single rose.

Is Your Grandfather Single and Looking for Love?

She wasn't a pathetic old woman who couldn't catch a man. She was a seventy-year-old woman who didn't want one. A woman who not only owned her own business, but had done it all—house, store, kids, grandkids—on her own for more than a dozen years. In the fall, she'd be in Europe for the first time in her life, having the *time* of her life. Embarrassed? Baffangul!

She returned to the store. Grabbing a red Sharpie from the pen cup, Varina slapped the flyer down on the counter, pressed it flat as it was going to get. She scrawled words in big, bold letters across the bottom.

If this is why you're here, go home. This senior bachelorette
isn't interested!

She taped it up in the front window, and there it would stay until the sun bleached it beyond reading. Maybe she'd even frame it, hang it up behind the register like the first dollar Palladino's earned.

The door chimed, signaling her first customers of the day. A group of young men looking for her locally famous egg sangweeches and coffee. Varina tied her apron, cooked up peppers and eggs on toasted hard rolls. Wrapping them in foil, she heard the bell chime again. More customers. It was going to be a busy morning.

menz'ammenz'

Italian: *mezza mezza;* "half and half"

It's usually used to denote "not good, not bad," but something in between. It's also used as an evasion, whether to avoid answering in the negative, or to promote a righteous appearance of martyrdom.

"How's that burst appendix feeling today, Aunt Angie?"

"Eh? Menz'ammenz'."

ghiacchiad'on'/ghiacchiad'elle
(key-yak-ya-DOAN/key-yak-ya-DELLE, the former being masculine, and the latter being feminine)

Italian: *chiacchierone;* "blabbermouth," "chatterbox"

Sylvia sat beside her John, in the chairs brought in for them, in this house she did not recognize. Despite the address, it was absolutely not the one she'd raised her family in, that Varina had likewise done. The aluminum siding she and Joseph spent a fortune on all those years ago had been pulled off, leaving the chipped, white boards they'd covered up in the first place. The front steps were gone. Dante said, during the tour he gave them all, he would be reintroducing the old front porch back into the structure, the one that had never existed in all the years Sylvia lived there. It had always been a front stoop. End of story. Apparently, she'd always been wrong, because her grandson went on and on about regaining the original integrity of the place, which also included a fireplace found behind a wall in the kitchen, and reconverting the whole structure to a single-family home, as it had been originally. He planned three bedrooms upstairs, with the addition of two not-original-to-the-integrity-of-the-home bathrooms. It seemed excessive to Sylvia. Dante was one man, even if Gabriella stayed with him from time to time. He should have stuck with the rental income, as far as she was concerned, though far be it from her to say so.

No beige walls and flowered wallpaper. Not a thread of carpet. Her bedroom, where she'd watched countless hours of *Murder, She Wrote,* had been swallowed by the living room. Varina's, too. And the third bedroom, always too tiny for its purpose, was to become one with the original bathroom, and far larger than was necessary. The small but sufficient bathroom had yet to be demolished, but would be after this family gathering. It currently stood out like a brown-paper package alongside all the foil wrappings under the Christmas tree—a time capsule to a past no one apparently wanted anymore. Sylvia was glad her Tommy wasn't there to see what was being done; he'd have plenty to say. Then again, she'd seen the pictures he sent from his new Floridian home, all tile and light, and pretentiousness.

"What's wrong, my love?" John touched her hand. "You look troubled. Are you feeling all right?"

"Menz'ammenz'." She waved it off. "It's nothing."

"Can I get you something?"

"No, really, I'm fine." Sylvia pulled a crumpled tissue from her handbag, touched it to her nose to stop the tingling there. "It's all just so . . . so . . ."

"I know what you mean." He squeezed her arm. "It'll be lovely. You'll see."

"I'm glad to see Vicky's window, at least. I should bring the old demon here. Let her see what's been done. Maybe she won't feel so sad about her new home."

"Vicky is not sad." John laughed, kissing her hand. "She's just getting used to things. Give her time."

He'd listened to all her stories, and never once scoffed. Sylvia loved him all the more for that. Joseph, bless his soul, never had patience for her thoughts on the Victrola. He'd never seen Vicky in action, or if he had, he'd denied it. Very Joseph. Varina was so like him. Sylvia was no fool; John was humoring her. She also believed he kept an open mind. The Chinese were like that, prone to believing in magical things. She never spoke that thought aloud, just in case it was accidentally racist.

"Looks like everyone is here," Dante called above the chatter. Davide, Donatella, and Paulie, of course, Pandora and her new beau—and wasn't that the strangest thing, with Dante right there?—and Gabriella, home for the summer. Last to arrive, Varina, who Sylvia still had a hard time looking in the eye, even if Varina had hugged her gently and told her, "I was really pissed off, Mom, but my ego's intact, and I had a little fun along the way." All was forgiven. She forgave too easily, that daughter of hers. Knew nothing about the fine art of holding a grudge while maintaining a civil tongue. It was a lost skill the younger generations didn't see the value of. At least Sylvia could thank the Virgin Mary and all the saints for that fact, considering.

Dante popped the cork from the champagne bottle, held it high when it fizzed over a little. "Pan, you want to help me?"

"Sure."

He filled. Pandora passed. Her beau popped two more bottles. All so friendly and nice. Sylvia knew she should just be grateful for this, too, and stop wondering what the devil was wrong with young people today.

"Thanks for coming, everyone." Dante cleared his throat. "It means a lot to have you all here to kick off the reno on this house we all grew up in.

"This place means a lot to all of us. Christmases and Easters. Everydays. Lots of good times, and not so great ones. On to bigger and better things, right?"

"Eh, ghiacchiad'on'!" Davide called out. "I didn't think we'd have to sit through these sappy speeches once Uncle Tommy moved."

"You hush," Varina scolded, but Davide was grinning and so was Dante. Sylvia shook her head.

"Since my tact-challenged brother can't be quiet, I'll get to the point." Dante looked from one to the other, his gaze ending and staying with Varina. "Mom, you made this place the best home any of us could have asked for. Including you, Paulie."

Paulie lifted his glass a little higher.

"Change is hard sometimes, but it's good. Nothing stays the same. Nothing should. That's . . . what's the word?"

"Stagnant?" Donatella offered.

"Unhealthy?" Varina.

"E'stupeed," Sylvia supplied.

Dante lifted his cup her way, winking. "Thanks, Nonina. It's stupid. We got to make the changes we need to be happy. Like you did. And Mom." He toasted in her direction, his eyes straying to Pandora—did they go a little sad?—and then Paulie, who didn't notice because he was trying to get Donatella's champagne from her without causing a scene.

"To change." Dante lifted his cup higher. "Achendan!"

Donatella lifted her cup. "Chin-chin!" And downed it before Paulie could stop her.

All cups raised, voices echoed. Sylvia couldn't decide if she was glad or sad or mad, or nothing at all, so she sipped her champagne and leaned closer to John. He kissed her temple.

Gabriella lifted her cup higher, cleared her throat loudly. The chatter fell silent. "Dad's right," she said. "Change is good for the soul. He and Mom, and Frankie"—she leaned closer to her mother's beau—"already know what I'm about to say, but . . . I'm not going back to college this fall."

"What?"

"No!"

"Are you kidding me?"

She waved them all silent in that Gabriella way, with a lift of her eyebrows and a quirk of her lips, so like her father. "I've decided to go to culinary school instead. Most of my credits from this year transfer. I start at the Culinary Institute of America up in Hyde Park come the fall semester."

"Congratulations!"

"That's wonderful!"

Varina nearly knocked Davide over in her efforts to reach her granddaughter. "I knew it! Haven't I always said her future is in food?"

"I always wanted to tell people I knew someone in the CIA," Paulie called out. Only Donatella laughed. Dante shook his head.

Sylvia tried not to make a face, but feared she failed miserably. Maybe they'd just think she had gas, like a baby when it smiled. Who needed to go to school to cook? Varina certainly hadn't, and she'd done well. It was probably backward thinking, like accidental racism, so she kept it to herself. Taking a sip of champagne, she patted John's knee, whispering, "I need to use the ladies' room."

"Oh, oh." John rose, helping her up from her chair.

"Something wrong, Nonina?" Davide asked.

"Mom? You okay?"

"I'm fine." She waved them all off. "Can't a lady need to use the facilities without everyone making a big deal about it?"

Some chuckling, but the chatter resumed. John leaned closer. "Shall I accompany you, my love?"

"No, darling. Sit. I'll be back in a moment."

Sylvia closed herself into the bathroom. She ran her hand along the chipped, Formica counter. The sink curtains she'd sewn herself were gone, but there was the yellow tile on the floor, and halfway up the wall; the ceramic towel bar and toilet roll holder; the handrail Varina had installed years ago, when it was only Sylvia who needed a little assistance getting into and out of the tub.

Enclosed within that time capsule, inside what was and would never be again, Sylvia Cioffi-Spini-kind-of-Yu closed her eyes and imagined. All of it. The holidays and everydays. The childhoods and teen years. The brides who had left this house dressed in white. Muted voices beyond the door were anyone and everyone. Any time. Her whole family, including Tommy, was just outside, gathered around banquet tables set end to end in the parlor. They were Joseph and the children, her sisters and their families. Her parents and aunts and uncles. Listening harder to those ghosts, she heard Vicky playing Bing Crosby and Jo Stafford. Songs of bygone years for most everyone now beyond the door, but from the heart of Sylvia's youth.

Dabbing water around her eyes and mouth, she checked her makeup out of habit, not need. She'd stopped wearing foundation after John, tracing the wrinkles uncovered by cold cream one of their first nights together, whispered, "You are so beautiful. So very beautiful."

Sylvia felt so very beautiful, lying in his arms, in the bed a little softer than what she was used to, as nervous as the bride she'd been at barely twenty. Joseph had been nervous, too, good inexperienced Catholic boy that he was. John did not seem to be, that first night. He'd touched her gently, and she'd touched him. Sylvia had no expectations of anything more, and it was quite enough.

A soft knock, then, "Sylvia, my love. Are you all right?"

His voice, dear and sweet. She opened the door, let him slip in.

"Is something wrong?"

Sylvia snuggled into his chest; his arms came up to hold her close. Her heart fluttered, the edges of her vision starting to blur with the headache coming on. A lifetime in the thick of her family's chaos, and a few months away had stripped all her immunity to it. "There is nothing left of me here. Of my life. It's like I got swept clear along with the debris."

He didn't tell her that was not so. John was old, too. Not as old as she, but close enough.

"They make their own journeys, just like we did," he said. "That's the way of things."

"I know. And I'm glad. I am. Happiness is all I wish for all of them, especially now that I am so happy, myself."

John's smile, those channels becoming chasms that never ceased to thrill, lifted Sylvia's heart. They returned to the festivities, arm in arm. To the chatter and laughter of family excited about what was to come. Her heart, that poor, sensitive thing, did a new sort of flip. Or a very old one. It felt like love and worry and sorrow and joy all at once, sort of like she used to feel when her children were too little to trust the world with them, too old to hold back.

PAULIE WASN'T FAST ENOUGH TO GET THE FIRST CUP OF CHAMPAGNE from her, but he managed to get the second.

"Knock it off."

"You can't drink."

"It's just champagne," she whispered. "A little isn't going to hurt."

A little would not. Donatella never stopped at a little.

"Oooo, the cookies are coming out. Let's go get some."

Paulie tipped back the cup of champagne he swiped from her, following in her wake. Cookies were okay. She ate them all day, most days anyway. He would not say a single word about the slightly more than baby weight she'd gained. He thought she looked extra cute, in fact. A lot more like he remembered Sylvia, when they were kids.

"Dante says he's doing the kitchen all in white." Donatella nibbled at a mini linzer torte. "You going to talk him out of it?"

Paulie shrugged. "It's his kitchen. There'll be red and black accents. I found this tile, hand-painted in Italy, to spot here and there among the white subways."

"Ugh. Subway tile?" Donatella took another cookie. "Isn't anyone tired of subway tile yet?"

"It's classic."

"It's boring."

Paulie agreed, so he let it go at that.

"Hey, little sister." Davide sidled up to the tray of cookies set on the sawhorse table. "You saving any for the rest of us?"

"Very funny." She stuck her tongue out at him. Paulie refrained from rolling his eyes. These two were childish separately; put them together and they were infantile.

"So, Dante tells me you two are shacking up in that duplex he bought a while back. That's the furthest out of town you've ever lived, isn't it, Paulie?"

"It's still in town."

"Barely." Davide took one cookie from the platter. "I've been meaning to tell you." He took a bite. "Dante showed me the work you've been doing. Man, you're good. Our Paulie. Who'da'thunk it?"

"Not me, that's for sure," Paulie said before the look on Donatella's face could turn into a snide comment. "I really love it, but I have a lot to learn, too."

"Then you're only going to get better at it." Davide looked up, down, all around. "All this renovation stuff is making me want to move."

"You have a gorgeous house." Donatella took another cookie. "Too big, but beautiful."

"Yeah, it is. Both. Mom's place has me thinking bigger isn't necessarily better, though."

"You thinking of buying one of the places your brother's renovating?"

Davide winked. "That little townhouse over on Bronson caught my eye."

"It's going to need a huge amount of work," Paulie told him. "But it'll be worth it."

"I bet you can sell your place and buy ten of Dante's houses here in Wyldale." Cookie crumbs flew from Donatella's lips.

Davide brushed them from his shirt. "Hey, be careful there."

"Oh, sorry. I mussed your cashmere."

"No one wears cashmere in the summer."

"Whatever." Donatella took yet another cookie. Paulie saw the remark in Davide's eyes before the words came out of his mouth.

"Hey, gavone, how about you take it easy on the cookies. You're starting to look a little pregnant, there."

Donatella froze, mid-bite. Her eyes narrowed. Paulie tried to put a steadying hand on her shoulder, but she shrugged him off.

"What did you say?"

Davide winked. "I'm just kidding."

"No, you're not. Who told you?"

"Told me? What?"

Donatella spun on Paulie. "What did you tell him?"

"Don, come on. Calm down."

"Don't tell me to calm down." Donatella threw her cookie across the stripped-down room. "What did you tell him?"

"I didn't say anything," Paulie tried, but she was having none of it.

"I never should have let you talk me into this!"

Tears stung, balled in Paulie's throat. He opened his mouth to speak, but nothing came.

"Hey, what's going on here?"

"Stay out of this, Dante. You, too, Pandora," she cut off her ex-sister-in-law, already at Dante's elbow. Everyone was looking now. Silently.

Varina moved a little closer. "Sweetheart. Calm down. What's wrong?"

"Davide said I look pregnant."

"So?" Gabriella snagged a cookie, took a bite. "Aren't you?"

No one said a word, except Sylvia, who whispered too loudly, "She is, isn't she? I thought she told me—"

"Hush, my love. Not now."

"How do you know?" Donatella asked, her voice so tight one could bounce a quarter off it. "Who told you? Mom? Was it you?"

"No, sweetheart. I haven't told a soul."

Donatella turned in a circle, that trapped animal look on her face breaking Paulie's heart.

Gabriella rolled her eyes. "Um, duh? Everyone knows. Well, apparently not Uncle Davide, but everyone else."

"What do you mean?"

"You kind of shouted it, that Sunday dinner," Pandora said. "Remember?"

"I didn't shout anything."

"Yeah, okay. Whatever you say, Don."

The lump in Paulie's throat threatened to choke him. It was coming. His moment of doom. He could see it in the tension of her body. Donatella closed her eyes. A tear slipped out. "How long have you all known?"

"What does it matter?" Gabriella asked. "You and Paulie? It's awesome! It's not like you could've kept it secret forever."

The hands coming to Donatella's face shook terribly. Paulie didn't know what to do. Comfort her? Leave her alone? No matter which he did, it would be the wrong answer. He took his chances.

"Get off me!" she growled, pushing through those gathered around her. "Everyone just leave me alone!"

Donatella blew out of the house; no one dared follow her. Paulie stood among them, unable to lift his head. It was too heavy. His shoulders weren't strong enough. An arm—strong enough—fell across his shoulders.

"Come on, kid."

And led him away. Paulie went. Just went. He didn't know what else to do.

Dante guided him out the door and into the humidity of a New Jersey summer. Paulie took deep breaths, wishing for the cold, or maybe the scent of something sweet. Only sticky heat. Only motor oil and exhaust. Paulie inhaled deeply anyway, trying like hell not to let go of the tears he'd been holding inside for months.

"Hey, it's going to be okay."

Paulie nodded. He swallowed and swallowed, but the lump wouldn't loosen. He leaned against the railing, head down and arms crossed. Dante's hands landing on his shoulders nearly toppled him.

That was it. The final straw. Paulie let go one sob, swallowed the rest, but they bubbled in his throat anyway.

The hands on his shoulders became arms around him, jiggling him in that masculine way of men uncomfortable with displays of affection. "It's okay, Paulie. It's okay." Over and over.

Sniffing, Paulie pulled away, pressed fingers to his eyes. "I think she stopped taking her meds."

"Damn. You sure?"

"No, but she's . . ."

"Her old self."

Dante handed him a napkin from his pocket; it smelled like coffee.

"Sorry. It's been . . . a lot, these last few months."

"It's always been a lot, with my sister." Dante smiled a half smile. "I don't know how you do it."

"She'd do the same for me."

"Yeah, I guess she would, but . . ."

"But?"

"But it always seems like you're the one doing, and she's the one doing it to you."

"It wasn't always. We go back and forth. Remember when I came out?" He blew again. "I probably would've killed myself, if not for her."

He'd actually tried. Once. Half-heartedly but desperately. Donatella brought him to the ER, held his hand after his stomach got pumped and dosed with charcoal, and never told a soul.

"Don't say that."

"Why not?"

"Because . . ." Dante took a step back. "I don't want to think about a world without Paul Vittone in it."

Paulie tried hard, but he couldn't force his heavy head up fast enough. Dante was already averting his gaze, but Paulie caught just enough to let him hope for impossible things.

The door opened. Pandora's boyfriend stepped out, pack of cigarettes already in hand. "Oh, sorry. I'll go out front."

"Hey, Frankie. It's okay." Dante pointed to the pack. "Can I bum one?"

"Huh? Oh, sure."

"Since when did you start up again?" Paulie tucked the napkin into his pocket.

"I never actually quit all the way." Dante lit the cigarette, blew out a long drag. He pointed it at Frankie. "Don't you tell my ex-wife. She'll kill me."

"I'd be more afraid of your daughter. I'm trying to quit. Today? Isn't happening."

"I hear you."

Frankie took two more drags, stubbed the butt on his heel, and flicked it into the pile of rubble in the driveway. "Hey, congratulations, Paulie."

"Thanks."

And back into the house he went.

"Nice guy," Dante said.

"It's cool of you to be cool with him."

Dante took a drag. "Why wouldn't I be?" Blew it out. "He makes Pan happy. If he hurts her, I'll break both his legs, but he's all right."

"Yeah."

Paulie wanted a drag of Dante's cigarette. He wanted the replacement joint in his sock drawer, back in the duplex. He wanted to finish off whatever champagne remained inside. Something, anything to close himself off from all he was feeling. "I better go after her," he said. "Sorry for ruining your groundbreaking party."

"You didn't ruin it."

"Sideways, sort of." Paulie grinned, shouldering past Dante on the stair.

"Don't." Dante grasped his elbow. "Don't go after her."

"I have to."

"Maybe that's the problem, Paulie. You got to stop letting her walk all over you."

"She doesn't." His shoulders slumped. "Not usually. I'm cutting her slack, because of the baby."

Dante let go of his elbow, bowed his head. "I'm here for you, kid? Okay? You know that, right?"

Paulie nodded.

Stubbing his cigarette out on the railing, tossing it into that rubble pile, he opened the door leading back inside. "See you tomorrow?"

"Yeah. Tomorrow. Steinhauser house, right?"

"Right."

Dante went back inside. Paulie trudged down the steps and no farther. He sat on the bottom one, rested elbows to knees and head to palms. How much longer could he do this? Hover over her. Make sure she took her meds. Texting her constantly to be sure she hadn't taken off, gotten into a car with some rando on his way to Texas.

"Paulie?" Her tiny voice. A sniff.

He bolted to his feet, spun this way and that. There she was, on the side of the garage. He clambered over all the rubble to get to her. "Are you okay?"

She nodded, then shook her head. "I don't know what's wrong with me."

"You're pregnant."

"No shit, Sherlock." Donatella almost smiled. "The medication didn't help. It's all still there, just . . . dulled. I want it to be gone, Paulie. I want to be normal."

He took her into his arms. "I don't think normal is in the cards for either of us. But we got this. You and me. Always."

She nodded, wiping her nose on the back of her hand, then on her jeans. "It's kind of a relief, you know? Everyone knowing."

"No one keeps a secret in this family. They only think they do. And maybe that's why you popped off in there," he said. "Keeping it in all this time. Let's be real, my darling. Anger is your go-to reaction. Maybe it was your reaction to the relief."

"Maybe. Or maybe I'm just a psycho."

"You're not a psycho."

"If you say so." She drooped. "I want to go home and snuggle the cats. Can we just go home?"

"Sure."

Arm around her shoulders, Paulie guided her through the rubble to the old Pinto out front. Getting in on his side, he spotted Dante in the window. The one Varina always said her demon of a Victrola liked best. He raised his hand. Dante did likewise. Paulie got into his car and drove away, back to the duplex that was home-for-now, the one farther outside of town, farther from the Palladinos than he'd ever been in his life.

32

'sgraziad'

Italian: *disgraziato;* "wretched"

In Jersey, it's often used as "dirtball," as in an underhanded villain with no morals. Though, sometimes, it's synonymous with *scumbari* when the level of messy rises above mild dishevelment, usually involving sweat, maybe some actual dirt.

H ey, stranger. How've you been?"

Varina tried not to stiffen. Though she'd forgiven her mother and her daughter, though the grandfathers were looking elsewhere for love, though she and Ruth had laughed about the whole thing to the point of it being a running joke, Varina still had a hard time looking Ray Pimintiero in the eye. Her last bastion of humiliation, clinging like mussels to a rock at Jones Beach.

Closing her car door to keep the air-conditioning in, she turned to him, smile fixed resolutely in place. "Hey, Ray. Long time no see."

"I was in the store the other day. A nice young lady took care of me."

"That's my granddaughter, Gabriella. She's helping me out over the summer. She starts culinary school in a few weeks."

"Apple didn't fall far from the tree, huh?"

"Not far, no."

"I was hoping to see you there."

"Well, I'm here now. What's up?"

"Nothing." He shrugged. "We really going to do this?"

Varina didn't realize how stiff she was between the shoulders until she let them relax. "No. Sorry. Still, you know . . . embarrassed."

"How about we make a deal? If you stop being embarrassed, so will I."

"You? Why would you be embarrassed?"

"For answering the dumb flyer to begin with, maybe?"

"Oh." Laughter bubbled in her belly. She kept it there. "You have a point."

"So, let's just move on. You here to see your mom? Dumb question. I'm making small talk. Tell me how subtle I'm being."

"Very subtle. I didn't even notice." Varina leaned against her still-running car. "Picking her up, actually. John's playing cards in the clubhouse. A friend and I are taking her out for lunch. Maybe a little shopping." She hesitated, then, "Ruth, that's my friend, and I are going to France at the end of September. I need clothes I don't work in."

"Oh, right. The cruise."

Varina's shoulders bunched up again. "How did you know about that?"

"Sylvia told me."

"I see." But she didn't. And Ruth certainly hadn't mentioned it to Mom. Had she?

The front door opened and Sylvia stepped out into the summer sunlight, shielding her eyes with one shaky hand.

"I should go help her. Nice seeing you, Ray."

"Nice seeing you, too."

She wanted to hug him, just a quick, friendly thing. Maybe a peck on the cheek. He was such a nice man, evolved in the same way Dino had been. Or just older, wiser, and oozing less testosterone.

"Hey, Ray!"

He turned back, shielding his eyes.

"How about we get together this week sometime? We can have dinner. Maybe Ruth will come, too."

"You trying to set me up?"

"With the Dragon of Fifth Avenue?" She laughed. "No way. I swear to Christ. Just dinner. Have some fun. What do you say?"

He grinned. "I haven't been to The Blue Pig in a while."

"Me either. Meet you there at seven on Thursday?"

"Seven on Thursday." He saluted, bowing just slightly.

"Varina!" Her mother called from the front steps.

She hurried to her mother, fussing on the top step. There were only two, but Sylvia always seemed sure she'd fall and break something. Honestly, Varina didn't know how John kept up. And then realized she knew full well, because until he came along, Varina had catered to her just as devotedly.

"There you go, Mom." Lovingly. Tenderly. Her mother, ninety-three years old, deserved every offered hand, every concession, every quelled eye roll. She led her—so slowly!—to the car, helped her into the cool interior.

"Could you turn down the air?"

Varina hadn't even closed herself in. She turned down the air. "Good?"

"Much better, sweetheart. Thank you."

"Ready for our outing?"

"I'm very excited. A day out with my girl and . . . and . . ."

"Ruth."

"I know that. Where are we going?"

"I just have to stop at the store first, then we'll meet Ruth at Panera."

"Oh, my favorite!"

She'd have the soup. Sylvia always got the soup. It had taken a lot of convincing to get Ruth to agree, but she had, in the end, because she was a good friend. And because Varina promised her a pound of the rigatoni she loved as a reward. Rigatoni she was *not* getting if it turned out she was the one who blabbed to her mother.

"So," she hedged, "I thought we'd do a little shopping, if you're up for it. I need clothes for France."

"That'll be fine, sweetheart. You need more than one nice dress for a cruise. I'd love to buy a new dress myself. For dancing. A blue one that swirls. Antonette thought she was so stylish in that black dress she wore last week. She looked like a buttan', I'll tell you. Twenty-year-olds and widows wear black."

No pretense. Not even a little.

Sylvia looked in the center console, took a mint from the tin Varina kept there. "Were there no cruises to Italy in your fancy book?"

Fancy book. Fancy book. What fancy book?

"Oh, Jesus. The brochure you caught me browsing through."

"Yes, in that brochure. There must have been trips to Italy."

Ruth hadn't told. No one had. Her mother had made an assumption that turned out to be right. It reminded Varina of being a teenager trying to outsmart her mother. It hadn't worked then. Apparently, it still didn't.

"The only Italy trips included other stops in the Mediterranean. When I go to Italy, I want to go to Italy, you know? Maybe next time."

Sylvia smiled in Varina's periphery. She patted her daughter's thigh. "Good for you, sweetheart. It's about time you started doing things for you."

"Even though"—she was playing with fire now—"the trip is roughly the same time Donatella is due?"

"Eh, babies are born every day. She'll be fine. So will you."

Varina had every right to righteous indignation. Her mother had spent a lifetime trying to mold her with shouldn'ts and couldn'ts, to the point that at seventy years old, Varina had kept her trip to France a secret. Maybe her mother's conscience was still prickling guiltily about advertising her only daughter like a weekly special, or maybe it was because of John. What did it matter now? Like her fury over the flyer, she could choose to prolong the agony or let it go. Varina let it go. Sylvia was Sylvia. Good, bad, or otherwise. And she loved her very much.

"Yeah," Varina said. "It'll all turn out fine."

"So . . ." Sylvia folded her hands in her lap. "Are you going to let Davide color your hair before you go? Not that purple, though. A nice, dark brown would be so youthful."

"I just have to run into the store and check on something." Varina pulled up to the curb. "Come inside and say hi to Gabriella."

"I'll just wait in the car, sweetheart."

Leave her mother alone in the car? Whether running with the

air on, or off with the windows down, to Varina it was a hard no. She pulled around back instead. "Come sit on the patio," she said. "I might be a few minutes."

Sylvia didn't object. Settling her into one of the faux-wicker chairs, Varina made sure the umbrella was tipped to shade her.

"Bring me a cold Pellegrino," she called. "And tell that grand-daughter of mine to get out here and give me a kiss."

Varina entered the cool, fragrant kitchen through the back door. Marinara still simmered over an almost nonexistent flame. Stir. Taste. Perfect. Splashing in the vermouth, she turned off the gas and put the cover on tight.

"What are you doing to my madinad'?" Gabriella stood in the doorway, hands on her hips. "I told you I'd take care of it."

"I know, I know!" Varina threw up her hands in surrender. "I swear I'll get better at this sharing-the-load thing. I just stopped in to get a package of rigatoni. Go out and say hi to Nonina."

Gabriella spread her hands wide. "I'm all 'sgraziad'. She's going to give me crap."

"You're perfect. And if you don't go give her a kiss, she'll never let you hear the end of it."

"She'll forget in five minutes."

"No, she won't," Varina told her. "She's an old Italian. She forgets everything but a grudge. Go."

Gabriella groaned, head back and shoulders exaggeratedly slumped, but she trudged out into the summer heat to give her great-grandmother a kiss.

Varina grabbed the pound of rigatoni, caught off guard by the sight of her store. It happened, when she wasn't paying attention, that shock and thrill. Palladino's hadn't even looked as good in their earliest days. Dino would be so proud. Of it. Of her.

She missed him intensely in that moment; always-uncomfortable tears tingled her nose. Where had all the time gone? Not just her youth, but even this single year? The store, the apartment, the renovation just about finished on the house no longer hers. Tommy was in Florida. Davide was talking seriously about buying one of Dante's houses. Donatella was having a baby. She and Paulie. Paulie was Dante's right-hand man. Sometimes, it all hit her so quickly, it nearly knocked her off her feet.

"Nonina says get a move on. She's hungry. Oh!" Gabriella snatched a slip of paper from the corkboard, handed it to Varina. "I had to sign for a delivery of jarred stuff from the distributor."

"This wasn't due in until the end of the week." Varina looked at the invoice. Jarred sun-dried tomatoes, eggplant, olives, jardiniere, roasted garlic. Staples in her store, and always running out. "Good. Did you stock the shelves?"

"Not yet, but I will before closing." Gabriella shifted, foot to foot. "I was thinking."

"Thinking?" Varina prompted.

"Just hear me out, okay?"

"I'm listening."

"What if we made some of this stuff in store rather than importing them from Italy? I mean, we're *Italian*. We both know how to make this stuff. It would be fresh, delicious, and way less expensive."

"As well as very time-consuming. Believe me, I've thought about it. Our customers like this brand. They know it."

"True. But you have me now, at least until school starts. And on the weekends. I can help. Or I can do it for you. A trial sort of thing. We can have both in the store, so if our . . . your customers still want the jarred stuff, they can have it. If they like ours, we can phase the imported stuff out. Or at least cut down on what we buy. That shit's expensive! What do you think?"

Varina still thought it was time-consuming, and probably not cost-effective, and that her customers were more habitual than most. But . . .

"There is a way to dehydrate using the convection function of the oven. I'll order a bushel of plum tomatoes from the market. Start with that, and then we'll see."

"And garlic," Gabriella said. "That's super-easy."

"Okay. But I draw the line at curing our own olives. Maybe in time."

"Thanks, Nonnie!" Gabriella clapped her hands, bouncing on her toes, just like she did when she was little and always getting her way and too cute to scold.

Varina's cell phone chirped. Pulling it from her pocket, expecting Ruth, she nearly dropped the phone when she saw Paulie's number on the screen. A call. Not a text. Everything turned on a moment; she tapped in.

"What's wrong?"

"I don't know." He was crying, she could tell, though his voice seemed overly calm. "A pipe burst in the duplex. She was helping me mop . . . and she . . . there's . . . can you please just meet us at the hospital?"

"I'll be right there." She tapped out. Dialed Ruth.

"Nonnie? What's wrong?"

She held up a finger. "Hey," she said before Ruth could joke. "I need you to come get my mother and bring her home."

"What's going on?"

"Nonnie?"

"I don't know. Something with Donatella. I'm heading to the hospital."

"Shit."

"Shit."

A unison of *shits*.

"I'll be right there," Ruth told her.

"Thanks. Gabriella is here until then."

"What do you want me to do?" Gabriella asked before Varina could jet out the door.

"Container the madinad', and keep an eye on Nonina until Ruth gets here." She yanked open the door. "Oh, and get her a Pellegrino. I'll call when I can." And she headed out to her mother.

"You forgot my Pellegrino."

Varina was leaning over Sylvia, kissing the line of white on the top of her unnaturally black head. "Donatella is in the hospital," she said quickly. "Ruth is coming to get you to take you home. I'll call you when I know something."

Now she was darting for the car, that ancient Buick, still cool despite summer's heat.

"It's too early," she said aloud, as if it might somehow alter the reality. "It's way too early."

And Donatella was so fragile. Medication. No medication. Eating to beat the band. Sleeping. Not sleeping. Calling in the middle of the night. Not calling or texting for days. All the years of not knowing where she was, what she was doing, until she turned up in trouble of some kind or another, Varina thought, had built up emotional calluses. But that was a lie she'd told herself often enough, forcefully enough to believe. The rush of anxiety she was feeling as she backed out of the drive brought it all back into clear focus. All of them. All at once. And now there was a baby in the mix.

The cornoot hanging from her rearview mirror swung, *clack-clacking* against the window. Varina reached out to steady it.

"Please," she said. "Please."

To the cornoot. To Dino. To God. To whoever, whatever would listen.

33

Com'sigiam'? *(com-see-gyam)*

Italian: *Come si chiama?; "What is it called?"*

The Jersey Italian version of *whatchamacallit,* which in turn can be used in all manner of euphemism. I thought *com'sigiam'* was the Italian word for vagina* until I looked it up for this entry.

*Note, a word I never used until my teens, and then only to see my family cringe. Always a euphemism, never the proper word. We called it a cookie for as far back as I can remember. You can imagine my horror when I heard my best friend in second grade was being sent to the principal's office for crushing JoAnn Venzano's cookie.

Varina was on her way. Everything was going to be all right. The EMTs, the nurses, all said so. They'd taken Donatella up to labor and delivery and asked Paulie to take care of registration while they saw to whatever needed seeing to.

"Mr. Palladino?" A nurse approached, tablet clutched to his chest. "You can come with me now."

"It's Vittone, actually." Though a man could dream. "Where?"

"Follow me."

"Paulie!"

Both he and the nurse turned to Dante's shout. Obviously still wet from the knees down, Dante pushed through the crowded waiting room, his hands coming up, reaching, grabbing Paulie by the shoulders. "How is she? Is the baby all right?"

"I don't know. I think so. This nice man here was just showing me in to her."

"Sorry. Sorry." Dante's hands fell to his sides. "Go. I'll be here."

"It's likely going to be a while. Your mom is on her way. The two of you should—"

"I'll be *here*."

Paulie started away, turned back. "The pipe?"

"I turned off the main valve."

"Is it bad?"

"It's bad, but don't worry. I got it covered. Just go. Tell my sister I love her."

Paulie gave him a thumbs-up. The strange calm enveloping him even let him smile encouragingly. Inside his head, the wailing and jabbering keened, but muffled. At arm's length. Like it wasn't his at all. Maybe he was holding on to it for Donatella, keeping it safe and separate, as he'd been doing since forever.

"Mr. Palladino?"

Sigh. "It's Vittone."

"Oh, sorry." The obstetrician smiled a doctor's smile, cool and warm at the same time. He made a note in the file. "I'm Dr. Iravani. I'll be taking care of your wife—"

"Not my wife."

"Oh, sorry again." His discomfort was kind of sweet, actually, with his round cheeks and round face and Harry Potter eyeglasses. Dr. Iravani couldn't be more than thirty. Was he even a doctor yet? Or a resident on rotation, or whatever it was called? Paulie couldn't remember; it had been a long time since he'd watched any of those hospital shows.

"But you're the father."

"I am."

"Okay, good. So, I'll be taking care of things here. We've stopped the bleeding, and stalled labor, we'll know soon if it takes."

"If it takes?"

"Sometimes labor can be halted. Sometimes it can't."

"Is she all right?" Paulie shuddered. "There was so much blood."

"It wasn't as much as it looked, I assure you. Her water broke. Do you know what that means?"

"Isn't it too soon?"

"Let me see." Dr. Iravani checked the chart. "I don't see any ultrasound results in here."

"Because she hasn't had one."

His eyes widened, but his lips pursed down on whatever words rattled about in his head. "The chart says she's only at thirty-four weeks, but there could be a miscalculation. That's why we do ultrasounds, to pinpoint—"

"There's no miscalculation."

"Oh." Dr. Iravani pushed his glasses up to the bridge of his nose. "Well, then. Thirty-four weeks is early, but we really should do an ultrasound so we know what we're dealing with, make sure the baby is big enough to deliver, and if it's not, to prepare for the best outcome."

"Let me talk to her." Paulie moved closer to the hospital bed, leaned low. "The doctor wants to do an ultrasound to make sure the baby is big enough to deliver. Okay?"

Donatella only moaned, a sound more contented than it should have been, just then.

"Does that count as consent?" Paulie asked.

"Not really," Dr. Iravani answered. "Unless she's completely unresponsive, we need her consent. The sedative we gave her should wear off soon. She'll be all right until then. Meanwhile, I'll put in the order. It usually takes forever to get a machine and tech in."

"And the baby is okay?"

"Being monitored." Dr. Iravani placed a hand on Paulie's shoulder. "Don't worry, Daddy. Your baby is in good hands. The nurse will be back to check on you all. If you need anything, or if she wakes, press the call button."

"Okay. Thanks. Wait. What about her medication?"

The cool-warm smile downturned. Dr. Iravani checked his chart. And again. "There's no medication listed here on her intake."

Paulie's face went hot, his fingers cold. "She . . . she takes lithium."

"Bipolar?"

"It's very new. Well, very old, but only newly being treated."

Dr. Iravani held out the tablet. "Well, she didn't list it. I'll ask her when she wakes. She'll be all right until then. Try not to worry."

Did those words ever work? Paulie could do nothing but worry. That his baby was too small to be born. That Donatella would die. That she didn't list her medication because she'd stopped taking it. And he'd known, dammit! He'd known. But he didn't want to, and so he pretended.

Why had he let her help him mop? Why had she insisted? Because she'd been less lethargic lately, more argumentative. Paulie's brain whirred. How much was real and how much made bigger by anxiety? And how much—dear, sweet Jesus!—how much more could he take?

The nurse returned to check this, tap that, take the other thing. Donatella was still pretty out of it.

"It's good she rests now," the nurse told him. "She'll need all her strength soon enough."

"Do you think it's safe for me to go get a cup of coffee?" Or a handful of Valium? "Maybe let the family know she's all right?"

"Sure." The nurse smiled the same sort of cool-warm smile, though his was more warm-cool. "I'm Brandon, by the way."

"Paulie." He stuck out his hand.

Brandon's eyebrows rose, but he shook it. "There's a coffee station right here, but it's swill. Go down to the cafeteria. They have the good stuff there. And while you're at it, get yourself something to eat. The cinnamon buns are ridiculously good. And, don't worry, I'll take care of her until you get back."

Muttering his thanks, Paulie darted out of the labor room. Varina, Davide, Pandora, and Dante gathered in the waiting room, poised to descend upon him like vultures on a dead squirrel.

"Is she okay?"

"What's going on?"

"Isn't it too early for her to be in labor?"

"Yo!" Dante suddenly stood between him and them. "Take it easy on the poor guy." And then to Paulie, "We're all a little stracciad', you know?"

"I know. Me too."

"Is she okay?" Varina asked. "And the baby?"

"Both fine, for the time being. We'll know more in a little bit.

They told me to go get a cup of coffee and something to eat from the cafeteria."

"I'll go," Dante said. "Cream and sugar, right?"

"No, it's okay. I need to . . . to walk it off a little."

"I'll go with you, then." Dante taking charge. *Thank Jesus, Mary, and all the saints.* "Does anyone else want anything?"

Dante, silent, stoic Dante, didn't try to engage him or encourage him or soothe him, and in this way was exactly what Paulie needed. Knowing the man would catch him if he stumbled, or put an arm around him if he cried, made those things unnecessary, and improbable. By the time they got back up to obstetrics, Paulie had eaten his—very delicious—cinnamon bun, drunk half his—also very delicious—coffee, and was as near to excited about the impending birth of his child as his anxiety would allow.

Paulie stopped Dante outside the swinging doors of the waiting room. "Thanks."

"No problem."

And that was all.

Heading back to Donatella, Paulie took deep, even breaths. He'd always thought it condescending, telling someone having an anxiety attack to "just breathe." Whether he wanted it to work, or there was actually some science behind it, Paulie could not deny its powers.

She was still conked out when he walked in. Standing beside her, a distracted tech fiddled with a machine that looked kind of like an old computer.

"What's going on?" he asked.

She startled, hand to heart. "You the daddy?"

"I am."

"Well, get ready to see your baby, Daddy." She smiled so big her eyes closed. "I have to do some measurements first, but you can watch if you want."

Paulie asked no questions, especially not *Did Donatella wake up and give consent for this?* Because he didn't want to jinx it. She couldn't be upset with him for something that happened—at least, partially—while he was out of the room.

Ah, the lies he told himself. Paulie was so good at it, he barely even felt guilty.

Donatella didn't wake, not even when the tech placed the gooped wand on her exposed belly. The fuzzy image on the screen cleared. Paulie dropped to the edge of the bed.

"Is that ... ?"

The tech chuckled. "I sure hope so."

His mouth hung open, and nothing about catching flies or looking like a mammone could convince him to close it. Arms. Legs. A head. And there, a face. Scrunched and grumpy-looking, but the face of his ...

"It's a boy," he said, because there was no denying what he'd just seen.

"You didn't know?"

"This is her first ultrasound." Donatella was going to be ... he hoped not pissed. She'd been so sure the baby was a girl. They hadn't even picked out any boy names. "Does he look okay?"

"I don't read them, I just take them."

"Come on. You have to know something."

She looked over her shoulder, lowered her voice. "Don't quote me, but he looks a little small. Not too small, though." A roll of printouts buzzed out of the machine. "You want a copy?"

"Absolutely."

And she printed out another set. Putting the first into the chart, she told him, "Dr. Iravani will be in shortly."

"Okay, thanks."

Paulie stared at the gray images of his son. His tiny boy. Tears he had no interest in denying rolled down his cheeks.

"Let me see."

He nearly jumped out of his skin. Turning slowly, bracing for whatever she would hurl at him, Paulie handed her the still-warm printout. Donatella stared at it, chewing on her lower lip.

"A boy."

"Yes."

More lip-biting. "Maybe that's a good thing. Maybe he'll be more like you instead of me."

"There's nothing wrong with being like you."

She snorted, held the prints out for him to take back. "We need a name. Just no Ds, okay?"

"Okay," he told her. "What do you have in mind?"

Her nose scrunched, and for an instant, Paulie saw their baby's scrunched-up grumpiness in her face. "Peter?"

"Peter Palladino?" Paulie laughed. "That sounds like a nursery rhyme."

"Peter Vittone," she corrected. "The baby always gets the father's name."

"How archaic of you." He laughed again, sat on the edge of her bed, took her hand. "If I could be a Palladino, I would be."

"Paulie Palladino sounds even more like a nursery rhyme."

"True." He kissed her hand. "He should have your name. My family didn't want me. I don't see any reason to give their name to my son."

"It's your name, too."

"What about Nicholas? Nicky. Every family needs a Nicky."

"Too Greek. Boris?"

"Too Russian. You know what name I really love for a boy? Warren."

"Don't be ridiculous. Warren." She chuffed. "What about Vincent? Remember Vincent Petrulo? He was nice."

Naming their son for an old schoolmate they'd never actually been friends with; how very Donatella. But he did like it. "I hate Vinnie, though. You know everyone will call him Vinnie. I can't even get you to call me Paul."

"Because you're a definite Paulie. And everyone always called Vincent, Vincent."

"True."

"Vincent Palladino." Donatella cocked her head. "I really love it. It has a ring, doesn't it?"

"Yes?"

"Well, considering I'm the one about to push him out of my com'sigiam', I should get my way."

"You always get your way."

"Then there's no point changing that now." She grinned, all dimples and round cheeks. Donatella. His beautiful, wonderful Donatella. A little while ago, he thought she would die. Now she was bossing him around, like always.

"All right," he said. "Vincent it is."

"I have to pee." She tried to sit up higher. "Do you think I'm allowed to get up?"

"I don't think the staff wants you to do it in the bed. Hang on." Paulie buzzed for the nurse. He was there in moments, assisting Donatella with all the drips and monitors hanging and attached. Waiting outside the bathroom door, his head cocked for any sound from within, he smiled at Paulie.

"Your first?"

"How could you tell?"

"Just a wild guess."

The toilet flushed. Donatella called for the nurse. He went in and helped her back to the bed, re-hooked the monitors and re-hung the drip.

"Can't I walk around?" she asked. "I read it's good to walk while in labor."

"Not until Dr. Iravani says so," Nurse Brandon answered. "Just hang tight until he looks at your ultrasound."

"Fine. Can I get something to drink?"

"I'm afraid all I can offer you is ice chips."

"Ice chips, but no water?"

"I know, sounds dumb. But the fact is, you'd drink a lot more water than you will suck on ice chips, so, you want some?"

"Yeah, sure. Thanks."

Paulie pulled a chair up to her bed. Donatella rested her head back, eyes on the ceiling or lights or whatever she looked at besides him.

"I okayed it."

"Huh?"

She leveled a gaze. "The ultrasound, Paulie. I told them it was okay."

He could lie to himself, not to her. "I was afraid you'd say no."

"It's good to know where your loyalties lie."

"Hey, that's not—"

"No, sarcasm. It *is* good. You thought of him first, even if you were afraid I'd be pissed. That's what a good parent does."

"Oh."

She sighed. "That's the way it's going to be, from now on. Me and you, putting Vincent first. Sacrificing for him, even each other."

"You're so dramatic."

She did not chuckle, or even smile. Donatella's lip trembled. She held out her arms and Paulie moved into them. Resting his head against her belly, he closed his eyes and felt the lumps of elbows and knees, balled hands and jutting feet, just under Donatella's skin. No amniotic sac full of water between them now. Just the three of them, in the bubble of the *before* making way for the *after*.

Paulie didn't ask about the medication. There was no point. Now was not the time, anyway. It probably never would be. And it wasn't the time to think about it either.

"Good news." Dr. Iravani burst in, barely looking up from the chart he carried. "The baby looks to be about six pounds, lungs look good, strong heartbeat. We're good to go if that's what you choose."

Paulie looked at Donatella.

Donatella looked back.

She bit her lip, tears welling. "This is happening."

"It is."

"Okay," she said. "Okay."

34

gabadigazz' *(gah-bah-DEE-gahtz)*

Italian: *capo di cazzo;* "dickhead"

Cazzo makes the rounds, doesn't it? Versatile word.

Amonini

Italian: *Andiamo;* "Let's go"

When I was a kid, I found an ancient VHS copy of *Yellow Submarine* in my parents' basement. I became obsessed. I watched it until the tape wore out, then kind of lost interest. I caught it streaming recently, shocked to realize the villains are actually called Blue Meanies, not Blue Amoninis. Being Jersey Italian is just weird sometimes.

Dante paced as if he were the expectant father, not uncle. Varina watched him, a little concerned but mostly puzzled. Always quietly intense, from the day he was born with that stern look upon his tiny face, her son seemed less in control of his emotions than usual.

"He's okay, Mom." Pandora. Of course, Pandora. "Try not to worry."

"I'm not."

Pandora snorted. "Okay."

"Don't be fresh."

"He's just invested in this baby. It's his sister. And it's Paulie."

"Well, of course he's invested. They're family. Exactly what are you not saying?"

"Mom." Pandora sighed, shaking her head. "You really need to speak with your son one of these days, and not just a hi-how-are-you. It'll do him the world of good."

"What does that *mean,* Pandora?"

"It means what it means." She kissed her mother-in-law's cheek just as Varina's cell phone pinged. Pandora smiled, leaving her to her phone call.

"How is she?" Ruth asked.

"In labor, apparently."

"I know that, but how is she?"

"No idea. Paulie says okay."

"Want me to come down?"

"What's the point? I'll probably head home. It's going to be a long while, and sitting here isn't going to make it happen any faster."

"Wow."

"Excuse me?"

"Nothing. I think you're right. How about I take you out for dinner, Grandma?"

"Nonnie."

"Right, I forgot. What do you think? Jade Fountain?"

"I think Chinese food is exactly what I want right now. I'll meet you there in half an hour."

Varina tapped out of the call, then into one with Gabriella, who'd closed up the store at five, as promised, and put up all the marinara. She'd probably need her to open the store instead of close tomorrow. At least, Varina hoped the baby would be born by then. What had she done before Gabriella started helping at the store? She'd done it all herself, of course. When her granddaughter started school, she'd have to hire someone, because returning to those backbreaking days was not happening.

"What do you say?" Davide had his arm across Dante's shoulders when she approached. "You can come back after."

"Nah. But thanks."

"Gabadigazz', you have to eat."

"I'll grab something in the cafeteria when I'm hungry."

"It could take well into tomorrow, or even longer," Pandora told him. "You can't just sit here. Come with us."

"Don't tell me what to do, Pan."

Hands up, she took a step back. "Call if you need me."

"Right." Dante's chin fell a little. "Sorry."

"It's okay. I get it." And she kissed his cheek.

You really need to speak with your son one of these days . . .

Varina had never been good at riddles. They required a more convoluted sort of thinking than she was capable of. It was one of the reasons she and Ruth got along so well—what you saw was what you got. No pretense. No secrets. It had been the same with Dino. She never had to guess what he was feeling. He felt it. He said it. She'd done the same for him. How had they produced beings like Donatella, who felt things out in chaotic rages, and Dante, who held it all inside until it bubbled under the skin? It was a little strange to discover, after close to fifty years of motherhood, that her hairdresser, fashion-loving playboy with a fondness for all things flashy and expensive was the least complicated child of them all.

"Mom? You want to come?" Davide was asking.

"I'm grabbing a bite with Ruth, but thanks, sweetheart."

"Guess it's just you and me, Pan," Davide said. "Unless you want to call Gabriella."

"Nah. She should spend some time with her nonina before school starts."

"You and me it is." Davide held out his arm, bowing dramatically. "Scordato's?"

After they had gone, Varina tried, "How about I bring you takeout?"

"I'll be fine."

"Sweetheart, there's really no point in you—"

"I can't leave him," Dante said. "I told him I'd be here."

"Oh." All the breath evaporated from Varina's lungs. She tried to pull it back in, but the sensation lasted long enough for Dante to turn away, to take from her sight the look in his eyes, that hunted, haunted, desperate look she had seen before but never understood. Until this moment. And, oh, how simple. How obvious.

"I'll call if there's any news."

"All right, son." She could speak. How miraculous. Kissing his cheek, she left him alone in the waiting room that used to house expectant fathers, in those days before fathers were allowed to bear witness to the very womanly occupation of birth. No one else was in there. Just Dante, his cell phone, and the emotions he held bubbling under his skin.

HE'D BEEN SO UNPREPARED. NO HOSPITAL BAG OF CLOTHES, SNACKS, bottles of water, the sort of bag he read about online, in mommy groups and daddy groups and on midwife boards. His contacts were killing him, and he didn't have his glasses. Paulie thought there'd be plenty of time. At least another month. Vincent should have been small, maybe underdeveloped, but he'd been born at 1:48 in the morning, six pounds, five ounces, nineteen inches long, with an Apgar score of eight, despite all measures in place to whisk the preemie off to the NICU.

"That's a big boy for being a month and a half early," Sherry, the nurse who came on duty after Brandon, told him. "You're sure about your dates?"

"Positive," Paulie answered, considering it was only the one time.

"He'd have been a ten pounder had he gone to term. Your wife is lucky."

"Not my wife."

"Right, sorry." Sherry's smile wasn't cool-warm, or warm-cool. Mostly, it was tired. "Go home, shower, get some things, and come back. They'll both sleep for a while. I'll have one of those chair-beds set up for you when you get back."

Paulie didn't want to leave. He wanted only to hold his perfect rosebud of a son and watch over Donatella, make sure they both continued breathing. Recognizing sense despite his euphoric wishing, Paulie nodded and left, promising to be no more than an hour.

He pushed through the swinging doors, into the waiting room, and flopped into a chair. Head back and eyes unfocused, he took several of those deep, maybe-wishing, maybe-scientific breaths. He'd already texted Varina, who promised to call the whole family for him. They'd all descend in the morning, he was certain. Dr. Iravani, who'd stayed even though his shift was up, said Donatella would probably spend a couple of days in the hospital, considering the circumstances in which she arrived.

Another moment within the silence, and Paulie groaned to his feet.

"Hey, kid. Don't be startled, it's just me."

Hand to heart, nevertheless. "What are you still doing here?"

"I told you I would be."

"But you didn't have to."

Pushing out of the chair he'd probably been asleep in for at least a couple of hours, considering the odd cant to his shoulder and neck, Dante held out his arms. Paulie did not hesitate, though he did pretend just a little.

"Congratulations." Dante clapped him on the back. Always that odd, uncomfortable embrace, but sincere, and absolutely cathartic.

"Thanks."

Dante let him go. "Vinnie, huh?"

"Vincent, and if you call him Vinnie, your sister will castrate you. What do you think?"

Dante chuckled. "Vincent Vittone sounds like a cartoon villain."

"Palladino, actually."

Dante only crooked an eyebrow. Paulie was too tired to explain what didn't need explaining. "I'm heading home to shower and get a change of clothes. You should get some sleep."

"I'll take you," Dante told him. "I had the guys take your car for detailing when I sent them to clean up the duplex. It was . . . kind of a mess."

A bloody mess. Paulie hadn't thought about his white leather interior when he put Donatella in the car and plugged it to the hospital. "You had the guys clean up?"

"My duplex. My responsibility. You should've called me in the first place."

"You've already done enough."

"Amonini, kid. It's late, and I got to get some sleep."

Too tired to explain, or to argue, or to figure out some other way to get home that didn't involve Dante, who'd sat there, alone, all this time, Paulie nodded.

Waiting outside for him to pull up to the curb, Paulie took out the contacts scratching the shit out of his eyes, flicked them to the asphalt to shrivel away. The world blurred, gentling with the harsh lights of the hospital entrance, the parking lot. He lifted his face to the cool-but-humid summer air. A son. His son. Vincent Palladino. They hadn't even discussed a middle name. It had all happened so fast. Thank goodness he was a good size; maybe it was all those cookies and shit Donatella ate. But six weeks early. Six weeks? Maybe it was five. He was supposed to have been born on the cusp between September and October. An autumn baby. Now he was a summer baby. Virgo? Or a Leo? Oh, Leo. That would have been a good name. Not Leonard, Leonides. Donatella would have told him it was too Greek, but she got to pick his first name, maybe she'd go for it as a middle.

Dante's truck pulled up to the curb. Paulie got in. The relief of this familiarity, this moment *after,* busted open a bubble he hadn't even realized was there, let alone close to popping. This family. Their protection. Their love. This man. The sob he swallowed back down made way for a future that would forever contain those things, however shifted. As Donatella said, Vincent was, now and forever, Paulie Vittone's everything.

"You okay, kid?"

"Emotional."

Dante nodded, pulling away from the curb. "Understood."

The duplex smelled like disinfectant, but it wasn't full of water. Thankfully, it had been the kitchen that flooded, and not the living area upstairs. Only when MaryJane, Pastafazool, and Chooch curled around him, meowing for a long overdue feeding, did Paulie realize he'd not only forgotten about them in the frenzy of the pipe bursting, but in all the drama that followed.

"You poor darlings. I'm sorry."

"You say something?" Dante asked.

"Just talking to the cats." He checked their litter boxes in the mudroom. Apparently, they'd been spared. "I better feed them."

Dante squatted, scratching Pastafazool behind the ears. "Cute."

"So, do you actually like cats?"

"I like them fine." Dante stood, stretched. "Why?"

"You gave them to me, remember?"

"What do you think, I'm oobatz'? I know I gave them to you." Dante straightened. "Mind if I use your bathroom?"

"Go for it."

Paulie fed his cats, leaving dry kibble in a big bowl. He got a bigger bowl from the cabinet, and held it under the tap for water; nothing came out. Shit. The main valve was turned off. Reaching across the kitchen counter for the half-full bottle of designer water Donatella insisted was good for her complexion, Paulie knocked over the basket there. Mail, his glasses, loose change toppled out.

And a prescription bottle, its contents rattling. Full.

Paulie put his glasses on. He checked the fill date. Opened it. Counted the pills. Thinking maybe, just maybe, he was wrong. There was something off about the pills on his palm, about the date on the bottle; they should have run out over a week ago.

Exhaustion crawled through him. He tipped all but one of the pills back into the bottle. Pinkish. Letters. Numbers. He looked them up on his phone. Hopes for *maybe, just maybe,* flew off like startled, cawing birds. Paulie popped the pill into his mouth and chewed, instantly recognizing the baby aspirin he had to use until he was well into his teens, because Paulie Vittone couldn't manage to swallow a pill without throwing up.

Donatella had gone through the effort of trying to fake it. Paulie didn't know if he should laugh or cry, rage or fear. He managed to feel all of them at once.

"You got hand sanitizer or something?" Dante asked, coming out of the bathroom down the hall. "I forgot about turning off the valve."

"Jesus Christ, Dante." Paulie darted for the door to the bathroom, pulled it closed. "You friggin' destroyed my bathroom."

"Ashbett', ah? I wasn't doing it at the hospital." But Dante smiled, the one he reserved for taunting Davide.

Paulie handed him the half bottle of designer water, went to the fridge for another for the cats. He took a swig first, washing away the taste of chewable aspirin. It was a relief to know rather than suspect. At least he was more familiar with the unmedicated Donatella than the medicated one; he knew what she was capable of, both in good ways and bad. He didn't hold out much hope that she'd try something different, now that she was no longer pregnant, but maybe she'd at least discuss it once—

"So, I been thinking." Dante dried his hands, head down. "You, Donatella, and the baby should just come stay with me until, you know, you decide whatever you two, three, are going to do."

Paulie's thoughts stumbled over one another, trying to keep up. "What?"

"Am I speaking Russian? You have no place to go right now. Not a place with water, anyway." He chucked Paulie's shoulder. "I got this big house, and no one in it but me. If you and Don and the baby moved in, even for a little while, it'd be . . . great."

Paulie's throat closed. Tears he barely had the strength to hold in beat the crap out of the backs of his eyes. All he could manage to say was "The cats?"

"Cats, too."

Something closer to a bark than laughter flew out of Paulie's face, but whatever it was worked to open his throat. "You and Donatella? Under one roof?"

Dante laughed, too, his regular, deep, almost-laugh. "She's my sister. And you're my . . . you're our Paulie. And that kid she just popped out is my nephew. You're going to need a, what do you call it? A support system. Mom's close. I'll be there. Pan and Gabriella. You won't be alone with this, Paulie."

"And Donatella."

"Well, sure, you have to ask her." Dante either didn't get the implication, or ignored it. "But she'll go for it. I know she will."

Tell him? Prepare him? Paulie tried to find the words. All he could manage was "She's off her meds."

"She's always been off her meds." Dante put his hands on Paulie's shoulders. "It's what I meant, kid. You won't be alone. We're family. We stick together, no matter what."

Paulie's chin ached from his efforts to keep it from quivering. "I'm scared."

—she won't be okay.

—she'll break Vincent's heart like my parents broke mine.

—she'll vanish.

—she'll vanish and take Vincent with her.

"I know," Dante said. "It's okay. I was scared when Gabby was born, too."

Got it? Ignored it? What did it matter? Dante was there. He'd always be there whether Donatella was the perfect model of motherhood, or flew a rocket ship to the moon.

Paulie wanted to stop thinking, thinking, always thinking. Forever thinking. He wanted to be happy. He had a son! A beautiful, healthy son whom he'd watched come into the world, a wiggly little worm covered in blood and goo, the most beautiful sight he'd ever seen in his life. Vincent and Donatella were safe, in the hospital, which is where he should be, not in this waterlogged duplex, waiting for the sky to fall.

"I'll talk to her," he said. "Thanks, Dante. I mean, really. Huge thanks. I don't know what I'd do without you."

Dante let his hands slide from Paulie's shoulders like a caress. "Don't worry, kid. You'll never have to find out."

No looking away. Not this time. Paulie held the gaze pinning him in place like one of those case-encapsulated bugs in science class, back when he was a sophomore in high school. Donatella had stolen one that looked like an emerald, saying she was having it made into a ring. She probably still had it, in that box of memorabilia she dragged with her from home to temporary home.

"Get whatever you need. We'll take the cats to my place, then I'll get you back to the hospital."

Had he looked away first? Or had Dante? Paulie didn't know. He'd never know. Just like he'd never know what he'd do without Dante Palladino, because he'd never have to find out.

35

pizzeel/s *(peets-eel/s)*

Italian: *pizzelle;* a light, crispy waffle cookie

Caveat—this is not what a pizzeel is in my world, only where
the name came from. A *pizzelle* (also pronounced peets-eel
by many; it has the same *t* sound, like the *zz* in *pizza*) is made
from eggs, sugar, butter, vanilla, flour, and baking powder, then
pressed in a waffle-iron sort of thing that looks like lace. A pizzeel
is fried pizza dough, sprinkled with powdered sugar. This was
the highlight of the church bazaar, every summer before school
started up again. My grandmother was always one of the fry
ladies, so I got as much as I wanted . . . from the other ladies,
because she knew I was a gavone who would keep eating them
until I puked. Which I did. Every year. You've never lived until
you've puked up half a ton of fried pizza dough, and orange
punch glommed straight from the machine.

T hree days after giving birth, Donatella was home with baby Vincent. She and Paulie had, for the time being, moved into Dante's house. He and Paulie surprised her with a purple and orange—her favorite colors—nursery, set up in the smallest of the three bedrooms. She seemed happy. Exhausted as any new mother, but happy.

Varina felt bad, really selfish, thanking her lucky stars for that burst pipe, and her eldest's generosity that probably had a lot to do with being lonely, but still. Her mother living her happily ever after with John in Sunset Downs, the new little family ensconced in the security of Dante's protection, and the fact that Vincent would be just over a month old by the time she left for France was allowing Varina to do so without the guilt she'd been avoiding—though she'd not avoided it at all—by not telling a soul. Except—unintentionally—her mother.

"Those pizzeels ready yet?" Davide hovered over the fryer. How her son stayed svelte was a mystery even his trainer couldn't explain.

"Another minute." Varina turned the dough. Gabriella, at her other elbow, watched carefully.

"And they're just pizza dough," she said. "No eggs or anything?"

"Nope. Just pizza dough."

"I always thought they had eggs and rigott' in them."

"That's zebbole."

"Oh."

"Back up, both of you. You'll get burned."

She had to say it. She really had no choice. That one was in his forties and the other was about to head off to culinary school had no bearing on her need to warn them from harm. It was too ingrained, and Varina figured she'd earned the right to give herself a break.

There was no room to sit them all to a Sunday dinner in her apartment over the store, but getting together was doable. Dante, Paulie, Pandora—no more Frankie; it hadn't lasted long. It took a special sort of stalwart to endure the Palladinos—and Donatella sprawled out on the sectional in Varina's living room. The baby slept in Varina's powder-blue bedroom, and Ruth would be there any moment, for moral support. It was time, past time, to talk to her family about France.

Varina had kept it secret so long, it seemed silly, now, that she had. She was embarrassed. Of course, they'd be fine with it. Maybe not Donatella; then again, maybe her most of all. Who the hell cared, anyway, what her grown children thought about her spending so much money on a week and a half in France, with a friend she met at the travel agent because she'd planned on going alone?

Varina did. She cared what they thought about her going, about her keeping it secret. She, who cared nothing for what others thought of her and never had, cared deeply what her children did.

Opening the door, Ruth knocked. "Hello, hello!" She waved both hands. "Am I in time for pizzos?"

Gabriella and Davide laughed.

"Pizzeels," Davide told her. "Can I get you a glass of wine?"

"I'd love it, thanks."

"Gabby, grab the sifter for me, will you?"

"Sure, Nonnie."

Alone at the counter, Varina leaned nearer to her friend. "You should have texted. I'd have sent my granddaughter down in the elevator to get you."

"I know. I need the steps. Getting ready for all that walking." Ruth leaned closer still. "You didn't tell them yet?"

"I'm about to ply them with sugar and grease, then I'll tell them." She looked beyond the kitchen island to the sitting room, where all her children sat together, chatting. "This is nice, isn't it?"

"Very. I'm envious, right now."

"What's mine is yours, my friend."

Ruth took the glass Davide brought to her, raised it just a little. "Chin-chin to that."

It didn't make sense, but Varina got the sentiment. Lifting the pizzeels from the hot oil, she set them onto a tray lined with a paper towel. Gabriella got to work, dusting them with powdered sugar. The family gathered around, pulling apart the too-hot slabs of greasy, sugary dough. Pandora snatched Davide's right out of his mouth. Gabriella laughed and threw pinches of powdered sugar at both of them. Donatella hoarded three all to herself, giving Paulie one because he had none. And Dante—without whom none of this would have been possible—stood back as Varina did, watching them all with a smile on his face and love in his eyes.

"I'm going to France at the end of the month!" There. She had said it. Laughter and chatter died away. Chewing did not.

"Wha'd'y'mean?" Donatella, mouth full of pizzeel, asked first.

"I'm going on one of those river cruises. With Ruth. Ruth and I are going to France."

Her daughter swallowed the wad of dough in her mouth. "Together?"

"Of course, together."

"I mean, *together,* together. You know." Donatella made a kissy sound.

Varina blushed from the roots of her hair to her toes. Ruth laughed, that jingling, musical sound she'd probably learned in some finishing school that taught girls how to laugh melodiously.

"No, darling. As bawdy-brilliant as that sounds, your mother and I are not going *together.* We met at the travel agent just after Christmas. Same place, same time. Kismet. The rest, as they say, is history."

"I saved up for years," Varina was saying. "I don't want you to think this was a frivolous whim I—"

"Mom." Dante, of course. "You can do whatever the hell you want with your money."

"Yeah, Mom." Davide put his arm around her. "You should have said. I'd've kicked in something."

Varina was pretty sure he'd have said the same were Ruth not standing right there, even if he side-eyed her a little.

"Oh, Jesus." Donatella paused, pizzeel halfway to mouth. "I nearly blew it for you, didn't I? With my court fines."

"No, sweetheart," she lied.

"I did. Of course I did. I don't just fuck up—sorry, screw up my own life. I nearly screwed up yours."

"But you didn't. I'm going? In just about a month. See?"

"And then . . . Vincent! Thank goodness he was born so early, right?"

"Not at all. Sweetheart, please." This had taken a turn. "I don't want you—"

"I have a lot of what I owe you," Donatella was saying, as if Varina hadn't spoken at all. "I was waiting to give it all to you in one shot. Tell her, Paulie. Tell her I have the money."

"She has some of the money?"

Donatella whacked him in the arm, half smile, half scowl. "You're not helping."

As if by some staged cue, Vincent started crying. Paulie darted for the bedroom. "Got him!"

"Pan, can you grab a bottle from the fridge?" Donatella asked.

"I thought you were breastfeeding."

"I tried. It's not for me. Don't you dare bottle-shame me."

"I wasn't going to." Pan handed her a bottle. "I didn't last long with Gabby either. She just didn't want to latch on."

"Gross, Mom."

"Yeah," Davide said. "Gross, Mom."

"Hush, you."

And, like that, Varina forgot her misgivings. The topic absorbed into common knowledge. Into no big deal. Like John Yu had. Like Ruth had. She was leaving in a few weeks, and her children's world would continue spinning without skipping a beat. Relief. And a little sorrow. Keeping them close had never been about keeping them close to one another, but keeping them close to her.

"That went over well," Ruth said.

"I knew it would." Varina shoved a bit of dough in her mouth. "Have a pizzeel."

Ruth shook her head, chewing. "You're one strange duck, Varina."

"Yeah, takes one to know one."

"Want to go shopping tomorrow? Get some clothes for the trip?"

"Sure. Lunch? We never did take my mother to Panera."

"And you never did give me the rigatoni."

"Tomorrow, then?"

"Tomorrow." Ruth raised her glass.

Varina touched her rim to it. "Chin-chin."

Would it have been this easy, way back at the turn of the year, when she went secretly and apprehensively to the travel agent? Maybe her kids, one or all of them, would have helped her do it all online. Then she would never have met Ruth. Easier or not, Varina wouldn't change it if she could. Fact was, Sylvia and John had changed a lot in her life; so had Donatella and Paulie having a baby; and Dante buying the house, which wouldn't have happened had Tommy not retired and moved himself to Florida.

Varina put a few more stretched-out bits of dough into the fryer. Life was like that, she supposed. Sometimes things happened that led to everything turning out right, and sometimes things happened that made everything go wrong. This was one of those right moments, and the last thing she was going to do was tempt any fates. In a few weeks, she'd be on a plane for the time of her life. She'd eat too much, dance every night, and walk her way through every city along the Rhône listed on the itinerary. She'd eat cheese aged in a cellar on a goat farm, and drink wine from vineyards that also kept pigs and dogs for hunting truffles. She'd see Roman ruins in the middle of the modern city of Lyon, and the bridge at Avignon, the one from the song she'd learned as a child.

Life was good.

Life was better than good.

Life was at least as good as it had been in the nineties, that Camelot of her life.

Knocking on her butcher-block chopping board, kissing the cornoot she always wore around her neck, Varina watched the hot oil change the white dough to golden brown, thanking every lucky star in heaven.

36

Veni qua *(veh-nee kaa)*

Italian: *Vieni qui;* "Come here"

It means the same, either way. J.I. just does the smoosh-it-to-something-slightly-different thing.

bicciurid' *(bee-choo-REED)*

Italian: *picciridu;* "my little boy/little baby"

Sylvia Cioffi-Spini-kind-of-Yu was losing touch with her family. At least, the day-to-day touch she'd always been in with the
whole bunch of them. Varina left for her big trip to France—though
why France and not Italy, Sylvia could not fathom; she'd ask Varina
when she got home—a few days ago. They'd had a bon voyage party
for her and Ruth, complete with travel-appropriate gifts and champagne. The gabaruss' cried, that silly thing, though she pretended
it was the champagne tickling her nose. Varina said Ruth had no
family of her own, at least none she was close to. The Palladino clan
had adopted another stray into the family. Sylvia was pretty sure it
wasn't kosher to refer to humans as strays, which is why she kept
that thought to herself, especially since she was also sure *kosher*
wasn't kosher to use if one was not Jewish. These days, she was
taking no chances. The last thing she ever wanted to be again was
accidentally racist.

The grandchildren, bless them, took turns calling her. She'd
learned the rotation at this point. Donatella started the ball rolling
that first Sunday, then Davide, Dante, Gabriella, Pandora, and even
Paulie. When the phone rang on the Friday before Varina's return,
Sylvia expected it to be Gabriella.

It was not Gabriella. Sylvia tapped into the call.

"Hello, sweetheart. It's not your turn."

"Huh?"

"Never mind. How's the baby?"

"He's great, Non. Good. That's why I'm calling, actually."

"Something wrong?"

"Yes. No. Not with him. I just ..."

Sylvia could feel her vibrating through the airways.

"I need to go out a bit. Just down to the bakery, you know? Hang
out a little, maybe get my hands in some dough. You know how it is

when you have a newborn. It's just . . . just for a bit. Could you come watch him?"

"Where's Paulie?"

Donatella's laughter shook a little. "Working, duh."

"Doesn't he usually take Vincent with him?" *Babywearing.* It was a term Sylvia would only think grudgingly, she certainly wasn't going to say it out loud. Paulie had been babywearing Vincent, at first, to give Donatella time to recover. A month later, he was apparently taking the baby to work most days, leaving Vincent home only when absolutely necessary. She heard Dante and Pandora talking about it at the bon voyage party. Strangely enough, it had been Dante who defended Paulie, not Pandora, who thought he was coddling Donatella way too much for her own good.

"He wants his kid with him," Dante had said. "It doesn't bother me, and I'm his boss. Besides, if he was a woman bringing her kid to work, would you say anything?"

Pandora hadn't responded. Dante had a point, alien as it was to admit. If it were Donatella wearing Vincent to the bakery every day to keep him with her, she'd have been proud.

"He couldn't take him today," Donatella said. "Something about asbestos, I think. It's okay if you can't. I just thought I'd ask so I could run down to the bakery for an hour or so. Never mind."

"No, no, sweetheart," Sylvia told her. "I'd be happy to come spend some time with my little great-grandchild. John's home now. I could have him run me over right away."

"Really?"

"Of course, sweetheart." *When have you ever asked me for something I didn't give you immediately?* But she left those thoughts in her head, too. Even at ninety-three, Sylvia Cioffi-Spini-kind-of-Yu was learning.

"You're the best, Nonina. The best! He's sleeping, and probably will stay asleep while I'm gone, but I can't just leave him alone, right?" More shaky laughter. "I'll see you in a few."

Sylvia put her teacup into the sink. "John?"

Her almost-husband put down his crossword. "What is it, my love?"

"Would you mind taking me over to the house?" Not Varina's house. She couldn't call it Dante's, either. Just, the house. That's what it would always be. "Donatella asked if we would mind Vincent for an hour while she went to the bakery."

"Of course." Tossing the paper onto the coffee table, he stretched his back. Instead of getting his keys from the hook by the front door, he went to the Victrola, and only then did Sylvia realize he'd been listening to music. She was so used to Vicky playing, she sometimes didn't notice it at all.

"Did you?" Sylvia pointed. "Or did she?"

He winked. "I was about to. She must have known."

He was probably humoring her. Vicky still wasn't herself, though she seemed a little less melancholy than she'd been. Maybe because Sylvia told her all about the changes in the house, though she made sure to assure her that her favorite window was still intact. And that she'd made Dante promise, when she was gone from the world, he would take Vicky and put her back in the window. It wasn't much of a legacy, but at least it would make the old demon happy. He'd never admit it, but Dante was sentimental like that. He, more than anyone, knew what *famiglia* meant.

It only took fifteen minutes to get from Sunset Downs to the house, but Sylvia stopped at Palladino's on the way to get a package of the dried figs she and John ate like candy, so it was half an hour later they finally pulled into the driveway. She hoped Vincent would wake while they were there, though she also hoped he didn't need a diaper change. Feeding was okay, but she'd sworn off diapers when her own grandchildren still wore them, and she really didn't want to break that streak. Maybe John would do it. Of course, he would. Her John would do anything she asked.

"Hey, Non! Hey, John!" Donatella met them at the door, kissed both their cheeks. Her hair was neat, her cheeks rosy, and she wore actual clothes, not sweats or maternity wear. "Vincent is sleeping in his Moses basket in the front room. Bottles in the fridge, diapers and stuff on the side table. I'll be back in an hour."

She trotted down the steps and half jogged down the drive before Sylvia closed the door behind them.

"She was in a hurry, huh?" John smiled, but it was a little strained.

"Yes, she was. That's our Donatella." Sylvia went to her great-grandson. Standing over his basket, she could have wept. Vincent was as perfect as perfect could be, with Donatella's fawn-colored hair, and her dimples puckering in and out of existence as he suckled in his sleep. It took her back to Donatella as a baby. Back further still, to Varina, who had looked nothing like either. She'd been a dark-haired, dark-skinned Palladino from day one. It didn't matter. Babies were babies, and *famiglia* was *famiglia*.

"I put the kettle on." John put an arm around her waist. "We can have tea and figs while we play cards."

"That'll be lovely. Thank you."

"He sure is cute."

"He is."

And he was soundly sleeping.

John made them tea. They ate their figs. They played cards. An hour passed. Donatella did not return. Neither of them mentioned it. Maybe John hadn't really noticed, or thought nothing of it. Sylvia had. She did. There was something off with Donatella since the baby's birth. A relief that somehow made her edges sharper. Sylvia noticed, because she knew the feeling. She remembered it more clearly when Donatella was in its grips.

"Why don't we watch a little television," she suggested. "Maybe the news?"

"I wouldn't mind finding out what's going on in the world." There was that smile. That channel-chasm smile. Sylvia's heart flittered and fluttered. She'd never tire of it, this love so big it made her cry.

John turned on the news; he never fretted over the remote control the way she did. Maybe because he'd been one of those early techies when still a working man, married to another woman who gave him all those children then died and left him alone. Sylvia made sure to thank her whenever she thought of her, because John had loved her. She helped create the man Sylvia would meet by accident at the age of ninety-two, when he was a grandfather looking for love and all she wanted was a man for her stubborn daughter. Her daughter, currently in France, hopefully having a grand time. Maybe she'd bring her back some chocolates. Or lavender sachets for her drawers. Varina was such a good girl; maybe she'd bring her back both . . .

SYLVIA WOKE TO THE SOUND OF A DOOR GOING *CLICK*. SHE KNEW BETTER than to bolt upright. Her muscles and bones would protest for days.

John was still sleeping on the couch beside her, his head back and his mouth open, soft snores more like puffed breaths she loved as much as his smile. Getting up as gently and quietly as she could, she went to check on Vincent in the front room.

Donatella was lifting him, still sleeping, into her arms. Sylvia's heart did that flitter-flutter. Was there anything as beautiful as a mother with her child? As Donatella holding Vincent, gazing at him so lovingly? Sylvia couldn't speak if she wanted to, and she didn't. She wanted only to watch, unnoticed, for as long as it lasted.

"I'm sorry, baby," Donatella whispered. "It won't be long. I swear.

I'll be back before you know it. Daddy will take care of you. He's the best daddy, the best person, in the whole world. He loves you so much. He loves us both. He'll be there for us no matter what, like always. Okay? All right, Vincent? Mommy loves you so-so-so much. I won't be gone long. I'll be back before you know it."

Sylvia backed away as silently as she'd crept up, her face aching with smiling and not-crying. She went back to the couch John slept on. Donatella came through the space, not sneaking but quiet, wiping the tears from her face.

"Are you okay, sweetheart?"

She stumbled, hand to her heart and eyes closed. "You scared the shit out of me. I thought you were asleep."

"I was. I'm sorry. Are you all right?"

"I'm fine." Donatella sighed. "Baby blues, I guess. I didn't mean to wake you. I only stopped back to get my purse. Some of the guys are going to grab food after work. Paulie'll be home in another half hour or so. Do you mind staying?"

Did she mind? No. Sylvia held out her arms. "Veni qua."

Donatella's shoulders slumped, but she obeyed. Sitting on the couch beside her grandmother, she let Sylvia hold her.

"Being a mother isn't necessarily instinctive," Sylvia said. "Not for all of us. It takes some getting used to."

"I know."

"You're doing great, sweetheart. It's no sin to need some time to yourself, away from the house."

Donatella sniffed, nodded against Sylvia's shoulder. "That's all I need. A break from . . ." She leaned away, hands in the air. "All of this. You understand, Nonina."

"I do."

"And you don't mind staying?"

"I don't mind staying."

Still sniffing, Donatella smiled a wobbly smile. "You're the best, Non. You always get me."

Sylvia patted her cheek. "Go on. I'll take care of our boy."

"Okay. Thanks." Donatella got to her feet. She picked up the backpack dropped when Sylvia scared her, slung it over her shoulder, and headed out without looking back.

John woke when the back door shut louder than it had opened only moments ago, puffed breaths snarling like a startled bulldog's as his head came up. "Something wrong? Is the baby awake?"

"No." Sylvia kissed him. "He's almost as adorable as you when he sleeps."

John smiled, cupped her cheek in his papery hand. He checked the time. "Still not back yet?"

"Here and gone again. She's going to grab food with some of her bakery friends. I told her we'd wait until Paulie got home."

John rubbed his hands together. "Maybe I should go to Palladino's and get something for dinner, just in case Paulie's late."

"You just want my daughter's arancini."

"It might be an ulterior motive. Don't tell anyone I said so, but Gabriella makes them even better than Varina. She puts peas in them."

"That sounds lovely. Should we go together? Take the baby for a walk? Fresh air is good for babies, and it's such a beautiful day. We won't have many of these in the coming months."

"Are you sure you can walk that far, my love?"

She'd spent years claiming she couldn't, mostly because she knew Varina would make her walk places instead of drive. Sylvia hadn't the energy, then. Or maybe it was the will. Now?

"If I can dance for two hours every Wednesday evening, I can walk a couple blocks to the store." She patted his hand. "What about you?"

John pounded his chest, gorilla-style. He walked the Sunset Downs grounds daily; he could walk to Palladino's.

"I think I saw a stroller in the mudroom," he said. "Do you think Donatella would be upset?"

"Donatella?" Sylvia waved off his concern. "She trusts me completely. I'll get the baby. You get a bottle from the fridge, and the stroller."

Sylvia lifted the Moses basket from the floor, her shoulder and wrists protesting just a little. After so many years of feigning frailty, she had to admit that it wasn't completely feigned. She was, after all, nearly a century old. Maybe it wasn't such a good idea to take the baby for a walk. What if he cried? Or pooped? Or wanted his bottle? What if someone knocked her and John down and stole him? And where had that come from? Old fears creeping up, threatening her good mood. That's all. Besides, if they got there and she didn't feel she could make it back, they could wait in Varina's apartment until someone came to fetch them. Having a big, loving, smothering *famiglia* had its downs, but it had many more ups.

"Veni qua, bicciurid'." She lifted Vincent from his basket. His little legs curled up underneath him; he didn't wake beyond a squirm. Baby in her arms, diaper bag on her shoulder, Sylvia followed the sound of John bumping down the back steps with the stroller. She glanced at the four steps that would take her from the mudroom to the driveway, only glanced. Hand on the railing, she took careful steps and made it without even a wobble.

John took the diaper bag, put the bottle inside, and placed both in the handy basket underneath. How things had changed, even since Donatella was a baby. Sylvia had seen some big things in her lifetime. Cars, computers, disposable diapers, formula. No more baby buggies, but strollers that opened with the flick of a wrist, and folded compact and lighter than air. Gay men having babies with their best friends.

Gay men, period. They'd always been around, of course, just not where anyone could see them.

"Ready?"

"Ready."

John pushed. Sylvia took his arm. Together, they walked slowly but sturdily down the driveway, to the sidewalk, to Palladino's.

37

Lascialu! *(lah-shah-loo)*

Italian: *Lascialo!;* "Leave him alone!"

Jersey Italians just change the final *o* sound, to an *oo*. Also, notice it's masculine. I never heard a feminine version of this. Kind of says something, doesn't it?

Nothing, absolutely nothing, was going to keep Paulie from a hot shower, something quick and easy heated up in the microwave—there was lasagna in the fridge, he was pretty sure—and sacking out in front of the television with his son in his arms. It had been not a day, but a *day*! His body had lost the muscle memory necessary to do the strenuous part of renovation without complaining. But if he hadn't gotten in that kitchen with the demo crew, it wouldn't have gotten done, which meant the floor couldn't get laid in the morning. Putting off the floor guys meant being sent to the end of their long list of clients. They'd contracted for this job at least a month ago. Without the floor in place, they couldn't do cabinets or backsplash or appliances; wasted time was money Timeless Renovation couldn't afford to lose. Dante was strapped tighter than he'd ever been. Without the cushion of Spini and Son, it was all on him.

He worked so hard, and Paulie worked hard alongside him. Every day. Vincent strapped to his chest. They rarely went home the same time, but they slept in the same house, got up at the same time, and often spent an hour or so exhausted on the couch together, Vincent between them, while Donatella went out with friends.

Paulie Vittone had never been happier.

"Donatella?" he called, not shouted, just in case the baby was sleeping. He hadn't wanted to leave him home, but she'd practically begged him to. As it turned out, it was a good thing. He never could have done the demo wearing Vincent. Paulie still feared more than he trusted, but she'd been trying so hard. Harder than he'd ever seen Donatella try anything. He had to start trusting her at some point. He had to believe in her, or how would she ever believe in herself? It'd have been easier if she'd agreed to try a different medication, now that she'd given birth, but Donatella was adamantly against it.

"The meds don't help me," she'd told him. "The meds help you.

They help everyone else, because they make me like a zombie. Controllable. You don't know what it's like to still be in there, screaming and unable to do anything about it."

The *controllable* had gotten him, as she had to have known it would. There was no reasoning with her, no amount of proof he could show her that the newer medications didn't have that side effect. She wasn't ready, and until she was, Donatella was Donatella, beloved and keeping him on the edge of fear.

But she came home after being out all day, and hadn't stayed out past eleven since moving into Dante's house. She'd even arranged to go back to work at Jumbaloon's when Vincent turned three months old, though she wasn't the one taking care of him on a daily basis. That wasn't her fault. It was Paulie's. She hadn't had Vincent all on her own, for any extended amount of time, since his birth. There was always someone with her. Until today, she hadn't even asked.

"Donatella?" He peeked into the nursery. No Donatella. No Vincent either.

"Donatella?" Their room, the one they platonically shared. No Donatella. No Vincent.

Don't. Panic.

He texted her. No response. Paulie did the never-done and called. No answer. He trot-stumbled down the steps, checked the Moses basket. No Vincent. No diaper bag. He looked in the mudroom; the stroller was gone. She just went for a walk. It was a gorgeous day. Indian summer weather. That was all. Donatella had taken her little son for a walk, probably down to Jumbaloon's.

He checked the time; the bakery would be closed. Maybe they were still in back, chatting. He tapped into the call. The phone rang and rang. He tapped out.

Taking a deep breath, letting it go in a long, long whistle, Paulie tried to collect himself. He couldn't do this to himself. Or to her.

She'd gone out for a walk. She had every right to take her son out in his stroller on a beautiful autumn day. Trudging up the stairs, he peeled his work shirt off. Dust flew. He'd take a shower. Donatella would be home by the time he got out.

She was not.

Now, he panicked. Paulie called the only person he could think to call.

"What's up, kid?"

"Donatella's gone. So is Vincent."

Something on Dante's side of the call banged. "I'll be right home. Stay put."

Paulie didn't know what else to do, so he did as he was told. He went back up to the room he shared with Donatella, checked her drawers. They seemed . . . light. Peeking into the laundry told him nothing, but her crappy, ancient backpack was gone, too. She used it as a purse, and never actually had anything in it; no credit cards and very little cash . . .

Cold heat shivered up Paulie's spine, made his hair stand on end. He tried not to dive for the box under the bed, the one he usually kept for her when she was between temporary homes. The one that held all her best memories. The one where she kept the money she owed her mother but still hadn't given her.

Cross-legged on the floor, Paulie opened the box. There was all her stuff. The *Yellow Submarine* VHS she'd been obsessed with when they were kids. How many times she'd forced him to sit through it. The "kindest student" award she got in fifth grade. Christmas cards she'd saved because she loved the velvety Santa coats and Frosty scarves. The emerald bug she'd stolen to make into a ring. Lots of stuff she somehow couldn't part with.

No envelope of cash.

Paulie was still sitting cross-legged on the floor, now with three cats curled against him, head in his hands, when the door opened and slammed closed downstairs.

"Paulie!"

"Up here."

Thumping on the steps. Dante blowing into the room. The avenging angel motif, as ever, in Paulie's brain, ingrained. Always. Dante dropped to his knees next to Paulie, put his arms around him.

"It'll be okay."

"She's gone, Dante. She's gone." Paulie burst, then, unable to say the next part. Unwilling to believe Donatella would do this to him. Not just leave, but take their son with her. The son she couldn't take care of on her own. The son she'd leave with strangers if there was someplace she wanted to be or go or investigate. His baby. His son. How could she?

"Hey, hey. Come on. You know Donatella. She'll show up with a—"

"Dad?"

Gabriella, but other voices as well. Dante and Paulie scrambled to their feet, stumbled over one another down the stairs. Paulie's vision narrowed to a tiny point, only large enough to see Vincent cradled in Gabriella's arms. He swooped in.

"Jesus Christ, Paulie! Take it easy."

"Hey, lascialu, ah? You have no idea what he's been through the last hour or so."

Paulie held his son close, sobbed into his baby body. Somewhere in his overwrought brain, he acknowledged Sylvia and John fretting quietly with Gabriella, and Dante explaining what had happened, what they thought happened. Mrs. Spini was patting his shoulder, telling him she was so sorry. She had no idea they'd be gone so long, but they'd gotten all the way to Palladino's and the walk back was just too much and they'd waited on Varina's patio for Gabriella to close the store.

"I called Donatella to tell her," she said. "She said it was fine, not to worry. Why didn't she call Paulie and let him know? Oh, I should have. I should have. I'm so sorry. So sorry. The trouble I've caused."

Paulie sniffed back what he could. "It's all right," he choked out. "It's not your fault."

Vincent was solid in his arms, eyes open and searching. Donatella was gone, but she hadn't taken their son.

She hadn't taken their son.

"Hey, give him here." Dante lifted Vincent from Paulie's arms, and only then did Paulie realize he was shaking so hard his teeth chattered. Gabriella led him to the couch, sat him down. A moment later, Sylvia and John were gone, and Gabriella was handing him a glass of water.

"I'm okay," he told her, even though he wasn't. The relief sat heavy, painfully so. He couldn't even worry about Donatella yet. He would. Later, alone in their bed. He'd worry about where she was, who she was with, what she was doing. How long she'd be gone this time, before blowing back into his life as if nothing had happened. All his research since her diagnosis had made sense of her swings for him. He could map out her patterns going all the way back to their teens. What pregnancy had done to that pattern, he couldn't say, but she'd been pretty okay, if antsy, these last weeks off her medication. Maybe she'd walk off her need to run, and come back home. All that mattered was she loved Vincent enough to leave him. Loved Paulie enough not to take him.

Gabriella was rubbing his back, making soothing, motherly sounds. Paulie didn't have it in him to tell her he was fine, she could go. It helped. It soothed. MaryJane jumped up on the couch on his other side. Chooch climbed across the back of the couch, and Pastafazool wound about his legs.

"You think they know you're upset?"

Of course they did. "It's past their suppertime."

"Oh, ha! I'll do it."

"It's okay. I got it."

Gabriella followed him to the huge, walk-in pantry, hands on hips and eyes everywhere. "You and Dad did some job on this place."

"I'd have done some things different."

She chuckled. "Dad likes white, huh?"

"How could you tell?"

"At least he let you do the red accents. And the downstairs bathroom is yellow."

"A little homage to the old bathroom." Paulie smiled. "And let's not forget the orange and purple nursery."

Gabriella's normal made him feel better. Like Donatella was off doing her Donatella thing, and everything was just fine. He grabbed a few cans of cat food and brought them to the marble island. MaryJane, Chooch, and Pastafazool proved hunger overruled their concern by meowing and circling his ankles. Setting the bowls onto the kitty place mat Dante insisted upon, he wobbled a little. Gabriella steadied him.

"You're really broken up, huh?"

"I'm fine."

"Oh, stop. You are not."

"Why aren't you in school?"

"I don't have class today. I took my mom's shift at the store. Why are you changing the subject?"

"There's no subject, Gabs. Donatella does this. I'm used to it."

"But things are different now."

"Apparently, they're not."

"You thought she took Vincent with her."

Paulie looked down at his cats, obliviously chowing down. "She'd never do that to me."

Gabriella put her hand on his shoulder. "For what it's worth, I don't think she would either."

"I wish she'd answer her cell phone."

"Give her a day or two, she will."

"Maybe." He groaned out a breath, rubbing his eyes. "I don't know what I'd have done without your brother. He's a rock."

"That's one thing he is." Gabriella chuckled. "Paulie, Paulie, Paulie. Do you have any idea how much he loves you?"

"He has to love me. Varina makes him." He tried to smile. "Honestly, I do know. I'm very grateful for—"

"Will you shut the fuck up."

"You kiss your mother with that mouth?"

She shoved him. "You're an idiot."

Normal, normal, normal. Paulie managed the smile now. Gabriella reminded him so much of Donatella, and of Pandora, and Dante, and Varina. She was the perfect combination, the best of all of them in one person. He pulled her into a hug, kissed the top of her head.

"I love you, you know."

"It's going to be okay, Paulie."

"Yeah."

She pulled away. "You want me to text Donatella? See if she answers?"

"It's probably best to leave her alone for now," he said. "You're right. She'll answer in a few days."

"Should we call Nonnie?"

"And ruin the last few days of her trip? There's absolutely nothing she can do."

"True." Gabriella checked the time. "I should take off. I have homework."

"What kind of homework does a culinary student have to do? Chop carrots?"

"Funny. You're a real clown." She sighed. "It's a lot to juggle, school and the store, but I love it. I really do."

"You're going to do great things, Gabs."

"Yeah, yeah. So I've been told all my life. I just want to do things, Paulie. They don't have to be great."

Wise. In all ways, wonderful.

"Lean on my dad," she said. "He's here for you."

"I lean on him too much."

"It makes him happy, believe me. Dad needs to be needed. Especially by you."

"I'm not *that* needy."

Gabriella shook her head, rolled her eyes. "You really have no clue, do you."

"About?"

"Aren't you supposed to have, like, a sense about this kind of thing?"

"What kind of thing?"

Another eye roll. "Good night, Paulie. Get some rest. Don't let my dad make you work this weekend. You know he will if you don't say something."

"There are no weekends in construction." But Dante wouldn't have anything pressing for him. He'd know. He'd understand.

Paulie walked Gabriella to the door. The buzzing in body and brain had dulled, though his fingertips still felt weird. Vincent was home, safe and sound. The weird would pass.

He took the container of lasagna from the fridge. Rather than heating it up in the microwave—so soggy and gross—he set the oven and put two servings into an oven-safe dish. The stove wasn't as massive as Varina's professional beasts, but it was the same brand, and way fancier than Paulie had ever otherwise had. Everything in the house was fancier than Paulie had ever otherwise had. And yet, it was home. The only home he'd known since he was a kid his parents no longer wanted.

Heading upstairs while the lasagna heated up, he heard Dante softly singing "Pepino Soolagil'" to Vincent. They started them early in the Palladino family, and Vincent was, indeed, a Palladino. Paulie walked slower, listening to Dante sing, letting the sound become sensation that eased the weird tingling from his fingers. It was near feeding time. They'd all eat together. Vincent, Paulie, and Dante. It was going to be okay. He and Vincent were going to be okay.

"You like that, little buddy?" Dante was saying. "I'll teach it to you, like I taught it to your cousin. Okay?"

Vincent farted.

"Whoa, whoa. You wait for your daddy for that, eh?"

Paulie swooped in, his turn to be avenging angel. "You've changed diapers before."

"Not for a little boy." Dante stood back, arms crossed. "I don't know what to do with that little pishadeel."

Paulie put Vincent on the changing table, checked his diaper. Explosion. *Normal, normal, normal.* "I put lasagna in to heat," he said. "You hungry?"

"Starving."

Diaper changed, Vincent buttoned up again, Dante put his finger into the infant's tiny, flailing hand, smiling when little fingers curled around his. "My nonina, huh? If I didn't love her, I might have strangled her."

"It wasn't her fault. She couldn't have known what Donatella was up to."

Dante grunted. He wouldn't say anything bad about his sister. Not now. In a few days, probably, right around the same time she started answering texts.

"But I should have," Paulie said, "when she asked if she could keep him for the day. I should have known she was planning something."

"How?"

"Because I know *her*. Your mom will be home in a few days. This was her last shot. She kept Vincent so she could get her grandmother here to babysit. No one would have known she was *gone* gone until later tonight, except Sylvia and John took him for a walk and . . . you get it."

"That's hindsight, Paulie."

He put the baby on his shoulder, patted his bottom. "I guess."

"You're never going to outthink her, kid. She'll always be at least three steps ahead of you."

He knew that. He'd always known that. Until now, it had always just been how things were. Until now, it was only his own heart, his own brain space he had to worry about whenever she disappeared. Paulie held his son closer.

Dante put his hand on the baby's back. "She won't take Vincent," he said. "Let's be real. She doesn't want him. But either way, we'll protect him. You and me. I swear to Christ."

Paulie's insides squirmed. His eyes stung and his nose tingled. No, Donatella did not want Vincent. She hadn't, from day one. But she loved him. Paulie knew beyond a shadow of a doubt, Donatella loved her baby boy. It was up to him to make sure Vincent knew that.

"Lasagna's probably ready," he said. "We should head down."

"I'll be there in a sec. I'm filthy." Dante leaned in, kissed Vincent's duck-fuzz head, his face so close to Paulie's he could have kissed him, too. Emotion balled in Paulie's throat. Want and need. Hope and relief. This tiny baby in his arms who was more than his whole world, his whole heart, his everything.

Dante's hand was on the back of his neck. He ruffled Paulie's still-damp hair. "It's going to be okay, kid."

And then he was gone, before Paulie could do anything to embarrass himself. Before he toppled a balance he'd never be able to put right again.

38

moolignan' *(moo-lin-yahn)*

Italian: *mulignana;* "eggplant"

There is another, unsavory way to use this word, but in my family,
it speaks specifically of a certain method of making eggplant,
and that's fried in olive oil and garlic, then salted, drizzled with
vinegar, and layered with fresh basil.

Moolignan, moon'jahn, or *moolie* is a racial slur for a person of
color. I did not know this until doing the research for this entry.
When I asked my dad about it, he got red in the face and asked
me where I heard it used this way and told me to never repeat it.
I include it only as a matter of scholarly interest.

Che cazz'? *(kay-kaahtz)*

Italian: *Che cazzo fai?;* "What the fuck?/
What the fuck are you doing?"

Same in either language.

ghistu gazz' *(gee-stoo-gahts)*

Italian: *questo o cazzo;* "this or nothing"

Don't you love how the term for "balls" literally means "nothing" in so many of these idioms?

I t was no use. Sylvia would never sit in this house and feel any sort of kinship with it. Maybe in the cellar, the only area that hadn't been renovated, aside from a new furnace and all that, but Sylvia hadn't paid attention to such things when the house was hers, she didn't really know the difference now. It was still dark, cinder-block dampness she wouldn't step foot into. Gabriella teased it would be a great place to age a certain kind of cheese with a tongue-twisting name. That great-granddaughter of hers, with a whole month of culinary school behind her, was making all kinds of changes at the store.

"Peas make the arancini pop, texturally," she explained when Sylvia complained. And—"Red wine vinegar is way too sharp. A balsamic and EVOO drizzle on the moolignan' lets the eggplant take center stage." Whatever EVOO was. There was also now lobster, pumpkin, and truffle varieties of ravioli on offer at Palladino's, catering to the younger crowd buying up Dante's newly renovated but affordable houses. All while Varina flounced around France with the gabaruss' Ms. Fancypants Moneybags.

"You look like you might bite someone," John whispered in her ear.

"There's always so much noise," she groused. "I don't remember it being this loud all the time."

"Oh, it was." John took her hand, kissed it. "The first time I met your family, I wished I wore a hearing aid so I could turn it off."

It was true; their life in Sunset Downs was largely quiet, accented by the Victrola or the television, occasionally by conversation. For the first time in her life, Sylvia Cioffi-Spini-kind-of-Yu didn't feel the need to alleviate the silence. She could simply be. With John. Reading together. Watching the television. Sitting in the sunshine or taking a walk—she'd begun joining him on his daily walks, ever since the drama with Vincent—or dancing, cheek to cheek, while Vicky played. John, her serene being, her love, somehow quieted the inner frenzy she'd always squelched, because he loved her just for her. He didn't expect anything more than her love in return. Or maybe she was just really old, and her brain was finally losing the race. Whatever it was, being among her family brought back all that old baggage. The wanting and needing, the simmering feuds and the little aggressions. The crankiness that made her want to criticize, even if only inside her head.

Or maybe it was the fact that Donatella still had not contacted anyone, not even Paulie. Sylvia alternated from angry to envious to a little proud. She didn't like to be used, duped, made to feel old and half senile, but Sylvia envied Donatella's ability to run and actually stay gone. Her nutty granddaughter didn't push it all down to play by the rules.

"I wish Varina would get here already," she said. "I thought she was due in at noon."

"That's when her plane landed," John told her. "She'll be here soon."

"She won't be happy Pandora closed the store early for a welcome home party."

"She'll be fine." John patted her hand. "It's important we're all here for her when she finds out about Donatella."

Sylvia wanted to say it wouldn't matter. Donatella had broken Varina's heart so many times, she was used to it; she also knew better. It broke fresh every time. Her daughter was used to the worry, knew where to keep it so it didn't shadow every moment of her day. But at night, when she was alone and staring up at the ceiling, the worry dropped on her like a ton of bricks. She imagined every awful scenario in a mother's arsenal. Sylvia knew this, because your kids were your kids, no matter how old they got.

"Try the mutz." Gabriella was suddenly squatting in front of her, a paper dish held out. "I pulled it myself. I also made the sun-dried tomatoes. In the oven, not outside. Gross. Tell me what you think?"

Sylvia picked up a toothpick. She handed one to John. Creamy mozzarella, a hint of salt, the sun-dried tomatoes slightly garlicky, and a single leaf of bas'nigol' topping it off. Perfection in a single bite. "Maybe a little less salt."

"Nonina." Gabriella groaned. "What do you think of the cheese?"

"Very delicious. Creamier than Varina's."

"I used buffalo milk, like they do in Italy. Good, right?"

And expensive, Sylvia was sure. "How did you get it?"

"You can find anything, these days." Gabriella kissed her cheek. "Can I get you something? I made goat cheese, caramelized onion, and fig tartlets. Want to try?"

"We'd love to," John said for both of them. Gabriella bounced off. Sylvia had never seen anyone get so excited about food.

"I don't like goat cheese."

"I'll eat yours." John patted his belly. "At least all the noise comes with good food. A silver lining."

Gabriella returned, handing them each a plate of food. More of the mozzarella skewers, tartlets, mini meatballs, stuffed mushrooms. She wanted to impress her globe-trotting Nonnie, that much was obvious. Varina would be, and maybe a little put out, because Gabriella's creations were better. The same, traditional fare, just different enough to be new. Exciting. Sylvia hoped her daughter wouldn't be stubborn about things.

And maybe pigs would fly.

She ate what she could, gave the rest to John. Sylvia felt a little less cranky. Pandora and Davide flirting like they always had, right there in front of Dante, who didn't even notice because he was yelling at someone on his cell phone, intrigued rather than upset her. Gabriella bouncing about, forcing food on everyone including Paulie, who took what she offered but still hadn't eaten a bite, didn't annoy, even if Paulie looked a little too skinny these days, a little too drawn. Sylvia wanted him to eat, she wanted to tell him he needed to keep up his strength for Vincent's sake if nothing else. But he hadn't been upset with her and John for giving him the fright of his life, so she didn't say a word about how his clothes hung on him.

Vincent's buzz-saw cry rose above the chatter. Paulie scooped him out of his Moses basket. "He just had a bottle." He checked his diaper. "Still dry."

"It's probably too noisy down here for him," Sylvia offered.

"I bet you're right." He glanced at the stairs, his lip between his teeth. And then he was no longer staring, but heading up them as if there were a barking dog at his heels instead of three black and white cats.

"I hope he doesn't let those cats in the nursery," Sylvia tutted. "They'll steal the baby's breath."

John popped the last skewered bite of mozzarella into his mouth. "I believe that's a myth, my love."

"It's no myth. Cats smell the milk. They smother babies. I know people it happened to. And they shed. All that hair. And what about their dirty paws digging around in the litter box? Schufozz'!"

"I'm sure they're very clean cats."

"Schufozz'," she muttered again. Sylvia had never liked cats. Baby-smotherers was what they were. She remembered, clearly, when Rosy Filetti's big orange cat smothered her infant daughter, before she could even be baptized. Poor little baby, doomed to Limbo, buried in unconsecrated ground. The doctors said it was crib death, not the cat, but Dom Filetti had shoved that cat in a bag and tossed it in the river. Babies didn't just die in their sleep. He knew what was what. Sylvia had felt bad for the cat, though. It probably had no idea what it had done.

"Dante." She stopped her grandson on his way past, his attention focused on the stairs Paulie had just climbed. "Tell him not to let the cats in the baby's room. Tell him."

"Okay, Nonina," he said, still staring. "I'll tell him."

"Good boy."

Dante was already moving. Up the stairs. Out of sight. Sylvia settled back into the couch. Nice couch, though leather squeaked a lot. She didn't want anyone to think she was passing wind. Wriggling a little, making sure to re-create the same sound, she took John's hand in hers. He brought their joined hands to his lips and kissed the back of hers. Chicken-kisses. He'd learned. He could even make the proper, smacking sound.

Leaning her head on his shoulder, Sylvia closed her eyes. It helped with the noise, strangely enough, dimming it to a dull roar. Her mind eased. She could have pretended the house was still the house, her family was still young. *She* was still young. The noise even bigger. Her son and his family. Her sisters. Her parents. All those cousins. But she didn't. Sylvia was happy being ninety-three, in the life she'd found so near the end of it with this grandfather who'd been looking for love. Varina's love, not hers. The thought still made her giggle, if under her breath. John had been looking, Sylvia had not, but they'd found one another nonetheless.

Her head on his shoulder, her hand in his hand, Sylvia Cioffi-Spini-kind-of-Yu let herself doze off without worrying about being caught.

VINCENT SETTLED AS SOON AS THE NOISE BECAME MUFFLED CHATTER below. He wasn't sensitive to sound; being on a construction site half of his days made him oblivious to it. It wasn't the too-loud talking, but the Palladino vibe. Maybe Vincent was half Palladino, but he was also half Vittone; Paulie had always been able to pick up the mood in a room better than most. It had made blending in easier, until it became impossible.

Varina was coming home.

Any minute.

They were all on edge, even Sylvia. Maybe not John. The man was as Zen as Zen could ever be. Paulie envied that. He'd have to ask him if it was a skill he could teach, or he'd just been born that way.

"Hey, buddy." Paulie bounced his son. Vincent stared at him with those wise, infant-gray eyes. He read all babies were born with those inky eyes. They'd turn brown over the coming months. No one in either family had blue eyes, as far as he knew. They did seem to be bluer than ink lately, though. He'd have to ask Varina who he might have gotten blue eyes from. If he got up the nerve to call his parents, tell them they had a grandchild from their fanook son, he could ask them if there were blue eyes in the family.

Rocking Vincent in his arms, swaying as he would forever sway when holding a grocery bag, a bundle of fabric, anything with heft, Paulie hummed "Pepino." He didn't know all the words the way Dante did; he'd leave teaching it up to him. Vincent's eyes batted, his fingers clenched into fists, unclenched, clenched again. Paulie watched the wonder of his son fighting sleep. Would it always be this way, marveling in every movement, in every glance? He couldn't imagine it not being so, and how had Donatella just given him up without a backward glance?

The thought, the fact he'd been avoiding for days, slammed into him. For a moment, he couldn't catch his breath. Paulie loved her. He would always love her. He understood she was who she was. But he'd never forgive her for breaking their son's heart. Vincent didn't know it yet, but she had. Paulie knew all too well what it felt like to be rejected by the one who was supposed to love you most. All the love otherwise surrounding him would never entirely fill the hole something like that left behind.

"Hey, kid."

Vincent didn't startle, little arms flailing outward. He knew Dante's voice almost as well as he knew Paulie's.

"He's trying very hard not to fall asleep," Paulie whispered.

"Curiosity is a sign of intelligence. Oh, Nonina said not to let the cats in here. I told her I'd tell you."

Paulie nudged his glasses farther up on his nose with the use of Vincent's shoulder. "The stealing a baby's breath thing?"

"She didn't say, but probably."

MaryJane, Pastafazool, and Chooch were sacked out on the lavender pillows of the window seat. Paulie had imagined sitting there, reading while his son slept, but the cats had collectively decided the window seat was theirs; he wasn't about to argue with them.

"Did you need something?" he asked.

"Not really. Checking on you, I guess. You nervous about my mom coming home?"

"A little. Not for me. For her. You know she's going to think it's somehow her fault."

"Because Donatella took off while she was gone?"

Paulie nodded.

"Like I said, no one's going to get ahead of my sister. We all got to accept that and not blame ourselves for the shit she does."

"I know. So does your mom. I wish I could be as cut-and-dried about it as you. Sometimes my thoughts run away with me. You know I can be dramatic."

"You're Paulie Fucking Vittone." Dante grinned. "Best designer in the tristate."

"Now you're the one being dramatic." Paulie bounced Vincent, now solidly asleep.

"Not really. Look what you did with this room. Orange and purple? I'd never have agreed in a million years if it wasn't for my sister. I knew you'd make it right."

It really was nice, more peach and lavender with accents of royal purple. "I'd never have chosen these colors," Paulie said. "But it turned out okay."

"What colors would you have chosen?"

"Blue and yellow."

"Then change it."

"I'll have it redone any colors you want, except white. I can't allow any more white in this place." He laughed, a little high-pitched but quietly. "Seriously, let me know what you'd like and I'll see to it before we leave."

"Leave? Che cazz'?"

Paulie's stomach lurched. "I know you'd never kick me out, but I should probably start looking for a—"

"Whoa, whoa. Where's this coming from?"

From necessity. From his hope for at least a little sanity left to him. Donatella had been a buffer between his heart and his hopes. Now she was gone. "Dante, look, you've been really great, but there's only so much I can take from you without feeling like an asshole. Now that your sister's gone—"

"You think I did this for her?"

There went Paulie's stomach again. "Well, yeah."

"I did it for you, too. And for that little guy. Fanabola." Dante's hand cut the air before he turned away, fingers pushing through his hair. His shoulders bunched. Fingers tugged at the hair between them. "I don't want you to leave, Paulie." He turned back, arms falling. "Don't leave. Me. Don't fucking leave me."

Dante's hair, thick like his mother's but only flecked with white, stuck up every which way. Shoulders high, hands clenched. Ready for a fight. Already waging one. Paulie knew what he was saying. His entire body vibrated with the knowing. He needed Dante to say it. Say the words. Do something to make it real and not wishful thinking that would take everything from him if it was only that.

But Dante never would. He'd said all he could say. It was up to Paulie to cross that fearful line drawn in a coat closet on New Year's Eve a million years ago. This was that now-or-never moment made famous in movies and books and folktales of heroes backed up to the edge of a cliff.

Ghistu gazz'.

Vincent in his arms, Paulie crossed the line, leapt from the cliff, more afraid than he'd ever been in his always-scared life, but Dante didn't pull away from him, from the hand on his jaw, from his kiss. Rather, his whole body eased, from lips to fists unclenching, and Paulie was in the coat closet again, all those New Year's Eves ago, being kissed by this then-newly-married man, this man he'd loved ever since and long before.

Dante's fingers threaded at the nape of Paulie's neck. Forehead to forehead. Breath mingling. Dante had smoked a cigarette, had eaten something garlicky his daughter made. To Paulie, there would never again be a sweeter scent, unless it was the scent of his son between them.

"I don't know how to do this." Dante's voice came rough, raw. "I don't know how to *be*. This."

"You're no different than you were thirty seconds ago," Paulie told him. "Except, maybe a little more honest."

"It's so . . . I'm just . . ."

"I know. Trust me."

"Always have." Dante lifted his head, but didn't pull away. The smile he gave took Paulie's breath away. Sad and relieved. And something that might have edged closer to happy than Paulie had ever seen in him before.

I've loved you since I was a kid.

The declaration stayed put in his head. There would be time, he hoped, for such confessions. Dante might be sad and relieved and somewhat happy, but he was also scared out of his mind. It wouldn't be easy. It was going to be damn hard. With the *famiglia*, with business, with the town of Wyldale as a whole. He was Dante Palladino, the man everyone had known all their lives, and yet no one, apparently, had ever actually known him at all. Except . . .

"Pandora knows, doesn't she."

Dante nodded.

Paulie smacked himself in the forehead. "And Gabriella."

Dante actually smirked. "She was hoping the cats would've done it for me last Christmas. It almost did."

"Me? Back then?"

"You, back then. Back a long time. Shit, Paulie."

Paulie grasped the back of his head, kissed him silent. He'd do that a lot. Daily. Hourly, if necessary. Hopefully, for the rest of his life. But he'd take right now, in the orange and purple nursery he'd repaint and refurnish blue and yellow. Not because Vincent was a boy, but because orange and purple were Mardi Gras colors Donatella had chosen because she was Donatella, still the only woman he'd ever love. Would always love. She'd given him Vincent. In a way, she'd given him Dante, because she crawled into a storm sewer when she was five years old, and made Paulie part of her aggressively beautiful life.

Vincent still and always between them, Paulie and Dante held on to one another. Face-to-face. Mouth to mouth. Everything that changed when Donatella told him she was pregnant was altering, morphing into something just as scary in the best way possible. It would do so again, and again. The first time she showed up in their lives, finding her best friend, their son, and her brother living as a family, in the home they'd built together. It would change again when Vincent went to school and found out most kids didn't have a daddy and an uncle Dante, then again when he was old enough to truly understand his mother's abandonment, and then when he realized it didn't mean she didn't love him. After so many years unchanging, Paulie saw his future stretched out as never-ending flux.

He was getting ahead of himself. Now was now. Downstairs, the family waited for Varina's return. To break the news. To hear of her travels. Everything the same, and yet forever different. The way ahead was going to be long and fraught, but it would be beautiful.

"Pepino Soolagil'"
(peh-pino soo-lah-jeel)
Italian: "Pepino Suracila"; "Pepino the Mouse"

It's a song about a mouse named Pepino who torments and humiliates the man of the house, who can't catch him, or kill him. His ultimate plan is to leave the wine out, get the mouse drunk, then do him in.

Yeah, weird, but it's a song that gets belted out at every family gathering. The youngest is always made to sing it at weddings, wakes, Christmases, and Easters. I've been the youngest pretty much since birth; as it was for the mouse-killer in the song, being made to sing it is humiliating. But the fun kind. I think you might have to be Italian to get that. Like I've said a few times, we are a complicated people.

O n the PNI—Palladino Noise Index—what came through the floor was about a seven. Downstairs, it had to be a full ten. Christmas Eve; the feast was in full swing. If the noise didn't attest to that, the overwhelming aromas of garlic and fried fish would have been enough. But they were all down there, even Uncle Tommy and Aunt Catherine, a pair of leather catcher's mitts, up from Florida. They'd been old as long as Vincent could remember, never really changing much. Longevity ran in the family; Uncle Tommy had another decade left, easy. Nonina Sylvia—whom he barely remembered outside of the pictures on the family wall in the kitchen—had lived to be ninety-six, outliving her second husband, John, whom he remembered better, maybe because he was Chinese, not another Italian, by a year. If he didn't know his Nonnie was eighty-five, he'd never have guessed it. No one ever did. She said it was traveling that kept her young. He thought, maybe, it had a little to do with Bubbe Ruth's creams and lotions. Nonnie's hair was as white as Santa's beard, but she no way looked almost as old as her catcher's-mitt brother, that was for sure.

"Hey, kiddo."

Vincent turned to the voice, his heart immediately in his throat. Not whom he hoped, but almost as good. "Hey, Gabby. Come on in."

She pushed off the door, sat cross-legged on the floor beside him, her back against his bed. "You should come on down," she told him. "Uncle Davide is eating all the shrimp."

"Dad'll save some for me."

"Don't you want to come down?"

He did, actually. Christmas Eve was his favorite holiday. The whole *famiglia* gathered in the huge kitchen. Eating, laughing, raising the PNI to the highest possible level. It was also his worst. He'd always been the only kid; his only cousin/sort-of-stepsister being Gabriella—who was in her thirties—but Vincent was used to being that. At family gatherings. At Dad and Uncle Dante's shop, the construction sites. Until he started school, he mostly only associated with other kids during the occasional outings to the park.

Vincent Leo—*nides,* though he rarely copped to it—Palladino didn't really like people his own age. They were sort of . . . dumb. They only cared about dumb stuff, like who liked who and what teams they were going out for. Vincent didn't like sports; he liked words. He liked history. He liked thinking about everything he touched, tasted, saw coming from the stars. That everyone was stardust, and they had no idea.

Uncle Dante always said he only had a few years to be a kid, but the rest of his life to be an adult. Vincent knew better, even at fifteen—Uncle Dante had never been a kid either.

"Your mom'll be here any minute."

Vincent looked away. Christmas Eve was his favorite holiday, and his worst. "Maybe," he said. "Or maybe not."

"She's really coming this time. Your dad just got a text. My dad's picking her up at the bus station right now."

Maybe she'd still be there. Maybe she'd have run into someone she knew from back in the day and gone off with them instead. Vincent tried not to care. "Your mom is your mom," Dad always told him. "She loves you more than anything. It's why she left, and why she stays away. You'll understand when you're older."

Dad said a lot of things. About Mom. Always good things. His stories about her were always from when they were young and always in trouble. Very few from the fifteen years since Vincent's birth. Uncle Dante called her oobatz'. Dad never corrected him. His mother wasn't crazy; Vincent didn't like that word. It was one of those over-simplified words, easily used and dismissed. Dad confessed, only a couple of years ago, she'd been diagnosed bipolar. Vincent didn't like that term either. Labels were usually more dangerous than oversimplification, putting people into categories and making them fit a different sort of norm. Vincent was all about coloring outside the lines. If being a Palladino had taught him anything in his short life, it was that normal didn't exist.

"I'm going back down." Gabriella patted his knee. "Don't be too long."

He slipped his word notebook in between the box spring and mattress of his bed. "I won't. Oh, hey, congratulations on your win."

"Who told you? No one's supposed to know until the show airs."

Vincent tried not to roll his eyes. As if a Palladino ever kept a secret.

"Dammit. I told Mom not to tell."

"Then you shouldn't have told her. She can't keep a secret from Uncle Dante. Or . . . anyone."

Gabriella bounced, clapping her hands. "The store and restaurant are going to blow *up* once the show airs."

"You'll be a world-famous champion chef."

"Well, maybe not world-famous." She got up, brushed off her red velvet Christmas slacks. "Do I have lint on my butt?"

Vincent would not look. "Nope."

"Good. Thanks. Come on down, okay?"

"In a minute."

Gabriella kissed the top of his head, like he was a child. To her, he was. To everyone. Vincent was close to certain he'd be considered *the baby* for the rest of his life.

"Love you, kiddo."

"Love you, too, Gabs."

Vincent watched her go; her butt did have lint on it, but he wasn't saying anything. His cousin. Because her dad was Uncle Dante, who had once been married to Aunt Pandora, her mother. Stepsister.

Because Uncle Dante, who was Vincent's mother's brother, had raised him as his own. Did that make Gabby his aunt, too? He didn't think so. Not that it mattered anyway. *Famiglia* was *famiglia*.

A cheer went up downstairs.

"Donatella!"

Unmistakable. Vincent's heart hammered. He hadn't seen her since last Easter, after she hadn't shown up for Christmas. She'd given him a chocolate bunny missing its ears, because she'd gotten hungry on the train. She held him and kissed him and told him how handsome he was, just like his daddy. Vincent loved her differently than he loved anyone else in the world, even when he hated her.

Getting to his feet, Vincent adjusted his jeans, tucked the long curls always in his face behind his ear so Nonnie wouldn't brush it back, tell him not to hide his handsome face before chicken-kissing both his cheeks. There would be no sad smile, because his mother actually showed up this time. He looked just like her, according to the family. Vincent acknowledged her dimples, her light-brown curls, but didn't see it otherwise. If anything, he saw more of Uncle Dante in himself. Nothing Vittone, though. Only the blue eyes his grandmother—who sent him ten dollars in a card every birthday, but whom he'd only met twice—said came from some long-dead aunt or grandmother he'd never met, or even heard of.

He paused at the top of the steps, the PNI already a nine. Above it all, he heard old-timey music trying to make itself heard from the front window with the cool, wavy glass. He knew all the records by heart, those hefty things in their paper sleeves, from a time long before even Nonnie was a kid. He loved them all, especially the Caruso recordings. Vincent couldn't sing, at all, but he'd tried, when he was little and oblivious to his own shortcomings, standing on the coffee table with his wooden-spoon microphone, singing make-believe Italian words until Dad or Uncle Dante caught him and made him get down. How he'd, back then, managed to put the record on the turntable, crank the crank, and set the needle in place, Vincent couldn't have said, even now. Mom once told him the Victrola was haunted. She called her Vicky. Nonnie denied it, to this day, though he heard her say the same.

On the landing, overlooking the big room that had once been— according to pictures on the family wall—closed off into several too-small rooms, Vincent Palladino searched the faces for his mother's. Uncle Davide was holding mistletoe over the head of his current girlfriend, a woman younger than Gabriella. Vincent hadn't even bothered to remember her name. Dad was helping Uncle Dante off with his coat. Nonnie and Bubbe Ruth, Aunt Pandora and Gabriella, hovered close to the stove, over some pot or pan. And who was that guy hovering close to Gabriella? Shaved head. Earrings. Wearing a T-shirt on Christmas Eve that displayed tattoos where pale skin should have been. Another chef. Of course. He wouldn't last any longer than one of Uncle Davide's girlfriends.

There was Uncle Tommy and Aunt Catherine with Mikey and one of the twins Vincent had never been able to tell apart from his brother. The twin's wife and kids. A sea of beloved Italian faces, but he couldn't find the one he wanted to see most.

And then, there she was, hanging her coat on a hook in the mudroom, turning to laugh at something Dad said to her. He was always so happy when she turned up. His best friend, all his life, even when she stayed away too long.

She saw him. She smiled. His mother. Donatella Palladino, for a while Quinn, and for a shorter while, Donatella Perez. He'd never met any of his mother's husbands; Dad said it was a good thing. Vincent's heart panged again. Threading her way through her loud, smothering, always-loving family, Donatella-once-again-Palladino's arms were opening. Vincent's foot came down on the next step and missed. He stumbled, tried to catch himself on the banister. And there she was, catching him before he could tumble.

"Umbriag'?" She laughed. "You better not be."

"Nah. I don't drink."

"I did at your age. Your dad and I, always sneaking whatever was left in everyone's glasses." She ruffled his hair. "Merry Christmas, Vincent."

"Merry Christmas, Mom."

She kissed his cheek, not the chicken-kisses Nonnie gave, but one warm, slightly-too-long kiss on his cheek. "I brought you something."

"Yeah?"

She reached behind her back, pulling a rectangular package from the waistband of her jeans. "Open it."

"Now?"

"I've been dying to see you open it for weeks. Please?"

"O . . . okay. Sure." Vincent turned the package over in his hands, looked for an edge to tear.

"Oh, here!" His mother laughed, tearing the paper to reveal a book. Vincent smoothed his hand over the dark-blue cover. *Jersey Italian Slang,* by Vincent Leonides Palladino. He flipped through the pages. Words. His words. His family's words. "Where did you get this?"

"I had it made," she told him. "Do you like it?"

"I . . . I love it. Mom, it's . . . Wow. But where'd you get . . . How'd you even know about it?"

"Vincent." She laughed. "Your dad and I were the king and queen of sneak. Besides, every kid keeps shit under their mattress. Dad found it and told me about it. He scanned me the pages, I transcribed it, and had it made with one of those publish-it-yourself places. Do you like it?"

Did he like it? Three years of collecting words, hunting down their meanings, their origins, scribbling them into a notebook he thought no one knew existed. A collection he'd hid under his mattress because he didn't want anyone to think he was making fun of them, even though he kind of was. In the most loving way possible.

"I love it, Mom. It's . . . it's so great."

"Do I know my son, or what?"

She didn't. Not at all. But she did, in ways that mattered. That would matter, as he got older. His mother was his mother. The woman who gave birth to him, who'd left—Dad said—to spare him her crazy. Brave, in her way, and selfish. Maybe they were the same thing. Donatella had never pretended to be anything else.

"Vincent! Sing 'Pepino'!"

His eyes rolled. His shoulders slouched. A chorus of "'Pe-pi-no'! 'Pe-pi-no'!" brought the PNI level to eleven.

"They're calling your tune."

Her arm around his shoulders, his never-there mother led him into the thick of the noise. Into the feasting and laughter. Into the loud, smothering, aggressively beautiful *famiglia* always happy to see her come home.

AUTHOR'S NOTE

Jersey Italian is a pidgin language with roots in both Italian and English, as well as all the beautiful mash-ups of all the other languages spoken by other immigrants in the given areas. Thus, Boston Italian will have different words and pronunciations, as will New York Italian. Even Jersey Italian varies, depending upon whether the neighborhood is closer to New York City or Philadelphia. The pidgin in this book is *my* Jersey Italian, that being the North Jersey Italian (specifically, Paterson) I grew up with. The research into the Italian equivalents is mine, and most likely fallible, but undertaken with the utmost respect and love. The myriad of dialects and minority languages in Italy, combined with not only the areas Italian Americans settled in but the other nationalities in any given area, makes some of the etymology fairly impossible to be 100 percent sure about. Thus, like Vincent's, I consider this an amateur attempt.

These words and pronunciations are still being passed down despite the fact I left New Jersey for Connecticut more than two decades ago. Don't offer my Yankee grandchildren maniCOtti; they'll have no idea what you're offering them. It's maniGOTT', and they probably still won't eat it, but they'll know what you're talking about.

If you have any words to contribute, drop by my blog at modesty isforsuckers.com. Leave them in the comments to *Jersey Italian Slang,* by Vincent Leonides Palladino, where you'll find more Jersey Italian words that appeared in this book. It'll be fun!

ACKNOWLEDGMENTS

First, thanks go to my Italian Connection—Flora Bellini, Angelo Benuzzi, GaryPeter Casella-Voccia, and Michelle Biddix-Simmons. Without their assistance on social media, I'd never have found the roots of many of my Jersey Italian headings. Thank you, a million times over.

Huge thanks to my large, insane, beloved Jersey Italian *famiglia* consisting of not only blood relations, but aunts, uncles, and cousins I didn't even know weren't biologically related until I was well into my teens. I love you all immensely. Especially the Van People.

To Mom and Dad, Michael, Karen, and Mark, thanks for being my forever-core. You're all my most cherished friends. You inspired this book more than anyone, anywhere.

Thanks to my editor, Rachel Kahan, for knowing I had the right "second book" in me. Working with her has been the stuff of dreams. Despite my whimsical personality, I don't say that lightly. Thanks to the amazing "behind the scenes" work done by the whole William Morrow team. Few readers know what goes into producing a book; I am humbly grateful to everyone.

Thanks, of course, to Agent of Wonder, Janna Bonikowski. We were both fledglings in the field when we first teamed up. I couldn't ask for a better advocate, or friend. A second thanks goes out to the Knight Agency, because I'm the lucky recipient of this village of agents raising their authors together.

Thanks to my own branch of the Jersey Italian *famiglia* who moved out of Jersey and into Connecticut more than two decades ago. Jamie, Scott, Christofer, and Grace, the words and traditions live on. And to Frank Jr., who stayed in Jersey, keeping the blood from seeping out entirely.

Last, my deepest thanks go to Frankie D. He has been part of my writing life from day one, encouraging me and inspiring me and never once considering what I do a hobby, even in those early days before ever being published. He's my biggest fan, ally, and advocate. And my love. Always.

RECIPES

Sunday Gravy

Gravy or sauce? Pasta or macaroni? The debate is real. In Jersey, we grew up having macaroni and gravy at our grandparents' house on Sundays, always around two in the afternoon.

INGREDIENTS

1/4 cup olive oil
1 large yellow onion, chopped
1 head garlic, crushed and chopped (yes, a whole head. At least. More, if you're so inclined.)
2 lbs meat, any cut, on the bone or boneless (pork makes a sweeter gravy, beef a heartier one. A combo of both is divine.)
3 28 oz cans crushed tomatoes (yes, canned. It holds up better to long cook times.)
1 6 oz can tomato paste
2 tbsp* dried basil
1 tbsp* dried oregano
1/2 tsp crushed red pepper (optional)
1 tsp salt
1 cup vermouth (you can use wine, red or white. I prefer vermouth.)
2 tbsp butter (optional)

Put olive oil, onion, and garlic into a heavy stockpot. Sauté on medium heat until translucent. Don't let them brown! It makes for a bitter gravy. Brown whatever meat you're using to sear in the juices, and so your sauce doesn't taste "bloody." You can use pretty much any meat in the gravy. Italians are a resourceful people. Whatever cut was available—usually the cheapest—went into the pot. Remove from heat (so you don't get splattered . . . but you will anyway at some point) and add the crushed tomatoes and tomato paste, basil, oregano, red pepper, and salt. Stir until well incorporated and return to heat. Keep it on medium until it's simmering, then set it to low. Put the lid on, but leave it tipped just a little to let some of the heat/steam escape. Now, the most important part— NEVER LET IT GET HOTTER THAN A LOW SIMMER. Boiling takes away all the flavor. Low and slow is key. Give it a turn every once in a while, but let it cook at least two hours before checking the meat for doneness and flavor. Thicker cuts (like braggiol' or a pork loin) will need longer. Something like Bolognese** will be just about done. Meat should be fork-tender.

Once the meat is fall-aparty, add the vermouth and butter. Let it simmer another ten minutes. If time allows, take it off the heat and let it sit, covered, for an hour (more or less is fine).

Mangia!

*When making Sunday gravy, always use dried herbs. Fresh herbs lose all their flavor over the long cook. The measurements above are rough ones, and probably on the too-little side. It all depends upon the palate in question, and the quality of the dried herbs. If you can't smell them when you open the container, you'll need more . . . or a new container of bas'nigol'.

**If you want Bolognese, use a combination of beef and pork three parts to one. Brown lightly at the outset. Drain the fat if you're a fool . . . I mean, if you want to be healthy and cut down on your fat intake.

Varina's Meatballs

Easiest thing to make; hardest to get right.

INGREDIENTS

2 eggs
1 cup *Italian seasoned** breadcrumbs
1 lb ground beef (85/15 is the leanest you should go)
$^1/_3$ lb ground pork
olive oil

And that's it. You make or break a meatball by how you roll them, the ingredients you use, and the proper sear before they go into the sauce.

Whisk the eggs and breadcrumbs together. Add the *cold* meat to the mixture. Do not overmix, or the warmth of your hands—yes, use your hands, so take off your rings—will break down the fat in the meat.

Once everything is incorporated, you roll. Ping-pong sized, or tennis balls, roll lightly. Pack them tight and you'll have dense meatballs. Sear in olive oil, getting a good crust but not cooking through, before adding them to your pot of gravy.

Whatever their size, let them cook at least a couple of hours for the magical transfer of tomato to meat, meat to tomato to occur.

*Italian seasoned breadcrumbs will have all the garlic, salt, onion, cheese, and herbs you need. The sauce will already be seasoned enough otherwise.

Varina's Chicken Picatta

This sounds fancy, but it's one of the simplest things to make, and doesn't take long at all.

INGREDIENTS

Four chicken breasts, pounded thin
Flour to coat (gluten-free option: almond flour)
2 to 3 tbsp olive oil
2 to 3 cloves garlic, minced
1 shallot, minced
1 cup chicken broth
2 to 3 tbsp butter
3/4 cup white wine (or vermouth—I always prefer vermouth)
1/2 tbsp cornstarch*
Juice from 1 lemon
1 heaping tbsp capers
A good handful of fresh (dry doesn't cut it) Italian parsley

Coat the chicken breasts in flour and give them a quick sear in the olive oil. Set them aside. Add the garlic and shallot to the pan, sauté until translucent (never brown). Deglaze the pan with the chicken broth, then return the chicken to the pan, along with the butter and wine. Bring to a gentle simmer and let cook until the chicken is done. If you've pounded the chicken thin enough, it won't take long. Maybe ten minutes. As always, never let it get above a simmer, otherwise you'll lose all the flavor of the wine and butter, and the chicken will be tough.

*If you like your sauce more brothy, skip the cornstarch.

Once the chicken is done, remove the pan from the heat. In a separate bowl, add about 3 tbsp of the liquid from the pan to the cornstarch, stirring until well incorporated. Slowly stir this mixture into the pan, along with the lemon juice, capers, and parsley. Put back on a very low heat, stirring until thickened (about three minutes).

ABOUT THE AUTHOR

Terri-Lynne DeFino was born and raised in New Jersey but escaped to the wilds of Connecticut, where she still lives with her husband and her cats. If you knock on her door, she'll invite you in and feed you. That's what Jersey Italian women do, because you can take the girl out of Jersey but you can't take the Jersey out of the girl. She is the author of the novel *The Bar Harbor Retirement Home for Famous Writers (and Their Muses)* and the Bitterly Suite romance series.